Fegnir

BOOK I

The Plight of Man

by

Will Abel

Edited by:
Paige Duke

Special thanks to
Dan Philipp, Karl Kropp, David "Dice" Latrell, Kevin Monroe, James Kirkpatrick, Brian Haines, Todd Thatcher, and many others in the old gang.

Cover: Lima Graphics
Johnathon Eakin
Cover/interior design: The Book Cover Whisperer
ProfessionalBookCoverDesign.com

For you, Mom.
You never stopped believing in me.
Soar high with the angels.
I will see you soon.
Miss you.

Table of Contents

Preface

At first there was darkness, nothing, and from this darkness arose a light, and out of the light appeared Eurek the Creator. Eurek's birth created both space and a comet. This comet crashed into Eurek and formed a sun. Angered by the comet, he hurled it into the sun, which exploded into planets, moons, and stars. The existing sun he called Sulo, and the planet closest to Sulo he called Iund, and the two sister planets he called Xie and Noar. But the last two planets Eurek could not name, so he decided to destroy them. He hurled himself into the two planets, but he did not foresee that the collision would destroy him along with both of the planets. From the fragments, three beings were formed, they called themselves Gods and the planet that remained they called Zor.

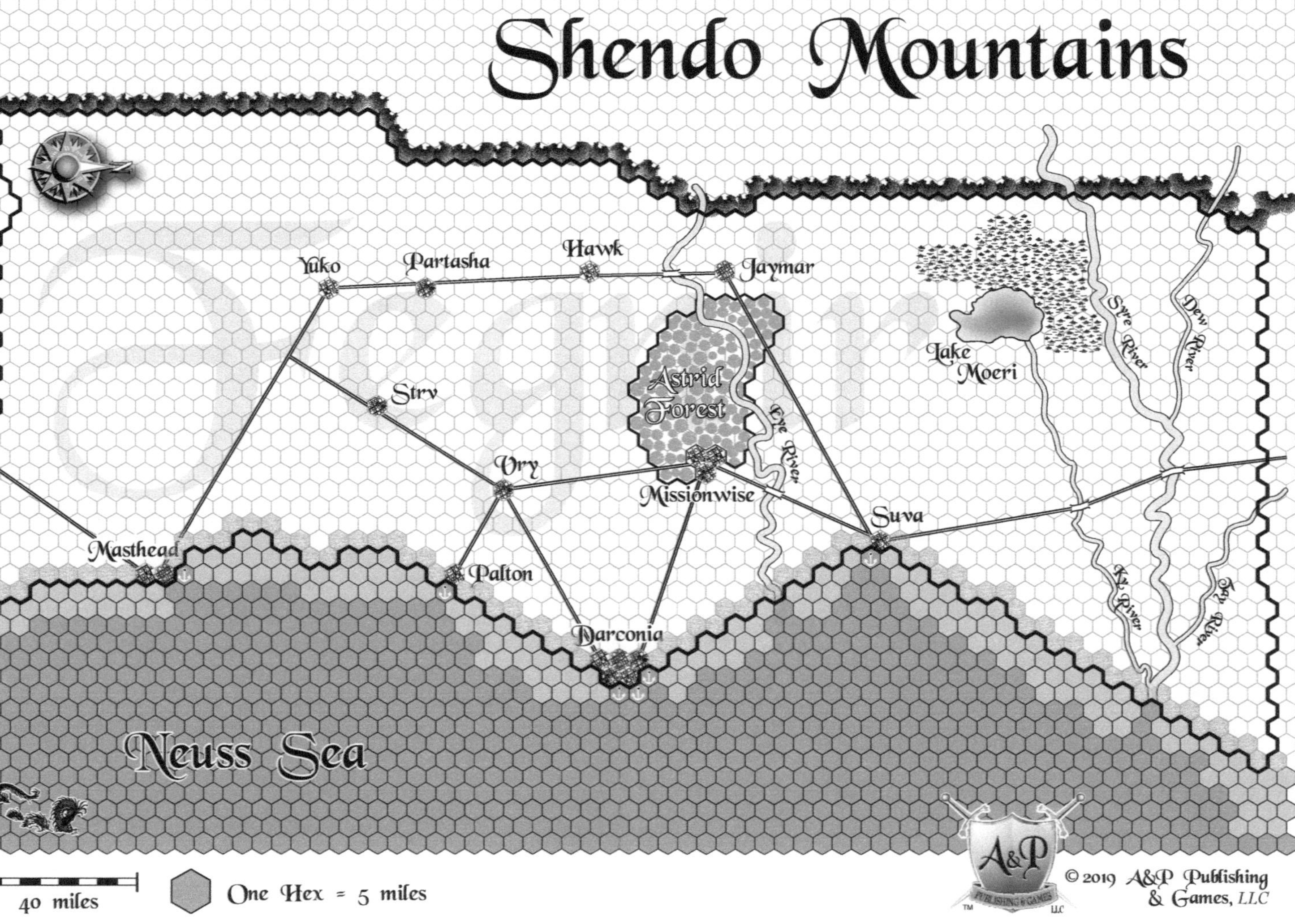

Shendo Mountains
Yuko
Partasha
Hawk
Jaymar
Lake Moeri
Syre River
Dew River
Astrid Forest
Strv
Eye River
Missionwise
Vry
Suva
Ky. River
Sey River
Masthead
Palton
Darconia
Neuss Sea
40 miles
One Hex = 5 miles
© 2019 A&P Publishing & Games, LLC
A&P PUBLISHING & GAMES

Chapter I
Those Putrid Beasts

Strategically positioned atop one of the snow-covered Villiashian Mountains of Fegnir, stands Guel Castle. It's an average-sized castle but a work of art in craftsmanship and design. The light-gray stone walls reach a height of twenty-five feet and together form a shape similar to that of an octagon. Forty-foot towers anchor each corner of the castle. Atop each of these towers, coat-of-arms banners of Duke Guel's most prominent knights (eight in all) snap violently back and forth in the cold, snowy wind. The surrounding mountainous terrain makes a moat unnecessary. Instead, the occupants rely on the cliffs for protection; this makes the east and north walls especially hazardous to invaders.

Despite the terrible weather, the castle compound is alive with activity this evening. Both servants and citizens of various trades are all busy preparing for the night's activities and feast. Guards impatiently pace back and forth at their posts awaiting the return of the final patrol.

Tonight, there will be a wedding between Duke Guel's grandson, Sargon, and his betrothed, Jessica, to unite the noble houses of Guel, Martox, and Zartharel. This of course, dictates that Jessica comes from noble blood on both sides of her family; her father was from the line of Martox, her mother of Zartharel. This fact sometimes troubles Sargon, whose grandfather did not come from noble blood but worked his way up the ranks through the knighthood of Darconia. Neither were Sargon's mother's forebears among the nobility; they were middle class tradesmen. His grandfather never mentioned how he came about "climbing the ladder," neither did Sargon's father. Duke Guel always insisted to Sargon that "nobility is not a birthright—it has to be earned every day." He would also add, "A good leader always leads by example." Sargon lives each day with these two thoughts in the forefront of his mind, drilled into Sargon's head all his life by both his grandfather and father.

Sargon and Jessica's wedding will be a most blessed event, for this day is the twenty-first day of Toystra, commonly called "The Scales of Love." It is a holy day for the Goddess Zura.

Sargon leans against a merlon above the east wall overlooking the darkening countryside. Sulo, their magnificent sun, must be setting behind the blanket of clouds. Blond-haired and blue-eyed Sargon is only sixteen and has already made squire to the knight Reaxl. Menarc, Sargon's father, ensured his son made it through the ranks like he did. He is very muscular and stands seven feet tall as he watches aimlessly over the horizon for the final watch to return, he tries not to think about how different his life will become after he marries. Although he realized his love for Jessica long ago, he can't help but feel nervous about tonight. He has not been able to hold down any food, and so all he can do now is quietly moan as his empty stomach growls.

Growing impatient of the late-returning patrol, Sargon leaves the guards on the wall and makes his way across the courtyard to the banquet hall. He passes the stable, where the stable boys are preparing the horses' final feeding. As he nears the banquet hall, the voices and noises of the many guests grow louder with every step.

Sargon stops just a few feet inside this massive hall, admiring all the banners and decorations. Against the north wall of this magnificent room stretches a long and narrow wooden table stacked with a fantastic variety of foods. Reaxl turns from a group of ladies he has been entertaining and joins Sargon. The knight's armor glistens in the candlelight.

Reaxl is the champion of the castle. He is not as good-looking as Sargon, but he is much older and charms all the ladies with his wit. He is very fond of Sargon and is amazed at his abilities and progress in training. He knows that Sargon will soon become the best knight of the castle.

"Made another trip to the east wall, did you?" laughs Reaxl.

"I'm still awaiting the return of the last patrol," Sargon shoots a searing glance at Reaxl; sometimes Sargon fails to appreciate his mentor's humor, especially when it is directed at him. The thought of blowing chunks and dry heaving over the eastern wall does not strike a pleasant image in Sargon's mind nor does his sore gut and ribs.

"Of course," Reaxl snickers, "when were they expected in, anyway?"

"Quite a bit ago," Sargon answers sternly. "Sulo has surely set by now."

Reaxl, now serious, says "Ah, nothing to be worried about, they're probably lost again. Most of our guards have the direction sense of a blind man. Then tag on this weather, hell, they could be in Vry for all we know." For a moment, Reaxl loses his balance and rests an arm on Sargon's shoulder to stabilize himself.

"By the gods ... you hit the ale already?" Sargon asks.

"Nope, but it sure has hit me!" Reaxl blurts out, laughing again, his alcoholic breath potent enough to bring a horse to its knees.

"I can't believe that you have been drinking so heavily this soon. 'Tis not even dark yet."

"Yeah ... yeah, whatever, a few more drinks and I'll drink myself sober. Come on, I have something to show you," Reaxl says with his arm around Sargon's shoulder while clumsily guiding him over to the banquet table. "Can you see the cook has chosen your favorite dish?"

"Oh, yes, I do love those roasted pheasants there." Sargon points out at the far-right corner of the table. "If only my guts weren't twisted in a knot, I would ..."

"No," interrupts Reaxl. "Look at the other end of the table."

Sargon's jaw drops open as his eyes fall upon the largest roasted pig he has ever seen in his life. He stands there speechless for a moment and then angrily begins to holler. "Who the hell is responsible for this?" Sargon points at the pig while looking around the hall.

Reaxl begins to laugh uncontrollably. Sargon abruptly turns away from Reaxl, causing the knight to lose his balance and fall. "Hey, hey, where are you going?" he asks, tears of laughter rolling down his face as he tries to pick himself up off the floor. "Wait up, pig boy."

But Sargon storms off, looking for the cook. Reaxl falls back to the floor as he laughs hysterically. This little episode has now started some of the guests laughing too.

Sargon thinks to himself, *I'll deal with Reaxl later*. About halfway across this massive room, Sargon spots the culprit and goes to confront him. "What the hell is the meaning of this? A large putrid beast on my wedding day?" Sargon asks sharply.

The cook is a short, bald, foul-smelling man that shows respect for no one. But despite his offensive manners and hygiene, the Guel family keeps him on, for there is no argument that he is a very fine cook.

"What's the matter, young master? Haven't you gotten over your hatred of pigs? Well, you'll have to talk to your father 'bout it, for I got lots of work to do." Without waiting for Sargon's reply, he walks off snickering.

Sargon stoically watches the chef disappear into the crowd of guests. He remembers the day that caused his hatred of these "putrid beasts." He was about eight years old at the time. On a typical day, he would practice the art of swordplay and balance—the two skills essential in training correctly to be a great fighter. His practice consisted of standing atop the main castle flagpole, which stood about twenty feet off the ground spiked to the castle wall. He would swing his wooden sword about, imagining a massive sword fight with a powerful enemy. Menarc did not take kindly to this escapade, and scolded Sargon many times for his insistence on such ridiculous and dangerous practice. But Sargon's grandfather loved the moxie of his grandson and thus encouraged it.

One day while standing atop the flagpole, Sargon felt an uneasiness inside himself; thinking the feeling to be an ounce of fear, he just swung his sword harder, refusing to climb down. Because Sargon was big for his age, over time his weight had slowly been pulling the pole loose from the castle wall. So the pole finally gave, and Sargon fell into the thick mud of the pigpen directly below. The startled pigs jumped back in surprise as Sargon landed in the mud.

Sargon slowly picked himself up, having the wind knocked out of him, only to be pushed back in the mud by a six-hundred-pound sow. Sargon attempted to get up again, but this time was attacked by all six hogs in the pen. The boy screamed as the beasts bit him, head butted him, and pawed at him. A couple of the castle guards that saw the young Sargon fall rushed to his aid. They pulled his bleeding and muddy body from the pen and carried him to Menarc. Despite Sargon's demands that all the pigs be slaughtered, Menarc chose to do nothing to the pigs or to Sargon for disobeying him. Menarc knew that the scratched and bruised young man had learned his lesson; as for the pigs, that was simply the way of those animals.

"'Tis a fine feast for a wedding, wouldn't you say?"

"Huh?" Sargon turns.

"I said it's a fine feast for a wedding!" Menarc has startled the day dreaming Sargon as he put his arm around his son's shoulder.

"Oh ... yes it is, Father, thanks." Sargon says, looking his father in the eye. "But why must a beast be served in my presence?"

"Look, Son, I love pork, and your mother loves roasted pig as well as the guests. Even your bride to be ..."

"All right, all right, I won't say another word about it. Besides, this is supposed to be the happiest day of my life, and I can't eat anyway," Sargon says as he puts a hand on his gut.

"Yes, Reaxl has told me of your repeated adventures to the east wall—a most amusing story he tells," Menarc snickers.

"What a drunken idiot. I swear he drinks more than a fish. I have a lot of respect for Reaxl, but sometimes he rubs me the wrong way."

"Now son," laughs Menarc, "don't worry yourself about such petty things. Tonight, there will be much merriment throughout the whole country of Fegnir. There is one thing I have to say to you." Menarc holds Sargon's shoulders while looking him squarely in the face, almost misty-eyed. "I am very proud of you, my son, your grandfather would have been proud too ..."

"Yes, I know. I miss him. I can't believe it's been two years," Sargon interrupts as he shakes his head.

"Please, let me finish. You have become the best swordsman in the castle, can handle a horse better than anyone in our kingdom, and have become quite the nobleman—"

Menarc's words are cut short. The banquet hall grows suddenly silent at the sight of beautiful Jessica walking down the stairway of the great hall. Trumpets sound, announcing her arrival, and the guests applaud enthusiastically.

Sargon turns from his father. "I know, Father, I know." Sargon looks over and smiles as he pats Menarc's shoulder. Sargon watches Jessica as she takes each step ever so gracefully. He can't help admiring her voluptuous figure and long, flowing light-brown hair. He reminisces about the day they met.

It was little more than a year ago. Sargon was in the castle courtyard sword fighting with Reaxl one afternoon when a caravan arrived containing a knight and his family. When Sargon first laid eyes on Jessica, her immaculate beauty paralyzed him. No longer paying attention to his training, he nearly got his hand chopped off because of his carelessness. She could not have been a day over thirteen, but she had a very mature body and could have easily passed for twenty. She snickered at Sargon's lack of concentration, as Reaxl easily knocked him to the ground.

"Now see how you made a fool of yourself in front of that beautiful lady. I could have cut off your hand if this sword was not dull. Remember, sweet lips, sharp or dull they both weight the same." Reaxl laughed.

Sargon gave a sneering smile as he wiped the blood from his lips before he got up. Reaxl swatted Sargon on his chain mail chest with the flat of his sword, nearly knocking the wind out of him.

"Remember, take care of your armor and it will take care of you," Reaxl said. "Hello? Hello?"

Sargon was too awestruck to pay anymore attention to Reaxl. As he walked toward the carriage, Reaxl rolled his eyes, dropped his sword, and walked away with his hands in the air.

The Martox family was to stay in Castle Guel overnight and then resume their journey in the morning. However, Tarco,

Jessica's father, contracted an illness sometime during the night. Menarc immediately sent for a healer from the nearby city of Vry—a day's travel away—and they all remained until Tarco was cured.

During those few days, Sargon and Jessica spent time together and soon fell in love. It was hardly surprising to anyone, for everyone who knew Sargon loved and admired him. Sargon made those around him feel really good about themselves, and he always put his own problems aside when someone else was in need.

The blaring of trumpets interrupts Sargon's thoughts, as they play the couple's wedding march. The guests watch in silence, and all eyes turn to Sargon and Jessica as the wedding ceremony commences. Ardox—a priest from the Temple of Zura, the Goddess of Love—conducts the ceremony. The fact that Sargon and Jessica love each other is only circumstantial, for Tarco and Menarc had arranged the wedding beforehand but did not tell the two lovebirds. They believed it was especially important for strong wealthy families to bond together because of the troubled times in which they lived. They both felt that it was best to keep it between them and see how the couple fared.

Menarc is suspicious and cautious of the nearby nobles, who are always looking for a way to put an end to those who do not support or approve of their business. Fegnir does not have a king, and so the law of the land is written by the nobles. Every six months all knights convene to discuss laws and problems throughout the country; they are overseen by the Duke of Darconia.

No one knows why a king has never been chosen, probably because so much money has been changing hands for so long that no one wants anything to change. Menarc and Tarco both hope that one day, the evil nobles would become the victims of their own greed, and a king would rise and clean house.

The ceremony progresses beautifully, and soon Sargon and Jessica are bonded in marriage. Afterward, several bards play delightful, fun-loving music as everyone eats, drinks, and dances to celebrate this happy occasion.

"Here darling," Jessica says, handing Sargon a piece of meat as she gives him a soft kiss on the cheek.

"Just as I figured, beast meat," Sargon mumbles to himself.

"What? Did you say something, honey?" Jessica kisses him on the cheek again before getting caught up in conversation with Sargon's parents.

"Thanks." Sargon smiles. He doesn't want to spoil her wedding day with something so petty. He waits for her to turn her back and then quickly feeds the meat to his favorite castle hound, Barnabus, whom he has raised from a pup. He pats the animal on the head and rubs its back to get the beastly smell off his hand.

Menarc makes his way from the wedded couple and up the castle's main gatehouse. Smiling and shielding himself from the cold wind, he calls out, "Sergeant, tell your men to come down off the walls and help themselves to the warmth and food inside the hall, I do not think we are under any danger in this terrible weather."

"Sire, the final patrol has not come in yet."

"I'm well aware of that, soldier. They have probably found shelter in one of the mountain caves. Now, tend to your men and invite them inside before someone gets sick."

"Yes, my lord."

After a full evening of dancing and merriment, Sargon and Jessica excuse themselves and start to make their way upstairs to their bedroom. On the way, they bump into Reaxl, who is clearly unsteady with drink.

"Ugh, my guts are rolling!" exclaims Reaxl.

"You must quit drinking so heavily." Now Sargon is laughing at the knight as he slaps him on the back.

"Yes, you will make yourself sick," Jessica adds.

"'Tis too late. Guess I'll be making it to the east wall myself," Reaxl replies. "By the gods, Reaxl, get one of your lady friends to help you get there before you fall and hurt yourself," Sargon suggests.

"I already had one of my lady friends, thank you very much. Ugh." Reaxl moans as he holds his stomach.

As Sargon and Jessica climb the stairs, Sargon glances over his shoulder and notices Reaxl is now choking and holding his throat, gasping frantically. Sargon darts from Jessica's side and leaps to the floor, catching the falling knight before he hits the concrete stairs. Other guests are falling all around him, choking just like Reaxl. But Sargon's full attention is on his friend. He puts his arm around the knight and helps him to sit up.

But it's too late. Reaxl mutters a final word, "Poison." He slumps in death in Sargon's arms.

Aching with the sudden loss of his friend, Sargon sets Reaxl down and scans the hall for his parents. A short time ago it was a place of joy, harmony, and love. The once beautiful banquet hall has now become a chamber of death. All around him, lifeless bodies are falling to the floor. He spots his parents lying together against a wall. Rushing to them, he trips over something. It is Barnabus, lying dead on the floor too. By the time Sargon reaches his parents, his mother has already passed. His father barely clings to life. "You must flee, my son," Menarc coughs. "Seek Calador ..." Menarc dies in mid-sentence.

Now panic-stricken, Sargon runs back toward the stairs.

"Jessica. Jessica!" Sargon screams at the top of his lungs. He runs as fast as he can, only to see Jessica lying facedown on the stairs. With lightning speed, he rushes to her collapsed body. He turns her over slowly, not wanting to see the death in her eyes. She is barely alive; a tear slowly drips down out of her left eye.

She looks up at him and tries in vain to smile. She whispers, "I love you. Love no other." These are her last words; then she is gone.

"Nooooooooo!" Sargon yells in a useless act of denial. He picks up her lifeless body and carries her down the stairs, tears of disbelief pouring down his face. He sets her down beside his father and mother, sobbing as he caresses Jessica's face. When he can see through the veil of his tears, he looks around at the hall. The floor is no longer visible under the carpet of corpses. He tries in vain to get himself together and search for any survivors: the cook, all the servants, Jessica's parents and family, even the castle guards are dead, some atop the castle walls.

After an hour or so of searching throughout the castle, he hears a faint murmur. It's coming from Ardox the priest, who is out in the castle courtyard. Going over to him, Sargon finds that apparently the priest did not consume enough of the poison to be fatal. Although Ardox is weak, he is alive at least for the moment. Suddenly in the distance, Sargon makes out the sound of horses and armor between the gusts of wind.

"Is that your men?" Ardox coughs.

"No, it's whoever is responsible for this treachery," Sargon answers.

"How do you know?"

"I just have a gut feeling. I learned a long time ago to trust it."

"Then we have no time to waste," gasps Ardox.

"When they arrive, I will be ready, and I will kill as many as those bastards as I can before I am felled," Sargon promises as he reaches for a guard's sword. "Another day, my son, dying today is just what those evil bastards have in mind for all of us. Think of Jessica—your death will only bring down some of the pawns in this evil game of chess. It will not bring down the one responsible for all of this. If you die, all will go unpunished." Ardox clears his throat.

"You are right. With his dying breath my father told me to flee. But I am a knight—well, almost a knight, and knights do not run away!"

"Yes they do, when they are outnumbered. Now let's make haste, for they will be here any moment. Maybe you don't care about dying, but I do. And knights are supposed to protect the weak," Ardox says as he stands and tries to regain his strength."You're right," Sargon agrees and runs to the stable. Sargon leads his horse, Tantor, to the priest. He carefully picks Ardox up and sets him on the animal.

"Can you hold yourself up, Ardox?"

"Yes, I think so. I'll try."

Sargon leads them to the portcullis at the main gate, letting go of the reins. He turns the crank to raise it—a test of his strength without another man to share the weight. After locking it open, he jumps onto the horse behind the priest. He turns back one last time and looks at the devastation.

All the lives lost—his beloved Jessica, his parents, Reaxl and all the other friends and family; it feels impossible to leave. But in the next breath, his sadness turns to anger, and Sargon realizes that Ardox is right. Perhaps the gods have spared his life for revenge, no ... justice.

Sargon says a prayer to Yahmar—Father of the gods—and Marxbaq, the Goddess of Honor, vowing that these deaths will be avenged and that all evil will pay.

Chapter II
Father Yor

S moking lit torches line the curtain walls of the town of Missionwise. Voices echo through the streets as cold, city guards change shifts. The Temple of Yahmar rings with the chanting of acolytes singing verses commemorating Zura. In a room adjacent to the altar stands a nervous young priest named Yor, who is getting ready for his part in the service.

"Everything will be okay," reassures Preador, High Priest of Yahmar, as he pats Yor on the back. "You cannot hide in the shadows of the temple forever ... you are a priest now."

"I hope you are right, Your Grace, many people believe that I am a reflection of my father," Yor says with a slightly pessimistic tone.

"Nonsense, Yor, most of those people have forgotten who you are. Besides, all of that happened before you were born."

"Perhaps you are right, Your Grace, but I am only eighteen, and many of the acolytes say that, at the mere mention of my name, some frown with disgust."

"Well, we will talk after the service. The choir has almost finished their last song. Now don't forget your cue. Right after the prayer, I will introduce you, then you come out and read." Preador reminds him, straightening his robe in front of the large full-sized mirror that Yor has been using.

"Yes, Your Grace, I know—I won't forget." Yor smiles at his mentor, who has been more like a father to him than just a teacher.

Preador walks out of the room and out behind the altar to

continue the service.

Yor thinks back to the stories of his parents that Preador has spoken of through the years.

Yor's father, Bargos, was the Captain of the Guard of Mission-wise for five years before Yor was born. He served under the rule of the Temple of Yahmar and did a great job. Crime was not much of a problem because of Bargos' strict discipline of his men; and also because he took it on himself to judge those accused, most found guilty and pronounce sentence—usually death. The high priest, Faustus, sometimes found this a little disturbing and often questioned Bargos' decisions. But in addition to being a great military leader, Bargos was a real smooth talker and could usually win any argument with the high priest, making the cleric believe that everything was being done for the benefit of the temple.

One day, Bargos came in and told Faustus that a group of clerics from the sect of Asberdies, God of Death, wanted to build a small temple inside the city walls. They claimed that they would give half of their collections to the Temple of Yahmar. "Have you lost your mind, man? That is the enemy of our god, and additionally those priests promote human sacrifices in their ceremonies, drink human blood, and are said to raise zombies from the dead." The high priest eagerly protested.

Bargos shook his head. "That's all superstition, I've been to an Asberdian ceremony and it wasn't at all like that."

"Was it on one of their holy days?"

"No, but ..."

"Then you haven't experienced their practices firsthand."

"That's right, I forgot that all priests know the calendar by heart, and I guess that would mean all the holy days too," Bargos said, changing the subject.

"Yes, that's our job, all holy days of all the gods, and to predict any bad forthcomings that may result from the cycles of Volutus and Pilutus, moons of Zor. It's like the old cleric Zeathara said, 'Each day is its own day.' We also heal the sick and diseased. But you know all this—you're just changing the subject, hoping I will say 'yes.' The answer is 'no,' and if you come at me with this utter nonsense again, you can find yourself another job."

"But Your Grace ..."

"That will be all, Captain."

With that, Bargos stormed out of the chamber and into the courtyard. Preador, who was the assistant to the high priest at that time, saw the fire in Bargos' eyes and warned his mentor, but Faustus thought nothing of it.

The next day, the high priest was found hanging atop the city flagpole, horribly hacked up. All of the priests knew without a doubt that Bargos was behind the slaying. Especially Preador, who thought he might be next and therefore, did not contest Bargos when he declared martial law over the city, vowing to catch the high priest's killer.

It seemed pretty ironic that after the high priest's death, the Asberdian priests moved in and began construction of their small temple. Bargos' wife, Clenok, was outraged to hear of the high priest's murder as well as Bargos' decision to permit the construction of an evil temple. She was very close to the high priest and attended all religious services without question.

"It will tear this city apart!" exclaimed Clenok.

"Nonsense, woman, it will bring religious freedom and extra commerce to the city ... as well as us," said Bargos.

"To us?" asked Clenok. "You mean those Asberdian bastards are paying you off?"

"Enough of this talk, woman, you are my wife and you should support me at whatever I do."

"What has happened to you?" Clenok asked as she softly caressed her husband's cheek. "You are not the man I married five years ago. You've changed for the worst," Clenok said, sobbing. "And what about our son? Will you want him to grow up worshiping the evil Asberdies?"

"Who he worships will be up to him," Bargos said, pushing Clenok's hand away. "But one thing's for sure—he will be a great fighter."

"You used to be as much a follower of Yahmar as I. What has changed your religion?"

"This is my religion now," Bargos said as he grabbed the hilt of his sword.

With that, Clenok came to realize the rumors were true—Bargos did have the priest killed. She waited until Bargos was asleep late that night, then snuck out of the house and to the Temple of Yahmar. Clenok, heavy with child, feared for her and her baby's safety. She decided that the best thing to do was to stay in the temple until the child was born.

Bargos apparently was not bothered by his wife's sudden absence, because the next night he was seen hanging around the Asberdian priests. Weeks passed, Clenok had her child, and the crude Temple of Asberdies was finished. Bargos began celebrating with the priests, in honor of both the birth of his son and the completion of the temple. He shared both the priests' wine and their women. Late that night, Bargos stood outside the Temple of Yahmar in a drunken stupor.

"Clenok!" he hollered, "I want my son." He took another drink of wine from the clay jug in his hand, spilling most of it on himself.

"CLENOK ... I WANT MY SON!" He hollered even louder in the middle of the street, barely able to stand up.

"My Lady, you must get up," a very scared priest called to

Clenok through the door of her chambers.

"Yes, I hear him ... I am coming," answered Clenok as she grabbed her baby and opened the door to her quarters.

"Here, you must take and hide him," Clenok demanded and handed the priest the babe.

But I, but I d-d-don't know what to do with the child." The worried priest stuttered, looking like he could wet himself.

Clenok shook her head, clutching her baby to her chest and walking briskly to a nun's quarters that she knew and trusted. She instructs the nun to hide the babe at all costs. The nun agreed and took the child to the catacombs beneath the temple and hid him there.

Two patrolling guards heard all the commotion from Bargos and went to see if they could render him aid and possibly walk him home.

"Captain, sir, 'tis late. Let me walk you home."

Bargos looked at the soldiers and attempted to straighten himself to attention. "My son ... *hiccup* ... is in that temple, and I want him."

"Yes, sir, I understand. Why don't you come back in the morning and see him?" the other soldier said.

"No ... you ... you ... don't understand, son, that's an order. I want my son now!" Bargos stated as he called for more guards. "Guards, guards come here!" He flagged them down from the city walls.

Soldiers assembled in front of the temple, about twenty in all.

"I want you to go inside this temple and bring me my son. If his mother resists ... kill her," Bargos sternly ordered.

The soldiers didn't blink an eye at his order; they marched into the temple. Priests walked out into the hall of the temple, objecting to such an intrusion, but the guards warned them to stay out of the way.

Bargos, thoroughly drunk and pissed off, paced back and forth, or rather staggered back and forth in front of the temple. He hollered out for Clenok again while standing in the middle of the road, oblivious to the late-arriving merchant wagon. The wagon driver did not see the drunken Bargos as he raced his team through town. Bargos was trampled to death before he knew what had happened. The soldiers never found the baby, though they ransacked the temple, knocking down priceless statuettes and killing a few acolytes in the process. When they do find Clenok, the soldiers slashed her to death because she refused to tell the whereabouts of her son.

Yor snaps back to the present when he hears his cue to join Preador. Some of the congregation gasps as Yor walks before them while reading from one of the holy books of Yahmar. Just then, Yor realizes that some people see him as his father; because, unfortunately for Yor, he looks just like Bargos. He continues to read while scanning the pews with his eyes, getting all kinds of looks ranging from interest to disgust. Yor fears that his unveiling may cause a lot of problems for the temple. He knew that he could not hide in the background forever, but he has always dreaded this day. When the service is over, Yor stands with Preador at the temple doorway to greet and thank people for attending. As people come by, one middle-aged woman says: "Father Preador and uh, uh, Father Yor that was a great service." Staring deeply into Father Yor's eyes, she says, "I'm sorry, but you look remarkably like your father." Then she walks away.

Another much older man says, "Thank ole blessed Yahmar for the two of you fine preachers. Father Yor, I think you did a fine job. And piss on any other who would say otherwise," he adds as he shakes hands with both of the priests.

Many more people compliment on the fine job Father Yor had done, and Yor realizes he is officially a priest now. He thinks it is true what the high priest told him, until he hears a comment from an apparent drunken old man. "Captain Bargos ... you might have everyone fooled, but you don't fool me." The man staggers while talking.

"This is Yor, Bargos died many years ago." Preador objects.

"Well you consp ... consp ... you were with the Asberdian priests before. Perhaps they raised you up from the dead," he adds.

"The temple to Asberdies has been closed for many years now, too," Preador says. "No use arguing with a drunk." He says to Yor as he motions to one of the temple guards.

"I think it's just a matter of time before you take over the town again and turn us all into a bunch of zom ..." the drunk gets interrupted as the temple guard grabs him under his arm and starts escorting him away. "Let me go ... here is what I think of all of you ..." The drunk lets out a big fart as he's hauled away. "You haven't heard the last of me ... you will all be sorry." The drunk says as he is dragged out the door.

"Don't let that bother you, Yor," Preador whispers to Yor as he fans his face "Ugh ... the stench is unbearable." Preador motions to an acolyte who is carrying burning incense, waving him over. They finish thanking the rest of the exiting congregation, who also are clearly taken back by the awful stench and fan the incense smoke around, and then they close the doors of the temple and depart.

Father Yor heads for the temple infirmary to tend to the sick and injured people. This was the thing that Yor really enjoyed about the priesthood. It warms his heart helping and healing people; it further strengthens his faith. As he walks down the steps to the chamber under the temple, he hears the groans of suffering people echoing up the stairs. Yor quickens his pace, the sound sticking him like a sharp thorn in the side. As he enters the chamber, he sees an old man on a table before him. This is a man Yor has been tending to for about three days, and today it does not look like he will make it. An acolyte has been tending to the suffering man as the service was being conducted above.

"How is he?" Yor asks.

"Well, I have given him some healing elixirs and holy water, but nothing seems to work," the young acolyte answers.

"I think he has the plague," Father Yor explains, and the young acolyte jumps back to get away. "See these sores he has," Yor points out. "Yahmar give you strength, young friar."

"Sorry ..." the young acolyte regains some of his composure.

"Help me, Father Yor, please ..." the old man groans.

With tears in his eyes, Yor hurriedly flips through an old manuscript he pulls from a nearby table. He found the book two years ago while cleaning out one of the many libraries of the temple and believes it to be the spell book of Bishop Solias, a very powerful priest said to have healed diseases, fought un-dead, and performed exorcisms. But all of that is pure legend now; the book is very old but is in remarkably good condition. The high priest told Yor that no priest in the last hundred years has been able to use it. It was stored away years ago and forgotten until Yor came upon it. No one has had the gift to make the spells work, or any type of holy magic for that matter. The temple has been relying on natural means of healing from wood, plants, trees, and powers of stones. Yor is down to his last straw with this old man; they have tried everything else. He stops at a page reads, then he grabs the old man's clammy hands. "Close your eyes and pray to Yahmar, for he rules the fate of us all."

The old man closes his eyes and nods.

"Rimuovere la malattia e andare nel fuoco," (*Remove the*

disease and go into the fire) Yor recites as he holds the old man's hand with one hand while extending his other to a torch hanging on a nearby pillar. A bright and deafening light flashes from the old man's palm to Yor's then out to Yor's other hand extended to the torch, which flashes a bright blue flame and then diminishes back to normal after about four seconds.

Yor slumps over the old man, weakened by the whole ordeal. "By Yahmar's holy brow!" says an awestruck Preador, who almost falls down the stairs to the infirmary.

Chapter III
The Third Watch's Demise

'm taking you to Missionwise, Father Ardox," Sargon says, the cold wind almost taking his breath away as Tantor races through the snow. "Do you know who Calador is? Or is it a city?"

"Lord Calador? Yes … of Du'tesh."

"Yes, yes, I remember now. He's east of Missionwise," Sargon exclaims. He looks over his shoulder to see that they are being followed by a hooded figure, probably a scout. Sargon knows that his great warhorse carrying himself and the priest cannot outrun this scout that's on a lighter, more agile horse through the snowy woods.

"Take these!" Sargon barks as he puts the reins in the hands of Ardox. "Get ready to stop the horse."

"I'll do the best I can," the priest, weak and half frozen, says as he braces himself on the bareback horse.

Sargon stands up and grabs a low branch. He pulls himself up, planning to land on their pursuer as he rides underneath. Apparently this scout is no amateur, though. He cuts his horse away from the branch that Sargon is laying on and up toward the priest who can barely stop the horse. Sargon's size doesn't help matters either. Even with the heavy snowfall and strong wind, a child could have seen him, Sargon thinks.

"Stupid, stupid, stupid," Sargon curses himself. "No … don't stop the horse!" he yells.

But it is too late. The hunter with sword in hand runs the defenseless Ardox through.

"Wait, my son …" Ardox says as he is gutted like a fish.

"Damn you! Come and get me, you cowardly bastard!" Sargon yells as he drops to his feet while Ardox falls lifeless in the snow. Sargon picks up a large snow-covered branch from the ground and charges the scout, who has circled around to finish him off. He swings with all his might, knocking both horse and rider to the ground. In his rage he easily pulverizes this murderer.

Sargon spits on the scout's head, grabbing him as the horse gets up and runs off. He then takes the scout's sword, turning him about to look for a coat of arms or some other clue to identify who this scout is working for, but to no avail. Sargon turns and looks at his horse, Tantor, standing by the slain priest. Shaking his head, he makes his way through the ever-deepening snow. He leans down and sees that every drop of life that Ardox had is now in the snow. Sargon makes a holy sign with his hand over the priest and then mounts his horse. Looking at the man he killed, Sargon knows that it won't be long before the scout is missed, even in this blizzard.

Snow flies as Tantor's hooves crash through the snow. Icicles form on Sargon's hair as it flows in the miserable wind. He finally begins to feel just how cold it actually is, having only wedding garb on, but at least he has his cape.

Looking back after fifteen minutes of hard riding, Sargon slows his horse to a walk. Tantor rears suddenly, spooked by a figure standing before him. Sargon easily stays on but is surprised too.

"Bellgrad, by the gods, you're alive. I totally forgot you were on the third watch!" Sargon replies as he sees a huge gash across his friend's forehead. He quickly slides off his horse and catches Bellgrad as the man slumps.

"Our patrol was ambushed …" Bellgrad mutters before he blacks out.

Sargon sets Bellgrad softly in the snow and leans him against his knee while tearing strips off his cape to bind his friend's wounds.

"It was made to look like a perq attack," Bellgrad says, regaining consciousness. "Someone ambushed us and laid dead perequine amongst us."

As Sargon rises to his feet, helping his wounded friend to stand, he sees over Bellgrad's shoulder the carnage that was once the last watch of his father's castle. It was easy to see that no perq attack could ever take out ten armored cavalrymen. Those creatures are too cowardly; unless they are in great numbers to stand against men on horseback, they tend to prey on weak and easy targets.

Someone went to a lot of trouble to make it look like a perq ambush, Sargon thought.

"Give me fifty men, and I will hunt down this vermin," Bellgrad says as he braces himself against Sargon. Gaining back some of his wits as he looks at the young nobleman dressed in wedding attire. "Why are you here? You're supposed to be at the ..." The cold wind takes his breath away in mid-sentence.

"I know, but it looks like everyone, but you and I are dead," says Sargon as his mind recalls the scene of his parents and his beloved wife. "*Love me, love no other*," the last sweet words of Jessica play again in his mind. The remorse turns to anger as he sees more death in the slain night watchmen.

"Bellgrad, we need to go. I killed a scout close to the castle, and I'm sure he will be missed soon," Sargon says as he boosts Bellgrad on the back of trusty Tantor.

"Everyone is dead, my lord?" Bellgrad asks.

"As we will be if we don't get going," Sargon says as he boosts himself behind his friend. He makes a holy sign in the air and says a prayer for his fallen comrades. He then spurs Tantor onward; he knows they must seek shelter for Bellgrad's sake. Sargon knows that he can make it, even dressed as he is, but Bellgrad won't.

They both travel for what seems to be a few miles, but it is hard to measure in the worsening blizzard. A light appears in the distance as the snowfall increases. Sargon makes out a cottage and spurs Tantor onward. When they reach the house, Sargon slides down and helps Bellgrad off the horse and to the front door. Sargon shivers as he knocks with one hand and holds up his half-conscious friend with the other. A man opens the door.

"Sir, we need lodging for—"

"By the gods, Sargon, come in out of this blizzard, lad," interrupts a familiar voice.

"Zeth!" Sargon smiles. "Thank the gods."

"Woman, fetch us some mead. Lassie," he says, looking at his daughter, "get some cloth, and bandage this lad's wounds." Zeth barks orders as he helps Sargon inside with Bellgrad. They both carry Bellgrad to the fireplace and prop him against a large stump in front of it.

"Boy, tend to Sargon's horse," Zeth commands his son. The boy nods, throws on a heavy animal pelt, and walks out the door.

"By the name of Yahmar, Sargon, what happened?" Zeth asks as they all three receive some nice warm mead.

Sargon and Bellgrad sip the nectar of the gods, or at least that's how it feels for a moment as the mead warms their frigid bodies. Sargon tells Zeth the horrible account of the night. Zeth's wife lets out a loud gasp, and Zeth himself is speechless. Three noble houses wiped out in an instant. Zeth has been living in the realm of Castle Guel since he was Sargon's age. Even now, at forty, he has never seen such deception. He followed in his father's footsteps as a blacksmith and has been a very loyal and dependable subject to Sargon's family for years, like his father before him.

"I believe this is the work of Heyrold of Vry," Sargon explains. "We were never in good standing with Vry. I never did like that bastard anyway."

"Young laddie, you are in no position to take on a whole city," Zeth advises.

"Yes, you're right, but I will exact my revenge on Heyrold and that assassin he planted in my family's castle … By the way, this is good mead."

"Yes … very good," Bellgrad adds.

"Like it, aye? I made meself." Zeth chuckles as he pats the young Sargon on the back and smiles at Bellgrad.

They both drink and watch as Zeth's daughter, Meg, takes off the blood-soaked cloth that Sargon put on Bellgrad's wound. She then takes a needle and thread, sews up the wound, puts a homemade salve on it, and wraps the gash with fresh bandages.

"Thank you." Bellgrad smiles at her while spilling a little of the mead on himself.

"Here, let me help you with that." Meg smiles softly at Bellgrad while she wipes off her hands. Then she gently holds the back of his neck as he sips.

"She looks like she has done that before," Sargon comments while he glances at the sewing kit next to Bellgrad.

"Aye, you don't stay a blacksmith long without getting cut from time to time," Zeth answers as he holds up one of his scarred hands.

"Get some rest, dear friend. We have a long journey ahead of us in the morrow," Sargon tells Bellgrad, leaning over him and putting a hand on his friend's shoulder.

Zeth cuts Sargon a look at that comment. He pulls Sargon aside. "Look, laddie, you'll be lucky if he makes the night, much less a journey in the morrow ... He needs rest," Zeth whispers.

"I know, but those men will be looking for me in the morning, and he needs a healer, so I'm taking him to Missionwise to the priests of Yahmar. If he stays here, he will surely die," Sargon states under his breath as he looks at his wounded friend.

"What about his armor, Da'?" Meg asks as she puts Bellgrad's empty mug upon the hearth.

"Leave it. We will take it off in the morrow. He should not be moved anymore. Let's lay him down and keep his head propped up. Where will you go from there, Sargon?" Zeth asks as he steps back to help Meg lay Bellgrad on the floor.

"Well, I know Lord Calador. He and my father were good friends, although it has been years since I have seen him. I know he will put us up for a while. He's about a day's journey south of Missionwise. Why don't you come with us? There is nothing for you here now, and I bet Calador is in need of a good weapon-maker."

"Sure ... I did some work for Calador some years back. Well, I have a couple of swords I need to finish up for a few of the locals, and it will take us a day or so to pack up everything," Zeth replies as he covers Bellgrad with a bear hide.

"Then it is settled. I will see you at Lord Calador's in three days," Sargon agrees as he lays himself diagonal to Bellgrad, up close to the fireplace, and Zeth throws him another animal hide.

Zeth tends to the fire and adds two more logs in the fireplace. Sargon closes his eyes, smiling at the sound of the crackling fire and the soothing smell of burning oak. He reminisces about being a boy in his family's castle, about the servants tending the fire in his room, but he quickly remembers where he is at the sound of Zeth's voice.

The older man lets out with some new words to their language as he drops a log on his foot. Sargon breaks into laughter, it's comforting in its own way, but only for a moment. As Zeth departs for bed, Sargon cannot help but think back on what happened earlier—his whole family murdered. He shakes his head and grimaces as the horrible sights run through his mind. He unwittingly drifts off to sleep, remembering ... *"I love you, love no other,"* ... Jessica.

Chapter IV
The Dark Figure

 ll the men are dead, my lord. We found a few men asleep in the bunkhouse that had apparently not eaten at the wedding. What should we do with them?" The soldier asks as he points to five half-asleep men escorted out of the bunkhouse. They're half dressed and astounded at all the death surrounding them.

"Kill them," a dark figure commands. "Kill them all. No survivors."

"I thought you were going to poison everyone." The commanding general says as screams of horror rise in the backgrounds as the defenseless men meet their deaths. "Heyrold will not like this ..." The cold wind breaks the general's words. "Let us get inside," the general barks as he gets off his horse. "See to my horse, Lieutenant."

"Yes, sir," the soldier replies. He grabs the general's mount and leads it to the stable as the rest of the thirty-man escort enters the castle.

The general and his adversary walk inside the great hall out of the snow-blown wind.

"Ah, that's much better." The general smiles as he warms himself in front of the great hall's fireplace. "Now, this was supposed to be clean without blood."

"Well, I guess we need to burn the bodies then, don't we?" The dark figure suggests.

"No ..." the general ponders, tapping his upper lip with his finger. "That will only make their families wonder what became of them. Leave the bodies where they lie. We will bury them in the morrow after their families have come to identify them. Did anyone else survive?"

"Yes, the son and the priest. I saw them take off shortly before you all arrived. They heard your horses running up the road and headed into the woods."

"The priest, you say? Well, isn't that just wonderful!" The general says sarcastically. "The boy's words would be easy to dismiss, but not a priest."

"Not to worry, General, the priest ate enough pork to kill two men. He will not survive the night."

"Well, hopefully some of the scouts have killed them by now," the general suggests. "We will blame all of this on the boy. Uh ... what's his name?"

"Sargon."

"Yes ... Sargon," the general mumbles, remembering. "We will tell the people that Sargon went mad and killed everyone at this wedding." The general smiles. "Including those men that most tragically met their deaths. He apparently planned a scheme that went wrong and had to kill five unarmed men that were not exposed to the poison."

"And stable boys," the assassin interrupts.

"And stable boys? Good ... then fled when he heard our approach. This is going to work out better than I planned." The general smiles, rubbing his hands excitedly. "That is of course if the priest dies. In the morning we will dispatch messengers to all of the guest's families to let them know of the murder that happened tonight."

"Well, we had better check around the area—he could have evaded your men." "Why isn't he dead along with the others?" the general asks.

"I didn't have enough time to poison the barrels of wine like I planned. The boy did not eat any of the pork ... he hates pork."

"How inconvenient for you. Are we sure that Heyrold has your undivided loyalty?" the general laughingly asks.

"Loyalty—hell, I'll have his undivided J'avins (gold coins). I poisoned a glass of Sargon's wine, but apparently he did not drink enough of it," the assassin says with a raised brow. "And he did not touch any of the pheasants like I thought he would."

"Well, with this weather he will either die or seek shelter." The general turns and faces the doorway. "Sergeant?"

"Yes, General." A heavily armored figure approaches.

"Have any of the scouts reported in?"

"No, sir, not yet. This blizzard has made it hard to see. They will probably be coming in shortly. The snowfall has gotten worse."

"Have one of your men send word to the Duke of Darconia that the whole of Castle Guel has been poisoned. We discovered the treachery upon entering the castle, having been late to the wedding due to the weather."

The sergeant gestures over to a soldier, who pulls out a quill and ink along with a rolled-up sheet of parchment out of his belt pouch. He then sets himself on one of the hall's tables and begins writing as the sergeant relays the message.

The general pauses momentarily then continues, "We believe that Sargon, heir to the Guel estate has committed this act. He fled upon our arrival, and we look to have him in our grasp on the morrow, once the weather has cleared. We will keep you informed, as Lord Heyrold would have it. Signed General Dytruik of Vry." Looking at the young soldier, he commands, "Deliver that in the morning, son."

"Yes, sir," the young man says pausing to look at the general.

Turning to the dark figure, the general asks, "What food has not been poisoned? I'm starved. And get these bodies out of here." He gestures to the floor.

"General, a horse has just entered the castle walls," a soldier calls from outside.

The general walks to the doorway and glares at a horse that the men are capturing.

"Hey, that's one of our horses," the general comments as he spots a brand on the animal's hip. "Sergeant, send a couple of your men to scan the area."

"But, sir, the weather is getting worse ..."

"I don't give a damn. Get someone out there to see where this horse came from, and see if we got that boy!" The general turns and faces the sergeant behind him. "As a matter of fact, Sergeant Trymith, you go out there too."

"Yes, sir," Sergeant Trymith reluctantly acknowledges as he proceeds toward the door.

The general goes back to his chair as soldiers start carrying bodies out to the snow-covered courtyard.

"Now, as I was saying, what can be eaten?" The general asks as he scans the table before him.

"Well, these hens have not been laced, nor the venison, nor did anything from the other table," the assassin points out.

Sergeant Trymith and three of his men ride their horses through the front gate of Guel Castle. The blizzard has turned the top of the mountain white, and the men are doing good to see five feet ahead of themselves. They start around a turn of the castle when a heavy gust nearly knocks the sergeant from his horse.

"Go around that way," the sergeant barks as he points to the west. The howling wind carries away his words. But one of his men sees his gesture west and begins out that direction. He disappears into the swirling snow. Only beyond the brief pauses between the gusts comes a faint sound:

"Aaaaaaaaaaaaaaaaaaaaaaaaaaaaaaaaaahhhhhhhhhhhhhhhh."

As the hapless soldier and horse fall to their death, Sergeant Trymith sees he was wrong. It would appear that Guel Castle is already seeking revenge. Completely disoriented, he jumps off his horse and sits on the ground, unaware of where he is and where the other soldier may be. He hollers out only to have his breath taken away by the frigid wind. He walks in the direction of where he thinks the castle may be; by chance he finds the wall before him. The howling wind begins to taper off, but the snowfall continues. He calls out to the men inside.

"Hey where's the gate?"

"Over here," he hears about thirty feet ahead of him along the wall. "Sergeant Trymith, is that you?"

"Yes." The sergeant smiles as he walks his way to the gatehouse.

"Herroth has returned, and so has your horse. We have not seen Melius, though."

"He fell off ..." A frozen gust breaks Trymith's words as the wind bellows again. He just speeds up his trek to the gatehouse through the knee-deep snow. He finally reaches the opening and makes his way into one of the guards' quarters within the gatehouse. He sees within a nice warm fire burning in a fireplace made in the wall and lunges for it like a madman. The four guards around it part like water to let Sergeant Trymith warm himself.

"Damn, it's cold! By the gods, I thought I was done for," Trymith says as he shakes the snow off his fur cape and field plate. He pulls off his frozen gauntlets and warms his hands. "Melius is dead. He fell off this cursed mountain. I'm glad to see you are still around, Herroth," he adds with a half-smile as he eyes the man next to him.

"Thanks. 'Tis a total whiteout, sir. Why did we go out there?"

"Just following orders. I told the general it was getting worse out there. But he ordered it still. So, as soon as the storm passes, we shall get underway again. Hopefully we will find this young murderer frozen out there."

"Do you think he really did it? I was one of the last to arrive."

"Yes," Trymith says hesitantly as he turns to warm his backside.

"Why? I wonder, what did he hope to gain?"

"You think too much soldier," Trymith barks as he cuts his eyes at Herroth. "You are part of the Elite guard. Don't you know you are not paid to think?"

"Yes, sir. I'm new to the guard."

A soldier opens the door.

"Damn that wind," Trymith barks as a frigid wind blasts through the small room "Close that door, soldier!"

"Sir, the general has called us all to the great hall."

"Okay, we are on our way," Trymith says as he points the other men to the door.

The soldier departs into the cold courtyard, followed by Trymith and the other soldiers. They walk into the crowded hall. The floor is vacant of any corpses, and the room is filled with soldiers eating and drinking. General Dytruik is standing atop a stage on the opposite side of the room with a large trunk in front of him. He looks at Sergeant Trymith and motions him in.

"Okay, men. Now that you have filled your bellies, not with the pork or the other tainted meat," the general jokes while others laugh in the background, "as I promised you before we left, I am giving you a bonus for all your help in this tragic event. In the morrow, we will put the Guel family in the crypt below the castle. We will also have the townspeople claim the other dead. The boy has escaped along with the priest ..."

"He won't talk," interrupts a figure entering the room.

"Riechter! Good to see you." The general smiles.

"I found the priest dead about ten feet away from Haeser; I brought them both. It appears someone bashed Haeser's head in with a massive tree branch. But I guess not before the priest got gutted." Riechter says as he walks toward the general, brushing the snow from the heavy animal pelts he wears. "It was the Guel boy on a large warhorse. I will go after him in the morrow after the storm clears," He adds as he grabs a roast quail from the adjacent table, sniffing it before he puts it in his mouth and smiles.

"How did you know that it was Sargon, the Guel boy?" the general asks, always impressed with Vry's best tracker. "Especially with all this bad weather."

"Well, you do not find a simple soldier with this elaborate garb on," Riechter says as he pulls a small piece of material out of his belt pouch. "I found this a few feet away from Haeser's body. I was amazed I found it myself with the heavy wind, but I managed to uncover it from about two inches of snow. It looks to be of ceremonial garb, possibly blown from one of the trees. Besides, I know that none of us have a horse that heavy ... Go on, general, it would appear that you have some J'avins there before you in that chest," he adds as he sits on one of the tables.

"How do you know I have gold in it? Is there some kinda way you can see inside it?" the general asks.

"No ... I can smell it." Riechter laughs, as do many of the soldiers at that comment.

The general laughs too, "Well, I will not hesitate any longer." He opens the chest and starts pulling out bags of gold. He throws the bags to all the men, who catch them without haste. "It's fifty J'avin, men." With that, the room really comes to life.

Calls of "Thanks, General," are heard throughout the room. It would take them ten years or longer to make that much. Sivs (silver) and Pens (copper) are the mainstay of their income.

Chapter 𝒱
The Morning

he smell of cooking meat tickles Sargon's nose, as does the spiced tea. It takes him back to when he was a child, waking in his nanny's quarters after a nightmare had drawn him there during the night. The servants' quarters were all close to the kitchen, of course, and she would be up with the other servants getting the castle ready for breakfast. She would bring Sargon a warm mug of apple cider and dress him while he drank it. She would then wrap him in a deerskin and carry him into the kitchen. The kitchen crew would then entertain him (or so he thought). He was fed roast rabbit and quail eggs while he laughed at everyone scurrying about getting everything ready before Lord Guel awakened.

"Aye, you're awake. Good," Zeth's wife, Myriam, says as Sargon opens his heavy eyes. "Like some tea, hon?"

"Yes, please," Sargon says as he tries to wake and peers over to see Bellgrad already enjoying a cup. "How's your head?"

"Feels like Tantor kicked it, but I'm okay."

Sargon looks at his longtime friend and sees that the gash is still bleeding, judging by the blood-soaked bandages that cover it.

"Here, dear," Myriam says to Sargon as she hands him a goblet of spiced tea. "Meg and I are cooking up your favorite this morning, Sargon—rabbit. Zeth tells me that when you were a wee one that's all you ate."

"That's right," Sargon smiles, peering over his shoulder to see Meg turning the handle of a skewer in the fireplace, "but how would he know?”

“He says whenever he visited the castle in the mornings, that’s what you were eating.” Myriam giggles. “He says that afterward you usually ran about the castle naked as day. You sure kept your nanny busy.”

“Yes, she was a dear sweet lady,” Sargon remembers.

“Yes, you had that whole castle in an uproar with all your running about,” Zeth adds with a slight laugh as he walks in the room.

“Yes, I’ve heard all the stories.” Sargon rolls his eyes.

“You’re looking chipper this morning, lad,” Zeth says to Bellgrad as he looks at his head.

“I’m alive, thanks to all of you!” Bellgrad says.

“’Tis nothin’, lad, you just get yourself better.”

Sargon tells Zeth under his breath, “He’s worse than you think, he just has the willpower of a bull.”

“Aye, ’tis a good thing, though,” Zeth comments as Myriam hands him a cup of tea.

“Here, hon,” Myriam says, handing Sargon a plate with half a roasted rabbit on it. “Careful, that’s very hot.”

The meat is still sizzling as Sargon looks at the delicious treat. “Thanks, Myriam.”

She scurries back to the fireplace and gets another plate that Meg has prepared then hands it to Bellgrad. “Here you go, dear. Eat up—you need your strength.”

“Thanks, milady ... mmm, nice,” Bellgrad acknowledges as the smell tickles his nose.

She then gets Zeth a plate and brings them all some bread with lard. She then gets food for her children and, finally, herself.

“This is good rabbit,” Sargon says. “Where did you get it?”

“From the cages in the stable. Joesef, our boy, cleaned them before you woke. You slept pretty hard, and I thought he would wake you with all his stumbling about, but you slept right through." Myriam comments as she eats.

"'Tis good meat, milady," Bellgrad adds.

After everyone has eaten, Meg rewraps Bellgrad's head then commences with taking off his armor.

"This armor's done for, must have been one hell of a fight," Zeth comments as he helps Meg.

"I don't remember much, except we were attacked from all sides," Bellgrad answers. "I was one of the first ones hit. If it weren't for Sargon, I would be dead along with the others," Bellgrad continues as Zeth tosses Bellgrad's breastplate aside.

"'Tis nothing—you would have done the same. Besides, it was a cherub of Marxbaq that had awakened you, else I would have never seen you." Sargon smiles.

"Yes, I believe you're right! Praise her great name," Bellgrad acknowledges as they make a holy sign in front of themselves.

"Hold still there, lad." Zeth grabs Bellgrad's chain mail shirt to remove. Looks like this chain mail has had it too, I'd say that armor saved yer ass ... Oops. Sorry, Wife," Zeth says, getting a glare from Myriam.

"I've heard worse from that mouth," Myriam snickers.

"Aye, that you have, Wife. Now hold him steady whilst I pull this over his head," Zeth commands as he looks at Meg and holds out the chain mail with both hands, trying not to touch Bellgrad's head as he pulls it over the wounded soldier.

"Yes, Da," Meg answers and holds Bellgrad with both hands.

"Now, you rest there, lad, whilst I go get you some fresh armor. I have a suit I think will fit you. Lars—one of the Guel knights—traded that in for his new set I made him last year, and he's as big as you." Zeth motions to Sargon, "Come, lad, I cannot carry all that armor meself."

Meg smiles at Bellgrad as Zeth and Sargon walk out the door.

"You are very sweet, milady," Sargon hears Bellgrad say to Meg before the door closes.

"Looks like Bellgrad has taken quite a fancy to young Meg," Sargon says.

"Aye, I noticed. Looks like every young man in the kingdom has."

"Well ... she has come of age."

"Aye, I know. Don't remind me, I feel like I need to carry an axe every time I open the door," Zeth says as they arrive at the doors of the armory to see there is only one door that is partially cleared from the heavy snowbank that blocks entry.

"Help me with this, lad ..." Zeth asks as he kicks snow out of the way. "That damn boy ..." Zeth grumbles under his breath.

Sargon helps kick the snow out of the way and then starts digging it out with his hands as Zeth opens both doors.

"Looks like the storm has passed," Sargon comments as he looks up at the starry sky.

"Aye, I know. We must hurry. Sulo is breaking through the trees," Zeth answers as he pushes the second door open and motions to the north with his head.

The two men walk inside the massive barn. Zeth walks over and pulls a chain on a huge bellows as coals start to glow.

"Wow, it's nice and warm in here," Sargon says, smiling as he rushes over to the forge and warms his frigid hands. *Man ... this is heaven!* Sargon thinks to himself as he briefly closes his eyes and inhales the smell of cedar, oak, coal, and iron. He hears the slight jingle from the chains and other tools hanging from the ceiling swinging lightly back and forth as the morning air draws in.

"Aye, I was here fairly late last night finishing up your armor. That's why I did not attend your wedding ... Sorry, lad."

"'Tis all right ... Whoa ... that is beautiful!" Sargon's eyes light up at the sight of a suit of field plate hanging on an armor stand and glistening in the firelight from the forge.

"Well, laddie, put it on. You can gawk at it later when you are far from here." Zeth lights a torch and puts it in a hanger on a post by the forge.

"Thanks." Sargon smiles as he puts on the padding and chain mail that goes under the armor then continues putting on the armor piece by piece.

"Come on, lad, you move like old people ..." Zeth holds his tongue. "Here, let me help you with that." Zeth hurriedly helps Sargon get armored up and grabs two gauntlets by the forge. "Here, put these on."

"These fit perfectly, thanks," Sargon comments as they slide snugly on his hands.

"There's the scabbard for your sword. Where is your sword?" Zeth says as he points to a sword scabbard hanging from a nail on a post.

"What Sword?"

"I made a sword for you, lad. You mean...oh that's right you never made it to your room." Zeth says referring to the tradition of a man receiving a sword on his wedding day, left on the wedding bed and accepted before consummating the marriage.

"No, it got left behind. I suppose Heyrold has it," Sargon says.

"Pity.... Here, take these inside," Zeth says as he throws Sargon a breastplate and leggings. Then he grabs the rest of the armor and heads for the door behind Sargon. Joesef opens the door as the two arrive; they rush in and set the armor next to Bellgrad on the floor. Then they both grab the young soldier under each arm and set him atop the stump he has been leaning against. Zeth puts on the chain mail over Bellgrad's padded shirt, which Meg had put on while they were outside. Sargon starts putting on the leggings as Joesef rushes out the door.

"Where is he going?" Sargon asks.

"To finish getting your horses ready," Zeth answers as he fastens Bellgrad's breastplate.

"There now, stand up," Sargon tells Bellgrad as he fastens the second leg.

They both help Bellgrad stand then continue attaching and fastening together his armor pieces.

Zeth tries to fasten one chest buckle but it will not fasten any tighter. "Well, I guess it's better than if it were too small. It will work."

"Thanks, but I can take it from here." Bellgrad reaches for the buckles of his armor and then for the two gauntlets in Sargon's hands. "I'm feeling better, my lord ... really!" Bellgrad adds as he looks at Sargon.

"Good, then let's get going." Sargon starts for the door.

They both walk outside and see two horses armored and saddled—Tantor and a horse of Zeth's.

"Damn ..." Sargon and Bellgrad say at the same time with gaping eyes. Sargon has never seen his great warhorse covered in full plate barding before. Bellgrad had seen his share of horses with armor before, but he is still impressed.

"You see why I kept Tantor over here for those five days now?" Zeth snickers.

"Yeah, well I sure did not see any damage on his hooves that you claimed happened when you shod him." Sargon smirks as he walks over and checks the intricate work of the barding.

"I guess that's what I get for letting you help me last year ... well, a knight needs those kinda skills ... your father agreed, but knights like Lars would never listen to me, felt it was beneath him," Zeth comments, shaking his head.

"Well, I for one sure do appreciate it, although I have to admit it was a lot of work." Sargon answers with a laugh as he runs his hands over the barding. "But well worth it … Wow, that was six months ago when I brought Tantor over here?" Sargon remembers as he jumps on his horse.

"To the day. It took a while, but it would have taken longer if I did not have Joesef," Zeth proudly acknowledges.

"Hey, you left those shields on the chest plate and buckle guards blank," Sargon says as he points to the front of his horse.

Bellgrad swings onto his horse easily, like he's not even hurt, but Sargon knows it's just for show. He knows his friend must see one of the healers in Missionwise fast before a fever sets in.

"Well, laddie, you know that's where your crest goes, not your family's … and you haven't made one yet, nor have ye been knighted."

"True. Well, thanks for everything," Sargon says as he eyes Zeth and Myriam, who has joined her husband on the front porch with Meg behind her. "We will see all of you in three days. You do remember how to get there, right?" Sargon asks, as Joesef ties a lead rope to the back of Sargon's saddle. He then grabs a lance from out of the armory.

"Aye, I do. We will figure some crest designs when we get there," Zeth answers.

"Thanks," Bellgrad says as he waves to everyone and smiles at Meg.

"I see that look in your eye, Sargon lad. The armor and barding are your father's gifts. The sword is our gift. As for the horses and Bellgrad's armor—you'll need 'em, don't fret none about the your sword either; it will turn up," Zeth says.

"Here, Sir Sargon," Joesef hands him the lance he brought. "You both have swords hanging on your horses, and there are more weapons including unpainted shields, which are on both packhorses, along with food and other supplies," Joesef adds as he points to Sargon and Bellgrad's packhorses.

"Thanks, Joesef. You could have made a good squire," Sargon says.

"Thanks, milord, but I would rather make armor and swords than wear and use them."

"Spoken like a true blacksmith." Sargon laughs.

Sargon and Bellgrad salute their friends and ride away.

"Let's get going, lad, we have lots of work to do," Zeth tells Joesef as they both walk into the armory. Zeth throws on his leather apron then fires up the forge as Joesef adds more wood to the fire. Zeth pulls a roughed-out sword he was working on a few days earlier from a pile of other sword pieces stacked in a barrel and puts it in the forge. Both work through the next hour as three riders approach.

"Hey, old man. Long time no see," the mysterious hooded man yells between Zeth's hammering. "Hey, old man ..."

"I hear you, Riechter," Zeth interrupts as he slowly looks up. His long red hair partially covers his eyes, showing only his expressionless face.

"Wow ... you remember. What's it been, twenty years?"

"Twenty four ... Well, I always remember the hiss of a viper. What is it you seek?" Zeth asks as he relaxes his hammer on the anvil.

"Ah, I'm disappointed, Zeth. No hugs or kisses? Still carrying a grudge, I see, even after all these years. Well, it wasn't my fault your brother went bad," Riechter says as he pulls back his hood and slides off his horse. He drops the reins as he lands on the snow-covered ground all in one motion, silent and agile as a cat.

"How's your father?"

"Been dead for five years now. What do you care?" Zeth says without hesitation.

"Shame—was a damn good bow maker."

"Aye, he could make any kinda weapon you like," Zeth remembers. "Well, he never forgave you for what you did."

"Where are my manners ... Garxe, Mychel ... this is Rylle's younger brother." Riechter points his open hand to Zeth.

"Rest yerself, lad," Zeth looks over his shoulder at Joesef, who is pumping the bellows. He stops and joins his father.

"Ah, Rylle's the one you followed from your home country of Kalamash?" Garxe asks.

"Yes, the reason I found a new home here in Fegnir. Well, I thought it was time for a change, anyway. Kalamash was so ... boring." Riechter's arrogant tone matches his movements; he slowly pulls off his leather gloves finger by finger and scans the armory and Joesef like a fox looking over a henhouse.

"Yes, you're right. It wasn't your fault he was a petty thief, but you did not have to follow him to Fegnir either. He was going to start a new life here with us," Zeth continues, staring Riechter directly in the eyes.

"Well, I always get my prize. Besides, he was—" Riechter stops.

"A horse thief!" Garxe interrupts. "Or ... that's what Riechter has told us."

"You were still tugging on your nanny's skirt back in those days." Zeth says as he breaks eye contact and looks at Garxe. "Or tugging on something else."

Laughter rings out from behind Riechter.

"And you did not have to shoot him in the back either," Zeth adds as he eyes Riechter again.

"He was running from the law," Riechter says and cuts a searing glance over his shoulder at Garxe's interruption and the other's laughter.

"You're not the law, you arrogant lil' bastard! You're a bounty hunter," Zeth says as he drops his hammer to the ground and starts for Riechter. Joesef shakes his head and puts his hand on his father's shoulder. Zeth's face is flushed red with rage. Joesef has heard that Riechter is a legend with knives and bows. Riechter stands only five foot five inches tall and is older than his father, but even standing with his father at over six feet, he fears for his father's life.

"Smart boy," Riechter smirks. The hand that caressed the hilt of a throwing knife hidden below his hood behind his neck moves to brush back his long hair.

"You know, you're not worth it," Zeth says as Joesef breathes a sigh of relief.

"Trymith? What the hell are you doing keeping company with this low life?" Zeth calls out as he eyes Sergeant Trymith riding up with some other soldiers.

"I'm here under orders from General Dytruik to escort Riechter," Trymith snickers.

"You know this man?" Riechter turns to Trymith.

"Hell, everyone in the region knows Zeth." Trymith smiles. "His skills have saved my ass a number of times," he continues as he knocks on his breastplate. "He is the best and fastest blacksmith I have ever seen ... well, next to his father."

Zeth smiles at Trymith. "Thanks, but you keep poor company."

"So what does Heyrold have his bloodhound and peons sniffing out this time?" Joesef interrupts. "Except for you, Sergeant," Joesef nods at Trymith.

"Peons? Watch your tongue boy! I have ten blacksmiths working at my castle," Mychel barks out.

"Having money and castles does not make you better than us," Joesef retracts.

"Hmmm, like father like son," Riechter laughs as he holds up his hand to Mychel to stop. "I think you know why I'm here,

Zeth."

"Well, let me guess, you are on your way to Darconia because you heard they were looking for a village idiot, so you thought you would apply."

Laughter rings out from behind Riechter.

"Very amusing. It's the Guel boy—he came by this way, right?" Riechter looks back at Zeth.

"I do not know what you are talking about."

"Don't play stupid with me. I see these heavy horse tracks that head away from this place as well as those drops of blood in the snow." Riechter points over his shoulder behind him.

"So? Lots of people have big horses. I have customers come and go all the time with big steeds. Maybe one of my customers cut himself. What do you want with Sargon anyway?" Zeth asks.

"Come now, Zeth, don't insult my intelligence," Riechter adds.

"That would not take much," Zeth snickers. "Be off with you, I have work to do. Go find someone else to brag about your ventures and money to." Zeth picks his hammer off the ground.

"Look, I have been patient long enough. More men are approaching. We can do this the easy way or the hard way— makes no nevermind to me," Riechter says as three more soldiers approach and stop their horses just behind his mount.

"Go soak your head," Zeth blurts out.

"Sergeant Trymith, arrest this man and his family! They have been helping the Guel boy. They sheltered him last night," Riechter orders as he walks toward his horse."

"My family? They have nothing to do with this ... I'll tell you what you need to know, let my family be." Zeth sighs.

"Too late for that now. Search the premises too—you might find some poison stashed away somewhere," Riechter says arrogantly. He smiles, looking over his horse at the men, and grabs the horse's reins.

Zeth's temper and his mouth have gotten the better of him again. He did not think they would do anything rash during the day, but he knows they will not bother taking his family to Vry, not while Riechter is hot on Sargon's trail. They will just simply take him and his family into the woods and execute them and anyone that stands in his way ... including Trymith. He had forgotten briefly that the only people close by that would stop Heyrold's ambitions died last night. If the charade that Sargon killed his own family and Jessica's is believed, then the Duke of Darconia will declare the land forfeit and give it all to Heyrold.

"Hold up!" Sergeant Trymith says, looking at his men. "Riechter, let's just move on. You have a trail—let's follow it. We are losing valuable time."

"I did not ask for your advice. You are in enough hot water with the general as it is. Had you gone after the Guel boy last night as you were ordered, we would have him."

"Hey, Riechter, burn in hell you perq shit son of a bitch!" Zeth barks as he launches his hammer with all his might toward Riechter's head.

Riechter quickly twists forward out of the way. The hammer barely misses his head and strikes his mount on the front left shoulder with a loud *pop* then tumbles across the horse's chest and lands in the soft snow beyond. The blow nearly knocks the animal to the ground. The horse jerks its head up and spins suddenly, pulling Riechter tumbling to the ground directly underneath his mount. The horse spins around trying to gain its footing, and its left hind hoof comes down sharply on Riechter's right leg just above the ankle, snapping it like a twig.

"Aahh!" Riechter shrieks out in pain and grabs his ankle while his horse limps off.

At the same time, Sergeant Trymith and Private Keagon, two soldiers across from Riechter, have to gain control of their horses. Corporal Herroth, who was behind Riechter's horse, is drug off when his mount spooks, his left foot hung up in the stirrup.

"Herroth!" Sergeant Trymith cries out as he sees the young soldier being drug away through the snowy woods. "Ah, Shit!"

Garxe drops the crossbow in order to control his horse, which lunges backward and spins around to run. Mychel, however, is not bothered at all by this whole escapade and keeps total control of his horse. He already had his sword halfway drawn when all the action started. He rides forward, but his horse balks at the entrance, refusing to enter the armory. He spurs it onward, and the horse complies.

The horse's slight hesitation allows enough time for Zeth to grab the sword he was working on and parry a blow from Mychel. Joesef grabs a spear and thrusts it from behind Zeth, but not before Mychel comes down with his sword a second time. This time, he hits Zeth in the left shoulder, cutting it deep. Joesef's spear glances off Mychel's heavy breastplate but manages to knock him off balance, giving Zeth an opportunity to strike back. Zeth swings upward with the dull sword. He hits the soldier in the bottom of the chin, breaks his jaw, and knocks him off the horse. A few teeth fly from his bloody mouth. Mychel's horse runs, trampling its master in the process.

"Kill that son of a bitch!" Riechter barks at the soldiers.

Trymith, Keagon, and Garxe jump off their horses, draw their swords, and move toward the armory.

"Myriam!" Zeth hollers out. "Run, girl, run!"

"Zeth ... drop the sword!" Trymith pleads.

"Too late for that now!" Zeth answers as he eyes the two soldiers next to Trymith.

Silence reigns. The only sound is the soft crunching of snow as the soldiers walk toward the armory. The front door of the cottage flings opens and a bolt flies out, hitting Keagon.

"Give it up, blacksm—" Keagon's words are cut short as the bolt penetrates the young soldier's armor and straight through his heart.

Garxe throws his bastard sword, hitting Myriam in the middle of her chest and nailing her to the front door. She drops the crossbow she was holding and dies instantly, her body slumped and nailed to the door.

"Nooo!" Zeth hollers out with sword in hand, charging forward to knock the shocked Trymith to the ground. He then swings the sword and almost cleaves off Garxe's head as the nobleman barely dodges the blow and falls backward into the snow. Zeth jumps onto Garxe's chest as he's pulling a mace from his belt and drops it in the melee. Zeth rears back to finish Garxe off when two daggers pierce his chest.

Zeth momentarily pauses. But then he hollers out and tightens his grip on the sword while looking down at the unarmed and panic-stricken Garxe. In the next moment, Zeth is finished off by two arrows—one to the chest and the other to his forehead. He briefly looks up to see Riechter holding a bow while balancing himself on one leg. The tough blacksmith mouths some words, looking like even this won't stop him. Then he collapses backward, dropping the sword behind him.

Riechter notches another arrow.

"Father ... no!" Joesef cries and charges the two soldiers at Riechter's side with another unfinished sword.

Riechter turns his bow toward the young man but is quickly blocked by one of his soldiers as they confront Joesef.

"No!" Trymith yells at Joesef as he is picking himself up off the ground.

"You bastards killed my parents ..." Joesef screams as he clumsily swings at one of the soldiers, leaving his back open to the other. A sword is thrust through the young man's body.

"Damn ..." Trymith exclaims as he bears witness to the event.

"Good job!" Riechter compliments the soldier.

"This was all your doing here, Riechter!" Trymith yells. "General Dytruik will hear of—"

The soldier's words are cut off as Garxe hits him in the back of the head with his mace.

"Good riddance," Riechter says to Garxe. Eyeing one of the soldiers in front of him, "Go look through the house. I got this," he continues as a soldier helps him sink back to the ground.

"Go find out what became of Herroth," Garxe commands two of the other soldiers.

"Find me some branches to fashion a splint," Riechter orders the soldier that helped him.

"Yes, sir," the soldier answers as he marches out to the woods.

Riechter looks at Garxe, "You know what to do as soon as we leave."

Garxe nods.

A brief time later, two soldiers exit the cottage with some bloody bandages.

"I knew it, I knew it." Riechter acknowledges. "You two help me get on this horse. C'mon lets move."

"But, sir, what about the others?" One of the soldiers asks.

"Garxe is going to stay behind and look after that." Riechter grunts, clearly in pain, as he is helped onto the back of Trymith's horse. "We have no time to waste."

"Sir, I have your splints," someone calls from the woods.

"Bring them. I'm after my prize," Riechter yells out as he rides away.

Chapter VI
Unexpected Guests

nock, knock ... Father Yor ... are you awake?" a young voice asks while slowly opening the chamber door. It's Phylax, the young acolyte that was helping Yor the previous night. He sees a silhouette of Yor sitting cross-legged holding a chesa. He cradles the holy symbol of Yahmar, an orb with sunbeams projecting from the top, in both hands resting in his lap. His right side faces the fireplace in his room, facing west toward the moon Volutus, which sets directly across from the door.

"I have been knocking for quite some time."

"Yes, I have been in prayer for most of the night," Yor states as he slowly opens his eyes then gets to his feet. He kisses the chesa, raising it above his head while muttering a small prayer, and then sets it on the mantel atop a wooden stand.

"How are you feeling? You were quite out of it last night. Me and some of the other fellows helped you to your chambers ... Oh I brought you some tea," Phylax says as he hands the goblet to Yor.

"Thanks ... I feel fine ... actually, I have never felt more alive than I do now." Yor takes a sip of tea. "How is Albrecht?"

"Who, sir?"

"The old farmer from last night." Yor makes a face as he sips more of the tea.

"Oh, he is sleeping ... sorry 'bout the tea—it was hot earlier."

"How does he look ... Well, come now?" Yor looks impatiently at the young man.

"Well, Father, his sores have disappeared and he's not

sweating anymore," Phylax answers with a puzzled look .

"Yahmar be praised," Yor says as he breathes a sigh of relief. "I saw a raven outside my window last night."

"A raven, sir?" Phylax looks even more puzzled.

"You know ... the bird of death? Haven't you been listening to your studies?" Yor asks sternly.

"I guess I missed that one," Phylax reluctantly answers.

"Yes, well, I guess it's a lot to take in with all the other important teachings like proper posture during services." Yor mocks him with a laugh. "You need to pay attention to omens. They are the gods' way of talking to us, relaying news of things to come or things that have happened elsewhere in the world."

Yor holds his cup to the firelight. "I guess we are going to get some rain or snow."

"Why do you say that, milord?" Phylax asks.

"Look." Yor holds the goblet at an angle so the young man can see inside it.

"What is that floating?"

"A dead beetle." Yor smirks.

"Yuck, let me take that." Phylax grabs the cup.

"Take it out to the courtyard and dump it out, else we will have about twenty of those things around here for its funeral," Yor stoically orders.

"More omens ..."

"Yes."

"By the way, what was that you read from that book?" Phylax asks eagerly.

"It was a Cuirre spell."

"Huh?"

"A Cure spell—it's Rokian."

"Oh ... okay, well are you hungry? It's almost midmorning. They probably still have some food in the kitchen."

"Starved, but I want to check on that farmer first." Yor smiles.

Both of the men walk out of Yor's room, which is at the back part of the temple and just a few steps from the kitchen. They walk around to the far-right back corner of the temple where the stairs are that lead down. All is quiet as they progress down the stairs, except for some kind of grumbling.

"Silverfish, it's sure good to see you. It's been about what, almost a year? Last I heard you were in jail." Yor smiles as he sees his three-foot-tall elvish friend sitting on a table, holding his badly cut hand. "Growing a beard now I see. This is Phylax, my understudy ... he's an acolyte."

"Wow, I've never seen an elf before." Phylax nods as he looks at Silverfish's tattered clothes.

"What were you expecting to see? Someone in tights with little curly shoes going 'tra la la' through the woods? I've heard it all, boy, sorry to disappoint you. But my feet are almost as big as yours and, yes, I know I'm a little heavy in the middle too," Silverfish acknowledges.

"You'll have to pardon Silver's gruff attitude, Phylax—but it kinda grows on you." Yor snickers. Who's your friend?" Yor asks, looking at a five-foot-tall man dressed in a silken robe standing next to Silverfish, who is still cradling his hand.

"This is Chan. He's not from around here," Silverfish says.

"Nah, really, what would give that away? He's just darker than any of us and has almond eyes and black hair. Well, pleased to meet you, Chan." Yor's sarcasm can be cut with a knife.

"He's a Euguadian monk of Fairwind. You know, the God of Fairness and Judgment."

Yor smirks at Silverfish.

"How am I supposed to know that?" Silverfish asks.

"Well, the scales that are embroidered on the front of his robe should have given that away."

"It is good to see you too," Chan picks his words carefully. "I mean ... meet you."

"You speak our language very well," Yor acknowledges.

"Thank you," Chan replies.

"A lot better than some of us here ... we won't mention any names," Yor says as he peers back at Silverfish.

"What's that suppose to mean?" Silverfish asks, looking a little bit irritated.

"Well, look at you, Silver. You cuss like a Fegnirian fisherman."

"The hell I do ... oops, sorry."

"You're an Evalie Elf, the race that has brought civility and unity to the entire human race—"

"Not that again," Silverfish interrupts and rolls his eyes.

"Okay. I won't start. So, how did this happen, as if I had to ask?" Yor asks with a smile.

"A knife fight again. That bastard called me an eble fart." Silverfish eyes a man with a bleeding leg who is being helped down the infirmary stairs.

"You mean Ealbhar ... it's an old Fegnirian word. Do you even know what it means?" Yor laughs as he shakes his head.

"No, but I know it can't be good," Silverfish answers.

"It means 'a useless fellow,'" a female voice answers. A woman approaches from a few feet away.

"Barb!" Silverfish's eyes light up as he turns his head to her. "Yor. I mean, Father Yor, this is my girlfriend Barbye. He says excitingly as he points with his head.

Father Yor turns around and sees a very beautiful, willowy five-foot-tall blond human female, apparently not what he expected. He momentarily stands amazed with his mouth open.

"Err uh ... nice to meet you, Barbye," Yor stutters.

"Nice to meet you too, Father." Barbye snickers as she

curtsies, holding the skirt of her peasant dress with both hands.

"You look familiar." Yor stares at Barbye.

"Yes, I come to all the services." Barbye answers, and then she smiles at Silverfish.

"Oh okay, that makes sense now. So, Silver, you never told me. I thought you were in jail?" Yor smiles as he looks at the farmer sleeping on the bed nearby then searches around some items on a nearby table.

"We were let out a few months back on the Days of Fairness," Silverfish acknowledges.

"We—you mean you and Barbye?"

"No, me and Chan." Silverfish smiles, "Barbye works across the street at the Green Griffin Tavern."

"Oh! What does she do there?" Yor asks.

"Uh ... she waits tables there. Anyway, it's all quite funny, we both were in the leather shop just minding our own business when the shop owner accused us of trying to steal a short bow."

"Just minding your own business? Why do I find *that* hard to believe? You don't exactly have a cherub's innocence or reputation around this town," Yor says.

"Yor, you don't know what it's like. I wasn't raised in a nice temple having all my needs met. I've lived all my life on the streets having to scrounge for everything I needed. Heck, I never slept in a real bed till I was twelve years old. You look at my race as something to be proud of, when it has brought me nothing but misery. I'm not admired by humans, but rather made fun of," Silverfish confesses.

POW! Barbye slaps Silverfish upside the head.

"What a total crock, Silver. You should be ashamed of yourself—lying to the good father. Your parents were jewelers in Jaymar, and as far as sleeping on the streets that's only because your dad caught you stealing gems to pay off your gambling debts and kicked you out. And as for the being made fun of part, you pick a lot of those fights."

"How do you know all that?" the startled Silverfish asks as he rubs his head with his good hand.

"You talk a lot when you drink mead," Barbye admits.

"Chan, what actually happened?" Yor asks as he finds what he was looking for.

"Well, I was in the shop looking at bows when Silverfish walked in behind me. He pushed me, and I fell into some leather pelts that fell on me and knocked me to the ground. I could not see real good, but I think Silverfish was running out with a short bow in his hands. The guards thought I was in with him, so they took me to jail too. There are not many of my kind in this town either. They would have let us go, but Silverfish called one of the guards a perq shit son of a—"

Yor interrupts, "I get the picture."

"What is perq?" Chan asks.

"A perequine—it's a creature like a human but with a wild boar's head with bristly hair. Kind of like our friend here," Yor snickers sarcastically. He holds a small club in his hand. "Are you ready?" Yor looks at Silverfish.

"Oh, not the club again. Don't you have one of those healing stones?" Silverfish asks, frowning.

"Yes ... do you have 2 Sivs?

"No."

"Then it's the club," Yor states as he raises the club.

POW! The blow echoes through the small room as Yor hits Silverfish's hand hard with the club.

"Damn." Silverfish grimaces with pain.

"They prey on the weak. Tend to be very stupid and war-like. It is said they were created by Asberdies to torment man, but I believe they began from pigs with the lycan disease biting men and women. Any armor or weapons they possess, they steal. They are not smart enough to make their own," Yor explains to Chan.

POW!

"Son of a—" Silverfish starts with tears in his eyes.

"Silver," Barbye interrupts as she holds him close.

"They usually stay together in small bands, are very cowardly, and will never attack any target that is superior to them." Yor raises the club again.

"Father … Father … YOR!" Silverfish yells.

"Oh, okay. Well, that's it, Silver. Look at your hand now," Yor says.

"Wow, the cut is totally gone." Silverfish looks at his hand and moves it around as he wipes tears from his eyes with his other hand.

"What is that club?" Barbye asks as she rubs Silverfish's back.

It's an ash club. It heals, but it's a little painful healing. Maybe Silver will think twice before getting in another fight."

"Doubt it," both Chan and Barbye say at the same time.

"Gee, thanks." Silverfish acknowledges as he looks at the two.

"Well, try to stay out of trouble, Silver. I'm going to attend to your friend over there who is bleeding all over the floor." Yor points to the other man with the club.

Silverfish looks at the man on the table a few steps away and spits on the floor as he, Barbye, and Chan make their way to the stairs. Barbye shakes her head and mutters something to Silverfish as they walk away. Silverfish laughs and swats Barbye on the butt.

"Okay, friend, do you have an offering to the temple?" Yor asks, tapping the club in his open hand as he talks to the stranger. The man is now sitting on a table and being attended by Phylax.

"I have about 5 Pens." The man pulls the coins from his trousers and hands them to Phylax. "Don't you have some other remedies?"

"Yes, if you want to be out for about a week, I can give you some elixirs you can drink. But if you walk on that leg, a fever will set in. Or if you have 5 Sivs, I can heal it with stones," Yor says impatiently.

"You just told that worthless fellow over there 2 Sivs."

"What? Were you just born stupid? That's my friend you just cut, you toad. The price just went up to 10 Sivs." Yor is steaming now.

"Well, can you at least put me to sleep then?"

"I'm liable to with this sleeper in my hand right now, friend," Yor says, gritting his teeth.

"Man, I thought you priests were supposed to be compassionate."

"Look, friend, I'm missing my breakfast right now. I'm not very compassionate about stupidity ... picking a fight with someone smaller than you. You're lucky I wasn't there. I would have walloped you so hard you'd be spitting teeth ... So WHAT'S IT GOING TO BE?" Yor hollers, losing his composure.

"Okay. Do it." The stranger gives in.

POW! echoes through the infirmary.

"OH SHIT!"

A loud laugh echoes from the stairwell.

POW! POW!

"Ahhhh!"

"Watch your tongue," Phylax tells the stranger.

"It hurts like—" the stranger is interrupted by another blow. *POW! POW!*

"If I hear you have picked on someone smaller than you again, you will wish for this pain. Now get out of here," Yor growls.

The stranger sobs as he hobbles out to the stairs.

"Wow, I've never seen you like that before, my lord," Phylax says.

"I can't stand bullies—drunk or otherwise," Yor explains. "Now let's get something to eat."

Chapter VII
Cross Country

"Whoa ... easy boy." Sargon pulls back on the reins, slowing Tantor to a walk. The horse snorts with fatigue, as do the other horses. "Slow them down, Bellgrad. They are getting winded, and we don't need to throw a shoe in these rocks." Sargon smirks. "Tantor is not used to wearing that heavy armor. Any-way, we are making good time—it's not even midday yet."

Castle Guel is about fifteen miles southwest of Vry, with Zeth's house being about five miles north of Sargon's home. They have been riding hard cross-country east to northeast for several hours. Sargon is tempted to head west and catch the road north, knowing it will be the fastest way to Missionwise, and riding as hard as they have been would put them in town late tonight. But he also knows he can't take the chance that Heyrold might have lookouts or assassins posted all along the roads. It's unclear how well-planned the scheme to murder his family is. Heyrold has a lot of influence and friends in this area of the country. So, instead, they will trek across the rocky mountainous plains to avoid detection, but it will cost them an extra day.

Sargon wishes he had about a thousand men to storm the town of Vry and put Heyrold's head on a pole, he knows alone he would not stand a chance against the army of the city. He would be cut down by the city's archers and crossbowman like a fish in a barrel. Even at that, he still considered it when he crossed the road leading west to Vry several miles back, but he saw his comrade in arms and knew he must take care of

Bellgrad. Once they reach Missionwise, they will be in a safe area; Heyrold has no influence around there, nor would he dare stand against the High Priest or worse still his Templar Knights, who were empowered after the murder of the last high priest. Missionwise is the oldest settlement in the whole country and has always been controlled by the theocracy.

"You're right … whoa, I was about to say something." Bellgrad, who was following Sargon's packhorse, slows his horse as well. The other horses seem to be breathing even heavier than Tantor—they are not used to the mountainous terrain like Sargon's horse. Then Bellgrad guides his horse around to ride beside Tantor. "How much further, do you think?"

"We should hit Missionwise about midmorning tomorrow," Sargon says as he grabs his waterskin tied to the saddle. "Want some?" Sargon holds the container up.

"No. I'm good," Bellgrad says as he wipes some of the drainage from his brow. "That tea still has me perked up. Actually, I need to take a break."

"Sounds like a good idea," Sargon agrees as he grabs a shot of water from the skin.

Both men stop their horses, dismount, and commence to relieve themselves.

"Phew … I'm good to go now," Bellgrad says as he resets his armor.

"Yeah, that tea seems to go right through me too," Sargon says as he resets his armor as well. "Let's walk them a bit. Want a biscuit?"

"Sure."

"That Myriam thinks of everything." Sargon chuckles and reties the waterskin then grabs two biscuits from a small bag tied to his saddle.

"I guess that storm didn't hit here—there's not much snow

on the ground." Bellgrad scans the ground.

Sargon tosses him a biscuit. "Mmm ... cinnamon. I see how Myriam landed Zeth," Sargon says after savoring a bite of the treat. He continues walking his horses.

"Wow. That's good," Bellgrad agrees, enjoying his biscuit and walking his horses beside Sargon's. "Of course that's why Zeth has that extra padding around his middle."

Sargon laughs. "Well, if we live to be his age, I imagine we will too."

"Do you think that Meg will be like her mother?" Bellgrad asks.

"Oh boy, here we go—" Sargon rolls his eyes.

"What?" Bellgrad interrupts, "You don't think I'm good enough for her?"

"Now cut that out. You sure don't know Zeth if you have to ask that!" Sargon snaps back. "Zeth thinks like me—nobility is not a birthright. He only respects those who have earned it."

"So what do you think?"

"Leave me out of this. You'll have to talk to Zeth when they get to Calador's castle. I think you need to be more concerned about Myriam than Zeth. Boy, you are feeling better, aren't you?" Sargon smirks.

"I told you I was."

"I think you are full of it. I see that wound is still bleeding. How are you feeling, really?" Sargon asks, glancing at his friend's bandaged head and then back to the path.

"Actually, my head is pounding, but I'm trying to keep my mind on something else," Bellgrad admits.

"I think you may get a worse pounding from Myriam if she hears you were even thinking about Meg. You forget Myriam is married to a blacksmith, and I think Zeth is even scared of her." Sargon snickers.

"What? She's five-foot-nothing and probably weighs less than my sword," Bellgrad says with a confused look on his face.

"You just keep your sword in its scabbard, if you catch my drift … look, I've known both of them all my life, and you won't find any finer people anywhere, so don't do anything stupid. Besides, you need to think about where you are going to be working next," Sargon acknowledges.

"True. All my money was in my locker in the bunkhouse."

"What, 2 Pens?"

"How did you know?"

"I just know how much you like to gamble—or, rather, lose."

"Well, for your information I actually had 5 Pens," Bellgrad boasts.

"Oh, look out, you're rich. Well, if you intend to make a life with Meg, it will take a lot more than that. Believe me, women are expensive to maintain, even the ones who are used to a meager lifestyle."

"How would you know?" Bellgrad asks.

"Oh, you think I was born with a Siv in my mouth. Ha! You apparently didn't know my father." Sargon shakes his head. "Don't believe all the rumors, I was paid just like everyone else. He believed all men had to earn their way in life … especially me." Sargon continues as he peers at Bellgrad occasionally while keeping an eye on their path. "I wasn't always making trips for the family, I made my own money on some jobs I did for some of the locals."

"No, I didn't know that, I guess I figured you had the run of your father's money," Bellgrad replies.

"Father's money? Man, my father had J'avins that were my grandfather's. Menarc was so tight he would squeeze a Pen until Lucan would scream."

Lucan was the long-ago king who once ruled the whole world

of Zor, and whose face is imprinted on the Pen.

Both men laugh.

"Well, I guarantee that Heyrold and his goons won't find it, not even bloodhounds could find it ... but I know where it's stashed. My father kept some money in the castle, but not the bulk of his wealth. And I'll use it one day to raise an army and crush that ... that ..." Sargon can't finish the thought.

"Yeah, I got it," Bellgrad acknowledges.

"Man, Bellgrad, you should've seen the plot of land I had my eye on just west of home, it had huge oaks and a spring-fed creek with a grove of apple trees." Sargon looks ahead, but he's day-dreaming of another place. "Perhaps Heyrold caught wind of that and it made him nervous."

Well, I'm sure that your inquiry into that property had nothing to do with what happened. I think this was all planned out. You know, I bet Calador pays well," Bellgrad says changing the subject.

"Well, it may not be as good as what my father paid."

"What? Thirty Pens a month ... that's not THAT good," Bellgrad answers.

"That's pretty decent wages, especially with free room and board, armor, weapons, and a horse. Heck, all you have to supply is yourself."

"And my blood."

"Man! There sure is a lot of crying going on," Sargon jokes. "Here, dry your eyes." Sargon grabs his cape with his free hand and holds it out to Bellgrad.

"Whatever." Bellgrad rolls his eyes.

"Hey, there's a stream up ahead." Sargon points with his left hand as he lets loose of his cape, looking downhill about a half mile. "We will water these guys and then get going again."

"Sounds like a plan. I wonder if there are any blue trout in that cold water?" Bellgrad asks.

"Oh, I imagine that water is full of them. It's their mating season, or so I've been told," Sargon answers. "But we really don't have time for that, we need to get you to that temple. You might be feeling better, but I can tell you it can turn bad. We are probably being followed, too. If I know Heyrold, he will have Riechter, or some other scouts of his, after us."

"Riechter ... oh crap!" Bellgrad exclaims. "We are in big trouble if he is on our tail. I have heard some horror stories about that guy—he shoots first and asks questions later."

"That's one reason I have been pushing us so hard. Look out, there's a hole right there," Sargon points to a spot a few feet in front of Bellgrad's path.

"Thanks." Bellgrad smiles as he diverts his horses around the three-foot hole.

"Let's ride on down there. This ground is too rough and steep to walk," Sargon says as he stops Tantor and mounts.

"Yeah, it's pretty rough," Bellgrad agrees as he stops and mounts.

Both men grab their waterskins and drink a few shots of water.

"I bet these horses are thirsty after all this time." Bellgrad says. "We can top off these skins too."

The two men direct their horses with packhorses in tow on down the hill. Riding the horses down turns into a wise choice, as they hit several patches of ice on some flat rocks. Had they been on foot in front of their mounts, the results could have been disastrous.

"What are you stopping for? We are almost there," Bellgrad asks, confused.

"Put your helm on," Sargon orders as he grabs his full helm tied at the back of his saddle.

"What? I have scaled worse."

"Don't argue with me. Just do it. You already have a busted-up gourd. I don't want these rocks to finish it off if you fall," Sargon barks.

"Okay, okay ... Mom." Bellgrad snickers as he unties his helm from the back of his saddle and slides it over his injured head. "Damn."

"Yeah, it will hurt a lot worse when I slap you upside that fat head." Sargon laughs.

They both continue downhill for what seems like an eternity. There are some hairy moments as the horses slip here and there on patches of ice.

"Phew. I was holding my breath on that last patch. Boy, I thought my horse was gonna fall that last time," Bellgrad admits.

"Yeah, I have to admit I thought I was going to have to clean my trousers. I didn't know it got so steep—the ground was hidden by that underbrush," Sargon says as both his horse and Bellgrad's almost lunge for the cold, flowing stream when they hit the bottom of the hill.

The two men dismount and untie their packhorses that eagerly pull on their ropes, hungry for that cold water as well.

"There you go," Sargon laughs as his packhorse almost pulls out of his grip until he lets the rope go.

"What ... what's wrong?" Sargon's smile disappears as he sees Bellgrad. His friend is white as a ghost and staring over Sargon's shoulder. Sargon slowly turns around to see a very large ice bear several yards away to the left catching fish as they swim upstream.

The bear is solid white and standing six feet high at the shoulder with paws that look to be twelve inches wide. Sargon knows these creatures can reach a height of fifteen feet when they stand on their hind legs, and some weigh as much as 2,000 pounds. The bear was hidden from sight by a grove of trees as they were coming down the hill.

"Oh shit. Well, he has not seen us yet," Sargon whispers as he slowly stretches over to grab the lead rope of his packhorse.

"That's not what worries me ... I wonder if there are any more we can't see," Bellgrad whispers back as he grabs his sword from his horse.

As if on cue, another ice bear strolls out from the grove of trees next to Sargon, unaware of their presence. Sargon's packhorse catches the bear's scent and instinctively bolts across the stream, but not before his master grabs the handle of a single-bladed axe. He holds it steadfast until the leather strap snaps, knocking some of their supplies into the water.

All in one motion, the vicious bear lunges toward Sargon as Tantor spins to the left, pushing Sargon gingerly back and lands a double hind kick square in the monstrous bear's jaw. The blow knocks a few of the bear's teeth out, and the horse quickly barrels forward out of the bear's reach then spins around. This momentarily stuns the bear, as it shakes its head while lapping its tongue across its bloody mouth.

Sargon wastes no time. He lunges forward and swings the axe as hard as he can at the beast's neck. He misses his mark but hits the bear in the left shoulder, cutting it deep and breaking a bone. A load *pop* resounds through the forest, and the bear lets out a roar, the axe wedged firmly in the animal's body. Sargon finds himself in a predicament—he tries to stay out of reach of the violently snapping bear, but he has to free the axe or risk the chance of being weaponless against this beast. Luckily the axe handle acts like a guard for Sargon. The bear can't turn its head, but Sargon still can't seem to grab the axe. If his hand gets in the way, the animal could sever it with its massive jaws.

Bellgrad joins the fight and slashes the great bear repeatedly with his sword. He keeps his distance from Sargon and the bear's head as it moves back and forth, trying to bite either fighter. The pelt tears with every slash, being tight against the animal's bone due to the weight loss of its recent hibernation.

The frustrated bear stands on its hind legs and swings its mighty paw at Bellgrad.

Sargon finally manages to grip the axe.

The beast tips off balance, missing Bellgrad and groaning from the pain of Sargon's hold on the axe. Sargon is lifted off his feet. Bellgrad seizes his opportunity and jabs his sword deep in the animal's belly, killing it instantly. The beast falls forward toward Bellgrad. He frantically backs up out of the bear's way. In the chaos, Sargon frees the axe and finds his footing. The bear lands on Bellgrad's legs, pinning him to the ground.

Out of breath, both men sit a moment, laughing lightly as Bellgrad sits up to free himself.

"Wow, what a day! Let's hurry and get you out of there," Sargon says as he sets down his axe and commences to lift the bear off his friend.

Too late, is the last thought going through Sargon's mind at the horrid event unfolding before his eyes. A great bear head lunges forward and sinks its teeth into Bellgrad's left shoulder, easily pulling him from underneath the dead bear and flinging him across the stream to the rocks on the other side like a dog flinging a rag doll.

"Ahhhhh!" Bellgrad screams in agony, flying through the air. There's only silence when he hits the rocks on the other side.

"Nooooo! You bastard!" Sargon screams as he drops the dead bear's arm and grabs his axe.

He swings with all his might, hitting his mark and driving the axe deep into the crown of the bear's skull, right between the animal's eyes. Blood gushes out of the wound, blinding the bear but not killing it. The bear roars in pain and swings its head, hitting Sargon in the shoulder and knocking off his helm. He goes tumbling to the ground, barely missing an adjacent tree. The bear spins its head around toward Sargon. The axe slams into a tree, breaking the handle and further injuring the bear.

Great, Sargon thinks to himself just as something catches his eye.

When the bear pulled Bellgrad from underneath the other bear, it overturned the dead animal enough to expose the hilt of Bellgrad's sword stuck in its belly.

The thought races through Sargon's mind, *I'm trapped. How can I get to that sword?*

Just as Sargon figures the animal is about to finish him off, something attacks the bear from behind, dragging it back about a foot or so. The bear roars with pain as he spins around to face its attacker. Because of the bear's massive size, Sargon cannot make out what the diversion is. But he seizes his opportunity, rolls toward the dead bear, and easily retrieves the sword from the animal's belly. He jumps to his feet and plunges the sword into the beast's left side, but the sword only goes part way in before hitting bone. Just as Sargon tries to retrieve the sword, he gets cow-kicked by the bear's left hind leg and knocked to the ground again.

Man, this bear is fast and strong, Sargon thinks to himself as he gets up. The noise of claws and teeth on armor rings through the forest. He looks down to see his armor on his right arm is torn through. His arm would have been ripped off if he had not had that armor to protect it. He painfully raises his right arm up and braces himself to drive the sword into the bear again. But a loud *pop* sounds from in front of the bear, and the beast suddenly drops dead.

As the bear collapses to the ground, Sargon sees who has

saved his bacon. It isn't Bellgrad, as he hoped. It's Tantor. The horse's armor has protected its chest and neck from the bear's teeth and claws. Sargon can see the evidence of a bite mark—that would have surely killed Tantor if it hit his neck or would have lamed his loyal steed if it reached the chest. Sargon throws on his helm and, with sword in hand, circles around the dead bear. There's a hoof mark in the center of the animal's head, and the axe head is driven almost completely through, splitting it wide open. Sargon rubs Tantor on the nose—the only thing not covered in armor. The bridle is broken, and there's bear fur in the horse's teeth. Sargon notices a sweeping blow on the left side of Tantor's head armor and blood on the other side. But it's not the horse's blood.

That was one hell of a fight ... I have never seen a horse do that before, Sargon thinks to himself, amazed at his horse's undying loyalty and protection.

Sargon's attention returns then to his other friend, and he runs toward Bellgrad. Puffs of steam betray Bellgrad's quick breathing.

"Thank the gods you are still alive!" Sargon smiles, but it disappears when he sees Bellgrad's shoulder wound bleeding badly.

"Yeah, I don't think this is a good spot for fishing, after all." Bellgrad laughs softly.

Sargon looks around quickly to be sure there are no more bears. Seeing none, he sets Bellgrad up against a big rock then scurries back to his horse and grabs a dagger and dressing from a saddlebag.

"I hate to do this, in case there are any more bears around, but I have to stop that bleeding." Sargon explains as he cuts the leather straps to Bellgrad's breastplate and leggings, throwing the armor aside. Deep indentions in the armor mark the place where the bear's teeth punctured Bellgrad's shoulder. If Bellgrad had not been wearing the armor, his shoulder would have been ripped off. Sargon removes his helm and gloves and uses the dagger to cut the cloth into strips.

Using the skills that Reaxl taught him about first aid, he rolls the strips into little plugs, lifts Bellgrad's chainmail shirt and padding with one hand, and inserts the cloth rolls into each puncture wound. Bellgrad's screams of agony pierce Sargon's heart like a knife, but he knows it's the only way to slow down the bleeding. He does this on both sides of Bellgrad's shoulder. Taking the remaining cloth, he lays it on top of the shoulder and gently releases the chainmail and padding.

"That should slow down the bleeding. Now, let's get the hell out of here."

Sargon tries to help his friend to stand, but to no avail.

"I'm done for, just leave me," Bellgrad says.

"No way. You are not dying on my watch. I'm going to get you to that healer."

"You're more pigheaded than I am." Bellgrad laughs then passes out, and Sargon leans his friend back against the rock.

Sargon goes to his trusty steed, unbuckles the leather straps of the barding, and drops the armor. Then he shucks off his own armor and throws it all aside, leaving only his chainmail shirt on. He cuts away Tantor's broken bridle, fashions a makeshift halter, and attaches the reins to it. He fills the waterskins from the stream then grabs his helm and fills it with water. Holding it to Tantor's face, he gently washes the bear fur from the animal's mouth. Next he sheaths Bellgrad's sword and slings it across his shoulder and grabs a pick and a mace to slide into his belt.

Never again, he thinks to himself. He will never again let his guard down. He curses himself, recalling Reaxl's words, *"Never be without your weapons or let your guard down. The world is a dangerous place, and it's better to stand there and have at least a dagger in your hand rather than just little stumpy."* Sargon smiles at the colorful memory of his dear friend and mentor, but the smile fades as he remembers Reaxl dead on the stairs.

He turns away and pulls a sack of feed from one of the packhorses a few feet away, cuts it open, and dumps three piles for the pack animals and Bellgrad's horse to eat. He then fills his helm with feed and goes back to Tantor, who is busy drinking from the stream. The animal lets out a soft whinny as he smells the feed and sinks his head into Sargon's helm, nearly knocking it out of his hands.

"You definitely deserve this, bud," Sargon says as he sets the helm down on the ground. Tantor devours the feed almost as quickly as Sargon filled the helm. Going over to the unconscious Bellgrad, Sargon picks him up. His arms shake under the strain of his friend's weight, and his right arm screams with pain. But he pulls with all his might and manages to slide his friend onto Tantor's saddle.

"No more biscuits for you." Sargon groans and laughs between his labored breaths.

Bellgrad stirs. "What are you doing? He cannot carry us both." He holds himself up and pushes away Sargon's steadying hand.

"Oh yes he can. He's tougher than the both of us. He's the one that saved my ass!" Sargon says, grabbing the reins and putting his foot in the left stirrup to swing himself up behind Bellgrad. He spurs Tantor onward. "I lost my family. I'm not going to lose you too. I'll die before I let that happen."

Chapter VIII
The Hunt

ir, we seem to have lost the trail," says a soldier as he rides up.

"What do you mean you lost it? It was just here. Hell, my grandma could follow that trail, and she's been dead for years," Riechter arrogantly claims.

"It was here in the snow, and then it was gone."

"Look, mushhead, I don't care if you got to get on your hands and knees. Find me that trail. We have been following it for the past four hours, and I'm in no shape to do your job."

"My job? But, sir, I'm a soldier, not a scout like you. I never had to follow tracks before."

"Oh, cry me a river. Just get off your horse and find footprints or hoofprints in the snow from where the trail ends." Riechter orders as he rubs his right thigh against the pain shooting from his ankle. He stops his horse and watches the young man ride onward to where the trail seems to end ahead.

Riechter reaches into a saddlebag behind him on his right side and blindly fumbles through it with his hand. *Where is that flask of Viko?* He thinks to himself as he finds the bag empty of contents. Then remembers he is not on his horse, which is carrying his ice berry brandy. He scans the other soldiers riding behind him.

"Does anyone have any wine, mead, or something stronger?" Riechter asks."I have some wine, sir," one of the soldiers behind him offers.

"Good. Bring it here and help me off this horse." Riechter commands.

Two soldiers dismount and help Riechter off his horse as another brings sticks and rope for a splint. They hold him under each arm as he hobbles to a nearby tree and help him rest up against it. He lays his swollen ankle, still in the boot, in some fresh powdery snow next to him. The cold seems to numb some of the pain as his boot chills in the frigid ice. The soldier returns with a half-full flask of red wine. Riechter gulps it down in a couple of mouthfuls.

"Ah! That's good wine!" he says as he wipes his mouth with his sleeve.

"That's from Lord Heyrold's vineyard." The young soldier grabs the empty flask from Riechter's hand.

"He does tend to take good care of his men, doesn't he?" Riechter smirks at the young man, who is not probably a day over sixteen years old.

"I have some dried rations in my saddlebag if you are hungry, milord."

"Sure."

The young soldier brings Riechter some dried fruit and other assorted items wrapped in a cloth, along with a small flask of Viko.

"Aye, now we're talking." Riechter's eyes light up at the sight of the flask. He uncorks it and takes a swig then unwraps the rations and takes a bite of a dried apricot.

"Damn ... this is awful. I was wrong to say Heyrold gives you good supplies—these suck! This must be held over from the Elven War, over 1000 years ago." Riechter grimaces and spits out the mummified fruit. "Heyrold will definitely hear about this. Thanks for the Viko, son, but I've had wood grubs with more flavor than that." Riechter acknowledges as he throws the other piece away.

"These are not so bad, sir." The other soldier snickers, grabs a piece of fruit from the cloth, and pops it in his mouth.

"You must have rocks in your head, son. I guess I'm spoiled from my own." Riechter gives the rude soldier a searing stare.

"You make your own rations, sir?" The young soldier smiles.

"Yes. And they're a hundred times better than this crap," Riechter says as he sorts through the other items in the mix while swigging down the rest of the Viko. "It's either that or hunt every day. When you are on someone's trail or on some task, you don't always have the time nor the coin to buy any in towns. And I like to avoid that anyway, because most taste like a wasp nest like this one. What do they call you, boy?" Riechter asks of the young soldier with the wood branches in his hands.

"Corporal Third Class Symon, sir!" The soldier's smile quickly disappears as he snaps to attention.

"Well, Symon, the next time you grab something off my lap that's not about to kill me, you will pull back a nub," Riechter threatens as he continues throwing pieces of dried fruit away after sniffing them one by one.

"Yes, sir."

"Oh ... I guess it's okay. I'm just grouchy from this damn leg. I tend to forget that you soldiers share everything. In my profession that's not very common. Usually everything comes with a cost, and anyone you run into is out to kill you ... even your own brethren."

"Brethren, sir?"

"Other scouts, son," Riechter says. His eyes glaze over for a minute, and he looks blankly beyond the young man, apparently recollecting a bad memory.

"You ready to secure that leg, sir?" Symon asks.

Riechter catches his snap, "Yes ... we need to get going. What's your name, son?" Riechter looks at the other soldier who gave him the rations.

"Private First Class Davyd, sir!" says the soldier, standing at attention.

"Well, Davyd, you need to help Symon splint my leg. It needs to be good and tight." Riechter moves his leg around as Symon kneels in front of him, dropping the rope and branches to grab the foot.

"Oops ..." Riechter says, almost falling over as he moves his foot while bracing himself again with his arms.

"Well, he's not feeling any pain," Davyd snickers.

"Oh, but it will hurt like hell when you tighten that rope." Riechter snorts and then laughs.

"Sounds like you've done this before, sir?" Symon asks.

"Quit. Quit shirring me," he slurred. "My name's Riechter—Master of the Hunt!" Riechter sticks out his chest in mock attention and tries to look stern. "You boys with your ranks and titles ..." Riechter waves one hand and laughs. "Yes, I have done this before, but it was the other leg, and I was by myself. I fell out of a forty-foot ironwood tree about thirty years ago while hunting some murdering scum in Kalamash. I damn near killed myself that day. I must have hit about ten branches as I fell, but I could not grab hold of any of them ... I went end over end." Riechter laughs as he motions with his hands. "I wasn't much older than the both of you ..."

Symon wraps the rope around Riechter's leg as Davyd holds the branches. He hands the rope ends to Davyd and then straightens the scout's foot as Davyd cinches and ties the ends together.

Riechter does not make a sound. He just sits there, supporting himself with his arms behind him propped in the snow. The only sign of his pain is his trembling and the tears pouring down his cheeks as he exhales a ragged breath.

"Wow! You are one tough bird, Riechter," Davyd says,

stunned. Symon only nods in agreement.

"Comes with the training," Riechter says stoically, suddenly sobered up.

"Training? At your age?" Davyd asks.

"Always." Riechter smirks. "Now help me up, and let's see what mushhead has found. Oh, in case you were wondering, I did get my prize—dead of course. He ended up with an arrow in his eye at 100 yards in heavy brush."

"Wow. That's amazing," Davyd says.

"Well, not really, I was aiming between his eyes, but he moved at the last minute. I wasn't about to try to take him in alive, not with a broken leg. Besides, he was twice my size and had two goons with him. Oh, I took them out as well. That score yielded me about 5 J'avins that day." Riechter stands and shrugs off his helpers.

"Wow ... that's a lot of money," Symon acknowledges.

"Aye. Well, needless to say I got a lot of work after that haul. I found out later that my bounty had killed about six people that happened to be a local nobleman's family—killed them with an axe if I remember right," Riechter continues as Davyd brings him his horse.

"Don't scouts usually start out as messengers?" Symon asks.

"Well, I did when I was a kid." Riechter mounts with Davyd's help. "That's when Kalamash was at war with Rokia. Boy, those were some good times. I can't tell you how many times I had arrows and spears—and the occasional axe—whizz by my head as I crossed enemy lines."

"Man, Riechter, what a life you have had," Symon marvels as he mounts his horse.

"Had? Heck, I'm not dead yet, boy." Riechter smirks. "Let's get going."

Davyd mounts his horse and follows Riechter and Symon.

The three ride on about five hundred yards when they see the tracking soldier about a half a mile ahead. The soldier spots them as they are riding up and waves them onward.

"The trail seems to zigzag," Davyd says, breaking the silence.

"Yeah, he's smart. Must have figured he would be followed," Riechter acknowledges. "That's why he went cross-country."

"Was your father a scout, Riechter?" Davyd asks.

"Hell no, he was a shopkeeper in a little town called Neptune, and I wanted no part of city life, so I spent as much time as I could in the woods. On my sixth birthday, my uncle gave me a sling. Of course my folks hated the idea, but they felt I would lose interest when I couldn't master the weapon. Well, let's just say I proved them wrong when I started bringing home squirrels at first, then rabbits and birds. Some I hit in midflight—I had a real good eye and could hit almost anything within fifty yards. My mother tried to further discourage me from venturing into the woods by telling me stories about perequine, bogeymen, and a story about Black Annis—a female ogre who eats children. But instead of frightening me, it made me even more interested to be in the woods. But what really piqued my interest was when I befriended an elfin boy—"

"Elfin boy," Symon scoffs, "those little people are useless. All the ones I have seen could not fight their way out of black-bird pie."

"Hold your tongue, my young rude friend. Not all races of elves are the small ones like the ones we all have seen in these parts. In Kalamash, elves have their own cities deep in the woods, and they are the same size as us, except most are very slender and of course have pointed ears," Riechter continues.

"Yeah, knife ears." Davyd laughs.

"Wow ... you two idiots amaze me. You both realize there is more in this world than what exists in Fegnir?"

"Well, I guess I never really thought about it." Davyd sounds regretful.

"Vous deux sont aussi interessants que un epouvantail avec diarrhee," Riechter insults.

"What the heck does that mean?" Symon asks.

"It's Maganese—the language of fairies and elves—and it means you two are as interesting as a bugbear with diarrhea." Riechter laughs and then spurs his horse onward.

"Now that's the Riechter I know," Symon remarks.

"Really?" Davyd says.

"I've worked around him on and off for two years, and he has never asked for my name before."

"Well, we sure did piss him off with those elfish comments. I wish I had kept my mouth shut," Davyd says.

"Corporal, what have you got?" Riechter asks as he rides up to the soldier he put in charge of following the trail.

"Well, the trail seems to disappear and reappear in different areas of the woods. It is never consistent." The soldier points to various spots in the forest behind them.

"You have a good eye. I was wrong about you, son," Riechter says as he scans the ground then up to the trees.

"What is it, sir?" the soldier asks, watching Riechter's actions.

"Something seems amiss." Riechter swings off his horse then scurries over to a small leaf in the snow. "Look at this ..." Riechter strains to pick up a leaf from the snowy trail.

"Sir?"

"It's an aspen leaf. There are no aspen trees around here— they are on the higher ridges." Riechter points to the surrounding trees and then up to the higher elevations many yards behind them. "There's no way this leaf could have gotten here on its own. It was brought here."

"How?"

"Think about it. You said the trail comes and goes, right?"

"Right."

"How could the trail just disappear?" Riechter asks while looking at the soldier.

"He is jacking with us and must be dragging a branch behind them ... then they must be closer than we thought 'cause that takes a lot of time."

I don't think it's the Guel boy doing it. It's too cleverly done to be a simple knight. He doesn't know enough to do it so well. I think it's another scout—look at those smaller horse tracks." Riechter points at the tracks in the snow. "Between the pain of this leg and that Viko I drank, I don't have my wits ... I should have caught this."

"Well, you see it now. So, what's the plan, sir?" The soldier asks as he walks over and joins Riechter, who is having a hard time holding himself up in the thick powdery snow. The soldier reaches out and gives Riechter a shoulder under his right side to support himself.

"Thanks." Riechter leans on him and surveys the surrounding woods. "We need to get back on our horses. These woods have eyes," Riechter whispers in the soldier's ear. In the silence, various subtle birdcalls and other sounds reach them from all sides. Riechter holds up a hand to Davyd and Symon as they approach, commanding them to stop.

"Help me get back on my horse," Riechter quietly orders the corporal.

The two make their way to Riechter's horse; the animal is nosing through the snow in search of some grass to graze on. Riechter grabs the reins out of the snow with one hand, pulling them over the animal's head and tight to the saddle as the soldier gives him a boost. The soldier then slowly makes his way back to his own mount and quietly swings himself on his horse—not an easy task in chain mail armor.

"That's rather pointless," Riechter smirks as he watches the soldier mount, then he spurs his horse back to the other soldiers.

"What's going on?" Symon asks as Riechter approaches, the corporal a few feet behind.

"We are being watched," Riechter explains.

"What?" Davyd goes for his sword.

"DON'T—don't do that," Riechter commands, lowering his voice and shaking his head. "I don't feel like being shot in the head today. Let's just make our way back into the clearing where we were earlier."

The four ride back south to where they splinted Riechter's leg. A rider approaches from beyond that point, apparently following their trail from Zeth's house. Riechter recognizes the rider long before the others.

"Garxe, looks like you made a trip for nothing." Riechter smiles.

"What? Why?" Garxe asks.

"Looks like the trail has gone cold, besides I need to seek the healers in Vry about my leg."

"Well, you could get healing in Missionwise."

"No, I'm not welcome there … nor would any of you be. Heyrold does not have any friends in that town, besides I need to clue him in on our progress. I haven't seen him since I got back from Xieg. Go back to Guel Castle and let the general know."

"Oh, okay."

"Let's get going. It's better if we ride together—we will split off when we get to the road. This is what we have found …"

Chapter IX
Racing to Missionwise

he warmth of sulo's light fills Sargon's face with joy, while birds in the nearby trees make their sweet songs. He watches his beautiful love as she pours them both a couple of goblets of wine as the two relax atop a soft blanket in a meadow adorned with flowers. The scent of honeysuckle and jasmine fill the air. Jessica leans over to hand him a goblet of wine, lingering to give him a soft warm kiss on the forehead.

"What are you thinking, my love?" Jessica asks as she slowly sits back and sips her wine.

"Just how much I love you. I can think of no other place I would rather be," Sargon answers as he sips on his wine and sighs with complete contentment.

"Good ..." Jessica softly giggles as she bites on a grape, squirting a small spray of juice on Sargon's cheek. They both laugh.

"Oh, you think that's funny?" Sargon laughs and throws aside his wine goblet then pounces on Jessica like a cat on a mouse. He lands a soft passionate kiss on her supple lips.

He holds himself up to look at her, admiring her beautiful face. She blows a cool breath and lands him a warm kiss on the right cheek. She then gives him a soft wet kiss on his right eye.

"My love ..." Jessica whispers as she caresses his forehead with a frosty touch.

The ground shakes.

"What the—" Sargon says, confused, as the ground shakes violently beneath them. Then all goes black.

Damn. It was just a dream. Sargon thinks to himself as he's jolted awake. Tantor is jumping holes in the road, his heavy hooves thundering against the rocks on the road. It's night, and both moons, Volutus and Pilutus, are three-quarters full, which gives enough light to make out the trees and surroundings. Tantor is running down the road at a full gallop with Bellgrad in front of him in the saddle.

"Man ... I can't believe I dozed off. Lucky we didn't fall off," Sargon thinks out loud, but is reassured when he remembers supporting Bellgrad with his right arm, holding the reins with his left hand, and all the while keeping his right foot in the stirrup to hold himself on. He feels warm spots on his cheek, eyelid, and forehead. Letting the reins slide loose, he raises his left hand up and wipes his face and forehead. Looking at it in the dim light, he sees blood. Bellgrad's shoulder is still bleeding, and the wind has been blowing it onto Sargon's face.

Getting his wits about him, Sargon realizes he only dozed off for maybe a minute; he remembers they only recently got on the road, maybe a couple of hours now. It took five hours of hard riding before that to get to the road. He slows Tantor to a walk.

"Bellgrad, are you awake?" Sargon asks his old friend.

There is no answer. Sargon pulls off his glove with his mouth then reaches up to Bellgrad's face to feel if he is still breathing.

"What ... what the hell? You trying to pick my nose?" Bellgrad mumbles as he swats Sargon's hand away.

"I wanted to see if you were still breathing, knucklehead," Sargon answers with the glove still in his teeth. He reaches back and grabs his glove from his mouth. "You didn't answer me when I called your name, so I wanted to make sure you were still alive."

"I'm alive ... I'm alive. Just sleeping, so keep your hands out of my face. I don't know where they have been."

"Just scratching me arse." Sargon laughs and slides his glove back on.

"That's what I thought. Man, I'm just so cold and tired."

"Well, it is colder since Sulo has set, but it's not *that* cold. You have just lost a lot of blood. Do you want to stop? I could build a fire."

"No, let's keep going. Those holes will just keep leaking whether we are stopped or not. And there are too many for you to hit with fire. How much further?" Bellgrad asks.

"We should be in Missionwise in a few hours. You just hang in there and stay awake, you can rest when we get to the temple," Sargon says as he pulls off his cape and throws it on Bellgrad's back. "There, that should help warm you up."

"Yeah, okay, thanks. It's a … good thing it's dark. Someone might think I'm your girlfriend the way I'm riding in front of you."

"Keep that up and I might have to find you a dress." Sargon laughs.

Bellgrad laughs then coughs.

"You've rested long enough, old man. Hah." Sargon spurs Tantor back into a gallop.

Sargon says a silent pray to Yahmar, Zura, and Euklor to watch over their journey and to keep Bellgrad alive. The two ride on for another couple of hours. All the while, Bellgrad talks about Meg, and Sargon decides to give him a pass. He knows it's better for his friend to talk about anything if it keeps him from falling asleep again. It helps Sargon to stay awake as well. They arrive at Missionwise's eastern city gate, which is closed.

"Who goes there?" A soldier's voice rings out from atop the gatehouse.

"I am Sargon, and this is my corporal. He is badly hurt, and we need to go to the temple," Sargon hollers out.

"Open the gate," a soldier calls. The outer portcullis opens, and the inner gate opens from inside. Another soldier comes out with torch in hand, motioning them onward as he sees Bellgrad's condition. He in turn waves his torch at a guard standing outside the temple, a quarter mile away on the western side of town.

The streets are barren of activity at this late hour. Sargon spurs Tantor, though he knows the horse is exhausted. His breaths come in heavy bursts as they ride toward the temple. One of the guards at the temple who has seen the city guard flag him down gets another guard to go inside the temple and fetch a small group of men to meet Sargon and Bellgrad at the steps of the temple. Four guards gently lower Bellgrad off the horse as Sargon helps from Tantor's back.

"Easy, easy," Sargon says as he holds Bellgrad around the back just below his shoulders then transitions to holding the back of his head. "His shoulder is badly damaged from a bear bite. He also hurt his head."

"We have him, sir," one of the guards assures Sargon.

Four guards carry Bellgrad's limp body up the stairs, where a priest motions them into the temple.

A stable boy approaches Sargon. "I'll take him, milord, you can pay me in the morrow."

"Thanks. Make sure he gets an extra ration of feed in the morning," Sargon answers without hesitation as he slides off Tantor's back. The boy leads the horse to the stable across the street.

Sargon hurriedly climbs the stairs to the front door. He walks inside to see Bellgrad lying lifeless on a table just inside the door. He sees the guards around the table and the priest holding one of Bellgrad's hands and looking into his eyes.

"He is dead, my lord." The priest looks up at Sargon.

"No ... no ... that can't be. I was just talking to him only moments ago." Sargon says, stunned, expressionless. He cannot move.

"He just lost too much blood, sir," explains a guard standing beside Bellgrad. Blood drips from the table onto the floor.

"Go wake Father Yor," the priest whispers to one of the other guards, who nods and rushes into the sanctuary of the temple, stopping briefly to salute the gigantic statue of Yahmar rising beyond the altar.

"I still cannot believe it," Sargon says, stunned and white as a ghost.

"Here, my lord. Rest yerself," one of the guards says, leaving the table to offer Sargon a chair. Sargon sits and looks blankly at Bellgrad, feeling he could pass out at any moment.

Within a few moments, a priest hurries from the back of the temple up to where Bellgrad's body lies. He opens one of the soldier's eyes with one hand then feels the side and back of Bellgrad's neck with the other hand.

"You spoke that this man was alive a few moments ago?" the priest asks Sargon.

"Yes. We were talking. His voice was a little weak, but he was very much alive," Sargon says with a slight tremble in his voice.

"Take this man to the infirmary," the priest orders.

"But, my lord—" the guards protests.

"Are you questioning me, soldier?" the priest asks with a raised eyebrow.

"No, Father Yor." All the guards answer in unison. Then they hoist Bellgrad in their arms and carry him to the back of the temple.

"Good," Father Yor says as he turns away from the guards and looks directly at Sargon. "He has not crossed to the other side yet. There maybe a chance I can bring him back."

"I will give all I have ... my horse," Sargon says as his eyes light up, "what little money I have on me, but I have a lot more after I clear up some problems I have."

"That won't be necessary. Come, follow me," Yor says, taking in Sargon's appearance for the first time. His eyes pass over Sargon's right arm and the blood dripping from his wound. "I can fix that too."

Sargon looks down at his arm for a mere second then follows the priest to the back of the temple.

"I'll be right back," Yor says as he disappears into a room.

Sargon looks in to see the priest grab a book, a holy symbol, and a scepter from the hearth. He puts the scepter in a holder in his belt and scurries back to Sargon.

"All will be well," Yor reassures Sargon with a direct look and a smile. "Let's go."

Sargon feels a ray of hope that calms his spirit.

The two walk toward the stairs and descend into the infirmary below.

"Take off his armor and all those bandages, even the one on his head," Yor barks as they hit the last step of the stairs. "I can see by your long hair and braid that you are a follower of Marxbaq, but a prayer to Yahmar is in order."

"I prayed to him, Zura, and Euklor as we were headed this way—for safe passage and for my friend's life," Sargon confesses as he watches the guards take off the chain mail shirt and padding. Next he removed the blood-soaked pieces of cloth from his shoulder wounds and unwrapped his head. They gently lay Bellgrad back on the table.

"Good, it's Zura's second holy day and she will surely hear your prayer," Yor says as he thumbs through the book, stops at a section, and sets the book down.

"I don't know if that's true. I was wed yesterday, and everyone was murdered but Bellgrad there and myself." Sargon points to his friend lying on the table before them. "They were all poisoned including my bride."

"By Yahmar's holy brow ..." Yor is stunned at such news.

"Bellgrad there was on a patrol of my late father's castle when he and the soldiers were ambushed. Then they had dead perequine laid around them as a ruse."

Yor looks up at Sargon. "The gods will surely be angered over such treachery—especially Zura, it being on one of her holy days."

"I don't know, Father ... I'm starting to question my faith."

"That's what brought you here," Yor states while scanning the book. He looks away from the book to search the room, spots an acolyte, points at a table, then nods his head. The acolyte throws Yor a shroud from across the room, which he drapes over Bellgrad. He then grabs the chesa, the holy symbol, and sets it on the table right above Bellgrad's head. The priest takes the holy scepter of Yahmar from his belt and sets it below Bellgrad's feet. He then grabs some small vials from a nearby table and starts muttering chants in a language Sargon cannot understand while slowly sprinkling the liquids all over the covered body. Yor then sets some lighted candles on the four corners of the table, still chanting all the while.

The acolyte approaches Sargon. "Take off your chain mail shirt and lay on this table, my lord."

"I'm okay," Sargon says, "I want to stay awake for my friend."

"I'm going to heal your wounded arm, sir."

"I said—"

"Shhhhh ... don't break his concentration," the young acolyte interrupts.

"Oh ... okay," Sargon whispers. He finally complies, pulling off his chain mail and lying down on the table, never taking his eyes off Bellgrad.

"This will not hurt," the young acolyte says, holding some stones in his hands. "These are blood stones. Let me have your arm."

Sargon painfully raised his right arm, and the acolyte starts rubbing Sargon's wounds with the stones. At first it hurts almost as badly as when the wound was first inflicted, but the pain quickly diminishes as a warm sensation comes over the arm. The acolyte gently lowers Sargon's arm next to him on the table. Sargon glances at his arm and is amazed to see the wounds have closed up.

"Rest my lord. Father Yor will be busy all night with your friend."

Sargon feels his eyes get heavy. He says a prayer to Yahmar, Zura, and Marxbaq. In the next moment, he's falling into sleep from sheer exhaustion and the late hour. The last sound he hears is Father Yor's soft chanting.

Chapter X
Bellgrad's Fate

e is dead, my lord."

"No. No ... that can't be, I was just talking to him not moments ago."

"Man, this guy is as heavy as a mule."

"Watch your step."

"Al ritorno nella terra dei viventi ..." The voice repeats the words: "*Come back to the land of the living ... Come back to the land of the living.*"

Sargon yawns and opens his heavy eyes, seeing an old cavernous ceiling with flickering firelight dancing overhead. For a moment he sits there looking at it, slightly confused. He then suddenly springs up, remembering where he is and looks over at the table where he last saw Bellgrad.

"Bellgrad! You're alive ... oh, thank you, almighty Yahmar," Sargon hollers as he sees his friend propped up on a pillow and drinking from a cup held by the acolyte from last night.

The sudden noise startles the acolyte, who spills some of the cup's contents onto Bellgrad.

"Yes—but almost deaf now ... and wet. These walls echo badly." Bellgrad laughs.

"Sorry. I hope that wasn't an important elixir," Sargon says as he gets up off the table.

"No, thankfully it's just water. But you scared the life out of me." The young acolyte laughs.

"Man, I can't tell you how glad I am to see you up and about,"

Sargon says with a larger-than-life smile as he grabs Bellgrad's left hand with his left hand and pats it with his right.

"Easy there. He doesn't have all his strength yet. He still needs several days of rest." The young acolyte snaps at Sargon's rough approach.

"It does me good to see you smile, but I don't see what the big deal is. I was just asleep," Bellgrad says.

The young acolyte gives Sargon a look.

"What ... okay ..." Sargon lets go of Bellgrad's hand. "Hey, what's your name anyway?" Sargon asks the young acolyte.

"Bob," he answers with a smirk as he gives Bellgrad more water from the cup.

"No, its not," Sargon says as he rolls his eyes.

"Well, that's what everyone calls me." He feels Sargon's stare. "Okay, it's Valpurio Antonio Phillogotti," the acolyte admits.

"Wow, I see why they call you Bob." Sargon smirks. "Why don't you get some sleep. It looks like you could use it. I know you have been up all night."

"And all morning, sir," Bob adds.

"What time of the day is it?" Sargon asks.

"It's midday, sir," Bob answers.

"Hmmm, I slept a lot. Well, go on, I can tend to him."

"Okay, but don't give him too much water. He's very thirsty. It's a side effect of anyone coming out of ..." Bob says.

"Anyone losing that much blood." Father Yor interrupts as he walks down the steps to the infirmary.

"Right," Bob says as he looks over his shoulder at the priest walking down the stairs.

Sargon comes to his feet and respectfully salutes Father Yor. "I cannot thank you enough, Father," Sargon says as he shakes the priest's hand.

"You are very welcome. I see your right arm is doing better."

Yor smiles wearily as he nods his head toward Sargon's arm.

"Yes. It's like nothing happened to it."

"Yeah, right. I know better than that." Yor smirks as he looks at Bellgrad.

"Well, it is a little sore, but that's nothing," Sargon admits.

"How are you feeling, Bellgrad? Be honest—I know how you fighter types like to exaggerate." Yor eyes Sargon as Bob backs away to let Yor in to look at the soldier.

"I'm still rather tired, but I have no pain from my shoulder or my head. I'm ready to go," Bellgrad says as he starts to get up.

"Hold on there." Yor puts a hand on the soldier's chest. "You just rest there. You need to stay here a couple more days."

"Oh ... okay," Bellgrad says as he lies back. "I sure could use some more water."

"In a while, try to get some sleep," Yor answers as he waves Sargon away from the table.

Sargon and Yor step about fifteen feet away from the table.

"Why is he so ready to leave?" Yor asks.

"We are being followed, and I think he's worried they might find us," Sargon whispers.

"Well, he doesn't need to worry, very few people know about the infirmary." Yor reassures him.

"A scout named Riechter might be following us," Sargon confesses.

"Hmm, I've heard that name. Well, he surely is not welcome around here. I'll alert the Templar Knights to be on the lookout. If there is even the slightest risk to us, they will take out any threat—no questions asked. One other thing, be sure not to let him know or think that he died ... not for a long while. If he finds out, he won't sleep or will be afraid of going to sleep."

"Why is that?" Sargon looks confused.

"He'll be afraid he won't wake up. I would wait maybe a

month, or maybe not even tell him at all."

"Did he die?" Sargon asks.

"I don't know." Father Yor hesitates.

"For now I'm just glad he's alive." Sargon smiles as he turns and looks at Bellgrad sleeping. "By Yahmar's holy brow, you are really something, Father. His wounds are completely healed too."

"It comes with a cost," Yor says under his breath.

"What?" Sargon turns his head back toward Yor.

"So, where are you two going from here?" Yor yawns.

"Lord Calador's castle."

"Calador! Good."

"You know him?"

"I don't, but he's good friends with the High Priest, they have known each other for years."

"Wow. That's great. Could I maybe talk to him?" Sargon asks.

"Here he comes now," Yor says and nods toward the stairs.

Preador walks down the stairs and makes his way to Sargon and Yor.

"This is High Priest Preador." Yor introduces the two men.

Sargon stands at attention and salutes the High Priest.

"I'm Sar—"

"Sargon, my son, what a terrible tragedy," Preador interrupts, pulling Sargon into a tearful hug. "Your father and grandfather were very dear friends of mine. I almost did your wedding ceremony, my boy. But Jessica's father, Tarco, insisted on a priest of Zura."

"As much of an honor as it would have been, Your Grace, I'm glad you were not there. The priest was murdered—not from the poison, but by a sword," Sargon says as they break their embrace. "Hey, I remember you now. You did my grandfather's ceremony when he died two years ago."

"That's right. He was a good man and a great knight. He won many battles when we were not much older than you, when Fegnir was at war with Xieg."

"Wow, I didn't know that."

"Yeah. He saved many lives. You know he started out as a cavalry soldier ..."

Yor rolls his eyes, glances back at Bellgrad, and smiles when he sees the soldier sleeping. "Your Grace ... Sargon ... I'm going to get some shut eye."

Preador and Sargon nod at Yor.

"Thanks again, Father," Sargon adds with a raised hand as he is caught up in conversation with the High Priest.

Yor makes his way back up the stairs, thinking of his bed. He is met halfway up by a familiar character.

"Oh brother, what is it now Silverfish?" Yor asks wearily.

"I'm not to blame for this, I honestly was in the tavern just minding my own business waiting for Barbye to close up when this crazy guy started blasting out some gibberish and tearing the place apart," Silverfish explains.

"Yeah, that's a nasty cut on your head—a few lumps too, I see. Go on down, and I'll sew it up, Lumpy."

"That's not funny. People tend to remember nicknames like that." Silverfish looks up at Yor while rubbing his head.

"Hey, no more freebies either," Yor adds as he points at Silverfish. "Oh, and don't wake up that soldier sleeping down there or bother the knight talking to the High Priest.

"What do you mean no freebies? You know I don't have any money."

"Well, I'll figure out something," Yor says over his shoulder as he continues up the stairs. "Oh dear ... Barbye, what happened?" Yor asks with a wide mouth as he sees a battered Barbye escorted down by two guards carrying her on either side.

"That guy behind me just went crazy and started throwing chairs and tables and stormed all about the place." Barbye jerks a thumb over her shoulder to indicate behind her.

Yor looks up the stairs and sees four soldiers carrying a large fellow adorned in animal skins.

"La meg gå ..." (*Let me go*) the big stranger mutters as he struggles to break free.

"Why didn't you take him to the jail?" Yor asks as he goes back down the stairs.

"LA MEG GA DRITTSEKKER ..." (*Let me go, assholes*) the stranger demands even louder.

"He ... has a bad ... cut on his leg ... HOLD HIM," one of the guards answers.

They struggle and make their way down the stairs as Yor clears the way.

"Put him on that table over there." Yor point to an empty table as he grabs a large ash club from an adjacent table. He makes his way to the table as the guards set the big man on it.

"DIN MOR SOVER MED GRISER" (*Your mother sleeps with pigs*) the stranger hollers and spits at the guard on his right arm. He pulls the guard around, knocking Yor down in the process.

"Slå seg ned min sønn. Vi kommer ikke til å skade deg," (*Settle down, my son. We are not going to hurt you*) Preador cries out.

Momentarily, the large man stops. But in the next second, he pulls the guard on his left onto his chest and bites the man's face. The guard releases the big man's arm. In one swift motion, he pushes the injured guard away with his freed right arm and punches the guard on his left, knocking him out; a few teeth go flying as well. He sits up and commences to punch out the men holding his legs.

The guard with the injured face quickly reacts and pops the barbarian on the back of the head with a club he pulls from his belt, knocking the stranger out cold. With that, the man goes limp and collapses on the table.

"Good ole Number Nine Sleeper works every time." The guard laughs while catching his breath and holding a hand to his bleeding cheek.

"You want to tell me what the hell is going on? Sorry, Your Grace," Yor demands as he picks himself off the floor.

"That's quite all right considering the circumstances," Preador laughs.

"Sorry, Father, but it took eight of us to tackle this guy and bring him here. We have been trying to get him for the past three hours," one of the other guards explains.

"Oh, so you thought it would be all right to bring a maniac in here?" Yor asks.

"Well, he's bleeding awfully bad, Father." the injured guard adds.

"And now you and Sleeping Beauty on the floor over there are hurt as well. But I guess it's okay ... at least now." Yor throws his club on a table close by.

Two Templar Knights run down the stairs, followed by four guards.

"Everything okay, Your Grace?" one of the knights asks.

"Yes, Gunther, everything is good. Go back to what you were doing," Preador says to one of the knights, and both head back upstairs.

"Go on back to your posts." Yor waves off the guards.

"Yes, sir." The guards go back upstairs as three acolytes descend.

"Care to explain?" Preador asks as he looks at Silverfish. "Oh sorry, Sargon. This is our village idiot."

Sargon looks on, enjoying the free entertainment. "Oh ... okay. Boy, you sure are a small fellow."

"Watch it, Bub," Silverfish warns as he looks at Sargon. "Like I told Yor—excuse me, Father Yor—I was waiting for Barbye to close the tavern when that guy who had been drinking very heavily wouldn't leave."

Yor beckons the acolytes over. "Sew the barbarian's leg and Lumpy's head."

"Barbarian?" Silverfish jumps.

"Yeah, you can't tell by the way he's dressed? I wonder if he was the only one drinking heavily." Yor smiles.

"Whatever." Silverfish rolls his eyes.

"Silver intervened after that guy pinched me. I slapped him, and then he backhanded me, knocking me down," Barbye interjects.

"That big guy hit you?" Sargon asks, his mouth hanging open in disbelief. "When he wakes up, I'll give him a walloping he won't soon forget; hitting a woman is a big no-no with me."

"What was he drinking?" Preador asks, waving his hand downward in a signal to Sargon to calm down.

Sargon nods in agreement.

"Mead at first, but then he got a bucket of Rokian Swill," Barbye recalls.

"Wow. How much of it did he drink?" Yor asks, as he makes his way to Barbye.

"The whole bucket, I think."

"That explains it," Preador adds.

"What's Rokian Swill?" Sargon asks.

"It's a drink with Fegnirian Viko, Xiegian Schnapps, Kala-mashian Gin, Zquirgian Vodka, Seznoian Mead, Rokian Beer, and fruit mixed in a bucket and aged for two weeks. Sometimes worms get on the fruit—that's why it's called swill. It is usually served to a table of six to eight people," Barbye explains. "Usually most people fall down before they can finish it."

"Those mountain people can't handle that much alcohol. You should've known better." Preador lectures her.

"She didn't serve it to him—he got it from another table. *Owww!*" Silverfish adds as he getting his head injury sewn up by an acolyte.

"Lesson learned, huh, Barbye?" Yor says as he inspects her head and face. "Drink this. It will help you feel better."

"Okay." Barbye nods.

"Here, Lumpy, drink this." Yor hands Silverfish a vial.

"Funny ... what is it?" Silverfish smiles sarcastically then grabs the vial.

"It's boiled cabbage, it will help with that hangover. It also has some flecks of ash wood in it that will help with that goose egg and the cut on your head."

"Good, no more clubs." Silverfish looks up at Yor. "Hey, are you feeling okay? You look like five miles of bad road." Silver asks, noticing for the first time some gray on the back of Father Yor's bowl haircut and wrinkles around the priest's eyes.

"I haven't gotten much sleep in the past few days," Yor answers

"All done, Lumpy," the acolyte sewing Silverfish comments.

"What did I tell you?" Silverfish looks at Yor. "Man, I should have stayed at home last night."

"We are going to take the crazy drunk to jail now that his leg is done," one guard says.

"Okay. I wonder who cut him ... three guesses." Preador waves them onward as the acolytes tending the barbarian collect their sewing kits.

"My baby did." Barbye giggles and then finishes her elixir, eyeing Silverfish. "My hero."

"Oh, brother. I think I'm going to be sick." Yor rolls his eyes. "Now I'm going to sleep. And unless the temple is on fire, don't wake me." Yor scans the room, looking at each of the acolytes as he makes his way to the stairs.

"Yes, sir," the acolytes say in unison.

Two guards carry the barbarian upstairs while Father Yor slowly climbs the stairs behind. The acolytes tend to the two injured guards as Silverfish and Barbye make their way to the stairs.

"Silverfish, that was a very brave thing you did taking on that big guy and defending your lady's honor," Sargon says.

"Well ... thanks ... I guess." Silverfish smiles, but he doesn't know exactly how to take that. He's not used to anyone other than Barbye giving him praise of any kind.

"You take care, Silver. Get some rest, Barbye," Preador adds.

"Thanks. Nice to have met you, Lord Sargon. Maybe we will meet again under better circumstances." Barbye smiles.

"Well, how about some lunch?" Preador asks Sargon after Barbye and Silverfish turn to go.

"Sure, you go on. I'll be up in little while—I'm going to sit with Bellgrad a bit."

"Okay, I'll have the kitchen prepare us some food," Preador says and starts for the stairs.

Sargon grabs a chair and sets it by Bellgrad, who never woke from all the noise and commotion.

"My lord?" Bellgrad wakes.

"Oh, now you wake." Sargon laughs softly.

"Can I have some water?"

"Sure."

Sargon finds the cup and a bucket of water. He dips the cup then helps his friend drink.

"Thanks. That's much better. How long have you been there?" Bellgrad is still groggy.

"Oh, I just sat down when you woke, but I have been down

here since you fell back asleep. Go on back to sleep. I'll be here for you." Sargon reassures him. "No bears here."

Bellgrad laughs. "What about Riechter?"

"Oh, we don't have to worry about him. He doesn't know about this room we are in. And besides, we are being protected by the Templar Knights—they are in charge of keeping the temple protected." Sargon gives his friend more water. "I'm not even sure we were followed at all. You just rest. You had a heck of an ordeal, and it takes time to heal."

"Okay, will you be here when I wake?"

"Oh yeah."

I will always be here for you. Sargon thinks to himself. Bellgrad is the only living reminder of his home.

Chapter XI
Riechter's Return to Ory

hanks again, Riechter. Those rabbits and birds you shot sure hit the spot this morning for breakfast," Symon acknowledges.

"You're welcome. Sure beats those rations you have been eating." Riechter smiles.

Both Davyd and Symon nod their heads. "Yeah, I still can't believe you shot two birds through the head with one arrow," Davyd adds.

"Those were doves. And, yeah, that was a good shot if I say so myself." Riechter laughs. "I had to wait till they moved their heads together just right to make that shot." He reenacts launching an arrow from his bow.

"Well, I did clean all the game." Garxe joins the conversation.

"Thanks also, Garxe." Davyd gives a half salute with his dagger in his hand.

Riechter stares at Garxe. "Wahhhh," he mocks Garxe, crying like a baby. "What, you want me to give you a metal for valor? They cooked the meat." Riechter points to Davyd and Symon. "Oh, by the way, you are lucky I didn't shoot you as well—sneaking into the camp earlier."

"You're right. I should've announced my arrival. But the general wanted me to relay a message to Heyrold," Garxe says. "I'm glad I caught you all still camped, but I forget old men need more rest." Garxe smiles at Riechter.

"Hey, toadstool, I was up way before Sulo was in the sky."

"Yeah, well, I do appreciate the breakfast," Garxe says. "Oh, I got your saddlebag. It has a bottle of Viko and some rations."

"You just so happened to remember that this morning and not last night before you left us?" Riechter shakes his head.

"I think you were still feeling no pain when I left," Garxe says, going to his horse and pulling the bottle from a saddlebag. "Here, crybaby." He tosses the bottle to Riechter.

"Thanks, jughead," Riechter says under his breath as he uncorks the bottle and takes a swig.

"I'll clean up the camp, sir," Corporal Wyther, the tracking soldier, states.

All the men gather their things and prepare to head out.

"How did you find all those animals this morning, Riechter?" Davyd asks. "It was dark."

"You just got to know where to look," Riechter explains while loading his gear on his horse. "Heck, boy, I could've tracked those rabbits blindfolded. It just comes with years. I'll show you sometime. I could smell those rabbits before I saw them."

"Oh, please. You just got lucky and stumbled upon their hole and knew they would be close by." Garxe rolls his eyes, earning a searing glance from Riechter. "What? I do know a few things about hunting too, grandpa."

"Yeah right. Your version of hunting is telling one of your castle servants to go kill a rabbit while you sip your morning tea." Riechter mocks him. He takes another swig of the Viko before packing it away in his saddlebag.

"Well, it gets the job done, doesn't it?" Garxe smirks.

"We all packed up?" Riechter asks. He looks around as he mounts his horse.

"Wow, you must be feeling better." Garxe looks amazed at how Riechter mounted without help.

"Come on, grandpa. Waiting on you now," Riechter says to Garxe as the other men mount their horses.

"I got your grandpa ..." Garxe swings onto his horse.

The men make their way onto the road and ride for about four hours to the city of Vry. But they find the main gate closed to the city.

"Who goes there?" a guard on the front gatehouse asks.

"Are you blind as well as stupid?" Riechter asks. "It's Riechter."

"Oh ... sorry, sir. Is that Garxe with you?" the guard asks.

"Yes." Riechter rolls his eyes. "This guy must be related to you two," Riechter adds as he looks over his shoulder at Davyd and Symon.

"Where's Mychel?" the guards asks.

"Open this damn gate before I shoot you off that gatehouse," Garxe orders.

"Okay, okay." The guard runs down the steps from the wall and opens the portcullis.

"If I wasn't so tired I would kick your teeth in, soldier," Garxe adds as they all ride through the gatehouse.

"He's not worth wasting your energy on," Riechter comments. "He's a prime example of why I would rather spend my time with animals in the woods. At least they aren't pretending to be something they're not. This Zom-Zom is pretending to be alive."

"Zom-Zom?" Davyd asks.

"See what I mean?" Riechter says to Garxe. "Zombie, dummy."

"Oh ..." Davyd answers.

"What's your name, soldier?" Garxe asks the guard as they ride by.

"Who cares? Come on," Riechter orders as he rides on.

Symon leans over to Davyd and nods toward Riechter. "See what I've been telling you? Watch your step. You think he went hunting on our account? Ha. He just knew he had help to cook and clean it. He can get as mean as a snake, especially if Heyrold gives him a chewing out."

"Yeah, well his leg is really hurting him. I don't think he's as bad as you say," Davyd says as the two lag behind. Riechter rides ahead and steers the men toward the town's temple.

"You'll see ... In any case, he will be laid up for two or three days. Those plants and stones the priests use don't heal instantly, although they do speed it up about ten times," Symon explains, still watching Riechter. "Wyther, why don't you go and let the Captain of the Guard know we are back in town. We will escort Riechter and Garxe to the castle."

"Sure, anything beats just waiting around. Need anything from the bunkhouse?" Wyther asks.

"No I'm good. We'll be along shortly," Symon answers.

Wyther rides off as the group approaches the temple. Riechter stops his horse, leaving it for Garxe as he makes his way slowly up the temple steps. Garxe looks over his shoulder and points to Davyd and then the horses as he follows the woodsman into the temple.

"You watch that kiss-ass too. He's even more dangerous—he has an agenda. Riechter's just in it for the money, but that guy's a powermonger," Symon warns as Davyd dismounts and hands him the reins of his horse, then goes and grabs Riechter's and Garxe's horses.

"How do you know all these things?" Davyd asks as Symon walks his horse up with Davyd's in tow.

"I didn't make Corporal by running my mouth. You learn to keep it shut. That gold the general gave us was not for our good work, it was to keep us quiet." Symon pauses and looks around them. "Don't tell anyone you know anything."

"Well, I don't know anything," Davyd admits as he peers around the streets as well.

"Good ... keep it that way," Symon comments. "Now look alive and be a good soldier."

"Yes, sir," Davyd acknowledges with a nod.

Riechter and Garxe are greeted by a young priest as they enter the temple.

"I'm Friar Yance. How can I help you gentlemen?"

"I'm Riechter. My leg is broken, and I need it healed," Riechter says as he limps over to a chair just inside the temple doorway.

"This is a Temple of Zura, Lord Riechter," Yance says.

"Please don't insult me, friar. I'm no Lord." Riechter groans as he sits.

"Sorry, Riechter, but you are not a follower of Zura either," the young priest states.

"I know that, but I'm prepared to make an offering." Riechter pulls a pouch with 15 J'avins from his belt.

"Wow, that's very generous, my lo—I mean—Riechter." The young priest's eyes light up at the sight of the gold.

"Well, I'm just a generous fellow." Riechter smiles.

Garxe barks a half laugh. "Sorry ..."

Friar Yance instructs some acolytes to cut away the splint and pull off his boot. They start rubbing the ankle with some stones while another gives Riechter a series of elixirs to drink. They then rub some ointment on his ankle.

"I have to say, it feels a lot better," Riechter says as he wipes tears from his eyes.

"I admit I'm surprised. You did not make a sound. Usually there is a lot of noise from a lot bigger fellows than you until the effects of the stones take away the pain." Friar Yance sounds surprised by Riechter's toughness.

"Yea, I've been told that." Riechter smirks.

"You need to stay off that leg for at least two days."

"Not gonna happen." Riechter shakes his head.

"But the bones won't heal correctly, and you could end up lame," Yance explains.

"That's a chance I have to take."

"Why are you so insistent to leave right away?"

"That is my business," Riechter answers.

"Well, all I can do is advise you. If you don't follow my instructions, that's on you," Friar Yance says.

"Can't you priests throw some kind of heal spell and it would be all normal?" Riechter asks.

"No one around here can do that."

"They can in Kalamash."

"Well this is not Kalamash. Does this have anything to do with the murder of Father Ardox? Horrible ... horrible. But I find it hard to believe that young Sargon of the House of Guel would have murdered him." Friar Yance shakes his head.

"That's what I have to find out," Riechter answers. "That's all I can tell you."

"I hope you can find the murderer."

"I intend to," Riechter states as the acolytes tending his leg wrap a fresh dressing and tie a fresh splint on his leg. "Thanks, friar." Riechter gets up from the chair and hobbles out of the temple.

"I would stay around town and let the wound heal," Friar Yance further advises. "Two days is not that long to wait."

"We'll see. I'll try to stay off it as much as I can."

"You might as well be talking to that stone pillar there, friar," Garxe comments as he points to one of the stone columns on the inside of the temple.

The two men exit the temple and walk toward their horses; Davyd hands the reins to the men and then mounts his horse.

"Nice touch, egghead," Riechter says to Garxe as he mounts his horse.

"What? I was just telling him the truth. You are not going to stay off that leg any more than I'm going to become High Priest of that temple," Garxe says as he mounts his horse as well.

"Your leg feeling any better, Riechter?" Symon asks.

"What's it to you, ratface? You my mother now?" Riechter laughs. "Yeah, it's a little better."

Davyd laughs as he gets a look from Symon. "Sorry, sir."

"Let's go see Heyrold," Riechter says as he spurs his horse.

The men all ride across the town and to the castle at the far side. They are all greeted by soldiers inside the gatehouse of the castle. As they dismount, stable boys take the animals to the stable just inside the walls and tend to them. Riechter leads the way as they walk to the main tower of the castle. The guards on either side of the doors open them and stand at attention as the men enter.

"Follow me, gentlemen. Heyrold is expecting you." A soldier wearing well-polished armor climbs the staircase ahead of them.

"Euuuwwww." Riechter rolls his eyes and shakes his head at Garxe as they climb the stairs.

"What, idiot? This is my domain. I'm in my comfort zone now, hayseed," Garxe smiles as he climbs the stairs next to Riechter.

"Like I said earlier about the rabbits …" Riechter adds.

Symon and Davyd both laugh under their breath, just glad they aren't the brunt of Riechter's jests. The four men continue up another flight of stairs, then to a hallway that leads to a great room. The soldier holds up his hand to the guards on either side of the doors as they approach. The doors open to reveal a large table with documents and maps scattered across it from end to end. A large armored man with long blond-and-gray hair with a well-adorned cape stands looking out a window as Riechter and the others enter.

"Riechter! Good to see you, my old friend," Heyrold says as he turns around. The men grab each other's forearms in the customary handshake. Heyrold pats Riechter's left shoulder with his left hand.

"Good to see you too, Heyrold. Still hard at work with matters of state, I see," Riechter acknowledges.

"Always. Garxe, I see Riechter has not bored you to death with all his stories—about himself, of course." Heyrold laughs and shakes Garxe's hand as well.

"Oh … he has been trying to," Garxe answers.

"That will be all, Captain." Heyrold dismisses the soldier who escorted the men. "You two can wait outside in the hall, but don't go anywhere. I need to talk to you both," Heyrold says to Davyd and Symon.

"Yes, sir," the men respond in unison and exit the room as the doors close behind them.

"You men want to tell me what the hell is going on? The Guel boy is not in our custody or dead, and Zeth the blacksmith and his family are dead, and his place burnt to the ground. I also heard that Sergeant Trymith turned against you and was killed in the melee, along with Mychel and all the other soldiers that died. And I heard all this from the general's messenger—a soldier reported to him the whole escapade."

Riechter looks at Garxe for an explanation.

"He rode off toward Guel Castle before I could stop him. He was one of the soldiers that helped you get mounted when you left," Garxe quietly confesses to Riechter.

"That little bastard …" Riechter says under his breath.

"Well, Riechter, you have something to add to that? SPEAK," Heyrold barks.

"My lord, Trymith did turn against me. And as far as the Guel boy, he had help. My kinda help—someone was covering his tracks and making it difficult to follow. We were being watched in the woods, probably by whoever helped the Guel boy, and that's why we turned back. As far as the blacksmith, he attacked us. He threw his hammer and hit my horse. I got pulled underneath the horse and broke my leg when it stepped on me. Mychel died while fighting Zeth in the blacksmith shop."

"My understanding is that you provoked that attack, Riechter. Were you honestly going to bring Zeth and his family back here?" Heyrold asks.

"Actually, sire, I intended to. I figured he would have told us all he knew," Riechter admits.

"Horseshit. You wouldn't have had him slow you down. I know you better than that, and apparently so did Zeth. You should have left him alone and gone after Sargon. You probably would've had him by now. Do you two magpies know how much I have risked in all this, not to mention money? I don't know if Sargon has a clue, but he's pretty clever. And if he gets to talking about his version of things—even though it's speculation—my enemies will just use this against me. I guess it's a good thing he did not stick around and see who entered his home," Heyrold says.

"Are you done?" Riechter asks as he pulls a chair up to the table, sits down, and props up his foot on the table. "You won't talk to me like that again. I don't give a damn how much money you pay me. I've been cleaning up your messes for years, and I will handle it in whatever way I see fit or you can do it all yourself, and I'll just disappear like a banshee in the mist and you'll never see me again." Riechter raises an eyebrow.

"Well, you're right, that was out of line. It's not your fault this plan all fell apart. It's just taken years for all of this to play out, and I guess I've gotten spoiled by you coming in and cleaning it all up." Heyrold looks thoughtful as he pours wine from a crystal decanter into three crystal goblets then hands Riechter and Garxe each a goblet.

"You should be looking at your other personnel. Someone is to blame for this, but it's not me or Garxe, we both came in from Xieg when all this happened. I was only given a day's notice by one of your messengers that my presence was required at Guel Castle. I wasn't brought up to speed by the general until after I arrived. I already had a pretty good idea after I found that dead priest in the woods … Mmmm, this is good wine." Riechter gulps down the nectar.

"Thanks. It's from my private stock, made from grapes I grew myself. This wine here is about ten years old, aged in iron wood barrels," Heyrold boasts as he sips his wine.

Garxe nods in agreement after sampling the sweet nectar as well.

"Look, I can take care of this, but it's going to take some time. I can't just go out and shoot an arrow in the Guel boy's head in the middle of town. Especially in Missionwise, I will have to catch him alone sometime in the middle of nowhere."

"Well, enough of that. How's that going in Xieg?" Heyrold inquires as he sips his wine.

"Good, my lord. You should have your trade agreement with Lord Oberon signed and in your hands any day now. Also, General Dytruik requests your presence. He thinks it would look favorable to the locals if you were there at Castle Guel at such a bad time," Garxe says.

"He's right. I'll go there right away. So, Riechter, what about the two soldiers in the hall? Have they been helpful to you?" Heyrold asks.

"Corporal Symon is the one who threw me my bow and quiver when Zeth was about to kill Garxe," Riechter says, earning a look of disbelief from Garxe. "You didn't know that did you?" He smiles at Garxe. "Everyone else was too far away in the chaos. He just happened to be closer to my horse than to the fight. With the way my horse was jumping around, I'm surprised he was able to snag it off and throw it to me before Zeth killed you."

"Wow ... I did not know that." Garxe looks stunned, staring blankly at the wall as he sips his wine.

"What about Private Davyd?" Heyrold asks. "I felt uneasy about having any privates involved in this, but he's good with a sword, and my men are spread out with that siege at Hiegar's castle." That's in Xieg, about fifty miles away.

"He's a good soldier, very loyal to you, Heyrold. Speaking of which, they have some sorry rations."

Yes, I know, but that's the leftovers. The good rations are with the men in Xieg," Heyrold acknowledges. "I knew they would not go hungry in your company."

"Well, that explains it," Riechter answers as he nods at his empty goblet.

Heyrold laughs and refills Riechter's goblet with more wine. "So what do you suggest?"

"Accommodation," Garxe adds.

"Really, skunk breath? How about promotions? You know, you fighter types like ranks and all," Riechter says to Garxe.

"Since when are you so concerned about soldiers? You didn't even know their names until you asked them?" Garxe asks.

"Oh, he knew their names. He just plays dumb. You forget what he does for a living. Nothing slips by him, Garxe," Heyrold interjects.

Riechter smiles. "I must be getting soft in my old age. Anyway, it's all about money. With promotions comes more money, right?"

"They already got that, with what I gave at Guel Castle," Heyrold reminds him.

"So? You will make a hundred times that with everything going on in Xieg," Riechter says.

"That is none of your affair," Garxe interjects.

"Oh shut up, kiss-ass. You are making some serious coin out of this too," Riechter barks at Garxe.

"Like I said, nothing slips by him, Garxe." Heyrold pats Garxe on the shoulder as he pours his friend more wine.

"Apparently not," Garxe answers with a raised eyebrow.

Riechter blows Garxe a kiss. "I got your number, fancy-pants."

"What about Wyther?" Heyrold asks.

"Him too. He was helpful with the tracking," Riechter answers.

"That doesn't sound like promotional action," Heyrold comments.

"It would have been had we caught the Guel boy. Look, you asked my opinion and I gave it. They are your men, not mine," Riechter states.

"Point taken. Garxe, tell those two in the hall to come in, then go find Corporal Wyther," Heyrold orders.

"I'm gone. I'll let you know what I find," Riechter tells Heyrold.

"Are you going to want those men to help you?" Heyrold asks as he points to the door. Garxe pauses to wait for Riechter's answer.

"No. I'm gonna work this one alone ... well, with *my* team. Tryton and Hogarth should be along in the next day or two. Their affairs in Xieg should be completed by now." Riechter sets his leg down and slowly rises to his feet. "Garxe, it's been good matching wits with you for the past ten days. Sorry about Mychel. I know you two were good friends," Riechter adds as he shakes Garxe's hand.

"Thanks. I'll convey your condolences to his family. I'll have some roasted rabbit waiting for you at my castle when this is all done."

The two men laugh as they exit.

"The captain has a package for you, Riechter," Heyrold announces.

Riechter smiles as he hobbles down the hall, as Davyd and Symon enter the room.

Chapter XII
Lord Valagar

AM ME DE CEENCHRS," SARGON says, his voice muffled by the nails in his mouth. He drives the last nail in. He quickly bends the nail over and downward with the hammer toward the bottom of Tantor's hoof like he did with all the other hooves. He then grabs the nails from his mouth with his free hand, releases his horse's front right leg, and spits all in one motion as Tantor sets his freed leg down.

"Did you say something, sir?" A young stable boy asks from across the stable.

"What's your name again?" Sargon asks the stable boy, catching his breath and stretching his aching back.

"It's Tat, sir." Tat says, making his way from stall to stall to give out the morning feeding.

"What I said, Tat, was: Bring me the clenchers. I left them on the ground over there just out of my reach on the other side of my horse." Sargon walks around the back of Tantor, patting the horse on the top of his rump as he passes. "But that's okay."

He pauses to spit. "I see you are busy now. You weren't earlier, you were watching me." Sargon grumbles under his breath as he grabs the tool off the ground next to Tantor, then circles back around the animal.

"I'm sorry, sir. I was just so amazed. I've never seen anyone shoe a horse that fast. I kinda lost track of time. All these horses should have been fed by now, Sulo is starting to rise." Tat says as he hurriedly dumps feed in the troughs of each stall. "If the owner stops by and sees that the horses are not fed before sunrise, he will run me off."

"Tis all right. I got it." Sargon spits again and taps the front of Tantor's right front hoof with his boot. In turn, the horse instantly raises his leg backward as Sargon grabs the hoof with his free hand, then gently squeezes it between his legs just above his knees. He repeatedly brushes away the white feathered tufts of hair that hang over Tantor's hoof, like he did before. He's careful not to pull or tangle them on the uncut nails, or—worse—cut them off while cutting the overhanging tips of the nails with nippers. He then cinches all the nails with a clinching tool then gives all the nails a final tap with the hammer and re-clench before Tat finishes feeding two stalls. He then in turn grabs a small bucket, picks up the leg, sets the hoof on it, and files all the clenched nails down.

"Phew. Finished." Sargon breathes a sigh of relief while taking Tantor's hoof off the bucket and setting it on the ground after filing down the nails. He picks up all the tools and returns them to their rightful place on a nearby post hanging on nails. Sargon grabs a brush hanging nearby, returns to Tantor, and grabs an apple from a nearby board of Tantor's stall that he had brought earlier.

"Here you go, old man," Sargon says to Tantor as he gives him the apple. He begins brushing the horse's cinnamon-brown back as the horse quickly gobbles down the apple and then turns his attention back to the hay he was munching on earlier between the planks of the stall's gate.

"You sure are an early riser, my lord," Tat says from across the stable as he continues feeding.

"I couldn't sleep, and I got those shoes ready yesterday when I noticed the ones he had on were in bad shape after that trouble we got into three days ago. Well, it was time to re-shoe him anyhow," Sargon says, spitting again.

"Is your friend okay? Remember, I was the one who grabbed your horse that early morning, I had just gotten here," Tat asks over his shoulder as he walks briskly to the back of the stable and refills his bucket with grain. "He looked like he was in a bad way."

"Oh yeah," Sargon recalls. "Much better. We should be underway today."

"Good. Is that tobacco?" Tat asks as he works his way closer.

"Aye. You want some? I got it in a leather pouch over there." Sargon points with the brush in his right hand to a shelf by the stable doorway as he spits out his chaw to the center of the stable.

"No. Brethel, one of the blacksmiths, gave me some to try a while back, and I got sick," Tat answers.

"I met him. He let me use his forge yesterday. Well, I was about your age when I first tried it. What are you, about ten?" Sargon asks as he gets a good look at the five-foot-tall blond kid. He is skinny and has shaggy hair and blue eyes. The boy, like himself, has had to grow up early in life. But Sargon understands the responsibilities he has grown up with are far different from those of this young man. For one, he has never had to worry about putting food on the table, or where his next meal might come from. His responsibilities were much vaster, like running a castle and the surrounding region that would all be his one day. Because of this, Sargon has a lot of respect for young Tat.

"Yeah. How did you know?" Tat asks.

"I was big for my age too. Funny enough, it was a blacksmith that got me started too, and I got sick my first time as well." Sargon laughs as he brushes Tantor's rump.

"I won't try that stuff again."

"Sure you will." Sargon snickers. "Ticklish ..." Sargon laughs at Tantor as he gently brushes the horse's soft white underbelly in front of his left hind leg. The horse lightly quivers his pelt with each stroke. "My father hated the fact that I chew tobacco. Felt it was a nasty habit."

"Finally. Phew." Tat breathes a sigh of relief as he wipes his brow with his tattered brown burlap sleeve while setting the feed bucket on a nearby board. He steps over to a frozen bucket of water near the entrance of the stable. Breaking the ice with a scoop, he dishes out some water. He gulps it down, then pouring a scoop of it over his head. "He's a really beautiful horse, my lord," Tat adds, his breath steaming. He slicks his hair back then wipes his face on his cloak while marveling at Sargon's three-thousand-pound warhorse while catching his breath.

"Thanks. He's quite an amazing creature."

"I love that blaze on his face and the fact he has one blue eye and one brown eye. It's a sign of a good horse, according to Father Yor," Tat says and blows his nose on the sleeve of his cloak.

"You don't say." Sargon smirks as he brushes out Tantor's black tail.

"He's very fond of you too, sire," Tat adds. "He's always keep-ing an eye on you."

"Really?" Sargon works his way up Tantor's right side to the horse's long black mane.

"Aye, sir. You don't notice it because you're around him all the time, and you fed him right before I got here, so it's not food he seeks. I'm around different horses all the time, and I notice things like that. Most horses don't pay much mind to their masters."

"Well, I raised him from a colt. His mother died when he was born, so I fed him milk from a waterskin three times a day. I got volunteered by my grandfather. He said it would build character, and he was right. Tantor's about ten years old now.

You know horses reach maturity by their fifth year. I trained him too—with some help. Yeah, he and I have kinda grown up together. We've seen a lot too, sometimes he's been the only company I've had in my travels." Sargon pats his friend's neck then lays down the brush on a barrel close by and starts working knots out of Tantor's mane.

"I still can't believe you know how to shoe horses, sir," Tat says as he starts back toward the back of the stable and grabs the empty bucket along the way.

"Why is that so surprising?" Sargon asks, almost offended. "Haven't you heard of field repair? What would happen if I was away from town and he threw a shoe?"

"I guess I never thought of that. Most men in your position think it's beneath them to do such work. Come to think of it, most men don't really talk to me except to ask for their horses," Tat explains as he takes a horse out of a stall then begins cleaning it out with a pitchfork.

"Oh. Well, I'm not most men. How do you know my position anyway? I don't have any armor on, and I am meagerly dressed. These clothes were given to him by the temple."

"The way you carry yourself, my lord. But it's also the way you wear your hair—long and braided in the middle. A follower of Marxbaq. Only knights follow that god."

"You are very perceptive. Any man who can't take care of his horse is not worth what you are shoveling out of that stall." Sargon smirks as he grabs the brush and finishes brushing out Tantor's mane.

"That's what Brethel says."

"Well, those words of wisdom aren't mine either. They are from a blacksmith as well, but I wholeheartedly agree with them." Sargon circles his horse to gather up the old horseshoes. He pauses when something catches his eye. He peers between

Tantor's legs and sees the Templar Knight, Gunter, standing halfway up the temple stairs shaking hands with a man in armor and then pointing toward the stable, toward Sargon.

"Looks like I'm not the only early riser. Who is that?" Sargon asks as he makes his way to the water bucket, throws down two of the horseshoes, and then scoops out a drink of water. Tat puts away the horse and makes his way over to Sargon.

Tat stands next to Sargon and looks outside across from the stable to the temple, completely lit up by the morning sun. "Oh, that's Valagar. He's Lord Calador's champion."

The two knights meet Sargon at the entrance of the stable along with Tat.

"Sargon, this is Sir Valagar." Gunter introduces the men.

Sargon is met with a strong handshake, which he meets with an even stronger one.

"Pleased to meet you, Lord Sargon. Good handshake." Valagar sounds impressed; he looks Sargon in the eye.

"Thanks, but I'm not a Lord yet, Sir Valagar. I haven't even been knighted." Sargon holds Valagar's stare.

"Well, that's a minor formality. You are still a Lord, in any case. And call me Val," Valagar says, releasing his handshake and patting Sargon on the shoulder with his other hand.

"Well, not earned yet, my lord." Sargon nods.

"I like the way you think, son," Val adds with a wink.

Two young men ride up to the stables. They're dressed in leather armor, and their horses are loaded with weapons and supplies. They dismount and approach.

"These are my retainers, Ari and Elof." Val smiles as he introduces them to Sargon.

"Pleased to meet you," Sargon says as he shakes their hands. *Wow they are not much older than Tat,* Sargon thinks to himself.

"Does Missionwise have a new blacksmith?" Gunter asks as

he eyes the two horseshoes in Sargon's left hand.

"Oh, no. Just replacing the damaged shoes I told you about, and I changed his back ones while I was at it," Sargon answers.

"On the bear-killing horse over there," Gunter says sarcastically as he points to Tantor.

"Really? Nice! Well, he is a big stud horse," Val says, clearly amazed at the sight of Tantor.

"He killed a bear?" Tat interrupts.

"Wow!" Ari and Elof say at the same time.

"Yep, if it weren't for him, I would be dead. He finished what I started—drove an axe head into its skull," Sargon acknowledges as he peers over his shoulder at Tantor, who is looking directly at him. *Wow ... Tat is right, he does watch me,* Sargon thinks to himself.

"Come now, Sargon, horses don't do ... that kind of thing," Gunter challenges then sees the indentions on the shoes as Sargon raises them in his hand.

"I told you—" Sargon smiles, stopping mid-sentence as he spots an approaching rider leading his and Bellgrad's packhorses with their armor, along with Tantor's barding on them. "Hey, that's my armor. I left that back in the woods."

"I know. I'm bringing them back to you, Sargon," says the mysterious hooded rider in animal pelts.

"How do you know my name?" Sargon is surprised and reaches for a sword that's not there. *Damn it, not again.* Sargon thinks to himself.

"I told him," a familiar female voice says, and its owner rides up from behind. "We followed your trail and came upon your horses, armor, and two dead bears. With all the blood we found beside the creek, it appears you left in a hurry. How's Bellgrad?" The woman continues as she pulls back her hood.

"Meg? He's fine ...Wow ... Where's Zeth?" Sargon smiles as he looks beyond Meg, scanning for other riders, then he peers back at everyone around him. They're all looking at each other. "What?"

"He's dead, Sargon," Val answers.

"What? When? How?" Sargon stands with his mouth open in total shock.

"He was killed shortly after you and Bellgrad left, along with everyone else in my family," Meg answers with tears in her eyes. "Exel here found me as I ran from my house. I climbed out a back window after my mom was nailed to the door by a sword." She dismounts and points to the rider as he pulls back his hood and dismounts as well.

Sargon walks over to the packhorses and starts to untie the armor pieces as he looks for his armor.

"What do you think you are doing?" Val asks as he steps to Sargon's side.

"I'm going to go kill that son of a—" Sargon says stoically as he goes over to the second packhorse.

"It won't do any good. Riechter has gone back to Vry," Exel interrupts as he makes his way to Sargon.

"I don't expect you to understand or to go with me," Sargon says to Valagar.

"Sargon, I do understand. I have lost family too. Tarco was my second cousin, but this is not the way." Val grabs Sargon's right arm under the shoulder.

Sargon winces slightly from pain. "That's not your parents and then your friends."

"True, he did not kill my parents, but Zeth and Reaxl were my friends too—long before you were born. Your father's as well," Val confesses. "Nothing would bring me more pleasure than to see Riechter's head at the end of my lance. Believe me, I would parade it around the whole country. But he's not the only one that needs to pay the price, he's just a puppet. We need to bring down the puppeteer. But we need proof. We can't just march into Vry and lope Heyrold's head off, although the thought has crossed my mind. He has been a thorn in my side for a long time. But the Duke of Darconia would back Heyrold, and this would bring on a bad civil war we could not win. Your word alone will not be enough unless you have hard proof that Heyrold did this."

"No, I left when I heard riders approaching at the request of the priest that did my wedding. I could not save him either, and he was cut down by a scout as I tried to jump down onto the killer from a tree. I did kill him afterward, but by then it was too late. The scout didn't have any kind of markings on him either. Wouldn't Riechter's pursuit of me be enough?" Sargon asks.

"It is for me and Calador and those who know you. But for everyone else, Heyrold's men have been sending out dispatches stating you killed everyone, including Zeth and his family," Val says.

"What? That's insane. What would I have to gain from that?" Sargon shakes his head.

"Well, I don't know—your family's land and her family's land. Her brothers died at your wedding as well, didn't they?" Val states.

"Yes, but—"

Meg protests, "I would tell them he had nothing to do with it. He loved his family and all the families involved." She joins the two men and puts her arms around Sargon in a soft hug from behind.

"That's admirable, but it will mean nothing to men who do not value the words of a young girl, especially one who just lost her family fighting Heyrold's men," Val explains.

"So when does it end? When he has killed everyone around me, taking them out one at a time? Or maybe when he has simply taken me out? I won't go down without a fight," Sargon says as he pauses and pats Meg's soft, dainty hands.

"I don't expect you to but going after either Riechter or Heyrold alone will get you nothing but dead. Heyrold has amassed a great many men. More men than Calador, Preador, or I have at our disposal. We need to give Calador time. He is gaining allies with the other noble houses all the time. Once Heyrold has gotten wind that you are under the care of Calador and me, he will not try to take you out directly. He'll know that he will be the first one we point a finger at if you are killed, and he won't chance that now that we know the truth about what happened to your family, and Jessica's family, as well as Zeth and his family. As far as I know, they don't know about Meg."

"So I should just stand by while he torches my family castle?" Sargon asks.

"He won't torch your home. He will keep it intact and give your family a proper burial in the castle crypt. He'll keep up the appearance that he has had nothing to do with it, same as he will with Jessica's family's castles," Val says.

"So what do we do?" Sargon asks.

"Let's depart to the temple. We can continue this conversation inside, I think the high priest would like to hear this as well," Gunter advises as he scans the streets, where he sees some of the locals looking on.

"Okay, okay," Sargon agrees and ties the rope holding the armor on the horse.

"Tat," Gunter clears his throat, "take these horses inside and unload that armor and lock it away." His eyes grow wide at the sight of the blood, scratches, and bear fur on the headpiece of Tantor's barding as he tosses the boy a Siv.

"I told you." Sargon smiles at Gunter. "Go on and put Tantor away as well. Give him another half ration of feed too," he adds as he tosses Tat a Pen he pulls from his boot.

"Yes, sir," Tat answers.

"Ari, Elof—give the boy a hand and grab my horse over there," Val says as he points across the street. The two young men nod in unison.

"What?" Sargon says as he sees Val smile at him as he pulls his pants back over his boot. "You can't be too careful."

"I didn't say anything. You are just being resourceful like your father." Val laughs and shrugs his shoulders.

"Wow, you weren't kidding, Sargon," Gunter says, blank-faced as he watches the horses being led into the stable. Val smiles and shakes his head.

"You got to start taking people at their word more often. Not everyone is full of gob droppings," Val says, grabbing Gunter around the shoulder in a familiar gesture. It's obvious they have known each other a long time.

"You're right. I'm just too used to hearing stories. It's hard to recognize the truth anymore. Most people get attacked by gobs or kobolds—something smaller than themselves. Next thing you know, they were attacked by giants."

"I think I would rather be attacked by a giant than some of the gobs that are out there ... night gobs come to mind," Val says.

"Night gobs? I thought all goblins come out at night?" Gunter asks.

"No. Forest gobs don't, but night gobs do, and they attack you in hordes. I ran into some of them one time when I escorted a shipment of iron ore coming from one of Calador's mines deep in the Shendo Mountains. They are vicious, terribly vicious. I lost some good men that night," Val recollects.

"I guess I got to get out more. Sure need to get my stories straight," Gunter says, a little spellbound at these words coming from a great knight like Valagar.

The party walks across the street and climbs the stairs to the temple. They all customarily bow their heads and salute the Statue of Yahmar as they enter the temple chamber and make their way to the back toward the kitchen area. When they enter, they see the high priest and Father Yor, with the barbarian sitting next to him. Silverfish, Chan, and Barbye are all there too enjoying some breakfast.

Stunned at the sight of the barbarian, Sargon goes before him; he sees the fighter looks rough even after three days. The barbarian looks like he was partying just the night before, but Sargon knows the man has been in jail.

"You and I are going to be having some words," Sargon says to the stranger, who looks up from his food.

"Sit down, pretty boy, before you get hurt," the very muscular barbarian says without expression as he eats and lets out a belch.

"Shut up, Bjorn. You don't want to end up on a warship as an oarsman like you were before, do you? Oh yeah, the captain of the guard has told me all about that. He says he has a permanent spot just waiting for you on one of the warships moored at Suva (a port city east of Missionwise)," Father Yor barks as he stands up ready for trouble, knocking over his chair in the process.

"No," Bjorn mutters as he peers up at Yor.

"Sargon, please sit. We don't need any more problems." Father Yor motions to the chair across from Bjorn.

"Sure," Sargon eyes Father Yor's other hand resting on the head of his scepter tucked in his belt, "Your Grace." Sargon nods respectfully at Preador.

"I would not fight here anyway. This is holy ground," Bjorn adds with his mouth half full of food.

Silverfish snickers.

"I'll have nothing from you either," Father Yor says as he looks at the small elf standing on the chair to his left.

"What? I didn't say anything," Silverfish says innocently.

Chan grins as he watches the exchange.

"Like looking after children. Sorry, Lord Valagar. Good to see you," Father Yor says, shaking his head in obvious embarrassment. Then he picks up his chair. "Please sit, join us. Who are your friends?"

"Oh, forgive me. This is Meg, daughter of Zeth the blacksmith, and—"

"Exel!" Preador interrupts, looking up from his breakfast. "Good to see you, old friend. Sorry, Valagar!"

"Your Grace." Exel nods, and Valagar salutes with his right arm and a closed fist across his chest.

"They arrived at Du'tesh Castle, Calador's castle, yesterday," Val says as he finds a seat next to the high priest.

"Zeth, his son, and his wife were killed fighting Riechter and Heyrold's soldiers. Meg here barely got away. I watched it all from atop a tree," Exel explains as he sits in a chair next to Val. "I was going to get some arrows and other supplies from Zeth when I heard Riechter's voice through the trees. I swatted my horse away and hid in a tree. When I saw Meg climb out the back window, I jumped from tree to tree and made my way toward her. I pulled her up into the trees with me."

"Sorry about your family, my child. Your father was a good man. I didn't know him personally, but I heard the soldiers mention his name from time to time. Too much death ... what a terrifying ordeal ... I bet you were scared, my girl," Preador says to Meg as she sits next to Exel and nods in recognition.

"Oh, I was terrified. Figured I was next. I bit Exel's hand as he covered my mouth when I started to scream. But I soon figured out he was not with Riechter when soldiers passed under our tree and Exel did nothing but keep us both motionless and quiet," Meg explains as she looks around the table.

"The one thing I failed to mention is that at least Meg's family took a few men with them, went down fighting, and Riechter did get his leg broken. Couldn't happen to a nicer guy," Exel says sarcastically with a smirk on his face. "I almost gave away my position with all my laughing when I saw his horse step on him. Luckily there was so much commotion no one heard."

"You know Riechter?" Sargon asks as everyone listens.

"Oh yeah, he's a real Lycan rat," Exel answers. "Gives a real bad name to my profession."

"He's a Lycan rat?" Silverfish asks, confused.

"No, buckethead! He's not really a Lycan rat, he means he's a real piece of trash," Father Yor tells Silverfish.

Yor shakes his head and laughs. "Sometimes you scare me." Then with his open hand he points to Exel. "You'll have to forgive our friend here. Please continue."

"Sorry," Chan interrupts. "What is Lycan rat?"

"It's a man that has been bitten by a rat infected with the Lycanthropy disease. His body changes and takes on the appearance of a rat-man. He also takes on a lot of rat traits—collecting things and living in garbage and its own dung. They basically become a monstrosity, not human or rat. But the Lycan disease affects all animals, in most cases killing the one bitten in a slow and painful death. I have never encountered such a person, just read about them in journals from a priest long ago," Father Yor explains.

"Oh, I have! I have seen them in Darconia. They disappeared off in the sewers below the city," Preador says.

"Well, most people have heard of werewolves. That's also from this disease," Father Yor continues.

"Yes. I grew up hearing stories, but it was about ladies with ...

a fox head," Chan recounts.

"Uh, okay." Father Yor nods. "So ... Exel, go on."

"Well, with Riechter hurt, that bought me some time to help Sargon after Meg told me the plight of his families. I knew Riechter would not be at his best, so we left shortly after everyone cleared out. Riechter was in hot pursuit even hurt like he was. Luckily, I ran into some friends of mine who were headed to Zeth's place as well. They were all too eager to help. Zeth and his kin have always treated me and my brethren like family." Exel clears his throat as sees the tears gently rolling down Meg's cheeks. "Needless to say, Riechter never did find Sargon's real trail."

"How's your hand?" Val asks as he dishes out some scrambled eggs from a bowl then hands it to Exel. Acolytes walking in from the kitchen hand him more bowls of food as well.

"I can help you with that." Yor points to Exel's wrapped hand.

"Don't let him use the club—" Silverfish warns, but Father Yor interrupts him with a slap upside the head. "Ow!"

"I'm gonna use it on you in a minute," Yor says through gritted teeth.

"Thanks. I'll live, but she can bite like those bears Sargon tangled with." Exel answers as he dishes out food on his plate.

The table erupts with laughter.

"Did someone mention bears?"

"Bellgrad!" Sargon, Meg, and Father Yor say at the same time as Bellgrad enters the room from the infirmary stairs.

Meg's eyes light up. She springs up from her chair and rushes to Bellgrad, gently hugging him and then helping him to the table. Father Yor moves to stand but is happy to let Meg take over the job. He returns to his seat and continues eating.

"I'm good, my lady, thanks to Father Yor. But I am always grateful to get help from you." Bellgrad smiles as they make their way to the table.

"You can have my chair. I'm done," Silverfish says as he jumps off his chair and pulls it out for Bellgrad.

"You can sit here, dear," Barbye says to Meg as she stands and steps back to allow the two to sit.

Meg thanks them and introduces herself and the others to Silverfish and Barbye. Silverfish in turn introduces Chan after getting elbowed by Barbye.

"We are going to get packed up," Silverfish explains.

"Hey, we aren't taking children with us," Val laughs.

"Very funny, me lard—I mean, milord," Silverfish laughs and makes a sarcastic salute and bow.

"What? Did I miss something?" Sargon asks, clearly confused, taking a bite from his plate.

"We are going with you," Father Yor explains.

"Huh? The barbarian too?" Sargon asks, almost choking.

"Well, I want to keep an eye on Bellgrad for a few days. And Silverfish, Barbye, and Chan want to look into work as well. Bjorn here has to pay off some debt for the damage he did in the tavern as well as the money I put up to get him out. That's not a problem, Val, is it?" Yor asks.

"Oh, no problem at all. There's lots of work to do at the castle," Val explains. "Pigs to slop and stables to clean."

"Great," Bjorn says under his breath and rolls his eyes.

"Oh, in case you were wondering, Sargon, Bjorn did apologize for striking me." Barbye winks at Sargon as she walks away. "Says he can't remember anything from that night."

"Well, good. But that still does not excuse him in my book," Sargon answers. He then leans over to Valagar, "Hey, I take it you know the little guy?" Sargon asks as Silverfish, Chan, and Barbye depart.

"Huh? Oh, Silver. Yes, a long time. What about him?" Val asks as he sips on some tea between bites of food.

"What does he do for a living?" Sargon asks with a raised eyebrow.

Val bursts out laughing, "You tell me and we'll both know."

"Oh boy, what a group," Sargon says, shaking his head.

"Hey, he's a good egg. He's a bit of a scrounger, but he knows a lot of people and is well connected, it's just ... he's got sticky fingers," Val whispers.

"Great." Sargon smirks.

"Don't sell him short. He's as perceptive as a bloodhound and good to have around. I've taken him with me on a few excursions, and he saved my ass a time or two by sniffing out booby traps some of my enemies had set for me," Val adds.

"Really? Well, what about his oriental friend?" Sargon asks, still eating.

"Oh, the Euguadian. I don't know, except he's a monk of Fairwind," Val answers and then turns to Gunter. "What do you know about the monk?"

"He just showed up to town a few months back, got into a bit of trouble with Silverfish. I just think it's a case of being in the wrong place at the wrong time. Of course there's a lot of that going on whenever Silverfish is involved," Gunter answers.

A temple guard walks over to the table and then to Gunter, leans over, and whispers something in his ear. Gunter nods, and the soldier departs.

Gunter finishes eating and wipes his mouth with a cloth. "Well, duty calls. I gotta go."

"Anything we can help with?" Val asks.

"No, not right now. Some dead bodies were found along the road a few miles apart, about ten to fifteen miles outside of town. The guard tells me they have been dead a couple of days or so," Gunter explains.

Exel looks at Val and smiles.

"You didn't run into any problems coming into town the other night, did you? I mean, after the bear attack," Gunter asks Sargon.

"No, I didn't run into any trouble at all. But I was pushing my horse real hard to get Bellgrad here," Sargon says as he sips on some hot tea.

"I didn't think so. They had arrows in them. What about you, Exel?" Gunter asks.

"We went cross country to Castle Du'tesh. We weren't even close to that road," Exel answers as Meg breaks her attention on Bellgrad and nods in recognition as Gunther looks at the two.

"Well, okay. I gotta check it out nevertheless. Good to see you again, Val. Your Grace," Gunter adds as he stands up, nodding at the high priest and then hurriedly departs.

"I wonder what that's all about," Sargon says, turning to watch Gunter leave.

"Could be random Perc attacks," Exel says.

"Please, they're too stupid to know how to use a bow," Sargon says, looking at the scout with a raised eyebrow.

Chapter XIII
Leaving Missionwise

"**W**here are my pants?" Silverfish asks as he stuffs clothes in a bag.

"You are wearing them, dear," Barbye says, smiling.

"Very funny ... my leather ones," Silver says.

"Your pink ones are in the closet," Barbye answers with a slight giggle.

"They are not pink. They are red. Well, they were red till the dye ran. Boy, you sure are feisty today. You just wait, I'm gonna get you," Silver says as he pulls the trousers from the closet.

"You already did," Barbye answers with a smile as she finishes putting her belongings in a sack.

"You little ..." Silver says, interrupting his packing to walk toward his girl.

Tap tap tap comes the sound of wood knocking against the door.

"Come," Silver barks as he goes back to his bag and stuffs his trousers in.

Chan slowly opens the door and softly says, "They are waiting for us out front."

"Okay, we are on the way. Go on ahead," Silverfish tells Chan, waving him on. Then he goes to pour water on the fireplace to snuff out the fire.

Chan turns and leaves with staff in hand, wearing a backpack. An occasional *clunk* can be heard as Chan walks down the hall using his staff as a walking stick.

Silverfish picks up his bag and throws it over his shoulder.

"Maybe, I'll get Mr. Nightgown to re-dye them for me. He's always sewing or meddling in some kind of tailoring."

"It's a robe, not a nightgown, dunderhead," Barbye says as Silver extends his arm out to allow her to go out the door first.

"I'll dunderhead you ..." Silverfish says. *Pop!* He slaps Barbye hard on the butt as she passes by him out the door.

"Ow! How come I feel like you didn't let me walk ahead because you are being a gentleman?" Barbye smirks as she starts walking down the hallway of the inn. She glances over her shoulder to see Silver close the door then walk behind her. Silverfish smiles as he watches his girl walk. Being only waist high to her, he enjoys the view. "You know me pretty good. Well, it's not every day I see my girl wear pants."

"Man! What's keeping those two? Sorry, Lord Valagar," Father Yor says as he and all the others wait on their horses in front of the Choking Gnome Inn.

"You should know by now that elves have no concept of time," Val states, his long brownish-blond hair blowing into his face. He looks up at the tip of the lance he's holding and watches the small flag start to flutter in the wind. "It's going to snow soon."

"Do you want me to go get Silverfish, milord?" Ari asks.

"No, antagonizing him will not speed him up." Val smirks.

"Here comes Chan," Sargon says as he points to the door. Tantor impatiently paws the ground.

"They are coming," Chan says as he strides toward Val and Father Yor.

"Where's your horse?" Val asks Chan. "If you don't have one, I can get another from the stable."

"I will run," Chan answers

The group bursts into laughter.

"Come on, man, it's a six-hour ride. Besides, all you have on is that robe and sandals. There are some areas where that snow can be waist deep," Val says.

"I run. I will stay warm and keep up." Chan is insistent.

"Okay, but if you fall back it's on you," Val demands as his gaze goes from Chan back to the group. "Boy, it's like waiting for my grandmother ... well, it's about time." Val spots Barbye and Silverfish walking out the front door. "I thought I was going to have to shave again."

"Oh, keep your dress on," Silverfish says as he and Barbye walk toward a horse tied out front to a hitching post.

"With you that would probably be a safe thing to do." Val smirks.

"I think I grew an inch taller," Elof adds.

"At least I have an excuse for being short, baby boy," Silver fires back at Elof.

"I warned you." Val smiles as he looks at Elof and shakes his head.

"I'm only thirteen," Elof says

"*I'm only thirteen,*" Silverfish mocks in baby talk and makes a funny face.

"You're lucky you have Barbye with you. If you were by yourself, little man, we would be long gone," Sargon sternly comments.

"I know," Silverfish laughs devilishly.

Silverfish and Barbye tie their bags to her horse's saddle then she climbs into the saddle as Silverfish unties the reins from the inn's hitching post and hands them to her. He then jumps up, lands his left foot in the left stirrup, grabs Barbye's left hand, and swings on behind his girlfriend, wrapping his arms around her middle.

"Very good, Lumpy. Wow, you can move when you want to," Father Yor comments.

"Lumpy—I haven't heard that one," Val chuckles along with the rest of the group.

"I told you not to call me that," Silver protests.

They all ride out of the city together. Once they pass through the city's main gate, the group spurs their horses into a brisk gallop. And just as Valagar predicted, a light snowfall begins. They ride on for about two hours and then slow their horses to a walk. To everyone's amazement, Chan has not fallen too far behind. He quickly catches up as the horses walk.

"How are you doing there, Chan?" Father Yor asks.

"I am okay," Chan answers, keeping up a brisk walk and staying in pace with the horses.

"Wow, I honestly did not think he would be able to keep up. But we have a long way to go yet," Val says over his shoulder to Yor.

"What is big deal?" Bjorn interjects. "My people run all day and all night to battle."

"Not keeping in pace with horses, I bet. Anyway, does it look like he's from '*your* people?'" Sargon asks.

"Oh, you talking to me now, pretty boy?" Bjorn looks past Yor to Sargon, who is riding behind Ari and Elof, who are behind Valagar, who is riding lead.

"Of course I'm talking to you. I just said we are going to have some words sometime, and we will. Just not today ..." Sargon answers as he twists around to look at Bjorn, "unless you call me 'pretty boy' again." Sargon turns back around.

"No, he is not like our people. He much smaller—*hva er ordet?* (what is word?), *ynkelig*—puny," Bjorn adds.

"Why do you keep calling Sargon 'pretty boy'?" Father Yor asks.

"Yeah, I'd like to know that too. Do you think he's cute?" Barbye asks. She and Meg giggle, riding side by side behind

Bjorn's horse. Silverfish is napping and misses the whole exchange.

"Yeah, I think he's sweet on you, Sargon," Bellgrad says with a slight laugh from his position riding behind the two women.

Bjorn is stunned and momentarily speechless. "No—I think he looks like sissy boy."

"Yeah, all that armor and weapons he's wearing, not to mention the armor barding on his horse, does kinda make him look like a princess," Bellgrad comments sarcastically.

What is it, Exel?" Sargon asks as he twists around in the saddle and sees the scout, who is riding tail, looking past everyone.

"There is something going on in the woods ahead," Exel answers as the riders turn their attention toward the woods a quarter mile ahead.

"Let's go. HAH." Val spurs his horse onward into a full run, and everyone follows his lead.

The group quickly reaches the lower edge of the small grove of trees to see Chan fighting a group of four perequine, which suddenly turns into a group of ten as more emerge from either hiding places or places they were bedded down. Perqs are known to be nocturnal creatures, so it's possible the others were napping and waiting for nightfall. The perq group quickly turns to nine as one of the creatures gets clubbed in the head by Chan's staff and falls down.

Crack. The sound echoes through the trees as the attacker gets knocked on the crown of his boar head. The staff rolls over the left side of its face, knocking out the left tusk. He staggers and falls backward three feet from where he was standing.

Snap. Snap. Crash. AHHH! *Thud.* REEEEEHHHH!

A horrid sound like a combination of a pig and a man echoes in the trees.

"*Don't* ride in there!" Exel barks as he lets loose an arrow, which finds its mark in the shoulder of one of the perqs. "There are pit traps in the woods like the one *that* perq just fell in," Exel explains, notching another arrow.

"We can't just stand here and watch him get killed," Val hollers and jumps off his horse. Sargon, Bellgrad, and Bjorn follow suit, drawing their swords as they run into the woods. "Ari, Elof, guard the women."

"Yes, milord," Ari and Elof say together as they dismount, grab shields, and draw their swords.

"Watch Meg ... okay ... watch Meg," Sargon commands Tantor as he catches up with the others, worrying that his big horse will follow him. He doesn't want the horse falling into any pit trap. Sargon smirks at the thought of Tantor acting more like a big dog than a horse as he peers over his shoulder and sees his great warhorse watching him leave. Then Tantor peers back and forth between Sargon and Meg while pawing the ground in frustration. Sargon is curious to know what will come of this experiment. He has never barked out this command to his horse before; he has never had to. Nor has he ever noticed until recently how protective Tantor is of him. He has, however, trained the horse very well in other areas of riding and warfare with the aid of his grandfather, father, and Reaxl.

"Yor, stay put," Val hollers over his shoulder as they make their way to do battle.

"Sure. No problem." Yor is none too eager to fight, as he's not wearing any kind of armor and has no protection; he knows he would get killed right off by these axe-carrying beasts. He pulls his scepter from his belt just in case he has to defend himself and the girls. "Hey, is Chan dancing?" Father Yor asks as he and the girls watch the monk fighting gracefully.

"Wow, he sure can move fast," Silverfish comments, being

awakened from the shriek of the fallen perq. He watches the monk momentarily study his opponents, oblivious to the arrow that just whizzed by his head. It only missed him by six inches, striking the perq to Chan's left in the shoulder. Chan shuffles his feet back and forth, as if he is running in place, then dodges the swinging axes from all three perqs that surround him.

"That's my buddy right there. Taught him everything he knows." Silverfish smiles while Barbye rolls her eyes. Meg and Father Yor shake their heads.

The six perqs seeing the approaching fighters and charge after them. One throws a spear at Val. It misses the knight, sailing over his head. They quickly reach the fighters and attack with axes in hand. The first one approaches Bjorn who is second to Val's left as the fighters are in a spearhead formation.

The perq swings and misses the barbarian by about six inches.

"My *amma* (grandmother) can hit better than that!" Bjorn boasts, but he is quickly smacked in the mouth by a backhand. "Oh, that's better." He spits out blood then swings his two-handed sword, hitting the creature in the left shoulder and cutting through the perq's breastplate, nearly cleaving the beast in half as the sword stops about center mass of the animal's torso. The perq falls to its knees. Bjorn puts his left foot on the creature's chest and pulls his sword out as the perq falls to the ground.

The next fighter under attack is Bellgrad, on Val's left. He is ready for anything, armed with a dagger in his left hand and long sword in his right. The perequine swings and hits the soldier across the middle of his chest, nearly knocking him back from the strength of the blow. Luckily for Bellgrad, Sargon had the armor repaired while the soldier was on the mend. The hit does not penetrate through the armor, but it sticks and the perq has to pull it out. This gives Bellgrad enough time to jab his dagger through the animal's lower jaw and into its head. The blade is stopped there by the perq's heavy bones. The jab is fatal, nonetheless, and Bellgrad twists the blade, pulling it out and dropping the perq where it stands. He pulls out the axe as the perq falls, bleeding out in the snow.

Val is the next one approached, but the perq turns and runs, seeing his buddies get taken out so quickly. Val tosses up his long sword, catches it like a spear, and hurls it at the retreating beast. It pierces the animal through its back, dropping it in its tracks.

Sargon tries making his way toward Chan, but he gets attacked on the way. He raises his shield with his left hand and blocks the hit. After learning his lesson with the bears, he's been wearing the shield on his arm the whole time. He swings his sword with all his might, cleaving off the animal's left arm at the shoulder. Then he pushes forward toward the monk, who is still surrounded.

Chan is still shucking and jiving, but, amazingly, he still has not been hit. He has managed to land a few blows on all three creatures that still surround him. Unfortunately, not with the same results he had earlier, but hits nonetheless.

Exel drops the perq to Chan's left, managing to shoot an arrow into the animal's right eye. But the slot is filled by another perq that seems to appear out of nowhere, apparently seeing Chan as an easier target than the knights.

Val pulls a mace from his belt and charges another perq standing still about 10 feet away from the knight, apparently in shock over the devastation of his comrades in arms. It's like shooting fish in a barrel for Val. He commences to beat the stew out of this perq, knocking loose the axe in the creature's hands at the same time as the animal falls lifeless in the snow. Val stows the mace back in his belt and grabs the perq's axe.

The fighters, having killed all the perqs around them, make their way to Chan. The two perequine on either side of the monk start running off, seeing the approaching knights. Chan trips the perq that is directly behind him by sweeping his staff under the creature's feet. The three fighters quickly come to Chan's aid. Bellgrad drops his long sword and grabs his dagger by the blade from his left hand. He lets it fly toward one of the fleeing perqs, hitting it in the middle of the back and killing the creature. The beast collapses and slides forward ten feet.

Sargon swings his sword at the first fallen perq as it jumps to its feet and goes after Chan. But the monk has pole-vaulted ever so gracefully about ten feet away from his foe, landing on his feet and facing his opponent. Sargon's sword glances off the right shoulder of the beast's breastplate. The creature quickly sees he is surrounded and makes a run for it. He darts toward Bellgrad's back.

Swoosh. Kerchuck. Valagar swings his axe, decapitating the creature as it runs by. Its head falls to the ground, followed by its body, which slides five feet away.

"I guess the other one got away," Sargon says as he catches his breath.

"It won't go far. I pumped a couple of arrows in its back as it ran," Exel says, riding out of the tree line just to Sargon and Bellgrad's right.

"Well, here's one that didn't get away," Val says, breathing hard and pointing to the beast with no head.

"This one didn't either," Bellgrad adds as he grabs his sword and walks over to the perq with the dagger in its back. He steps on the body with one foot and pulls out his dagger, then he overturns and searches the creature.

"Is it safe?" Barbye hollers from the edge of the trees, where the horses were left.

"Come through here where Exel rode in and bring the horses around," Sargon barks out. "Oh, sorry, Lord Valagar," Sargon says as he looks at Val kneeling down to inspect the dead perq at his feet.

"That's quite all right. A good leader needs to take charge. I guess it's okay for a squire to speak in my stead." Val smiles up at Sargon.

"Your ... squire?" Sargon asks, amazed.

"Unfortunately, no—Calador's. That's why I came for you." Val explains. "I wanted to see if you were up to the challenge. And it appears you are." Val winks at Sargon.

"But I only dropped one of those creatures."

"Well, you would have dropped the second one, had your hit connected. Besides, it's not all about what you take," Val continues.

"Sir?" Sargon questions.

"Son, you didn't hesitate a bit when danger showed its ugly head, and you kept trying to get to Chan's aid. That says a lot for a knight," Val reassures him.

"But, milord, you already have a squire—Haldor," Ari says as he walks up.

"I know, jughead. Calador's squire. Geez, if you are going to eavesdrop on someone you should learn to listen better. Where is Elof?" Val barks.

"He is coming around with the horses." Ari looks relieved.

"Is Silver with you?" Father Yor hollers out.

"No," Sargon answers.

"No, he's not," Val answers as well.

"Haldor is Ari's older brother." Val explains to Sargon. "He worries like a mother hen. I would love to have you as my squire. But, honestly, it will take a lot of pressure off me, having you as Calador's squire."

"I'm here …" Silverfish's muffled voice answers.

"He's in the pit over there," Exel says, pointing to the open pit.

"What the heck are you doing down there?" Sargon asks. He and Val walk to either edge of the pit, seeing the perq at the bottom of the ten-foot deep pit trap. Silverfish is pilfering over the dead perq's body, where it lies impaled on three-foot punji sticks at the bottom of the trap.

"Do you see anything out of the ordinary there, Sargon?" Val asks.

"Well, other than junior there, no," Sargon answers. "Wait—the armor they are wearing …"

"Yes?" Val smiles.

"It fits them. Perqs don't make armor … they don't know how. They just simply steal it off their victims," Sargon continues.

"True."

"Someone has made it for them."

"Exactly." Val smiles as he continues to look in the pit. "You coming, stinky?"

"That's not me that stinks. It's him. Boy the stench is almost unbearable. My eyes are watering. Hey, help me out of here," Silverfish asks.

"Oh no, little man. You got down there on your own—you can get out the same way," Sargon answers, smiling at Val, who just smirks.

"Man, I think I'm gonna puke," Silverfish adds.

"Quit your crying, baby. Here," Chan says as he walks to the edge of the pit, kneels down, and lowers his staff for the elf to grab.

"I see Father Yor is rubbing off on Chan now," Silverfish comments.

"Look out over there, it's another pit trap," Exel tells the group as he points in the direction of a snow-covered patch about ten feet from the fighters.

"I guess that should teach you about investigating places you can't get out of," Sargon says as Silver picks himself off the ground, brushing the dirt and snow from his clothes.

"I doubt it," Val and Barbye say at the same time. Barbye, Father Yor, Meg, and Elof ride up with the other horses in tow, just outside of the tree line behind Exel.

"Hey, where's Bjorn? I thought he was here with all of you. I saw him fighting a perq earlier, but it's hard to see through the dense brush," Father Yor asks Sargon and Val, who goes and retrieves his sword and Bellgrad. They all start walking toward the girls and Father Yor while shrugging their shoulders as they look around for any sign of Bjorn.

"I'm here!" Bjorn crashes through the snowy brush with his bloody two-handed sword in his left hand as he chunks the last dead perq off his shoulder and into the other pit trap.

"Wow. Hey, wait ..." Silverfish marvels at Bjorn carrying the heavy perequine through the woods. Most perqs stand as tall as a man but weigh twice as much. Silver tries to stop the barbarian warrior, but he is too late; the animal is already flying into the pit.

"You wanna go down there and pick him clean too?" Sargon asks, smiling.

"No," Silverfish answers with a bad expression on his face.

"The curiosity just kills you, doesn't it?" Val laughs and rubs Silver's head as if he were an old dog.

"I already searched him. He had two Sivs and three Pens on him. Here, *Hellig Mann* (holy man)," Bjorn says, handing the coins to Father Yor.

"Thanks. So what did you get off that one in the pit, Silver?" Yor asks.

"Nothing ... oh okay, I got four Pens." Silverfish winces.

"Is that all?" Yor asks with a raised eyebrow.

"Hey, it's a group fund. I'm gonna share," Silverfish says with an innocent look on his face.

"What, with you as the treasurer? I don't think so. Come on, cough it up," Yor insists, getting off his horse.

"Let him keep it. I hate seeing a grown man cry ... well, semi-grown," Sargon says as he makes his way to Tantor, who has followed the other horses.

"Hey!" Silverfish gives Sargon a dirty look.

"Come on, stinky, you owe me remember?" Father Yor says as Bellgrad walks over and hands off his bootie of three Pens and 1 Siv.

"Okay, okay. Here, I hope you choke on it," Silverfish says as he hands the priest his pillage sum of four Sivs and six Pens. "I liked it better when you called me lumpy."

"If it makes you feel any better, you can go search the other perqs we dropped," Sargon tells Silverfish.

"Oh goody, goody." Silverfish's eyes light up as he rubs his hands together. He eagerly runs over to all the other fallen perqs with a devilish laugh.

Father Yor glares at Sargon. "Do you think that's smart? Wow, I've never seen him move that fast before," Yor adds as he peers back to Silver, who is bouncing all around.

"Oh, let him have his fun. Less for us to do," Val interjects. "Besides, he can only hide so much coin."

"Oh, knowing him he's likely to swallow some of those coins," Yor says as he walks over to the closest fallen perq Bellgrad had killed and starts muttering some words and motioning his holy symbol in the air over the body while sprinkling water from a small vial.

"Eww," Sargon says, making a disgusted face.

"What are you doing?" Bellgrad asks. He mounts his horse while Father Yor walks over to the two pits and repeats the action.

"It's called the 'Rites of Rest.' You don't want to fight them again as something more sinister than they were," Father Yor explains as he continues the ritual, making his way to all the other fallen creatures.

"Huh?" Silverfish asks with a puzzled look on his face as he pilfers the last perq.

"He means they could come back from the dead," Val says and mounts his horse. "All except the one I cut the head off of."

"Yes, that's a guarantee they won't come back. It's about releasing the animal's spirit and protecting the body from evil spirits entering after their death," Father Yor answers as he finalizes the ritual then makes his way back to his horse. "The only other sure way is to burn the bodies, but that would not be prudent in these woods."

Silverfish makes his way back to the group with a small sack full of coins tied on his belt and an armful of axes that he drops at his feet. "Sounds like a load of sh—"

"I have seen it firsthand," Bjorn interrupts him. "A good friend of mine had fallen in battle. We had no holy man with us. Three day later he came back from dead. I had to kill him—he was no longer my *bror*, he was ... *skrímsli*," Bjorn recalls as he mounts his horse.

"Monster ... yes, but zombie is the word you are looking for," Father Yor says as he saddles up after putting the vial and his holy symbol in a saddlebag.

"Yes," Bjorn acknowledges. He leaves out the part that this action was the reason he fled from his clan and, furthermore, the reason he is not still with his people. They are the clan that took him in after he ran away from a merchant family that had found him after the death of his parents.

Bjorn recalls the stories that his father told him about his family from before Bjorn's birth; that they were once part of the Ziona clan. His father, Deblask, was once a great blacksmith for the clan, following the same life path as his father before him. Deblask was banished from the clan after being framed for a murder of the clan's chieftain by a so-called "friend" named Rector. Deblask had caught the man trying to have his way with Bjorn's mother, Niona, after she refused his advances to claim the beautiful woman for himself. Deblask had fought the much smaller barbarian with the intent of killing him and took out one of the man's eyes in the melee.

Rector ran off, but not before grabbing Deblask's dagger. Rector eluded Deblask's pursuit and hid in a hut, which turned out to be the chieftain's. Rector killed the man in his sleep to silence him while hiding from his pursuer. Deblask entered the hut and saw his dagger sticking in the chieftain's chest right before being knocked unconscious.

The new chief wanted Deblask's head but was talked out of executing him by both Niona's claims as well as Deblask's parents, who were well revered by the tribe. So, instead, they were banished. They left the Shendo Mountains for the city of Vry, where Deblask set himself up as an apprentice for one of the town's blacksmiths. They stayed there for many years, during which time Bjorn and his younger sister and brother were born.

But Deblask was not happy after many years of discrimination and the high taxes of the city. So, Bjorn's family fled Vry for the small hamlet of Strv only to be killed along the way, some said by Vyrian knights for unclaimed taxes.

Bjorn, who was eight years old at the time, was left for dead. That was when he was found by a passing merchant family who nursed him back to health and took him to their home in the city of Palton. But being taught by his father to trust no one, he fled after being frustrated by these people who tried to teach him to read and write. He knew he could make it on his own with his father's teachings. During his drifting from place to place, he managed to come upon a barbarian tribe that took him in. It was there he continued for the next few years the training that his father had begun.

In a battle against a warring tribe deep in the Shendo Mountains, is where he had the experience he would not forget. No one believed that his friend had been killed days before and had come back from the dead; some thought he was captured by the enemy and escaped. Many of his people had only seen Bjorn strike the young man down; this was only made worse by the fact that the frightened Bjorn burned the body of his friend to prevent the creature from coming back again, so no one could witness the grisly look of the zombied form of his kinsman.

Bjorn snaps back to the present as a cold gust of wind punches him in the face and his horse begins to grow restless from standing with the heavy warrior on its back.

"Wow. What about my family?" Sargon asks.

"Like I told you before, Heyrold will give them a proper burial. Besides, it doesn't always happen," Val answers.

"It happens more than you know," Father Yor confesses as Silver hands the priest the bag of coins. "We don't have room for those axes."

"It's a shame to leave them," Silver says with a sad look on his face.

"Here, tie them to my packhorse," Elof says as he throws a short piece of rope to Silverfish.

"Why bother? They are worthless. Hurry up, stinky—I mean, Silver—it's getting late," Sargon tells Silverfish, who is the only one not mounted, other than Chan, who is siting on a log with his staff leaning against a tree.

He is sewing a tear in his robe; it appears he may not have taken any hits, but his robe apparently did.

"See what I was telling you?" Silverfish says to Barbye as he jerks a thumb over his shoulder. He's finished tying the axes and jumps on the horse behind his girlfriend.

"I'll take point this time. Should've done that from the start," Exel tells the group as he starts out.

"No harm done. How did you know there were pit traps in the woods anyway?" Val asks.

"Just a gut feeling. I've seen them making those traps before. They stop by from time to time to check them. The traps are very crude and not well concealed, but anyone riding through or not on the lookout will fall in. There must be a lair close by, but honestly, it's not to kill humans—that's just the icing on the cake for them. They want horses. They love horsemeat. They don't eat human unless they have nothing else to eat," Exel explains and then starts riding out.

"Should have seen those perqs earlier, but I admit I was distracted by everyone talking until I saw Chan hurry his pace once he approached that grove," Exel shakes his head, mentally beating himself up.

"Not a well traveled path they put them in, in the middle of a grove," Sargon says.

"Well, like you pointed out earlier, they are not very smart," Exel says over his shoulder.

"Speaking of which, I admire your courage, Chan, but unless you want Father Yor to be saying those words over you, I suggest you let us do the heavy lifting from now on," Sargon says as he knocks on his breastplate.

"He who hesitates does not get the worm," Chan recites as he packs away his tailoring in his backpack and grabs his staff.

"What?" Val and Sargon look at each other and then among the group. Everyone just shrugs their shoulders at the comment as they all fall in line.

"I'll take tail this time," Sargon states as he waits for the others to pass. Tantor impatiently stomps the ground. "It's okay, old man," Sargon calms him. "Sometimes you have to follow."

Chapter XIV
Lord Heyrold's Deception

hank you, milord, for letting us know of the death of my cousin Jessica—second cousin, actually." A middle-aged woman says as she stands in the courtyard of Guel Castle, talking to Heyrold as many families tend to the other victims. "I am pleased to hear that you are having her put in the crypt at Zartharel Castle. I think that's what her family would want."

"That's what I thought as well. I don't think it would be appropriate, considering the circumstances, even though she did marry Sargon." Heyrold says with a somber look on his face. "What is your name again, milady?"

"It's Laurel, milord," Laurel says as she shakes her head in disbelief.

"Ah, yes," Heyrold remembers with a slight smile as he holds her hand in a consoling fashion.

"It just does not make any sense! Sargon loved her dearly. I got a couple of letters from her telling me how much in love they were." Laurel recounts.

"We are still trying to ascertain the events of that night. We think that perhaps Sargon was poisoning Jessica's family, but his plan went horribly wrong and he poisoned everyone at the wedding, including his new bride. But we don't have all the facts yet. Or perhaps that was his plan all along," Heyrold says as he shrugs his shoulders. "I am having my men comb through everything here in this castle to try and find it all out."

"What became of Sargon's parents?" Laurel asks.

"They were laid to rest in the castle crypt below two nights ago. Some priests of Zura from Vry did the ceremony," Heyrold says.

"Did you know them?" Laurel asks.

"Yes, they were dear friends of mine. 'Tis a horrible tragedy," Heyrold says with a sad look on his face. "I have had my masons working day and night to finish their sarcophaguses. They were already set, just not completed. I am sparing no expense."

"That is very good of you to look after them like that ... so, what will become of the estates?" Laurel asks.

"That will be up to the council of nobles to decide," Heyrold answers.

"Where is Sargon now?" Laurel asks.

"I don't know, but I have my best scouts searching the countryside to find him and bring him to justice," Heyrold answers. "If you will excuse me, milady, I have other families I have to attend to."

"Sure. Will you do me a favor and let me know when you catch this vermin? I would like to be there to see him hang," Laurel says with fire in her eyes.

"Yes, I will send for you," Heyrold adds as he bows and leaves the woman standing alone in the middle of the courtyard. She walks toward the front gate to the people she traveled with, gets into a carriage, and leaves.

Heyrold makes his way to some of the other families. He peers up at the castle wall and nods at a scout standing there. The figure gives a nod back while Heyrold converses with the families of the other soldiers of the castle.

"There has to be something sinister here. My Jerel was a good man, he knew Sargon personally ... I still can't believe it," an older woman says, apparently the young man's mother.

"We will find out all the answers. We will have to trust in the gods to guide us," Heyrold continues as the woman nods in recognition.

"There are still so many unclaimed men here," the woman continues.

"My men will stay here until all are claimed by their families," Heyrold states.

"What if no one claims them?" an older man asks.

"We will bury the remaining victims outside in the local graveyard," Heyrold reassures the man.

General Dytruik walks over from about ten feet away in the courtyard and motions to Heyrold.

"If you will excuse me ..." Heyrold nods to the families he was talking to, then walks to the general.

"We have a problem, my lord," Dytruik whispers to Heyrold.

"What is it?" Heyrold quietly asks.

"Some of General Devalar's men are here inspecting the castle," General Dytruik whispers. General Devalar is the Duke of Darconia's general, a well-known hero of Fegnir, loved by the people and well respected by all the nobles of the land. Devalar served with Sargon's grandfather Guel when the general was very young.

"Great," Heyrold says sarcastically, letting out a troubled sigh.

"Here comes one now," Dytruik says as he steps a few paces back from Heyrold.

The captain walks up with two men at arms and respectfully salutes before introducing himself. "Lord Heyrold, I'm Captain Vlaskar."

"Captain," Heyrold nods.

"What happened here, milord?" The captain asks as a scribe follows in behind.

"This is General Dytruik," Heyrold introduces with an open hand. "Perhaps he can tell you better."

The captain nods in recognition, eyeing Dytruik.

"Well, like I said to the duke in my letter, we came to the wedding in Heyrold's stead. We arrived late due to bad weather and found the whole castle dead. An apparent poisoning, except for a handful of men we found slain in the middle of the courtyard—half-dressed and unarmed," the general explains.

"Hmm, so what happened to these murdered men?"

"Their families that live outside the castle claimed their bodies yesterday. They were hacked up pretty badly," Dytruik states.

"Hacked up by what? Sword? Axe?" the captain inquires.

"Sword, I think. Why is that important?" Dytruik asks with a raised eyebrow.

"I heard tell that you had a scout with a crushed head from a tree branch," the captain continues.

"Okay?" the general says, even more confused.

"Well, doesn't it seem a little odd that if this boy had hacked up some men before he left, he would have used the sword on the scout instead of a tree branch?

"I suppose. Where are you going with this, Captain?" says the general, getting a little agitated.

"Well, I just find it hard to believe that if Sargon had planned all this out that his sword would still be in his room," the captain says as one of his men produce a sword from under his cloak. Heyrold cuts his eyes to the general.

"Okay. Well, how do you know that is Sargon's sword just because it was in his room?" Dytruik asks.

"It has his name inscribed on it," the captain says as he pulls the sword from its sheath, then points to the inscriptions on the blade. "I suppose that's an easy item to overlook, but I guess no one here can read Ber-Ber either? You know, the old Fegnirian language still used by the barbarians of the Shendo Mountains."

"You forget your place, Captain," Dytruik reminds.

Captain Vlaskar nods. "My apologies, General. Just doing my job and stating the obvious."

"Yes. Well, you are right, though. Not too many people can read that script besides the well-educated or those from the Shendos," Heyrold says as he steps up and reads the inscription.

Vlaskar sheaths the sword and hands it back to his man. "Or those who are history buffs such as myself." Captain Vlaskar smirks.

"Perhaps he did not have time to grab it. Anyway, I never said that Sargon did it ... but, just like you said, I'm just stating the obvious." Dytruik smiles.

"Well, that's the word on the street, and I kind of overheard some of the locals discussing with each other how none believe him to be the killer. How do you know that maybe the killer did this deed then kidnapped the young nobleman? Or maybe this young man is dead, and the killer took his body as proof of his deed to show his employer?" Captain Vlaskar states.

"Because one of our scouts found material—silk, to be exact—at the place where our murdered scout was found. That's way too expensive a garment for an assassin, especially in this cold," Dytruik says.

"Who is this scout, and where can I find him?" Vlaskar asks.

"His name is Riechter, and he is hot on the trail of this killer. We will know soon enough if it is the Guel boy," Heyrold interjects.

"Riechter. I have heard of him," Vlaskar states.

"Most people have. He's one of the best trackers in the kingdom," says Dytruik.

"What do you know of the blacksmith called Zeth?" Vlaskar asks.

"He has done some work—"

"He does work for the Guel family," Heyrold interrupts, "and, like the general was about to say, some work for us as well. Why do you ask?"

"We passed by his place on the way here. It was burned to the ground. And it would appear his whole family is dead," Vlaskar answers. "Someone that popular getting wasted doesn't go unnoticed."

"True. Perhaps the same murderer did this deed as well, leaving a trail of death in his path. I haven't heard any news of it," the general adds.

"You sure have a loyal following of men, General," Vlaskar says.

"Thanks. Why do you say that?"

"Every soldier I ask any questions to, say that I need to talk to you or Lord Heyrold," Vlaskar says with a raised eyebrow.

"Well, there has been a mass murder. There could be spies for the killer asking questions," the general answers.

"True. Well, I am almost finished. What—"

"No, Captain, you are finished," Heyrold commands. "You go tell General Devalar that I am investigating this matter and that we appreciate his concern. But we have this well in hand and will let him know once our investigation is complete."

"Yes, my lord, I will let him know," Captain Vlaskar nods and motions his men to follow. They all walk to the front gate, where the group's horses and wagons are tied up outside. They all mount up and give a wave as they leave.

"You can't let that Lycan rat push you around, General. You work for me, not that two-faced general nor that captain," Heyrold reminds.

"Yes, sir," Dytruik answers. "I just did not want to offend the duke's men."

"Oh, the hell with them. The duke is nothing but a pushover

… oh, the arrogance of that captain just pisses me off. He acts as though he works for a king. The duke did not send that man, the general did. I will have some words with Devalar before it's through. I'm going back to Vry," Heyrold says.

"What if the captain talks to Riechter?" Dytruik asks.

"Oh, I'm sure Riechter will give that man an earful, if he could find him," Heyrold says.

"I bet." Dytruik laughs.

"Wait until the morrow for all the dead to be claimed then bury the rest. I have twenty-five soldiers that will be here to guard the castle, so you can go to Zartharel Castle to place Jessica in the castle crypt and secure that castle as well. Then off to Martox Castle to place the rest of the family within that castle's crypt."

"What if the captain comes back, or some other men of the general's come to investigate further?" Dytruik asks.

"I have given specific instruction that no one is to be permitted in either this castle or the other two castles until after all the family members have been laid to rest. They must obtain my written consent and await the decision of the counsel. Being that these lands are in my realm, there should not be any problem that they fall into my custody, but until then we need to 'make nice' with the other noble houses," Heyrold instructs. "I just wish I had that Guel boy out of the way. With him alive, this process will be delayed, but I do have other spies in some key areas."

Heyrold makes his way to the castle stable, where a soldier walks out his horse, retightens the saddle, and then holds the reins as Heyrold mounts. He nods at the soldier then rides out the front gate. He rides out about a mile, where he is met by a young messenger boy wearing animal pelts.

"This dispatch arrived earlier for you, my lord," the

messenger says as he hands the letter to Heyrold.

"Thank you, scout, that will be all," Heyrold says as he nods. "Oh, go see if General Dytruik has anything for you."

"Yes, sir," the scout nods and then rides onward to Guel Castle.

"Son, do you know if Riechter was still in Vry?" Heyrold asks as he turns his horse around to face the scout after skimming the letter.

"I did not see him there, sire."

"Well, if you happen to run into him in your travels, let him know I need to see him. Okay, that will be all." Heyrold gives a wave as he turns his horse back around and heads to Vry.

Heyrold rides hard for about two hours and then slows his horse to a walk to give the animal some rest.

"'Tis not safe for you to be traveling the road alone, my lord, this late in the day. 'Tis almost nightfall." The voice comes from up in the trees.

Heyrold grabs a crossbow that is tied at the back of his saddle. The weapon is preloaded and wrapped in a cloth so the bolt does not dislodge. He pulls the wrapping away and aims in the direction of the voice in one swift motion. "Hogarth, you bastard. You're lucky I didn't shoot you," Heyrold announces as he spots the scout in a tree.

Hogarth laughs, jumping from branch to branch and then to a low tree branch and onto the road as Heyrold stops his horse. "You're pretty fast for an old man."

"Yeah and damn accurate. I could part your hair with this thing. Is Riechter with you?" Heyrold asks as another scout walks out from behind a tree. "Tryton, good to see you."

Tryton nods.

"He should be along shortly—thought we would surprise him. Then you happened by." Hogarth smiles.

"Well, I'm glad it was you two. I really did not feel like fighting," Heyrold says with a sigh of relief.

Tryton makes some signs with his hands, a silent language as Hogarth and Heyrold look on.

"Slow down. I know a little of the signs, but it's been a while since I had anyone sign," Heyrold says.

"He hasn't spoken for three days now. Actually, it's been nice to live in silence for a while," Hogarth smiles.

Tryton signs again.

"What was that?" Heyrold asks.

"You don't want to know," Hogarth smirks.

"I said Hogarth is right. You should not be traveling alone, milord," Tryton says.

"I appreciate your concern. But, son, I'm not so old that I can't take care of myself, as you just saw. Besides, I don't wear this armor just because I look good in it." Heyrold laughs as he pulls out a small flask of Viko from a saddlebag and tosses it to Tryton. He catches it, uncorks it, and takes a swig before throwing it to Hogarth.

"Nice," Hogarth says as he catches the flask, uncorks it, and takes a large gulp.

"So, I take it your business in Xieg is taken care of," Heyrold says as he gets the flask tossed back to him.

"Of course," Hogarth says.

Heyrold tosses him a small pouch with coins in it. He then pulls another pouch and tosses it to Tryton as well. "Good. Well, I have another assignment for you."

"Aye, I've heard ... the Guel boy," Hogarth says.

"Oh, so you have talked with Riechter?" Heyrold asks.

"Aye, we ran into him yesterday afternoon shortly after you left," Tryton says.

"You two saw me leave, crafty devils," Heyrold laughs as he

shakes his head. "So where are your pets?"

Tryton motions with his eyes above in the trees.

"Oh, I see Theo perched on that branch. Where's the cat?" Heyrold says as he looks up in the trees at Hogarth's pet, a snow-white falcon with brown on his wings. Then of Tryton's pet, he says, "Oh wow, that snow leopard blends right in with the white bark of those aspen trees. What's her name again?"

"Cat." Tryton laughs as the leopard leaps down and sits next to Tryton to rub its head on her master's leg.

"Well, I have a different assignment, much more interesting. But I'll wait till Riechter gets here to tell all of you."

"You don't need to wait."

"Riechter? Damn," Hogarth barks.

Riechter steps out of the trees. "I could hear you a mile away with all that noise. Heck, my mother could've snuck up on all of you—"

"Yes, I know, and she's dead," Tryton interrupts as he rolls his eyes. "You really need to come up with better sayings."

"For your information, elf turd, I was going to say crippled." Riechter laughs.

"Whatever," Hogarth scoffs.

"Where's that Viko?" Riechter asks Heyrold.

"So you have been here the whole time?" Heyrold smiles as he tosses his flask to Riechter.

"Longer." Riechter snickers as he catches the flask, uncorks it, and finishes it off.

Both Hogarth and Tryton shake their heads.

"I knew I should not have let you feed the cat yesterday. She would have alerted me otherwise."

Riechter smiles as he points to his head. Tryton replies with the same sign he gave Hogarth earlier.

"I just got this dispatch—iron ore shipments from one of my

mines in the Shendos has been getting attacked by some local barbarian tribes," Heyrold tells the men as he pulls the letter from a saddlebag and hands it to Riechter.

"Isn't that a Dwarf problem?" Riechter questions as he scans the letter.

"No, it's my problem. It's my mine, my iron ore. The dwarves don't transport the ore—they just mine it for me. Although I think their village outside the mine could be the next prime target ..."

"So what do you need us to do?" Riechter asks.

I need you to talk to the barbarian clan chieftain, to find out why they are making these attacks, and then negotiate a peace agreement. I don't know if it's something the dwarves have done or what, but I need it stopped. I've already lost a dozen men in the last attack," Heyrold says.

"What if we can't reach a peaceable solution?" Tryton asks.

"Do whatever it takes, I don't care. I just want those shipments to keep coming to Vry," Heyrold says as he starts to ride off. "Let me know if you need me to send some more men up there. I got thirty headed back with the caravan in the morrow. Oh, by the way, how come you are headed east? The Guel boy was headed north," Heyrold adds as he stops his horse and turns around.

"I wanted to see Zeth's place one last time. Real shame ... I really liked the guy," Tryton says.

"Oh, dry your eyes. You only met the guy one time, and he would not have helped you had he known you were working for me at the time," Riechter says.

"Wow, that was last year. Yeah, well I still wanna see it," Tryton says.

"Quit your crying. We are headed that way after we are done here." Riechter smiles.

"You know, Riechter, you never cease to humor me." Heyrold laughs then rides off.

"How's your Dwellvinar?" Tryton asks Riechter, meaning the language spoken among Dwarves and Bogey Classes, as well as many subterranean creatures that can talk. There are of course many dialects, depending on the region and creature speaking. But when this language is known, it is fairly easy to communicate with other dialects.

"As good as the both of you. How's your Ber-Ber?" Riechter asks.

"*Gott* (Good)," Tryton says in Ber-Ber.

"*Nógu gott* (Good enough)," Hogarth answers in kind.

"*Gut, dann können loslegen* (Good, then let's get going)," Riechter says in Dwellvinar as he whistles for his horse.

Riechter carefully mounts his horse, holding tightly on the reins as he lands in the saddle while his two scout brethren grab their horses from the woods and mount up, following close behind him.

As they get about fifty feet down the road, two more scouts emerge from their hiding places in the foliage next to the road where all the men were talking earlier and begin following.

Riechter smiles.

Chapter XV
Bugbears, Bogeyman, and Bucca-boos

hey all ride hard for another two hours without any encounters, unlike before. Exel keeps a close look for anything out of the ordinary. Suddenly, the scout pulls his bow and shoots it twice as the others stop a few yards behind. He holds his hand up for all to stop and then proceeds to where he shot his arrows about 100 yards from the road.

"Everyone stay here. I'll ride out and see what it is," Sargon tells the group, handing Bellgrad the rope to his packhorse. He draws his sword and spurs Tantor onward into a hard run so the animal has to leap through the thick powdery snow. "What is it?" Sargon asks as he approaches Exel, who is dismounted and scanning the ground.

"Dinner," Exel says as he puts his bow across his right shoulder. He holds up two white rabbits as he pulls the arrows from their bodies, plunging the tips into the snow to wipe the blood off and then returning them to his quiver.

"Wow, you shot those on the run. I'm impressed," Sargon comments.

"It comes with lots of practice." Exel smirks as he holds the game with one hand, grabs the reins of his horse with the other, and quickly mounts to head back to the group. Sargon in turn heads back as well, scanning the woods and sheathing his sword as he leaves.

"Everything okay?" Valagar asks with sword in hand as Exel reaches the front of the party.

"Just got us some fresh meat. I figure we will have to camp

with it getting dark soon. I judge we have about another couple of hours of riding ahead to get to Calador's," Exel explains as he rides up to the front of the line.

"I was thinking the same thing. That's what we did last night. Had we gotten an earlier start and not had to wait on Sir Naps-a-lot back there or run into those perqs, we would be there already," Valagar says as he and Exel look at Silverfish napping behind Barbye, both sharing a heavy animal pelt. Barbye is busy talking to Meg,

"You know, I just don't get it. A beautiful woman with that little guy," Exel tells Val.

"I know what you mean, but I hear tell what those little guys lack in stature they make up for in length ... if you know what I mean." Val smirks.

"Really?" Exel says with a raised eyebrow.

"Well, it's just what I heard. It's not like I have been meat gazing or anything," Val says as Elof and Ari bust out laughing.

"Uh huh." Exel smiles.

"Whatever. Just find us a good spot to camp," Val adds as he rolls his eyes and laughs.

"Sure thing." Exel laughs as he rides on ahead.

"We are going to camp for the night," Valagar tells the group as he starts out again.

"Good," Barbye says with a relieved look on her face. Father Yor smiles and nods with a relieved look as well.

"Duft blása," Bjorn comments.

"I heard that," Father Yor says.

Sargon laughs.

"What did he say?" Bellgrad asks.

"Powder puff," Sargon answers.

Bjorn twists around in the saddle and gives Sargon an astonished look. *"Du snakker mitt språk?"*

"*Ja*," Sargon answers as Bjorn twists back around. "*Sumir* ... Val, are you sure it's a good idea to camp? We could still make it. It's going to get pretty cold when it gets dark. Besides, we don't know what else might be out there tonight."

"What did Bjorn ask you?" Bellgrad asks as he slows and rides next to Sargon. "I didn't know you could speak the barbarian's language."

"Apparently he didn't either." Sargon smirks as he continues looking forward at Valagar.

"Precisely why we should camp and travel in the daylight," Val says over his shoulder as he looks ahead and waves at Exel off in the distance. "Let's go. Exel has found us a good spot." Val spurs his horse onward.

The group rides to a spot with a small opening surrounded on all sides by trees. Exel has dug a three foot-by-three foot hole in the snow and is setting up a campfire as the group arrives.

"We don't ride as much as you do, Sargon. Actually, it's been about a year since I rode in a saddle," Father Yor comments as he slowly dismounts his horse.

"I would expect talk like that from Barbye, but not you, Father." Silverfish laughs as he yawns and jumps off his horse.

"Shut up," Barbye and Father Yor say at the same time while looking at the small elf.

The fighters all laugh at the entertainment as they start unloading gear from their packhorses and Sulo begins to set.

"Sargon, give me a hand with this," Val commands as he unloads a tent off his packhorse while Exel gets a fire going and commences to gather more wood.

"Help me gather some wood, stinky," Exel says to Silver.

"It's Lumpy ... I mean Silverfish," Silver answers, shaking his head. "See what you started?" Silver looks over at Father Yor as he walks under the surrounding trees looking for fallen branches in the snow as Chan arrives with an armful of wood.

"Well, boohoo. I think I'm going to start calling you 'Babyfish.' It seems more fitting than Lumpy," Father Yor says over his shoulder as he joins in the quest for fallen tree branches.

Val lets out a great laugh. "Boy, Father, you come up with some real doozies." He shakes his head and almost drops the wrapped-up tent and poles as everyone else joins in the humor.

Elof and Ari gather wood as well.

Bjorn sits on a nearby fallen tree after he unloads a few things off his packhorse.

"You aren't gonna help with the fire?" Exel asks.

"That's *vinna konu*!" Bjorn says.

"Woman's work, huh? Well, if we were in town or at someone's home, I would agree, but we are setting up camp, and we all pitch in. So, here," Exel says as he steps to his horse and grabs the rabbits and tosses them on the ground in front of the barbarian. "Clean these. Oh, and here you go." Exel grabs two grouse on the ground next to his horse and throws them to Bjorn as well.

"Wow, look at that!" Bellgrad adds as he drops off a load of wood by the campfire. "When did you get those?" Bellgrad continues as oohs and aahs come from the rest of the group.

"I spotted them in the trees before I started the fire. Guess it's just our lucky day," Exel says as he goes and adds more wood to the fire.

"Looking at them is not cleaning them, drippy. Here, you can use my knife," Silverfish says as he pulls a knife from his belt and throws it, sticking it in the fallen tree Bjorn was sitting on earlier. Now he's standing in front of it with the rabbits in his hands. The knife sticks in the wood dead even with Bjorn's crotch.

"Thanks ... what is this ... drippy?" Bjorn asks with a confused look on his face and a raised eyebrow as he pulls the knife out of the tree, seeing where it landed.

"Well, you are going to be dripping with blood as soon as you finish cleaning our dinner." Silverfish snickers.

"I though you meant what happens to you when you lay with lady of evening, then you have to eat moldy bread for a month." Bjorn says as he starts cleaning a rabbit.

"Oh...that works too." Silverfish adds while walking over to Val and Sargon as they finish setting up the tent they are working on. "Do you need any help?"

"That's about right, Sargon. He shows up as soon as we are done," Val says as he finishes tying the last rope to a stake.

"Well, it's not completely done," Sargon says as he ties back the entrance flaps to the small tent. "You can clean out all that snow inside there."

"Oh." Silver's smile disappears. "Okay." He walks inside and starts kicking out the snow. "I might as well clean it out since I'm going to be sleeping in it."

"Oh no, little man. This is for the girls," Sargon states.

"Oh, come on. It's cold out here. Besides, I don't take up much room," Silver says with sad-puppy-dog eyes.

"Have you ever seen anything more pitiful in your life?" Val says as he looks at Silverfish and then to Sargon as he rests his hand on one of the front ropes securing the tent.

"Not since our cook had to tell my mother he ran over her cat with a wagon. Okay, okay. You can sleep in the tent. Geez, just quit your whimpering," Sargon says as he looks over his shoulder at Barbye, who is laughing and shaking her head. "Barb—" He stops mid-sentence as he sees Exel looking out at the woods to the west of their camp across the road about 1,000 yards away." Sargon walks over to Exel.

"I swore I saw something move out there. I guess it's

nothing," Exel softly answers, looking at Sargon.

"Keep me posted. If you think we need to, we'll go take a look." Sargon smiles as he pats Exel on the shoulder.

The scout looks out again, then turns away and throws more wood on the fire. Then he starts stripping down some long branches for skewers. "Man aren't you done yet?" Exel asks Bjorn, who has just finished one rabbit. "We'll starve before you get those finished." Exel grabs the finished rabbit, stabs the branch through the meat, and sticks it in the ground, leaving the rabbit roasting over the fire.

"This knife is dull. Elf probably been cleaning his toenails with the blade," Bjorn says as he looks at the knife.

"Gimme that." Exel impatiently jerks the knife out of Bjorn's hand. "Your hands aren't broken. You could've sharpened it ... here." Exel grabs a knife from behind his neck and hands it to Bjorn. "This one isn't."

Bellgrad walks over as Sargon and Val cut down some low branches and uses them to make more skewers. Bellgrad pulls his dagger and helps Bjorn clean the game as Ari and Elof pitch in as well.

"Ew. Is that the dagger you killed the perq with?" Silver says as he looks out from the tent.

"Man, what a big baby. I cleaned it ... I think." Bellgrad smiles as Bjorn, Ari, and Elof snicker.

The two women pitch in as well in cleaning the game, and soon all the meat is cooking. Father Yor walks around the campsite, apparently blessing the area with his holy symbol in his hand and reciting some words from his book.

Exel pours some wine and rubs some spices all over and inside the game, while Sargon and Bellgrad place some old logs around the campfire for everyone to sit on. Ari strings up a rope for tying the horses to, then he and Elof commences to unsaddling and feeding them.

"Hang on there. I want to keep Tantor saddled and armored, as cold as it is. It will help cut the wind. Besides, I like to be ready for anything. I think we should all sleep in our armor as well," Sargon says as he goes over to the horses after setting the last log, interrupting Ari's work to remove Tantor's armor barding.

Val walks over. "Okay, like he said, it's plenty cold. Don't take any more of the gear off. Just feed them," Val tells his two retainers.

"Okay," both young men respond, shrugging their shoulders with a little attitude.

"These men have got this. Go sit and rest." Sargon smiles while patting Val on the shoulder as he leans up against a tree next to his new mentor.

"Squire, I'm not *that* old," Val says with a raised eyebrow. The knight is in his mid thirties.

"I did not say that, milord. It's just the fact that we will need to take two-hour shifts on night watch, and I figure I'll take first watch, you second, Bellgrad third, Bjorn fourth, then Exel on the last watch.

"Wow, you already thought that through. I'm impressed. You are a good leader." Val smiles as he grabs a small flask from his horse's saddle bag, uncorks it, and takes a swig. Then he passes it to Sargon.

"Thanks," Sargon gives a nod as he takes a drink. "That's good Viko. Exel says he wakes up early anyway, so it will work out for him. I cannot sleep right off, so first is best for me. And Bellgrad has been a soldier for a long time, and he can sleep on a whim. He's had lots of practice at guard duty," Sargon explains then takes another drink and passes it back to Val.

"What about the barbarian?" Val asks as he peers over his shoulder at Bjorn sitting talking to Bellgrad.

"Well, he doesn't really have a say in the matter. Besides, he'll complain no matter what shift he gets." Sargon smirks.

"True. What about them?" Val asks lightly, pointing to Ari and Elof with his head as the two continue feeding the horses.

"Too young. Maybe once I have been around them longer," Sargon explains.

"Good point. What about twinkle-toes over there?" Val asks as he nods in the direction of Silverfish, who seems to be dancing on one of the logs and entertaining the rest of the group sitting around the fire.

Meg, who is sitting next to Bellgrad, peers over her shoulder at Sargon.

"He might have the heart of a giant, but not the strength nor the will. He's as likely to run off scared if something big and bad comes into the camp before even giving us a warning," Sargon confirms, totally oblivious to Meg's glare as she smiles and looks away.

"True, what about the monk?" Val asks as he glances over at Chan, who is busy sewing a shirt, then gets confronted by Exel for cooking some stinky tea in a small pot next to the fire. The group around the fire complains that it smells like troll droppings or something to that effect.

Sargon laughs as he momentarily enjoys the free entertainment. "I admire his courage, but without armor ... I mean, he may be fast and all, but depending on speed alone will eventually get him killed. I sure would not trust that, especially on a night watch when you can get blindsided by something he can't see in the dark." Sargon watches Bjorn get up, grab Chan's small pot, then throw it out away from the campfire. With lightning speed, Chan grabs up his staff and wallops the barbarian upside the head.

Meg lets out a scream.

"True. Time to break up a lover's quarrel," Val says as he and Sargon rush to hold back Bjorn.

"Children, stop this crap," Sargon says as he arrives at the fire. Exel and Bellgrad have already grabbed the dazed Bjorn under each shoulder. The barbarian shakes his head as his face turns red with rage.

"Crap is what that so-called tea smells like," Silver acknowledges. "I told Chan not to cook that stuff."

"Shut up, Silver! You instigated the whole thing," Father Yor tells Silverfish.

"I will kill *litli maðurinn* (little man)!" Bjorn says as he tries to shake loose from the men's grasp.

"You will not touch Chan. I would have done the same thing had you thrown something of mine like that," Barbye says as she stands between Bjorn and Chan, who stands at the ready with his staff.

"Sit down, Chan. I could smell that awful stuff from where I was," Val says as he looks at the young monk then to the barbarian. "You too, Bjorn. Or I'll put a wallop on you that you won't forget."

"Why you mad at me? He hit me," Bjorn says as he jerks out of Exel's and Bellgrad's hold and rubs his jaw.

"Oh, quit your crying, baby. I barely hit you," Chan says as he sits back down to his tailoring.

"Enough, Chan. I see what Father Yor means. You two are insufferable," Sargon says as he shakes his head. Chan sticks his tongue out at Bjorn. "I saw that. Now, Bjorn, go get that teapot."

Bjorn gives Chan a dirty look then walks out and grabs the pot as Father Yor walks out with him.

"Let's eat. The meat is ready," Exel says as he grabs the first cooked rabbit and hands the skewer to Meg and Barbye. "Here you go, ladies. Watch it—it's hot."

"Thank you," both women say at the same time.

The rest of the game gets pulled off the fire and passed around to the others, along with a jug of mead. Everyone eats, and it seems Bjorn and Chan resolve their differences after a long talk with Father Yor.

"Why do you have your feet buried in the snow?" Barbye asks Chan as she stands next to the monk while he eats. "Aren't your feet cold wearing those sandals?"

"I have to stay in balance, while part of me is warm, the other part is cold. It is the way with Fairwind, God of Fairness and Judgment. Besides, it is part of training of my head ... I mean mind ... over body," Chan says as he seems to shiver slightly.

"Sounds silly to me and a quick way for you to get a sickness," Barbye says and hands Chan a pair of boots. "Here, put these on. They should fit you."

"I cannot." Chan smiles gratefully.

"I think you have practiced your discipline enough with the trudging through the snow you did today," Father Yor adds, commenting at the nice gesture from Barbye.

"Perhaps you are right." Chan pulls his feet out of the snow and warms them by the fire.

"Yes, you are no good to us if your feet are frozen and you cannot fight," Valagar adds as Chan puts the boots on, knowing the monk does not want to appear weak. "It's good training for you to learn to fight with boots on anyway."

Chan smiles and nods.

Sargon starts walking around the campsite with a torch in his hand, looking out as far as he can. The surrounding forest is all black with the heavy cloud cover masking any moonlight from either moon. Everyone starts bedding down as the two women retire to the tent, followed by Silverfish.

"Hey, Silver, no funny business," Sargon warns the elf, who

nods with a smile as he goes into the tent.

"Not to worry, Sargon. I gave Meg my club to keep with her," Father Yor tells Sargon as the priest makes his bed next to the fire and sits cross-legged to pray silently.

"Bjorn, Val will wake you after his shift. You need to watch the camp for about two hours," Sargon instructs.

"Okay ... how will I know when two hours have passed?" Bjorn asks.

"The good Father has an hourglass next to the fire," Sargon says, amazed he did not get any bad reaction from the barbarian. He points to a rock by the fire where the hourglass sits. Bjorn nods in recognition while he lies down and covers himself with an animal pelt. "Bellgrad, you'll have your shift after Bjorn."

"No problem," Bellgrad answers as he covers himself and falls asleep almost immediately.

"See what I was telling you?" Sargon softly whispers to Val, who beds down next to the fire as well and smiles, closing his eyes.

Sargon walks the perimeter, turning the hourglass whenever it empties. His shift goes by without any encounters, much to his delight because he is very sleepy by the end of his shift. He wakes Val and then commences to lie down after stoking the campfire. Val walks the perimeter, same as Sargon, trying to walk in the squire's footsteps.

Just the same as Sargon, Val, Bjorn, and Bellgrad have no encounters other than the hooting of owls and an occasional howl from wolves off in the distance. Bellgrad goes to wake Exel but finds the scout is not sleeping where he was bedded down close to the fire earlier.

Exel gives a soft birdcall from up in a nearby tree. Bellgrad glances up then quickly looks down and nods as if Exel were in his bed, understanding the stealthy illusion the scout is enacting.

The soldier throws more wood on the fire then turns in for a short nap before dawn.

Exel watches over the perimeter as the camp grows deadly silent. The only sound is the crackle of the fire. He smiles, pulling out a piece of venison jerky from his belt pouch that he had cured about a year ago. *Yum, it's still very good*, he thinks to himself while slowly munching.

An unfamiliar scent catches his attention from the west, as he is downwind of a strong gust. His smile fades as he watches the woods where he thinks the scent came from. It's very difficult to see, as the night is almost pitch black, but then the cloud cover breaks, and pale moonlight illuminates the woods.

He makes out a silhouette of an upright figure bigger than a man moving away from a tree. It appears as though it may have been hugging it, perhaps to camouflage itself. Amazingly, the creature makes no sound. Exel slowly climbs down from his perch in the tree. There are too many tree branches blocking a shot from his bow, if need be. He has to investigate further to see what it is—perhaps only a hapless creature meaning no harm to anyone. The scout doesn't kill senselessly for any reason; the preservation of forest life is sacred to him and his kin.

He makes it to the bottom of the tree, quietly slips his bow off his shoulder, and then notches an arrow as he slowly progresses forward toward the area in which he saw the creature; the scent of the animal becomes stronger with every step. He catches another silhouette, but this time he makes out what appears to be bear claws as the animal stands next to a tree.

Oh, that's not good, he thinks to himself, realizing he has to take the creature out for the safety of the party. The moonlight fades again as clouds mask both moons. Exel closes his eyes, relying on his sense of smell to guide him; he is still about 100 yards away from his target. He lets loose his arrow and then smirks as he opens his eyes to see the silhouette come into sight again. The moonlight appears momentarily to reveal that his arrow hit the creature in the eye. The creature grabs the arrow and falls to the ground. Perhaps Elktor, God of the Forest, is smiling on him, the nineteen-year-old scout thinks to himself. Or not.

The hair on the back of his neck stands up as he hears a twig snap from up above; his smirk fades as he quickly crouches and grabs a dagger from his belt. He twists around and stabs one of these creatures through the mouth as it lunges from the branch of an adjacent tree. The creature collapses next to the scout as he sees what it is that attempted to attack him.

Its head looks like a cross between a wolf, bear, and man. The head is twice the size of a man's, with long canine teeth for ripping meat off bone, and it has pointed humanoid ears on either side of its head. The claws are twice as long as a bear's with heavy pads in the palms of its lower paws for quiet move-ment. This must be why he did not hear any sound from the one he saw in the woods. The animal's fur is long and shaggy, changing color from white to brown or black as the creature dies. It's hard to know for certain in the inconsistent and waning moonlight.

The arms of this creature are as big around as one of Exel's legs but much shorter than its back legs. And, much like a man, the animal's musk is very subtle. Even standing right next to one, the scout might not have caught the scent if not for the heavy wind.

Bugbear. I'm very lucky it did not take my head off, he says to himself. "BUGBEARS! BUGBEARS!" Exel hollers as he runs as hard as he can back to the camp.

Bugbear. It sounds harmless, like a stuffed bear for a child to sleep with for comfort. They are anything but. They are classified by his kinsmen as "buggarts" or "bogeys." Sometimes called "boogeymen," these creatures hunt humans, targeting mainly defenseless children and snatching them from their beds in the night as they sleep. They have been known on occasion to snag young women or take on single targets as well, as the scout just found out.

They must have been watching the group for hours ... must have been what I saw earlier, the thought flashes through Exel's mind as he runs.

He understands these creatures' tactics, even though he has never encountered them personally. All buggart types are high on the training agenda for his profession because they are man-eaters. Bugbears are crafty and can shape change at will, changing into harmless objects like a sack of grain or, as he just saw, enveloping themselves around a tree.

Sargon instantly wakes up from Exel's hollering alarm, but he struggles a moment to get to his feet because of the heavy armor he wears.

A blood-curdling roar rings through the woods. Silverfish stabs one of the bugbears in the left hand/paw while being pulled out from under the tent with Barbye in tow as she holds onto the other arm of the creature.

"Let him go, you bastard," Barbye says as the creature spins, flinging her loose from his arm like a rag doll. She plows into Sargon, knocking him down as she lands on both the squire and Bellgrad.

Val jumps to his feet as he sees another bugbear run off with Meg, who screams then passes out apparently from shock. The creature with Silverfish in his claws swings the elf around and slams his head into a tree. Silverfish's body goes limp, he drops his dagger, and the monster throws him over its shoulder. The creature runs off before anyone can reach them.

Exel lets an arrow loose at the creature with Silverfish.

"NO!" Val hollers as the creature twists around and the feathers of the arrow graze the elf's ear.

Bellgrad pushes Barbye off of him as he sees Meg being carried away. "Meg! Noooooooo!" He gets to his feet and chases after the creature. Bjorn throws an axe, which the quick animal easily dodges, and the axe sticks into an adjacent tree.

Sargon gently pushes Barbye off of him.

"I'm okay. Go after them," Barbye says, struggling to catch her breath.

Sargon races off toward the horses.

Father Yor struggles to look for his book in all the chaos. He was bedded down next to Bellgrad, and the book is buried under animal pelts after Barbye landed on top of the fighters.

Val grabs up his weapons and starts out but pauses as he looks at the black woods.

"Going after them on foot is pointless. They can run as fast as a horse, and it's much too dark to see. We need torches," Exel says as he and Val race toward the horses.

As if on cue, Bjorn is already grabbing torches off the pack-horses and tossing them to Elof, who races to the campfire and lights them.

"Here," Elof hollers, throwing the first one to Val.

The knight catches it while making his way to his mount.

Sargon races by on Tantor, grabbing a lit torch that Elof throws his way.

Sargon looks over his shoulder and calls, "Going after Meg."

"We got this. Go, go, go!" Val yells out as he flags the young knight forward. He looks at Ari, who is saddling and gearing the horses. "Follow him."

Father Yor looks on, amazed. "He's crazy ... he's going to get knocked off running full blast like that."

"Perhaps, but he will get them or die trying. It's in his blood," Val says as he and Exel quickly saddle all the horses.

Ari races his horse, packhorse, and Bellgrad's horse while catching a torch from Elof as he goes by. "Besides, we won't be far behind him."

"Let me help you." Barbye rushes over after a brief recovery and helps Val by holding the knight's torch.

"Thanks," Valagar hurriedly finishes, as thoughts of Silver and Meg's demise run through his head. He jumps on his horse then grabs the torch from Barbye.

"They are carrying them off to their lair to waiting hungry mouths. If we keep up the chase, they will not stop to snack!" Exel adds as he mounts his horse and Elof hands the scout a lit torch. He knows these creatures live together in family pods with as many as twenty in a lair. They will always feed the young first. Usually they are very cowardly despite a large size. They will not go against any armored foes, so they must be extremely hungry to have taken the chance of stealing Meg and Silver.

"Hey, where's Chan? I did not see him leave," Yor adds as he looks around. He accepts a torch as he mounts. "Think those creatures grabbed him?"

"I don't know," she says, looking at the pallet where Chan was sleeping. All that's left are the boots she gave the monk. She mounts her horse as Elof gives her a torch and then mounts his horse to head out with Valagar and Exel.

"Bjorn, watch over Barbye and Father Yor while we ride. We don't know if there are more out here," Val says over his shoulder.

"Okay, go ..." Bjorn hollers out as he stops and waits for the priest and barmaid.

"Let's go! No time to waste." Barbye spurs her horse.

Bjorn grins admiringly at her comment, and Father Yor nods

in recognition.

Chapter XVI
The Chase

hoo ahh, phoo ahh, phoo ahh, phoo ahh, phoo ahh, phoo ahh, phoo ahh. Tantor's heavy breathing is the only sound Sargon hears as his horse runs full speed through the deep snow-filled woods, other than the occasional jingling of the chain mail of the plate barding.

Branch, branch, branch ... the thought races though Sargon's head. He quickly leans over to the left, ducking a low branch as it grazes the torch in his hand. Sparks fly to the ground, but they're quickly extinguished as they hit the snow, and the faithful steed lunges onward. The woods briefly end as the landscape opens up to a small clearing about three hundred yards across.

Sargon momentarily stops Tantor. He looks to the right and then the left as he holds up his torch, scanning the ground at three sets of tracks that lead into the clearing ahead. One splits off from the other two, heading across the field about one hundred paces east of the other two. He spots Bellgrad in the middle of this clearing, bent over and apparently out of breath. Sargon is amazed at the soldier's stamina, running this far wearing all that armor and then wading through knee-deep to waist-deep snow in the field.

Close to two miles—Bellgrad must be ready to pass out, Sargon thinks to himself.

"Are you all right?" Sargon asks.

Bellgrad nods as he puffs.

"I figured right! These are tracks of the bugbear that has

Meg," Sargon says as he presses Tantor onward through the waist-deep snow.

"They are ... one hundred paces ... ahead." Bellgrad nods, catching his wind as he stands pointing. "I ... have never seen ... bugbears run this far ... before. They must ... be winded."

"Well, you sure are. Stay here and rest. The others will be along shortly. Stay here so they see you. Go after Silver."

"Damn it, Sargon. I'm going after Meg too," Bellgrad hollers as Tantor plows by through the snow.

"So be it," Sargon stares ahead, trying to catch a glimpse of the creature as sunlight begins to break through the trees behind him, throwing shadows in the early morning light while his horse strains with every leap through the clearing's deep snow.

"Sargon ... hey!" Ari yells as he reaches the clearing, but the knight apparently does not hear him as Sargon and Tantor disappear in the woods beyond the clearing.

"Boy ..." Bellgrad hollers as he waves his arms at Ari.

Ari rushes forward. "Here is your horse, milord," Ari says as he jumps off his horse about ten feet away from Bellgrad. Ari wades threw the deep snow, unties Bellgrad's horse from the back of his packhorse, and meets the soldier halfway with the reins in his hands.

"Let's go. *HAH*!" Bellgrad says as he mounts, spurring his horse onward after Meg, throwing his torch and drawing his sword.

"What about the other bugbear?" Ari asks.

"The scout is behind us. If they can't figure that out ... well, that's not my problem," Bellgrad says, still breathing heavy, but he stews over the monster having Meg, wondering if she is still alive.

The creature stops behind a tree, winded and trying to catch its breath while hiding. The heavy snow of the clearing has tired the creature out. It takes the unconscious Meg off its shoulder and lays her across its left knee while crouching. The bugbear holds its head up to catch the scent, but without success. The wind is not in its favor today, blowing toward its pursuers. It does instead hear voices off in the distance and the hard breathing of a heavy horse as the horse and rider make their way into the woods. Maybe two hundred paces back, the heavy horse has not moved any closer. The creature hears the snorts of the exhausted horse as well as its fast-beating heart. It also hears the heavy panting of the other bugbear that is resting about one hundred paces away in the woods.

Something wet and warm drops onto Meg's back, waking her up. She hears the creature's heavy panting and instantly remembers what happened to her. She realizes the liquid that woke her is the creature's slobber. She believes the only way to stay alive is to play dead; she is very scared, but if her capturer knows she is awake, she fears she might die or get pummeled against a tree.

The bugbear with Silver rests behind a tree as well, more winded than his brethren, having run farther in the snow-filled clearing. Silver is still on the creature's shoulder; he's out cold. The bugbear pants and looks back nervously every few minutes as it rests. The young male looks at its left paw; it hurts to shape change it into a hand. The injury still drips blood, but nothing as bad as when it was first stabbed. His nervousness eases some when he hears the other much older bugbear's breathing.

"We need to follow those tracks over there," Exel tells Valagar. "Sargon went that way." Exel steers his mount toward the other set of track in the clearing.

"Wow. Really? You must be a master tracker," Valagar says sarcastically with a ridiculous look on his face, seeing the numerous tracks heading in one direction as well as the tail end of Ari's horse going into the woods as he and Elof follow Exel cutting across the clearing.

"*Far holde på sal og anspore den jævla hest.* (Father, hold onto your saddle and spur that damn horse)," Bjorn barks out while looking over his shoulder at Father Yor, who has fallen behind.

"I can't with this torch in my hand," Father Yor nervously says while clumsily riding in the saddle.

"*Da mister det. Har Sulo kommet opp.* (Then lose it. Sulo has come up)," Bjorn states as Barbye has progressed fifty yards further ahead. "Kvinnen er for langt unna. (Woman is too far away)," Bjorn continues as he turns his head forward.

Bjorn and Father Yor watch in horror as a bugbear attacks Barbye's horse. The creature swipes and slashes the throat of her mount, killing it instantly, sending horse and rider tumbling to the ground.

"AH SHIT!" Bjorn hollers out as he spurs his horse to a full run, dropping his torch. He pulls his axe from the right rear of his saddle, breaking the leather straps holding it as he approaches the bugbear.

"Yahmar protect her," Father Yor prays while dropping his torch and grabbing the saddle with his freed hand, spurring the horse to a full run and presuming the worst.

Barbye is thrown fifty feet away from the horse as it flips forward. She barely misses a tree as she hits a thick snowdrift then rolls another ten feet and lies motionless in the snow. The bugbear wearily staggers over to Barbye and momentarily looks at its prey as the horse's blood drips from its strong sharp claws.

"HAAAAHHH!" Bjorn hollers a war cry as he jumps from his horse with his battle-axe in both hands as it rides by the creature. Bjorn swings with all his might in midair at the bugbear's head, splitting the skull in half and going halfway through the body of the monster. It collapses backward. Landing on his feet, Bjorn instinctively pulls his two-handed sword from his back as he goes to Barbye. He crouches, ready for any other bugbears that may attack.

"I'm ... okay," Barbye strains to say, recovering from having the wind knocked out of her.

"Good," Bjorn smirks as he grabs his sword by the dull lower part just above the hilt. "I feared the worst." He scans the surrounding woods while helping Barbye get to her feet with his freed hand. She clumsily falls up against the solid-as-a-brick-wall barbarian warrior. Standing face to face with her rescuer, she looks briefly like she might kiss him; but the image of Silverfish being taken off flashes through her mind.

"Thanks ..." Barbye says as she slowly pushes away with both hands, gently patting his chest. She stands and brushes the snow from her hair and face, gaining her composure.

"Are you hurt?" Father Yor worries as he rides up.

"I'm fine, just rattled from being thrown. That creature would have killed me if Bjorn hadn't taken him out." Barbye half smiles at Bjorn. He leaves her side and goes to retrieve his axe, returning his sword to its sheath along the way.

Father Yor breathes a sigh of relief while making a holy symbol in the air and thanking his deity.

"Perhaps ... or more likely it would have taken you to hungry mouths at 'her' lair," Bjorn says over his shoulder as he pulls his axe from the bugbear's body while holding it down with his left foot. "Tis female. They must be starving for females to hunt ... they usually stay behind with young. It would not have gotten far, though ... has broken off arrow in eye."

"We must hurry before the others make it to their home with

Silver and Meg," Barbye says as she grabs the reins of Bjorn's horse and quickly mounts. Bjorn jumps on behind her.

"You have rested long enough, old man," Sargon tells Tantor as the horse has regained most of his wind. *I regret leaving that heavy armor on you now,* Sargon thinks to himself. "It couldn't have been easy going through that heavy snow in the clearing."

He tosses the torch, which extinguishes immediately, then draws his sword as the sun is now delivering enough light to see. Even though there is still a mist in the woods, Sargon wants to be ready for anything. He does not want to repeat the same scene he had with the bears. He leans over, watching the tracks on the ground as Tantor trudges onward.

"Come on, come on. We can't slack up," Bellgrad tells Ari as they continue into the woods, following Tantor's heavy tracks.

"Keep going. My horse is spent. I gotta rest him. That heavy snow back there was too much. I'll catch up," Ari says, stopping the horse. The animal puffs and snorts with exhaustion.

"Mine is too, but I got to press on. I'll walk him a bit to give you a little time and give mine a chance to catch his wind," Bellgrad says as he looks down at the tracks in the snow. It kills him to no end to slow down, but it would be really bad if the horse gets totally winded and drops dead. Then he may never catch up to the creature that has his girl, Bellgrad thinks to himself.

The creature with Meg has caught some of its wind and starts moving again, throwing her over its shoulder and running through the woods. Meg happened to scratch something in the snow earlier when the creature was busy looking back at the riders behind it. Meg is amazed at how fast this bugbear can run; but it can only run for short bursts—it doesn't have the endurance of a horse. This gives her hope. She knows that neither Bellgrad nor Sargon will stop until she is rescued, or they are both dead. The creature lets out a grunt, which is answered by the other bugbear as the two get closer to their lair. Meg hears it but cannot see the other creature through the snow-covered heavy brush. They proceed for another one hundred paces, and it rests again.

"We have to rest these horses. They are winded from that heavy snow," Exel says as they reach the edge of the trees.

"Okay, but not for too long. I know those creatures have to rest too—that heavy snow tired them out as well. But they do this all the time. They will get too far ahead of us if we let up for very long," Valagar says as he stops his horse.

"Well, they usually don't have someone chasing them," Exel answers.

"There are the others. They only have two horses. That can't be good," Elof says as he waves at Bjorn and Father Yor reaching the other edge of the clearing.

"There they are," Bjorn says as he waves back at Elof, spying them across the snowy clearing. "Let's go, Father."

"Right behind you," Father Yor says as he smiles at Barbye.

"What is it, old man?" Sargon asks as he sees Tantor's ear perk up. *We must be getting closer*, Sargon thinks to himself as his steed picks up his pace to a light gallop, seeming to catch his second wind.

"They stopped here," Bellgrad says as he stops his horse and waits for Ari, who is just a few paces back. Bellgrad breathes a sigh of relief as he sees the word *ALIVE* scratched in the snow next to the tree. "Come on. Let's go. She is still alive!" Bellgrad says to Ari as he spurs his horse onward.

"They have rested long enough. Let's go, let's go, let's go," Valagar orders, spurring his horse and drawing his sword.

POW. Sssscccrrraaaapppeeee. The sound echoes through the woods.

A bugbear ambushes from behind a tree. It swipes at Tantor's neck, but the armor barding absorbs the blow and protects the animal from the bugbear's deadly claw. Sargon is unfazed by the attack. He swings his sword, missing a clean shot at the creature's paw. But the strike cleaves off the animal's claws.

ROAR! The bugbear cradles its paw in pain. It drops Meg off its shoulder as the bloody tips of its paw hit the ground. With lightning speed, it takes a blind swipe at Tantor's rear with its good paw, grazing the back armor of the horse. It doesn't do any harm, but Tantor feels the blow.

"Run, girl, run!" Sargon hollers at Meg as Tantor skids to a stop, stands on his back legs, and spins around toward the monster. He snorts and shakes his head then chases after the bugbear.

It's like déjà vu. These were the last words Meg heard her father yell out at their house. She picks herself off the ground and runs as fast as she can back toward the clearing.

In the blink of an eye, the creature lunges after Meg, who screams and ducks behind a tree.

The bugbear misses its target but keeps running with the heavy warhorse at its heels. Sargon sheathes his sword and steers Tantor to the other side of the tree, scooping up Meg as they pass. He easily swings Meg one-handed in front of him onto his faithful steed. He pushes himself over the back of the saddle, giving the seat to Meg while keeping his left foot in the stirrup.

He immediately steers his horse away from the danger, heading back toward the clearing as he holds Meg tightly against himself with his right arm.

Not knowing who has been following him, but figuring it to be Bellgrad, Sargon hollers, "I got Meg ... kill that son of a ..."

"I got him, I got him," Bellgrad answers from no more than one hundred yards away. "Hah! Damn it, I missed."

Confused, the bugbear doubles back and heads toward Sargon and Meg. Tantor slows to a stop with his ears perked up, watching the woods ahead of them, then he lets out a snort while stomping the ground with his left hoof. Meg and Sargon can't see anything ahead of them in the dense woods. The horse sidesteps and spins slightly to the left while apparently following the sound of the creature as it runs through the woods.

"What is it? Is the horse scared?" Meg asks, confused.

"Oh no, he's not scared. He's pissed." Sargon smirks. "He wants that bugbear dead more than we do. He has a score to settle."

"I don't care. Let's go. I don't want that creature getting me again," Meg says as she kicks the horse with her short legs, but to no avail.

Neither of us will let that happen. Tantor really likes you. Watch him every time you talk—his right ear goes back.

Meg giggles, and just as Sargon said, the horse's right ear twists back.

"I'm not going to fight the horse on this. I learned that a long time ago. We have to finish this, or the bugbear is going to keep coming after you," Sargon confirms as he draws his sword. Just then Tantor blasts off, picking up speed as the bugbear comes into view.

"Hold on," Sargon barks out. As Meg grabs the saddle with both hands, Sargon grips with his legs and readies his sword.

"Lean forward," Sargon commands while covering Meg with the shield. Tantor bows up his neck and leaps into the air at the same time as the bugbear reaches the warhorse. Sargon wonders fleetingly if perhaps the creature means to jump over the horse and grab Meg.

Tantor head-butts the creature, gouging its left eye with the ornamental horn in the center of his armor faceplate and smashing the creature's nose. It breaks the bugbear's jaw, and its teeth fly out. This sends the bugbear tumbling backward as the heavy horse steamrolls over the monster, planting a front hoof in the middle of the bugbear's head, which makes a loud pop as it hits the ground.

"Yeah!" Sargon rejoices as they continue onward out of the woods and into the clearing, seeing Bellgrad as they pass.

"Wow ..." Bellgrad says, amazed as he rides over to the bugbear. He jumps off his mount and stabs the creature in the heart for good measure, even though it's obvious the bugbear is dead. Its skull is crushed, and its body mangled.

The bugbear with Silverfish zigzags through the woods and toward his fellow hunter to give aid after hearing all the commotion. It stands on a fallen tree while looking at the bugbear about one hundred yards away and lets out a deafening roar.

Bellgrad looks up to see the other creature looking at him over the dead bugbear.

"Come on, you bastard, let's dance," Bellgrad adds as he pulls his dagger with his left hand and slices through the air with his sword.

The creature with Silver on its shoulder keeps looking at Bellgrad; then suddenly its big eyes get bigger as it seems to jump slightly. It roars then breaks and runs back deeper into the woods. When the creature turns and runs, the soldier understands why it jumped slightly—it has two arrows in its back.

Bellgrad hears the thunderous sound of the hooves of Valagar and Exel's horses as they follow the creature in hot pursuit. He mounts his horse to join the chase.

"You saved me ..." Meg tells Sargon as she twists in the saddle and plants a passionate kiss on his mouth. The knight can do nothing, as both hands are full—his left holding his shield and the reins while his right grips his sword.

"Wow ... you're welcome," Sargon is stunned at the loving gesture. He pulls back as she starts to give him another kiss. "I can't," he says, as images of Jessica run through his mind. He steers Tantor back around. "We need to save Silver," he says, spurring the horse forward, still shocked at Meg's kiss.

"Hey!" Bjorn says as he catches up to Bellgrad, with Father Yor and Elof following behind him.

"Follow me. They are hot on the monster's trail," Bellgrad says with sword in hand as he spurs his horse into a run. "Exel planted two arrows in its back."

"Good," Barbye comments as they follow. "Pity it didn't hit it in the head."

The exhausted creature rests behind a tree; it cannot shape-change with the elf on its shoulder. It can, however, change the color of its fur to match the tree's bark.

Exel holds his hand out while he stops his horse as Valagar follows the scout's signal. Exel looks back at Val with his finger over his mouth; then he points, signaling the creature is five trees ahead.

Val nods silently. Exel motions that he is going to circle to the right and Val to circle to the left; Val nods in acknowledgement then spins in his saddle as he hears the others approaching, quickly holding up an open hand to stop. Bellgrad, who is in the lead, quickly follows suit and stops the others behind him.

"I think they have spotted the creature," Bellgrad whispers to the others. "We might want to fan out to surround it."

Bjorn, with axe in hand, nods as he steers his horse with Barbye far to the left, walking slowly as he signals to Barbye to be quiet.

She nods in agreement.

Father Yor pulls out his scepter and begins riding slowly to the far right.

The creature pants heavily from being winded as well as from fear and the injuries to its back. It can hear the crunch of the snow under the hooves of all the approaching horses. It decides to stay hidden while catching its breath. It takes Silver off its shoulder and lays him in its lap, hiding the unconscious elf with its arms.

Sargon rides hard, following the tracks of all the others.

Exel continues circling around, getting closer to the tree that the bugbear is resting against. He cannot quite make out the creature just yet, but he can hear the heavy breathing. Falling leaves and snow from the trees momentarily draw Exel's attention away, but he quickly looks back at the tree. Val cannot see the creature at all as he continues moving in, but he does occasionally hear the creature's panting. It suddenly goes silent.

Here we go, Exel thinks to himself as he has heard the panting cease as well.

Everyone is silent but can hear the distant thunderous sound of Tantor as Sargon gets ever closer. This is apparently what has struck fear into the creature; this was the last sound it heard before the demise of its brother. The creature cradles Silverfish in its arms then breaks and runs. Exel was right about the location, but the camouflage of the creature's coat matches the tree exactly, which explains why it was so hard to make out.

Val spurs his horse after the monster. Exel notches an arrow, but he cannot get a shot. The others have encircled the bugbear.

The creature backs up against a tree, seeing nowhere to run. It holds up Silverfish to shield itself.

"*Yn ôl i ffwrdd* (back off)," the bugbear warns.

Shocked, Bjorn hollers to the group, "Wait ... it said back off. Hold up, everyone."

"You understood that?" Exel says as Val stops his horse and

the others hold their positions.

"It's Dwellvinar ... very broken," Bjorn says as he dismounts and walks closer to the creature.

"*Gadael neu ddifa* (Leave or devour)," the bugbear says as it caresses Silver's head and licks its chops.

"It is saying eat or leave ... no, leave or eat," Bjorn translates.

Suddenly Chan comes out of nowhere. He drops out of the tree and lands on the shoulders of the unsuspecting bugbear. With lightning speed, the bugbear grabs Chan by his right leg and flings him like a rag doll into a nearby tree before the monk has time to strike with his Euguadian short sword. Chan's back and head slam against the tree, knocking him out cold. He falls bloody and lifeless in the snow.

The creature stands up with Silverfish in hand and spins around the tree as Exel lets an arrow fly, hitting the tree where the bugbear was seconds earlier.

Silverfish awakens. Coming to his senses, he pulls a dagger from his boot and drives it into the neck of the monster. As the creature raises its head in pain with its mouth open, apparently going to bite the elf in half, Sargon rides up and spears the monster through its mouth, nailing it to the tree with his sword. Sargon releases the sword as Tantor thunders by, knocking the knight temporarily off balance, as he didn't know the weapons would pierce through the tree.

"I didn't know those creatures could speak," Exel says.

"Some can. Why don't you go ask him his name?" Bjorn smirks.

"Funny," Exel answers.

Chapter XCVII
The Lair

ow are you feeling? You took a heck of a smack to the head and back when that creature threw you into that tree," Valagar asks, taking a knee next to Chan, who is propped up against a tree.

Father Yor and Meg are administering first aid.

"I am better now, a little sore in the back, though," Chan says as Father Yor stands up and closes his book, putting it in a pocket of his robe with one hand as he puts some stones in another pocket with the other hand. He smiles at Val.

"Good … you just sit there and rest," Val continues. He pulls an animal hide over the young man and pats him gently on the shoulder.

"Good work, Father," Sargon says, leaning against an adjacent tree. "Yeah, I smell it too." Sargon looks over at Exel, who is sniffing the air.

"Think it's the lair?" Sargon asks.

"Oh, no doubt."

Bjorn walks toward the tree where the bugbear lies dead. He looks at Sargon, points at his nose, and nods his head. Bjorn grabs Chan's small blade from the snow.

"Hey, what about me? I got my melon smacked against a tree as well," Silverfish says. He's sitting on a log, Barbye gently holding him against her chest.

"You got a hard head, Lumpy. Probably just took the bark off that tree back there," Father Yor says, pointing behind him with his thumb, in the direction of their camp.

"Here, let me kiss it and make it all better," Val says sarcastically, blowing kisses.

"No, thank you. I got all the kisses I need right here," Silver says, holding Barbye close as she caresses his head. "Owww."

"Let me look at that, you big baby," Father Yor says as he walks over to the two and looks at the elf's head. "Nothing that my club can't cure." Yor smiles.

"Oh no ... I'm fine," Silver says as he pushes Father Yor's hand away.

"Just kidding, my friend. Here, drink this." Father Yor chuckles as he pulls out a small vial from his robe and tosses it to the elf.

Silverfish uncorks the vial and downs the elixir.

Bjorn walks over to Chan, holding the monk's small, short sword. "Nice sword, if you can call it that." Bjorn laughs and lays the blade next to Chan. "More like a long-bladed dagger."

Chan smirks at the comment and the fact that the barbarian has no idea what he is looking at. The same may not be true of Val and Sargon, as knights are well educated, and many have a worldly knowledge and interest in weapons. He grabs the sword and slides it back inside his staff when everyone is preoccupied.

"I'm glad you are okay ... I was worried." Bellgrad smiles at Meg.

Sargon walks over to his soldier friend and leans down. "Look after Chan and the girls. We are going to check something out," Sargon whispers in Bellgrad's ear.

"I am very grateful for the both of you." Meg says as she puts a hand on Sargon's shoulder then hugs Bellgrad.

Bellgrad winks at Sargon as the squire grabs his shield and helm then makes his way toward Val, grabbing him under the shoulder without saying a word.

Valagar nods in recognition, grabbing his gear as well.

Father Yor grabs a handful of snow and blows it over the

fighters as they leave. "*Benedizioni a voi* (Blessings to you)" The snow turns to a gold shimmer and disappears as it lands on the men.

"Thank you, Father," Sargon smiles as Val, Exel, and Bjorn nod.

"I'm very happy it was Sargon's horse and not yours that the bugbear attacked. Without armor, your horse—and perhaps you—would be dead. I could not bear that thought," Meg continues as she nuzzles her face into Bellgrad's neck.

The fighter picks her up, holding her tightly and well off her tiny feet.

"You four make me sick. We don't have time for all this lovey-dovey business," Bjorn says as he shakes his head and looks at Silverfish, Barbye, Bellgrad, and Meg. "You can do all that when we get to the castle."

"You're just jealous because you don't have someone to hug on as well," Barbye says as she strokes Silver's hair.

"I'm sure Sargon will be your 'pretty boy'. "Why don't you go give him a kiss?" Silverfish comments as the four burst into laughter. Father Yor chuckles too.

Sargon looks over his shoulder then shakes his head.

"Oh, you're giving me I'm number one ... so that's how it's going to be," Silver comments at the international gesture Bjorn gives him.

The four fighters walk about fifty yards away from the others, coming upon a hole in the ground with snow-covered branches across it. Suddenly, Elof emerges from the hole. The stench following the young man is potent enough to knock an average man to his knees.

"Oh, that's awful—smells like something dead," Sargon says as he breathes into his armored sleeve.

"Terrible," Exel says as he backs away.

"Oh, that's wretched." Val takes a step back too. "Man, that brings back memories ... not good ones either."

"I know, I know. An animal must have crawled down there and died," Elof says as he coughs and fans his face while walking away.

"What's down there?" Exel asks.

"Some farmer must have made a cellar to hold supplies. Nothing in there but barrels and sacks of grain," Elof says as he breathes in the fresh air.

"Do you see any farmhouses around here?" Sargon comments as he steps back.

"Where's Ari?" Val says, surveying the area.

"Oh, he's still down there trying to find the dead animal," Elof says.

Bjorn makes a face. "This is it."

"GET OUT OF THERE, ARI. NOW!" Sargon says as he walks over to the entrance and looks down the hole, seeing a torch waving in the darkness.

"Just a little longer. I'm getting closer to the source—ugh, that stinks," Ari says calmly.

"Don't go in there," Bjorn says as he puts a firm grip on Sargon's shoulder.

"Get your hands off me," Sargon pulls his shoulder away as Val hands the squire a torch. He has two more torches he lights from the one he hands to Sargon, then Bjorn.

"Wait." Val hands Sargon an oil flask, which the squire quickly stows away in his belt pouch.

"Just a little longer ... found it. It's guts of a ... little *girl*," Ari says as he spots a little girl's half-eaten head. He jumps back and slips in the ooze that is a mixture of blood and excrement, dropping his torch as he hits the ground.

"Wait ... females right inside entrance, that's their way to ambush you as you come in," Bjorn says as he pulls away the loose branches covering the entrance. He steps one foot inside and swings his great axe at the left wall. The gray wall changes to a dark brown covered in blood. A large female bugbear collapses forward as Bjorn pulls out his axe.

"Look out!" Sargon warns as he sees another bugbear appear from the right-side wall. He jumps in front of the creature, thrusting his sword deep in the animal's chest. "RUN, ARI, RUN!" Sargon hollers as the bugbear lets out a roar of pain. It swings its mighty claw at the squire, hitting his shield and knocking Sargon back a few paces.

Swoosh. Ker chuck. Valagar lopes the creature's head off as he lunges forward into the lair. "Come on."

"Thanks," Sargon says as he regains his footing on the slick ground.

Ari sees the sacks change into small bearlike figures standing on two legs. Barrels and large sacks come to life as well—momma bugbears. The babies are cute until Ari sees their razor-sharp teeth. He gets up on his feet just as four babies try to jump him. He draws his sword and slashes down two of the vermin. Grabbing his torch, he swings it feverishly at the other two bucca-boos, lighting the fur on one of them. He quickly kicks it away as he runs toward Val.

A great roar sounds as the baby on fire drops dead.

"COME ON, BOY!" Val hollers as he runs toward his young retainer. All the walls seem to come to life, appearing to be nothing but eyes as the knight gets ever closer.

Sargon lunges farther into the *hornet's nest,* that's how he thinks of it. He's just a couple of strides behind Valagar now.

"Back up toward me, Sargon. Don't expose your back and keep mine protected. We have got them stirred up now, boy," Val laughs as he kills another bugbear in front of him.

Exel stands at the mouth of the cave, shooting arrows at bugbears as they attack the other fighters.

Bjorn drops his torch in the middle of the cave. It's too hard fighting one-handed with his two-handed axe. He swings at one, attacking him in front. The creature dodges the blow; but Bjorn hits another on his left. The bugbears are surrounding the barbarian. A creature at Bjorn's back is shot with two arrows fired at once, hitting it in the head and shoulder, interrupting a swiping attack. This gives enough time for Bjorn to dodge the swipe and swing around, loping off the monster's left leg. It falls on Bjorn's torch and bursts into flame. This in turn catches two more bugbears on fire and lights the whole cave as the flambéed bugbears drop in their tracks.

It appears that the cave is not as small as they once thought. It is about 100 feet across and vastly wider than the light can expose. Everyone also sees that the stench of death is from far off to the right of the cave, where dead bugbears are piled up and half eaten. It is apparent, too, that there are more than fifty bugbears in the lair.

The bugbears shield their eyes from the bright fire. Ari takes advantage of the pause and fights his way to Val, killing a few more bucca-boos along the way. His escape is stopped by a large momma bugbear that swipes the young boy in the back, tearing through the soft leather armor.

"NOOOOOOOOOOO!" Val hollers as he bashes the bugbear in front of him with his shield, knocking the creature back. He throws his sword, piercing the large mamma bugbear through the head as Ari falls, dropping his sword and torch as he hits the ground. He is quickly overtaken by six bucca-boos; the creatures tear off the young man's leather armor and eat him alive.

"Oh NO. NO. AAAHHH." Ari cries in agony while swinging his arms wildly, but to no avail. One of the creatures at his neck bites through his throat.

CRUNCH. CHOMP. CHOMP. SMACK. SMACK. SMACK.

CRASH. Sargon hurls the flask of oil onto Ari's torch as all the bucca-boos and bugbears burst into flames, including the ones between Val and Ari. All the bugbears surrounding the retreating fighters, but not before the one Val knocked back takes a swipe at the unarmed knight. His attention is on his dead retainer, and he's knocked unconscious.

Bjorn rushes to his aid, chopping the bugbear in the back. Then he goes to help Sargon carry the knight out.

"Let's get the hell out of here," Sargon assures as the two grab Val under each shoulder and retreat to the entrance.

"Look at this happy horseshit," Silverfish says, sitting up from Barbye's warm lap as he spots bugbears storming out an adjacent hole about sixty yards north of their resting spot.

Bellgrad turns away from Meg, hearing Silver's comment. He draws his sword and charges the creatures, grabbing his shield along the way.

"Girls, climb up out of harm's way until the danger has passed," Father Yor instructs as he stands next to a tree with low branches.

Meg and Barbye comply as Silverfish joins Bellgrad.

"Where's Chan?" Barbye asks as she looks at the spot where the monk had been resting.

"Here, milady," Chan answers from the tree they are about to climb up with his hand outstretched for her to grab.

"Thanks," Barbye says, grabbing the monk's hand. Barbye is amazed at how strong Chan is; the shorter man literally sweeps her off her feet and swings her to a nearby branch.

"Thank you," Meg says as she gets pulled up the tree as well.

"HAH!" Bellgrad hollers as he attacks the closest bugbear as others rush from the lair. He slashes, disemboweling the animal while dodging swiping attacks from two others.

"Heads up!" Silverfish announces as he firebombs the exiting monsters from atop a huge boulder above the entrance with an oil grenade—an oil flask with a lit cloth wick. The grenade quickly engulfs about six exiting bugbears and bucca-boos, three of which fall back inside the hole.

PSST. PSST. PSST. Silverfish hears a noise from inside the lair.

"Ah, hell! FIRELINE! FIRELINE!" Silver hollers as loud as he can, knowing it to be a crag emitting vapors from the ground just inside the lair. He dives off the rock, away from the hole.

KABOOM.

Chapter XCVIII
The Aftermath

"Swil wer ... awe woo wotay?" Silverfish hears some muffled words from Barbye as his ears ring. He is facedown in the snow-and-dirt mixture, and his left arm is hanging off next to him. At first, he thinks he's in bed. But as he slowly lifts up his head, he gets a shock; he is lying next to a twenty-foot drop-off. He quickly rolls a couple of times to his right then onto his back. He sees light glistening through some snow-covered tree branches, briefly feeling a sense of peace.

Barbye runs to his side, grabs his hand, and kisses it as she kneels next to him.

"Wow ... what happened?" Silver asks, shaking his head as the ringing subsides. He sits up and is met with a tender kiss.

"You saved Bellgrad's life, that's what ... he dove for cover after you hollered and just before fire shot out of the cave and exploded."

Barbye smiles lovingly at her man.

"Is everyone okay?" Silver asks.

"Everyone except the bugbears, little man," Father Yor answers with a smile as he extends a hand. Silver grabs hold and pulls himself up to his feet.

"Whoa!" Silver says in astonishment, seeing the whole bugbear lair caved in. He eyes Sargon, Valagar, Bjorn, Elof, and Exel standing on the other side, looking slightly scorched but alive. "How long was I out?" Silver smiles as he brushes snow and dirt from his hair.

"Oh, just a few minutes, dear," Barbye says as she waves at

the others.

"Are all the bugbears dead?" Silver asks, still getting his wits.

"Just a handful ran off. The others were still in the cave. Any that survived the fire were crushed by the cave-in," Bellgrad says as he walks up.

"Come on, let's go get the others." Father Yor brushes debris off Silver's clothes as Meg and Chan join the group.

"MMMuah." Meg gives Silver an exaggerated kiss on the cheek.

"Thanks ... What's that for?" Silver asks with a confused look on his face.

"For saving my man." Meg smiles as she looks at Bellgrad. He glances back at her and smiles.

"How many bugbears were in the cave?" Chan asks.

"Too many to count. Can you walk?" Bellgrad asks as he steadies Silver.

"Oh, I'm all right. Just a little dazed from the blast," Silver answers as he starts to walk.

"How did you know there was a fireline in the cave?" Bellgrad asks, walking beside Silverfish.

"I heard it hissing. You didn't hear it?" Silver asks, picking up the pace.

"No, I guess I was too preoccupied with fighting those nasties." Bellgrad smirks. "I'm glad I heard you, though. That fire shot out about twenty feet from the hole. I would have been burnt to a crisp if I hadn't dove for cover. I know those bugbears where I was standing earlier were torched," Bellgrad answers as they approach the others.

"I guess the cave-in plugged it off. I don't hear it hissing anymore," Silver says.

"Sargon, are all of you okay?" Father Yor asks as the group gets closer to the fighters.

"We're alive. We made it right to the entrance just as it blew. It shot us about fifteen feet outside," Sargon says as he looks around.

"Where are the horses?" Meg asks.

"Probably halfway to Missionwise by now," Elof answers with a slight laugh.

Sargon whistles loudly.

A distant whinny is heard as Tantor answers his master's call. Just then, Silverfish and the others arrive.

"Ari is dead," Val states as he rests on a fallen tree. His face is marred by deep claw scratches, and the cape on his back is burned. He rips it off as Father Yor approaches.

"Oh, how horrible!" Barbye exclaims.

"I was wondering. I just figured he was going after the horses," Bellgrad states.

"He and Elof were stupidly investigating the cave, unaware they were in a den of death. Even I did not know those creatures could shape-change that well. I should have kept a closer eye on them. In any case, we were overwhelmed when we tried to rescue Ari. He couldn't get to us, and we could not get to him before he was eaten alive," Val somberly states. "I tried to get to him, but I failed."

"Hey! We all tried to reach him," Sargon says to the glum knight. "We all failed. It was his time—there was nothing we could do. When it's your time, it's your time."

"Oh, that's a load of horseshit!" Valagar fires back as he slams his fist into the fallen tree beneath him. "Sorry, Father," Val adds as he eyes Yor.

"No need to apologize, Val," Yor says.

"What is wrong with you?" Bjorn asks angrily as he looks at Val, Sargon, and Father Yor. "You should not disgrace his death with sadness."

"How can you say that, you barbaric pig? Don't you have any feelings?" Barbye goes to sit next to Val and comfort him.

"Feelings are for women. I know, I know, 'twas a horrible way to die. But he still died with honor. He went down fighting. This ensures his way to the Hall of the Fathers," Bjorn states stoically as he beats his chest with his sword hand.

"You are very wise, Bjorn, although not very sympathetic," Father Yor states as he hands the knight a vial. "Here, drink this." He goes on doctoring Valagar's facial cuts with a salve. "But you are both right. Ari should be riding the golden chariot about now to the Hall of Heroes, or Hall of the Fathers. Whichever you want to call it, he's going to Volutus directly and not the netherworld. Marxbaq is good not to keep the dead waiting; you two know this." Yor eyes Val and Sargon, and both men nod in recognition.

"Mmm, cabbage juice, but I don't have a hangover," Val says, sounding confused after downing the elixir.

"You like that? Yuck! He gave me that skunkweed earlier too. I didn't have a hangover either," Silverfish says.

"Does your head hurt, Lumpy?" Yor asks

"No ... now that you mention it." Silver smiles as he rubs his head.

Father Yor glares at Silver. "Too bad it can't help with your rudeness, ungrateful pup."

Silver sticks out his tongue at Father Yor, earning him a smack on the back of his head.

"Ouch."

"Be nice," Barbye says as she sits back down next to Val, glaring and pointing at Silver like a mother disciplining a child.

"For the most part, our fates are sealed. The thread is woven at the time of our birth. Yahmar does hold the threads of all of us; he can lengthen or shorten them as he sees fit, unless Lauralye was holding them," Yor continues, shaking his head.

"Who is Lauralye?" Val chuckles at the slight comedy of Silverfish and Barbye.

"She is Yahmar's most trusted archon. She holds on to the threads whenever Yahmar needs to rest or travel, but she cannot alter them," Yor explains. He finishes, wipes his hand on an old cloth, and wraps the vial of salve with it.

"Really? I didn't know that," Val says.

"There are some priests who believe the weaves cannot be altered, but I beg to differ," Yor continues, eyeing Bellgrad. "And there are still others who believe that Lauralye can change them as well because she is sister to the fates—the two maidens that spin the threads of life ... So how many bugbears were in the cave?" Yor changes the subject as he stashes his kit in a pocket of his robe.

"As many as fifty, I saw," Bjorn answers.

"Oh my!" Meg sounds shocked.

"They scattered when we set a bunch on fire," Sargon says, setting a hand on Val's shoulder.

"Father, I still don't see what your explanation has to do with what happened. Who held the threads of life ... what difference does it make? Ari is still dead," Val says, watching Yor.

"Oh, but *you're* not, are you? Nor anyone else. Perhaps you are looking at this all wrong, Val," Yor says with a grin. "Maybe it took Ari's death for the gods to get involved."

"Maybe so ..." Val nods.

"Besides, you will see him again after you pass this world, which I hope is a long, long time from now," Yor continues.

"We will see you there too, Father," Sargon smiles as he sits next to Val.

"No, I will be attending Yahmar's court in the Palace Vespar like all the other priests. But it is next door to the Hall of the Fathers," Father Yor contends as he taps a finger on his lip.

"Well, hopefully, I won't need to make that decision for a while."

"Thanks for getting me out of there. I thought I was done for," Val says, eye to eye with Sargon.

"Well, it was a group effort," Sargon explains. "Bjorn helped me drag your heavy carcass out of there. Without Exel and Elof shooting the occasional bugbear out of our way, we wouldn't have made it to the entrance."

"Elof? He's never shot a bow in his life," Val says with a raised eyebrow.

"He's a natural. That young man shot as good as me when you were being dragged out," Exel says, leaning against a nearby tree.

"Really? I guess I can't be too sore at Elof then." Val smirks.

"Let's get back to the camp, get our stuff, and then make way to the castle," Sargon states as Elof stands, holding all the reins and lead ropes of the horses.

"Uhh," Val groans as he gets to his feet and seems to wobble a little. Sargon and Barbye brace him on either side. "That smack on my head was worse than I thought, and my back is sore as well."

"I'll ride with him," Barbye says as she pats the knight's breastplate. "You won't get too lonely, will you, Silver?"

"I'll get over it." Silverfish smiles.

"I'll keep him company," Yor states as he climbs on his horse.

"Gee, thanks," Silver says sarcastically, smiling.

Father Yor says a prayer for Ari. Then Bjorn tosses an open vial of holy water to the area of the lair where the young man died.

"Before we go, I just want to say thanks for coming after us," Silverfish says, almost misty-eyed.

"Oh, I feel a tear." Val laughs. "You're welcome, fathead. I'm sure you would have done the same for us." Val jumps on his horse with help from Elof.

"No, he wouldn't have," Father Yor and Barbye say at the same time. Barbye mounts the horse behind the knight.

"Boy, I really feel the love around here," Silver says as he swings onto Meg's horse. "But you're right, I would have said good riddance." Silver bursts out laughing.

"Hey," Meg interjects as she mounts behind Bellgrad.

"Well, not you, sweetheart." Silver smiles and winks at Meg. "I would've come after you."

"Yeah right. I had my rescuer come for me," Meg says, hugging Bellgrad. Sargon scoffs as he glances at the maiden with a raised eyebrow.

"Oh, please," Bjorn says from atop his horse as he rolls his eyes and mimics vomiting.

"I guess we know who is going to be sleeping alone tonight." Barbye smiles as Silver cuts a sharp glance at his girlfriend.

"Let's go," Sargon stoically states as he mounts Tantor after retightening his saddle. "Elof, go on ahead and alert the castle of our upcoming arrival."

"Yes, sir." Elof spurs his horse.

"I really like this knight," Val says with a slight snicker. "Reminds me of myself when I was his age."

"Yes, I like him too. He'll make a great leader," Barbye says from behind Val.

"He already is," Val adds.

They all ride back to the campsite, where they are met by two men on foot.

"Febor! How are you, my friend?" Silverfish smiles and jumps off his horse, moving to hug the young swordsman. "Everyone, this is Febor ... the Simpleton?"

"The Splendid," Febor corrects, smiling and shaking his head.

"Simpleton—isn't that your surname?" Val smirks at Silverfish from atop his horse.

"Right. Febor the Splendid," Silverfish announces, ignoring Val's comment.

Febor bows to the group.

"This is my friend Friar Truvey," Febor introduces the other man.

Everyone acknowledges him as all dismount except Val and Barbye.

"You are a priest of Elktor," Father Yor surmises, eyeing the pine tree on the young man's shield. He gathers up the bedding and such from their camp.

"I am a friar not yet a priest, Father," Truvey says.

"Well, you are most welcome to travel with us," Father Yor says. "Friends of Silver can't be too bad."

Sargon and Bellgrad look at each, other rolling their eyes, then they look to Bjorn.

"What? Another holy man can be a good thing, especially one of the forest," Bjorn says. Bellgrad and Sargon nod to each other.

The group quickly polices the camp and then head to the castle. They keep the horses at a casual walk, mindful of Val's condition.

"You are a monk of Fairwind?" Truvey questions as he walks next to Chan.

"What a genius," Silver says, riding just a few feet ahead.

"Shut up, idiot," Yor scolds. "You'll have to excuse our friend's rudeness. He didn't know Chan was a monk of Fairwind either.

"I am Chan," Chan answers Truvey with a nod.

"I saw another Euguadian in the town of Jaymar a few weeks back. There are not too many of your people from the far east in these parts." Truvey says to Chan, inquisitive.

"No, not many."

"So what brings you to this part of the world?" Truvey asks, keeping pace with the monk.

Images flash through Chan's mind: his monastery back home; a man tied to a chair in a vacant warehouse; a shipwreck and the dead body of a small girl about six years old on a beach tangled in the wreckage. He shakes his head, "I'm here to one day become a diplomat."

"Oh, okay," Truvey says as he eyes Febor and shrugs his shoulders Knowing that all monks study to become diplomats. It's like saying grass is green or the sky is blue.

"The netherworld ... what's that? I heard you all talking about it earlier," Silver asks as he looks around the group.

"You want to answer that, Chan?" Father Yor asks over his shoulder.

"It's where we all go after our death to be judged by my god, Fairwind, who sits on his throne on his porch of judgment. Unless you are fortunate enough to die valiantly and go directly to the Hall of the Fathers like they were saying earlier. Or if you are a devout follower of Elktor and die protecting the forest or in his name, you could go to the Forests of Iund to live in peace forever. You will be picked by the Great Spirit horse ..."

"Named Zarthanon," Truvey interrupts. "Oh, my apologies."

Chan nods. "Upon your death and whisked away to Iund or taken to the netherworld by said spirit horse." Chan continues, ignoring the interruption.

"The same is true for Hefnor's followers, except the devout followers can live among the clouds of Iund forever. And are transported there by a flying unicorn named Parthegus," Father Yor adds.

"What about someone like me who doesn't follow any god?" Silver questions.

"I thought you followed Yahmar?" Yor asks. "You and Barbye go quite often to the temple."

"She does. I just take a nap," Silver smiles.

Father Yor just shakes his head.

"Your fate will be decided by Fairwind, depending on the kind of life you have led," Chan explains.

"I guess that kinda narrows it down, doesn't it, Silver?" Father Yor says. Silverfish shrugs, unconcerned.

"After we get ourselves settled in at the castle, I think you, Bellgrad, and myself will go after those bugbears that got away before they kill anyone else in the morrow," Sargon says, approaching Exel at the side of the group, letting the others slowly pass.

"Sounds good to me," Exel answers then swiftly rides back to the front of the group.

"Does this bring back any old memories ... me drinking too much mead?" Val says softly to Barbye as they ride ahead of Silverfish, in line just behind Meg and Bellgrad.

"Yes, but I remember it was Rokian Swill, not mead. Well, that was a long time ago," Barbye softly snickers at the memory. "That won't happen anymore. I'm spoken for now."

"Pity." Val smiles as they ride on, Barbye's arms wrapped around him.

"Hey—"

"He's a good man and you deserve to be happy," Val interrupts.

"Thanks." Barbye smiles as she lays her head on Val's back.

They ride on for another two and half hours without any encounters. Exel keeps a close eye on the group and the woods around the road as they travel, riding ahead occasionally to make sure there are no more surprises. When they arrive at the castle, soldiers are waiting at the gatehouse with Elof and an older gentleman in armor.

"Lord Calador, this is Sargon," Val says wearily as he points to the young squire.

"My lord," Sargon says, dismounting quickly and standing at attention with his sword arm across his chest.

"Oh, I like him!" Calador looks at Val then back to Sargon. "Come here, my boy." Calador opens his arms to Sargon.

Sargon proceeds forward into a strong hug. "'Tis a horrible ordeal what happened to your family. Your father was like a brother to me … you are all welcome here … my castle is your home now," Calador says and nods at the soldiers, who help Barbye down and then Val.

"My lord, I am Febor the Splendid," Febor says as he bows in front of Calador.

Calador nods and smiles in recognition.

"Corporal Bellgrad, good to see you," Calador smiles and his eyes light up to see the young soldier. "How are you, son? I heard you were in a bad way after a bear attack."

"I am fine, sir, thanks to Father Yor," Bellgrad says, standing at attention.

"Relax, son. Go inside and rest yourself," Calador says as he shakes the young soldier's hand.

"Everyone go on inside. My men will tend to your mounts and gear. Even you, Silver, my little court jester."

"Funny," Silver says as he dismounts.

"Oh, I like it. Court Jester Lumpy!" Father Yor says as he dismounts and smiles at Silver.

"I knew it … I knew it." Silverfish fumes with a disgusted look on his face until Barbye runs her fingers through his hair.

"Hush, lover," Barbye says softly as she grabs Silver's hand and walks with him through the gatehouse and into the castle courtyard.

Chapter XIX
Payback

Morning!" Calador says as he walks into the castle's dining room, at which point Sargon, Bellgrad, and Febor stand up from their breakfast.

"Morning, sir!" All three men say in unison as they stand at attention.

"Please, sit ... sit." Calador smiles as he motions with his hands for the three men to take their seats.

The three fighters go back to their food as the rest of the group, minus Silverfish and Val, enjoy a fine setting of eggs, liver sausage, and biscuits with maple syrup.

"Have you sampled the coffee?" Calador asks as he sits at the head of the table.

"No. It smells nice, though," Sargon answers as the others also shake their heads.

"Try it, it's quite wonderful. Comes all the way from the island of Krau," Calador says, enjoying a cup poured by his servant as he motions to the other servants.

"Wow, this is a treat. I have never had this before," Father Yor states excitedly as a servant pours a cup before the priest.

"It is a lot stronger than tea." Sargon smiles as he sips the hot liquid.

"Tasty," Bellgrad says.

Meg and Barbye nod in agreement. Bjorn makes a grimace after he samples the drink but says nothing as he feels the gaze of Father Yor upon him.

"I haven't had this since I was home ... is quite expensive," Chan says.

"Oh it is, but it's worth all the Sivs I paid for it. There is some maple sugar on the table and cane sugar for anyone to use in their coffee, and there's cream as well." Calador points to the items on the table, and Bjorn grabs some sugar.

"So where is our little friend?" Calador asks Barbye.

"He's not really an early riser," Barbye says. Meg giggles in the chair next to her then gets elbowed.

"What?" Calador asks, looking at the two women.

"Nothing, my lord ... he should be down soon." Barbye smiles as she briefly glances at Meg then back to Calador.

"Okay ..." Calador smirks as he receives his food.

"How is Val this morning?" Sargon asks.

"Resting well in his room, sire. Elof took him some breakfast earlier," one of the servants answers.

"He will need to rest for a couple of days. He was fairly beat up, mainly from the explosion. Must've been a hell of a blast—shook the ground here. Well, after a few times in the hot baths, he will be as good as new," Calador says.

"You have baths here?" Sargon asks as the others look on, puzzled.

"Oh, yes, down below. A wonderful Rokian invention. We also have running water," Calador answers.

"Baths should not surprise me. The servants showed us the gabinettos last night like they have in Missionwise. I've never seen a single castle with that before," Sargon says, describing the restrooms.

"How old is your castle, milord?" Father Yor asks.

"Please call me Cal," Calador says. "It's five hundred years old. It was built by my great-great-great-great-grandfather Du'tesh. He was a powerful Rokian general."

"Wow. I knew this place was old, but not that old." Yor smiles. "Du—"

"What is that awful stench?" Silver interrupts as he walks into the room with bed-head while fanning his face.

"It's you, little man, I smelled it when you walked in the room," Bjorn answers.

"Funny," Silver says as he makes his way to a chair next to Barbye.

"Yes, you smell like a bugbear." Chan smiles from his chair next to Bjorn, across the table from the couple.

"Really?" Silver pauses, believing it for a second, then he scoffs and rolls his eyes.

"It's coffee. Try some." Calador offers.

"No thanks, smells like vomit."

"Silver!" Barbye says, blushing with embarrassment.

"You'll have to forgive him, Cal, he would not know a good thing if it hit him in the nose," Father Yor apologizes.

"Oh, I know how he is, he hasn't changed a bit." Calador laughs. "I would be worried if he had."

"Quit touching me!" Silver brushes Barbye's hand away from his head as she straightens out his hair. "Sorry, I just didn't get a lot of sleep last night ..." Silver yawns then quickly cover his mouth as he cuts his eyes at Barbye.

POW! Silver receives a hard slap to the head.

"Ow! I'll have some tea, please." Silver winces. "Okay, okay ... I'll try some of that coffee. There, you happy now?"

"I've known Silver since I was your age, Sargon." Calador laughs. "He was friends with my father. How old are you now, Silver?"

"Sometimes I feel like I'm a thousand years old. I'm twenty-eight." Silver yawns again as he receives a cup of coffee.

"You are not. I just got through telling Sargon I knew you when I was his age. How old are you, Sargon? Sixteen?" Calador asks, and Sargon nods. "I'm sixty now."

"I knew your father before you were born, Cal. I am twenty-eight in elf years, but that's equal to three hundred and ninety-two human years." Silver sips his coffee, grimaces, and grabs some cream and sugar. "It takes fourteen of your years to equal one of mine," He explains as he receives some breakfast.

"Whoa. I guess I forgot how long your people live," Calador states as he shakes his head, looking somewhat stunned.

"That is a long time. Well, for us it is." Sargon raises his mug for more coffee. A servant arrives and refills his cup.

"Yeah, I have seen a lot of good people grow old and die," Silverfish says.

"Not to mention the women," Bjorn says with a sinister laugh.

"You better hush if you know what's good for you, mister!" Barbye says as she points at Bjorn. Silver smiles.

The rest of the group laughs at the free entertainment.

"So what's on the agenda for today, milord?" Sargon asks.

"First things first. I have some papers drawn up signifying that you are my squire," Calador says as he motions to one of the servants, who disappears from the room.

Sargon watches the man leave and finishes his breakfast and coffee, leaving the liver sausage. "Was there something you needed me to do?

"What's on your mind?" Calador asks as the servant returns with a bone scroll case.

"Well, I figured we would go hunt down those six bugbears that got away yesterday." Sargon points to all the fighters at the table. "I fear they could kill some of the local farmers around the area, and most definitely their children."

"I don't see a problem if you think the five of you can take them out," Calador says as he receives the scroll.

"You gonna eat that?" Silver asks, looking at the liver sausage on Sargon's plate. He shakes his head no, and Silver pounces on it like a cat.

"On horseback? Please!" Bellgrad adds to the conversation.

"They will go back to the area where the lair is by habit for a few days. But if we wait too long, they will be gone," Exel adds.

"Well, count me out!" Silver says. "I had enough of them yesterday."

"I didn't say you, squirtal," Sargon says. "We need *real* men on this mission."

"I got your real man hanging," Silver bounces back.

"Silver!" Barbye says, shaking her head. "Sorry, Father, Friar."

"Oh, I'm used to that knucklehead," Yor says as the friar laughs.

"Father, I thought it would be best if you and the good friar stayed behind. You as well, Chan. I plan on us riding hard and being back here midafternoon, and we don't have time for your running, and Father's not a good enough horseback rider to keep up. Besides, it would not be safe for any of you going without some armor," Sargon explains.

"Oh, I have a cure for that already in the works," Calador states. "I have some chainmail for you, Yor. I want you to put it on and wear it around the castle to get used to the weight. And for you, Chan, I have some soft leather. It won't slow you down. I hear you dance around a lot when you fight." Calador winks at Chan as the monk lightly nods and smiles.

"Sounds good to me, Cal. I don't like the feeling of being vulnerable like when those creatures came out of their hole and all I could do was climb a tree. That's quite all right, Sargon. Go on and go. I eyed an ash tree outside of the castle, and I need to make some more elixirs," Yor says.

"Good. We might need some when we get back." Sargon smirks. "Here, I'll take that," he adds, holding his hand out to Cal.

"Keep it with you at all times. You cannot be jailed for your family or anything else as long as you have it," Calador says, handing the scroll in the bone cover to Sargon. He also places some coins in Sargon's hand. In turn, the squire feathers them in his one hand, out of sight of the others—six J'avins.

"Aren't you going to look at the scroll?"

"I'll look at it when I get back. Let's go." Sargon smirks at Calador as he puts the bone container and coins in his belt pouch, putting on his armored gloves as the other fighters start to leave the table.

"Wait. Father, aren't you going to give them a blessing before they go?" Calador asks as the fighters pause.

"No," Father Yor answers as he continues eating.

"What? Why?" Calador asks, shocked as is everyone in the room.

"Yeah, why? I thought that was your thing?" Silverfish asks while he stuffs his face like a pig.

"No need. They will have success," Yor answers as he raises his cup for more coffee, while everyone's eyes are on him. "Okay, okay, I'll tell you before I get flogged. I saw signs this morning. Guess I should've mentioned it earlier."

"You think? What did you see?" Sargon asks.

"I saw a hawk with a snake, and then I saw a cat with a rat and a spider with a moth," Yor discloses.

"What a crock of sh—"

Barbye interrupts Silver with a pop upside the head. The biscuit Silver was eating gets knocked out of his hand and falls on the floor.

"I was eating that!"

"We are gone." Sargon smirks and shakes his head at Silverfish's antics.

The five men walk out to the castle courtyard then over to the stable where they all see their horses saddled and geared up.

"Good job, Tymothy!" Sargon states as he hands the young stable boy two Pens.

"You already planned this out ... I should've figured." Bellgrad smiles as he mounts his horse.

"A good leader doesn't wait for things to happen—" Sargon is interrupted as he gears up. He takes the additional sword hanging on his saddle and throws it across his shoulder, attached to a long belt. He grabs a mace tied to the saddle and runs the handle through his belt on the left side just behind his sword. He throws a belt with three sheaved throwing knives across his other shoulder, and finally grabs his shield and mounts up.

"Yes, I know, he makes things happen. I heard that from your father too." Bellgrad smirks as the other men mount up. "Are you sure you have enough weapons?"

"I have a crossbow as well on the other side ... What? I just like being prepared. I'm not going to be caught off guard again," Sargon says as Bellgrad and the rest of the men smile at the squire.

"You have been awful quiet this morning, Splendid," Sargon says as they make their way through the castle gatehouse.

"Just taking it all in, sir." Febor smiles.

"More like not speaking unless spoken to. You must have served," Bellgrad says.

"Yes, three years in Jaymar," Febor answers.

"Three years? You don't look much older than me," Sargon says.

"I'm eighteen. I lied about my age. I had a drunk for a father ... it's a long story," Febor explains.

"Say no more—just glad to have the help. Let's ride," Sargon says as he spurs Tantor.

Exel takes point as they all run their horses for a time on the road leaving Calador's castle. Then they trek cross-country as the road ends through the snow-covered mountainous terrain. They ride hard for about an hour and a half. Then Exel signals the group to stop as he jumps off his horse.

"What was that other sign he gave?" Sargon quietly asks the group as they look at Exel, who is about one hundred feet ahead.

"Get off our horses," Bjorn says while he dismounts as Bellgrad and Febor nod.

I've got to go over these signs with the scout. Sargon thinks to himself as he dismounts and realizes he is the only one who doesn't know what Exel signaled. The fighters all walk their horses to Exel, keeping as quiet as possible. Exel is squatting down, looking ahead as the other men approach.

"Look at that small hill," Exel softly says as he motions with his head.

"I don't see anything," Sargon says, squatting next to the scout.

"Well, there is one over there. The lair is just beyond that hill. I'm going to get a closer look. Leave your horses," Exel says, pulling an arrow from his quiver and proceeding forward in a slight zigzag pattern. He drifts from tree to tree, and a light snow begins to fall. The men all watch Exel as the scout gets closer to his target.

"Let's go," Bjorn says softly as Sargon walks over to Tantor.

"Guard the horses, okay? Guard the horses," Sargon tells his horse.

"What's he doing, asking his horse's permission?" Bjorn says as they wait for their leader.

"No, he is just making sure his horse doesn't follow," Bellgrad answers.

"Okay," Sargon says as he gets back to the others.

"Are you sure you don't want to tuck him in?" Bjorn asks.

"Funny. Let's go," Sargon says, motioning Bjorn and the others forward as he covers the rear.

Bjorn proceeds forward with great axe in hand and two-handed sword over his back, followed by Bellgrad with his sword and shield, Febor with a sword in his right hand and a dagger in his left, followed by Sargon with sword and shield. Exel proceeds forward after seeing the fighters approaching. Bjorn stops, motioning the others as he watches the scout in the distance. Bjorn signals the others to approach as he waits, and Exel disappears behind the small hill. As the others approach Bjorn, Sargon peers over his shoulder to see if they are being followed by either his horse or something else. Luckily for him and the others, they are not being followed by either.

Bjorn puts his finger over his mouth in a shushing motion as he signals everyone forward. The fighters quietly proceed toward the hill, walking through three-foot snowdrifts.

"Look out!" Bjorn hollers as he lets his axe fly toward a bugbear that came out from behind a tree as Sargon passed by. The creature dodges the axe as it hits a tree, nearly splitting it in half. "Damn, he's fast," Bjorn adds as he pulls his two-handed sword off his back.

Another bugbear shape changes and appears from a tree next to Sargon, trying to slice the knight with its sharp claws. But the creature hits the steel of his shield instead, doing nothing but breaking a couple of the animal's nails.

Sargon bashes the animal in the face with his shield, momentarily stunning the bugbear. "Nice try, you sneaky bastard." Sargon jabs his sword through the animal's gut, almost lifting it up. Then he twists it and pulls it out as the bugbear falls lifeless in the snow.

"Hhhaaahhh!" Bjorn charges the creature with his two-handed sword but misses as the creature runs off through the deep snow. "Oh, that's how you want to do it, a little hide and seek." Bjorn smiles as he loses sight of the creature that possibly blended into one of the trees. "I like games."

Rooooaaaarrrr! A bugbear hiding in the snow two feet from Bellgrad grabs the young soldier's right leg, pulling it out from under him, knocking him down and jumping on top of the soldier all in one motion. Bellgrad covers himself with his shield. He slashes wildly with his sword. The bugbear dodges the young man's many attempts.

Whoosh. Kerchunk. Sargon decapitates the creature with his sword. "Try dodging that!"

Whoo, whoo, whoo. Thud. Febor throws his dagger up in the trees, hitting another bugbear that was apparently going to attack from above. The creature falls to the ground only to find Febor there to finish it off.

"Come here little buggy," Bjorn taunts as he proceeds forward, following the creature's prints in the snow. *A child could follow this stupid creature*, Bjorn thinks to himself

"Well, that was unexpected," Sargon says, helping Bellgrad up from where he is buried under the body of the bugbear he was fighting.

"Everyone okay?" Exel asks from about ten feet away, startling the trio.

Sargon puts his finger over his mouth and points to Bjorn, who is still inching along.

"Apparently they caught our scent or heard us. That noisy armor doesn't help," Exel explains.

"Bellgrad and I would've been gutted like fish without this armor," Sargon interjects.

"I found the bugbear I saw earlier, nailed it with some arrows— four, to be exact. Something else—"

A bugbear appears out of nowhere, interrupting Exel and

taking a swipe at Bellgrad from behind, hitting his plate armor and knocking him off balance. He falls headfirst into the snow. Exel lets go of three arrows. Two of them hit—one in the eye and the other in the back of the head as the creature turned to run. The animal drops in its tracks.

"I saw tracks of four more, perhaps a hunting pod." Exel softly explains as he climbs a tree.

"Humph." Sargon scoffs.

"Come here, little friend, Uncle Bjorn has some love for you." Bjorn gets a swipe attack from behind a tree, the creature's claws missing his face by inches. "You not friend I saw earlier," Bjorn says, stabbing his two-handed sword through the bugbear's gut. He twists the blade and it then pulls it out. "But I play with you too. Got lots of love," Bjorn continues as he makes his way to where the tracks end. Bjorn rears his sword back.

Thwack! An arrow pierces the hidden bugbear's head, hitting the creature in the eye. The monster roars in pain as it stands up from a crouched position and changes back to its brown color, blood gushing from its eye socket.

Whoosh. Kerchunk. Bjorn decapitates the creature then shoots Exel a dirty look over his shoulder.

"Oh, I'm sorry, did I steal your thunder?" Exel laughs.

"You could've shot me," Bjorn hollers.

"Not likely. Quit your crying, there are four more we have to find," Exel says as he jumps out of the tree.

"Oh, okay, not so bad then." Bjorn smiles as he makes his way to retrieve his axe that is stuck in the tree where he chopped the creature's head off.

"Yeah, there are more to kill. You're welcome, by the way," Exel says as he shakes snow off his cape.

"Yeah, yeah, maybe I bake a cake," Bjorn says.

"I'm surrounded by children," Sargon mumbles as he whistles

for his horse.

Tantor and the other horses run to the fighters and stop next to Sargon.

"Your horse is well trained. I would have had to catch mine if I was here alone," Febor says as he grabs the reins of his horse.

"Oh, that's nothing, he killed an ice bear," Bellgrad says as he mounts his horse.

"Really? Wow." Febor sounds astonished.

"Yeah, and I have castle I want to sell," Bjorn says sarcastically as he makes his way back.

"Were you there? No, I saw it," Bellgrad says.

"Well, he just finished what I started," Sargon says as he checks the tension of his saddle then mounts his horse. "I stuck an axe in the bear's thick skull, he just drove it in the rest of the way. Saved my life."

"Amazing!" Exel says on top of his horse, waiting for the others.

"He saved me too, ran for twenty miles or better to the healer," Bellgrad says.

"Let's go!" Sargon smiles at the memory.

They all fall in behind Exel, who follows the tracks in the snow from atop his horse. This goes on for the better part of an hour until they all come upon a farmhouse with smoke coming from the chimney. A bugbear runs off the front porch, limping as it goes.

"Don't follow. It's trying to lure you away like a mother bird would from its nest," Exel clarifies as Bjorn's confused look disappears.

"Ride around back," Sargon orders Bellgrad and Febor while dismounting. He nods and rides on around the other side of the house. "Stay here and guard the front. I'm sure our friend will return," Sargon says as he looks at Bjorn, who jumps off his horse and runs to the porch with axe in hand.

Sargon and Exel burst through the front door to find a farmer facedown with a deep wound in his back. The man is lying in a puddle of his own blood in the middle of the dirt floor. Exel rolls the man over to show the poor guy has had his face ripped off as well. Apparently, he did not go down without a fight, though; the farmer has an axe in his hand but did not stand a chance against these faster creatures. It's obvious he faced more than one opponent. Neither fighter makes a peep, though Sargon is seriously steamed. He manages to keep his composure and just nods then motions forward as he stands ready with his sword and shield. They both proceed forward as they hear screaming and crying coming from the back room. Quickening their pace, they come upon a bugbear eating what appears to be a little girl off to the left as they enter the kitchen; a much larger bugbear stands a few steps directly in front of them.

"YOU SON OF A BITCH!" Sargon loses all composure, he throws his sword up in the air, catching it by the blade just inside the hilt then throwing it like a spear at the bugbear to his left. The creature has already spun around to make its way to the door as the sword spears it in the back. Sargon takes his shield and throws it at the much larger bugbear, an obvious alpha male, hitting it on the back of the head. The animal hesitates and looks over its shoulder at the squire. Sargon lunges at the creature, which has turned its attention back to its prey—a mother who is cornered and protecting her other daughter. "Oh no you don't!" Sargon pulls the creature away just in time before it lands a bite. He throws the bugbear with all his might into the wall behind him and actually launches the creature midair. The creature busts through the wall and rolls another five feet.

Exel goes after the other bugbear running for the back door.

The creature smashes its head on the low overhang of the back door. The stunned creature falls backward, driving the sword all the way through. "GET OUT!" the scout yells to the mother and daughter, who scurry out the door. "COMING TO YOU, BELLGRAD!"

"Okay," Bellgrad hollers back.

The alpha male looks at Sargon coming toward it with a mace in his left hand and a sword in his right, then at its prey as they run from the house.

"Hahaha. *Ni fydd eich arfwisg diogelu chi* (Your armor will not protect you)."

The creature laughs at Sargon.

"*Ni fyddwch yn lladd dynol arall* (You will not kill another human)," Sargon tells the surprised bugbear, eyeing the silver hue of the creature's claws.

"*Ni allwch gael i ffwrdd, rydych darn llwfr o cachu* (You cannot get away, you cowardly piece of shit)," Sargon adds as he inches closer.

"*Dydw i ddim yn bwriadu rhedeg* (I'm not planning on running)," the creature says, slowly getting to its feet. "*Rydw i'n mynd i fynd â chi allan o un i un* (I'm going to take you out one by one)."

"Oh, enough of this," Sargon says and charges the creature. He swings his sword, and the creature dodges the blow but manages to land a hard hit with the mace to the middle of the bugbear's back.

SSSCCCRRRAAAPPPEEE. The bugbear swings around, tearing into Sargon's breastplate with its claws. Four deep gouges pierce the armor.

"Whoa!" Sargon says in amazement as he sees the peeled away steel fall to the dirt floor.

RRROOOAAARRR. The creature bellows in pain as Exel cuts a

deep gash into its back. Then all in one motion the bugbear backhands Exel, sending the scout flying across the room, then it spins around, dodging another sword swipe from Sargon.

By this time Bjorn walks through the front door, Febor through the back door. Sargon jabs with the sword rather than slashing, cutting the creature as it spins to dodge. It is only a superficial wound with minimal damage.

Well, it's something! Sargon thinks to himself. The creature hits Sargon upside the head, dislodging the squire's helm and sending it falling to the floor. The young man is seeing stars momentarily but manages to land a hard blow with his mace to the side of the creature's head, sending blood flying through the air.

RRROOOAAARRR. The creature steps back in pain and swipes blindly at Sargon, who easily dodges the blow. The creature looks toward the front door but sees the barbarian there with his great axe in hand. then glances at the back door but sees the soldier there with two weapons in hand.

The creature attempts to jump through the thatch roof overhead, Sargon is too quick. He drops his weapons, grabbing the large bugbear and body-slamming it to the ground, landing on top of it. The creature attempts to bite Sargon's face, but instead gets a hard hit to the face by an armored fist dislodging a few teeth.

With its mighty arms, it throws Sargon off about five feet away then manages to swiftly get to its feet as Bjorn now approaches.

"STAY WHERE YOU ARE! He's mine," Sargon barks as he jumps to his feet. With that, Bjorn backs up to the front door, making sure the creature doesn't get away. Exel stands off to the side with a bloody lip and a couple of bruises, but otherwise okay.

SNAP. The creature tries in vain to bite at Sargon's face. But the courageous squire moves out of the way in time.

POW. Sargon lands a haymaker punch to the bugbear, breaking its jaw and knocking it back. Sargon doesn't let up. He proceeds forward, attempting to hit the creature again. But instead he gets grabbed around the neck by the bugbear, shape-changing its right claw into a hand and holding Sargon about two feet off the ground.

Sargon feels the strength of the monster as it squeezes hard on his windpipe, almost causing him to black out. He grabs the creature's arm with his left hand as he attempts to pull a knife off his back with his right, but he cannot reach it.

Bjorn throws his axe, but the bugbear spins out of the way, almost putting Sargon in harm's way. At the same time, Febor also attempts a rescue but receives a hard kick from the creature, knocking him to the ground. Exel jumps on the creature's back with a dagger in hand but gets flung off by the bugbear's free hand, nearly hitting the axe sticking in the wall.

Luckily for Sargon, all the shucking and jiving has drawn attention away from him. The bugbear has loosened his grip on Sargon's neck, and he can breathe a little. Sargon grabs the creature's right arm with both hands bracing himself and kicks the bugbear with all his might in the chest with his armored boot.

POP. The creature releases Sargon, holding its broken ribs with its paw, now back to its natural shape. It drops to its knee, clearly winded. Sargon coughs and breathes freely while on his knees. He holds his hand up for everyone to stop; he wants to finish off this monster.

Febor gets to his feet and guards the back door, noticing the bugbear eyeing a way out. Exel grabs Sargon's weapons and throws them on the dirt floor in front of Sargon. Bjorn stands fast, blocking the way out the front door. Sargon grabs his mace and sword, slowly making his way to the creature. He's winded too.

Sargon musters all his strength and willpower, attacking the creature again. The monster spins, dodging an attack from the mace but opening an opportunity for Sargon with his sword hand. But instead of dodging sideways, the creature lunges forward as it brushes the sword away from its body. Sargon gets knocked down and drops his sword. The bugbear lunges toward the front door with all its might as Bjorn rears back with his two-handed sword, but he gets knocked back by the determined creature too.

"DAMN IT!" Bjorn hollers and swings at the bugbear as it runs away.

"WHAT THE—" Sargon coughs as he rushes to his feet.

"Sorry, he is faster than—

POW. POW. KAPOW! The sound echoes outside, interrupting Bjorn. He and Sargon emerge from the cottage and bear witness to the large bugbear getting three double hind kicks from Tantor about twenty feet away. The last kick sends the creature flying back about five feet and hitting a tree hard. The horse rushes over to the creature, rears up, whinnies, and commences to trample the animal into the ground.

SNAP. SNAP. POP. SNAP. KERSPLAT. KERSPLAT. SPLAT. SPLAT.

Sargon rushes to his horse, and the others follow.

"Easy there, old man. I think you got him," Sargon says softly as Tantor snorts and stands trembling, looking at his master. The horse instantly calms down as Sargon pats his friend on the nose and grabs the reins. Sargon looks down to see the mangled body and broken skull of the creature ground into mush by the gigantic hooves of Tantor.

"No wonder he asks horse's permission," Bjorn says in shock.

Chapter XX
Returning to Castle Du'tesh

hey have returned, sire," a guard from the main gate-house reports to Calador in his study.

"What time is it, son?" Calador asks as he looks up from a parchment he is reading.

"Nearly nightfall," the soldier answers.

"That will be all, Sergeant."

"Sir." The soldier puts his fist to his chest in a salute then heads back out to the gatehouse.

Calador gets to his feet and makes his way to the courtyard in time to see Sargon and the other fighters arrive through the main gate.

"By the gods!" Calador says as he sees blood splatter all over Tantor's front legs.

"No worries. It's bugbear blood," Exel says as he hands off his horse to one of the stable boys.

"There won't be any bugbears around for a while," Sargon says hoarsely.

"What happened?" Calador says as he looks at Sargon's neck and damaged breastplate.

"He was nearly chocked to death by a very large bugbear. I was not there in the house to help. I was protecting these ladies here," Bellgrad says as he helps the mother off his horse. "My lord, this is Sylphie and her daughter, Kye," Bellgrad continues as he points to a little girl sitting in front of Bjorn on his horse. He hands the little girl to her mother on the ground. The little girl starts to cry as she looks back at Bjorn.

"I'll be along, little one," Bjorn smiles at the little girl. "My lord, we were with Sargon, but you know how fast those creatures can be, the last one we faced was an alpha male almost making lunch out of the two ladies. Sargon saved their lives."

"Ben, take care of them," Calador orders one of his soldiers, who nods and escorts the mother and daughter inside. "I would expect nothing less from Sargon. It's in his blood. Let's get inside—we have food on the table, and I'm sure you are all hungry." Calador puts an arm around Sargon as they walk up the steps to the hall.

"Hey, there are our heroes," Father Yor says as the fighters all arrive in the dining room. Meg, Barbye, and Friar Truvey clap. "Uh oh ... are you okay?" Yor asks as he sees the bruises on Sargon's neck and gouges in his armor.

"Who gave you the hickeys, Sargon? Did Bjorn finally express his undying love for you?" Silverfish asks as he walks in the room.

"Oh shut your pie hole," Father Yor says to Silverfish.

"Oh, don't make me laugh." Sargon laughs then coughs as he makes his way to the table. "I'm okay," Sargon adds while refusing help from Bellgrad and Meg, who try to help him sit. Meg hands Sargon a goblet of mead. "Thanks ... really, I'm okay."

Exel, Bjorn, and Febor tell the rest of the group the account of what went on as supper is served and before Sylphie and Kye arrive. After everyone has dined, Father Yor hands Sargon a flask.

"What is it?" Sargon looks at the glass flask with pieces floating in it.

"It's a healing elixir. It will help you with your throat."

"What's in it? Oh ... yuck," Sargon asks as he uncorks it and frowns in disgust at the odor.

"Smells like elf's underarms." Bjorn, sitting two chairs away, fans his face.

Silver raises his hand but quickly acts like he's combing back his hair after he receives a glare from Father Yor.

"It's Dog Rose," Yor explains.

"Smells more like dog—"

"Nah uh uh," Barbye interrupts and warns Silverfish with a wagging finger.

"Drink half now and half when you get up in the morrow," Yor says, giving Silver a dirty look.

Sargon drinks half the liquid. "Ugh, it tastes as bad as it smells," Sargon says with a sour look on his face as he chases it down with mead.

"Not too much of that." Father Yor points at the mead. "Oh, and you need to drink it after breakfast, or it could give you the running off."

Silverfish laughs then stands on his chair, holds his butt with both hands, and mimics running as he says, "Oh no, oh no, oh no. Better not put on your armor till midmorning, Sargon."

The whole room erupts with laughter.

POW. Barbye pops Silver upside the head. "That's just mean."

"I'm getting mighty tired of—"

"You better hush if you know what's good for you, lover," Barbye interrupts, whispering into his ear and then kissing him on the cheek.

"Yes, ma'am," Silver says and sits down.

"Silver, my little court jester, you keep me young," Calador says through tears of laughter. Calador turns to Sargon. "Why don't you go soak in the baths? The water should still be warm. The servants put the fires out only a little while ago."

"Sounds good." Sargon smiles and stands up to leave.

"Hang on, I'll go with you," Exel says as he stands and walks with Sargon.

Calador catches the two as they leave. "I have some business to discuss with you in the morrow."

Sargon nods.

"Hey, what's all this noise? Sounds like a party, and I wasn't invited."

"Val, come join us." Calador smiles. "We still have some food here."

"No, thanks, I ate already." Val slowly walks to the table with Elof by his side. "But I will take some of that mead." Val smiles as he sits in the chair that Sargon was sitting in.

"I haven't eaten yet," Elof says.

"Hang on, I'm coming too," Bjorn says as he jogs over to Sargon and Exel. "Elf annoys me."

"Hey, Sargon. Look out, I saw lust in his eyes," Silverfish yells from across the room as he points to Bjorn.

"See what I mean? He never lets up," Bjorn complains.

"You bring some of that on yourself. But don't let his demeanor or size fool you, that little guy may damn well save your life one day, maybe even all of our lives," Sargon tells Bjorn as they walk out the door and down the hall to the steps. Two servants follow the three men as three other servants scurry down the hall.

"He will have his uses," Exel adds to the conversation as the stairs end about ten feet away from a thirty-foot square pool with steam still lightly rising. The smell of jasmine and other fragrant flowers fills the air. Sargon sees the flowers floating in the water.

"Lord Sargon, I am Niles, your personal valet," one of the servants that followed them down tells Sargon. The young man is maybe a couple of years younger than him. "Do you want to use the changing room?"

"Are you kidding me?" Sargon looks at the boy.

"Then let me help you with that, milord." Niles grabs Sargon's armor and helps unbuckle it.

"Let me help you as well," the other servant says to Bjorn as he helps the fighter out of his armor. He then goes to help Exel, but the pathfinder has already shucked off his armor and clothing and is headed to the pool.

"Ahh, the water is nice and warm," Exel says as he sits on an underwater seat just beyond the three steps that lead down into the bath.

"Nice." Bjorn enters the water after getting undressed then dunks himself completely. "This reminds me of the hot springs up in the mountains. Of course, they had a fowl odor to them."

"Sulfur ... oh, that does feel good," Sargon agrees as he squats down in the five-foot-deep pool and rubs his right shoulder under the water.

"What?" Bjorn asks.

"It smelled bad because of the sulfur." Sargon smiles. "You know, the yellow substance that smells like rotten eggs."

"Oh, right," Bjorn answers.

"Would you men like some soap?" Niles asks, holding out three chunks about half the size of a brick.

"What is that?" Bjorn asks.

"It is for cleaning your body," Sargon answers as he nods and holds his hands out to catch. Exel follows suit.

"Wow, soap. Calador is indeed very wealthy," Exel says.

"That may be true, but he also has a candlemaker working here. That is where the soap comes from."

Niles throws the men each a bar. "Would you like me to bathe you, milord?"

"Hell no, leave us be ... Wait, I appreciate the offer, but no thanks." He realizes Niles was not being rude; he is just doing his job. Niles nods and walks up the stairs with the other servant.

"Just rub it all over yourself," Sargon instructs Bjorn, who looks confused.

"It appears the bugbear's claws managed to scratch you after all," Exel says, pointing at Sargon's chest.

He looks down to see superficial scrapes across it. "Huh, I hadn't noticed, but now that you mention it, it does kinda burn a little. Well, it could be a lot worse. How was he able to penetrate my armor anyhow?" Sargon says as he enjoys the warm water while soaping down. He looks around and spies some sponges next to the bath. He throws one to each of the other men.

"He had what is called iron claws. It's a rare mutation that happens when a creature has been drinking water from a stream that has a vein of iron upstream. Getting doses of iron for years, I suspect. Their teeth get the same way as well," Exel says as he scrubs down.

"Well, that was my first run-in with that. I will know next time to be more cautious when I see that silver hue." Sargon slides back and immerses himself in the water after soaping down.

"You are lucky it didn't kill you. I will not hesitate next time," Bjorn says as he bathes himself.

"I suppose that was stupid to try to take on that creature by myself. I was just so enraged seeing the other monster eating that little girl," Sargon says.

"Not stupid, understandable. I have been there too. But you just cannot fight a creature the same way as you would a man, especially an alpha male. They have no honor, so you cannot fight honorably. Not your fault, it is just the way you were taught to fight," Bjorn says and then dunks himself.

"Well, next time say something," Sargon says.

"Not my place. You are our leader," Bjorn says.

"Of course it is your place. I respect your advice."

"Okay, but all in all you fought well."

"I think you did a great job," Exel interjects. "We are all young, Sargon, even though some of us won't admit it. We all make mistakes with our inexperience, so don't beat yourself up. Great leadership takes time. Look on the bright side, no one died."

"True, not like Ari did the other day," Sargon says.

"We have already crossed that bridge. Besides, you were not leading the group that day," Exel says.

"Right." Sargon walks up the steps out of the pool and over to where his clothes were. "Where are my clothes?" Sargon looks at Niles, who has returned with fresh linen.

"I brought you clean clothes, milord. We will wash the soiled clothing. We also took all armor to your rooms." Niles hands Sargon a towel to dry off as Exel jumps into the pool on the far side.

Splash "DAMN!" Exel hollers as he surfaces, restraining himself from hollering more. "It's cold on this end. There is a dividing wall that separates the cold from the hot."

Bjorn climbs out of the hot side and walks over to where Exel jumped in. *Splash.* "Oh ... *hressandi* (refreshing)," he says after coming up from the frigid water.

"Refreshing?" Exel shivers. "Are you kidding? I knew it would be cold, but not this cold." Exel jumps out almost as fast as he jumped in. "Look, there is ice in it." Exel points then quickly jumps back into the warm side. "Ah, much better."

"You cry like a woman. I thought you were a pathfinder," Bjorn says, dunking himself again.

"Hey, I like the cold ... but not that cold," Exel says.

"There's a fire over there, cream puff," Bjorn says to Exel as he points to the far wall while bobbing up and down.

"Thanks, but I'm fine now." Exel makes his way out of the warm bath.

"Should I have the servants bring you a dress and apron?" Bjorn asks Exel while floating on his back.

"You would like to see me in a dress, wouldn't you, you sicko?" Exel says as he receives a towel from one of the servants.

"Not hardly," Bjorn says.

"Whoo hoo," Silverfish hollers as he runs into the room and to the pool that Bjorn is in.

"NO ... WAIT," Bjorn warns, but it's too late.

"ROCKFALL!" Silver yells as he tucks his legs under his arms and jumps into the pool. *Splash.* "HOLY SHIT THAT'S COLD!" Silver screams like a little girl as he emerges from the frigid water and dog paddles towards the stairs. Silver is shivering when Bjorn quickly pulls the elf out and sets him on his feet next to the pool like a child. Silver rushes toward the fireplace in the wall on the far side of the room containing a roaring fire.

"How can you swim in that? Look—there's ice floating," Silver says as he points to a small iceberg.

"Why didn't you warn me?"

"I tried, but you jumped in so fast," Bjorn explains as he makes his way to the stairs of the pool.

"According to Bjorn, the water is refreshing," Exel says.

"Refreshing ... my ass. That water is downright painful. I thought I was going to die." Silver warms himself by the fire.

"You weren't going to die." Bjorn rolls his eyes and climbs out of the pool. A young servant approaches with a towel.

"I am Kreel," the young man announces.

"So?" Bjorn says as he grabs the towel and dries off.

"I have your clothes over there." Kreel points to where Sargon is standing.

"How can that water be so cold?" Silver shivers as he continues to warm himself by the fire.

"It comes directly from an aqueduct fed by the Eye River,

which in turn is fed by the Shendo Mountains. You see, it exits out to the sewers quickly as well to keep the water from freezing and back out to the river. If the aqueduct freezes, we are out of water," Niles says as he goes over to attend to Silver.

"I'm fine." Silverfish looks up at the servant. "Thanks for savin' my bacon, Bjorn. I won't forget it."

"Thank me when I save you from a pack of goblins, or perqs or something. That water doesn't count."

"I could've drowneded," Silver says with sad puppy dog eyes.

"Right." Bjorn shakes his head.

"What was all that screaming, did someone get hurt?" Barbye asks, descending the stairs.

"No, it's just your husband there screaming from the cold water," Sargon says as he points to Silverfish.

"Oh, husband. I like the sound of that," Barbye says as she walks toward Silver.

Silver looks up with an expression of pure terror. "I almost froze in that water. Look, there is ice in it. Bjorn saved me." Silver points, ignoring Sargon's comment.

"Thanks for savin' my man," Barbye tells Bjorn as she wraps her arms around Silverfish, kissing his cheek and giggling as Silver whispers in her ear.

"Sure." Bjorn avoids gazing into Barbye's pretty eyes while he heads toward Sargon. He passes the squire, who is standing next to Exel. They are discussing scout signals, nodding as he walks by and quickly gets dressed, his clothes handed to him by Kreel.

Making his way up the stairs, Bjorn passes other servants. He opens the door and is startled by a servant girl in the room attending the fireplace.

"*Ég er Helga, Silverfish segir þú vildi eins og mig* (I am Helga. Silverfish says you would like me.)

Bjorn smiles as he closes the door.

Chapter XXI
Damsel in Distress

ess ... Jess ... no ... noooo." Sargon wakes in a cold sweat from another dream about his beloved. He sits on his bed with his feet on the floor, getting his wits back as he trembles slightly. A knock comes at the door of his chamber.

"Come."

Niles walks in with a cup of tea. "Here, milord," he says, handing it to the young nobleman.

"Thanks."

"Rough night?" He says, looking at Sargon's face and messy hair.

"You could say that. I could soak in a barrel of this," Sargon says as he gulps the tea, feeling like he got about two hours of sleep.

"I heard you shouting. Are you okay, milord?

"I'm fine. Tell no one, understood?"

"Yes, milord. That is why I came to wake you, so you did not disturb the others. Do you need help getting dressed?" Niles asks.

"Not since I was three. What time is it?" Sargon asks as he yawns.

"Sulo is about to rise. What about your armor?" Niles asks while pointing at an armor stand with Sargon's armor on it.

"I'm good, thanks," Sargon says as he hands his empty cup to the valet. Then he walks to the closet and grabs some pants and a tunic. He slides the pants on. "How did you know my size? These fit perfectly."

"'Tis my job, sire," Niles says as he helps Sargon pull the tunic over his head.

"Wow, I'm impressed."

"Thanks, milord." Niles smiles as he looks over the fit of the clothing, brushing fuzz from Sargon's shoulders.

"Since you are going to do it anyway, go ahead and grab my armor."

"Sure, milord," Niles grabs Sargon's breastplate, setting it aside and taking the chain mail tunic beneath. "You know, Garth the blacksmith can fix that for you." Niles points to Sargon's damaged breastplate. He grabs the padded shirt underneath the chain mail and takes it to Sargon.

"Thanks, but there is some pressing business I need to take care of today. Besides, I'm going to mend it myself," Sargon says as Niles slides the padded shirt over Sargon's head.

"You mend the armor?" Niles says surprised.

"Yes, I was taught by the best," Sargon boasts.

"But of course, milord," Niles says as he grabs the chain mail tunic and slides it over Sargon's head and over the padded shirt. Next Niles grabs the breastplate, unbuckling the leather straps and separating the two halves. He sets the front on Sargon's chest as the squire slides his arms into the plated sleeves of the armor. Niles pulls the backside across the squire's back, then fastens the pieces together. Niles grabs a pair of chain mail britches, wrapping some leather around Sargon's ankles to hold his pants down as Sargon slides his legs into the chain mail. Niles then goes and grabs the leggings and boots, setting the armored legs over Sargon's boots so the squire just has to slide his legs and feet through and into his boots all in one motion.

"Thanks, I got it from here."

"Milord." Niles bows then exits the room, taking the empty cup to the kitchen.

Sargon grabs his belt, with long sword in its scabbard, and belt pouch, buckling it as he goes for the door. He throws his shield over his shoulder and his helm on his head and then grabs his gauntlets along the way, tucking them under his left arm. Then he closes the door behind him. He walks downstairs and to the dining room, where he sees Exel at the table. The scout gives the squire a sign; Sargon returns the sign. Niles walks into the room and makes the sign as well.

"I know a little." Niles smiles.

"Very good. Do you know what it means?" Exel asks.

"Good morning."

"Excellent," Exel compliments.

"What are we having?" Sargon asks.

Exel signs again.

"It's too early for all that," Sargon says as he shakes his head while setting his shield and helm on the floor.

"Eggs," Niles says.

"Wow, you do know some signs!" Exel says.

"Coffee, milord," Niles says as he pours Sargon a cup.

"Thanks." Sargon sips the morning nectar.

"There's the early riser," Valagar says as he walks into the room and sits across the table from Sargon. "You look better. Those baths do wonders, don't they?"

Calador walks into the room, looking at Sargon. "Oh, good you are up."

Sargon stands at attention. "Morning, milord."

"Yes, yes, sit." Calador nods as Sargon sits back down.

"We have a problem. Beloges's niece has been missing for about five days now," Calador says as he lays a scroll on the table.

"That's terrible ... who is Beloges?" Sargon asks as Valagar snickers.

"Oh ... sorry. He is the overlord for the city of Jaymar," Calador explains. "This could go a long way to cementing allegiance between us, Jaymar, and Palton, if we can find the girl."

"The port city of Palton?" Sargon asks as breakfast is being served.

"Yes. Natanio, son of Helios, the lord of Palton, is due to marry the young maiden."

"I know Nate. You think they would stand with us against Vry?" Sargon asks.

"Well, if you know the guy, you tell us," Val says.

"I don't know. He must be going mad wondering where she is or if she is still alive. Was she kidnapped? Is there a ransom?" Sargon asks.

"We don't know," Calador says. "Nothing has been said of any ransom." Calador points at the message.

"Well, hell, she could be anywhere," Sargon says as a servant tops off his coffee.

"I doubt there would be a ransom. You see, there was a dead perq at the location where her wagon was attacked," Val continues.

"Hmm, so where was this attack?" Sargon asks.

"On the road halfway between Jaymar and the port city of Suva," Father Yor interjects as he walks in the room. "Sorry, I overheard you talking earlier, milord," Yor apologizes as he looks at Calador.

"Nonsense, Yor, you are part of Sargon's team. You look good in that chain mail, son," Calador adds as he looks at the priest.

"I like it. You will be wearing field plate before you know it, Father," Sargon smiles as he eats.

Father Yor rolls his eyes as he sits at the table, where a plate full of food is placed before him. "The couple's wedding will be at Missionwise, done by yours truly."

"You know Nate?" Sargon asks.

"Yes, very well. I imagine he is busy searching the area west of Missionwise," Yor answers.

"Wow, this is good rabbit," Sargon compliments between bites.

"Thanks," Calador says. "I forgot that you don't like pork. Then with what happen to your family, who could blame you. Tell the cook to come here," Calador tells one of the servants.

"You don't have to do it on my account," Sargon says.

"No, you are going to like this," Calador tells Sargon.

"Aye, you called for me, lord?" A large redheaded Kalamashian man walks into the dining room.

"Red, this is Sargon, my new squire."

"Pleasure to meet you, milord," Red says as he bows.

Sargon sits there somewhat awestruck. The man looks just like Zeth. "You don't know a blacksmith—"

"Zeth, aye. Second cousin. Makes me sad what hap'n to him and his family," Red interrupts.

"You know his daughter is here," Sargon continues.

"Aye, I saw the young lassie yester morning," Red says.

"This rabbit is excellent. What did you season it with?" Sargon interrupts.

"Just a wee bit o' sage, young master. Well, I got to get back to it. Glad to meet you, laddie," Red says and scurries off.

"Wow. Small world. Thanks, I needed that." Sargon grins then gets back to his breakfast.

"Back to business," Calador says. "Val tells me that the perqs you all fought the other day had gold and silver on them."

"They like the shiny stuff," Exel joins in.

"There may be more to it than just that," Calador says.

"Could be. It's worth checking out," Sargon says. "They must've had a lair close to where we ran into them. You going to join us, Val?"

"No, I have to get back to my castle, then I figure I'm going to meet up with Natanio and check out the road south of Missionwise."

"So be it. I'm going to get everything ready to go," Sargon continues as he sees the elixir he drank the night before. He downs the other half of the horrible liquid then washes his hands in a bowl of water at the table, grabs up his shield and helm, and then exits the room, headed outside.

"I think he is a welcome addition around here," Calador says as his squire leaves.

"I agree. Do you think he is going to be ready to take on the games?" Val asks.

"Someone say games? Dice?" Silverfish asks as he walks into the room.

"No, Valor, girdlehead—of which you have none," Val answers.

Calador laughs. "Yes, I think so."

"What, that I'm an idiot?" Silverfish asks.

Calador and Valagar bust out laughing.

"Yes, you are an idiot," Chan says as he walks in.

Calador laughs so hard he almost falls out of his chair. "Oh my little friend, you are not an idiot. A fool perhaps."

"Well, I'm glad I can entertain," Silverfish says as he stands on a chair at the table, getting a plate of food while Chan sits next to him getting food as well. "Darconia sounds good to me."

"What are you talking about?" Chan asks.

"What Lumpy is saying is that the games are in the capital city of Darconia," Febor explains. "Super crowded streets, not to mention the arena packed to capacity where someone of his nature can have the time of their lives gambling, pickpocketing, and just causing general mayhem."

"I don't pick pockets," Silver protests. "Not anymore," he adds under his breath.

Bjorn walks in and sits at the table, getting breakfast. He looks up to see Silver grinning across the table at him. He just nods at the elf as Helga walks behind the barbarian's chair, dragging her hand across his shoulders as she walks by and into the kitchen.

"He needs to start practicing," Val tells Calador.

"Practicing what?" Silver asks as he stuffs his face.

"Joisting," Val answers.

"How good is he with a lance?" Calador asks.

"I know a few years back he unhorsed Nate," Father Yor chimes in. "I don't know the full story, but Nate and Sargon were fooling around one afternoon, both had decided they wanted to joist. Sargon knocked Nate clean off his horse, breaking the young man's arm in the process. Their friendship has been at odds ever since. Perhaps this can bring them together if his bride to be is found."

Sargon goes to the stable and leads Tantor out of his stall. "Tymothy, I see you are hard at it this morning," Sargon compliments the stable boy, who is busy feeding the other horses. He grabs a brush and begins brushing his horse's back. He opens up his belt pouch, grabs a little bag of tobacco, and stuffs the chaw in his left cheek.

"He has already ate, milord. I washed the blood off his legs yester night," Tymothy says.

"Hmm, looks good," Sargon adds as he looks at his horse's front legs. "Where is his armor?" Sargon spits as he finishes brushing the saddle area of Tantor.

"Locked up in the back room ... here," Tymothy grabs a key on a chain around his neck and hands it to the squire.

"That was your cue to go and get it for me," Sargon spits as he hands back the key. "I have something I need to check out."

Sargon taps the left front hoof with his boot. "Toss me that shoeing hammer hanging on that post over there." Tantor raises his hoof up and Sargon puts it between his legs. He catches the hammer midair as Tymothy lightly tosses it to him. He taps the shoe to make sure it did not work loose after his horse stomped the bugbear last night. *Still good and tight,* Sargon thinks to himself. He goes around to the other front hoof and does the same thing. *Good.* He thinks to himself as he lets the hoof loose.

Tymothy is too caught up watching Sargon.

"The armor and saddle. Today, boy!" Sargon says impatiently. *Spit.*

"Oh, sorry, sir!" Tymothy conveys as he hurries to the back room. "I just have never seen anyone other than the blacksmith concerned about their horse's shoes."

"Is everyone in this country an idiot?" Sargon asks.

"I don't know. I don't think so," Tymothy says, Sargon's saddle in his hands.

"Well, the stable boy at Missionwise had the same reaction when I shod my horse the other day," Sargon says. "Have you ever shod a horse before?"

"No, sir. But I saddle them."

"I will show you sometime. Although I don't recommend it with armor on," Sargon says as he pulls off his gauntlets and reaches inside his leggings to rub his legs. "You can pinch the inside of your legs if you are not careful, like I just did." *Ahh, much better,* Sargon thinks to himself as he stops rubbing his legs and puts his gauntlets back on.

"Here is your saddle, milord," Tymothy says as he sets the saddle on the top board of the stall that Tantor is standing in front of nibbling on some hay through the boards. He takes

Sargon's saddle blanket and places it on the horse's back, and then he grabs the saddle.

"Here, let me have that. Tantor is taller than you," Sargon says as he grabs the saddle from the young stable boy.

"I can do it," Tymothy protests.

"I know you can, like you did the other day, but I'm here and I need to cinch it tight. Don't want our boy here getting a saddle sore," Sargon says as he tightens the saddle. "Besides, sometimes this smart guy holds his breath and you have to go back and recheck it. Can you put his barding on?"

"Sure."

"Then get those other five horses ready," Sargon says as he points to his party's horses. "Do you have any ponies?"

"You mean for Silverfish?

"Yes."

"He won't ride one. It makes him feel smaller than he already is," Tymothy explains.

"Then better make it six," Sargon adds as he wonders about how the small elf gets on and off the horse without help. "Don't forget about our packhorses." Sargon walks back inside to the dining room. Once there he sees everyone eating. He looks at Bellgrad, who is busy conversing with Meg. "I don't know if Calador has clued you in on what we need to do.

"Yes, he has. I'm almost finished."

"Same here," Meg says.

"You are not going ... it's much too dangerous," Sargon says to Meg. "Where is Barbye? He asks as he scans around the table."

"She is in the kitchen helping out," Silver answers.

"Good. Finish up there. I have your horses ready. I need you on this one, Father. If we find the girl, she may need your help. Always expect the worst. Friar, I think you should stay behind as well," Sargon continues as he looks at Friar Truvey, who just nods in recognition.

"I want to help," Meg says as Bellgrad stands up and wolfs down his food.

"Just be ready in case we find this girl. What is her name, milord?" Sargon asks as he looks at Calador.

"Emma," Calador says, consulting the scroll in front of him.

"Well, perqs are not like bugbears. Unless they have nothing else to eat … they don't usually eat humans. So there is a good chance she could be alive, even after this long of a time. That's not to say that they might not have had their way with her. Disgusting animals … Let's go," Sargon says as he walks out of the room. Bellgrad and the other men follow behind.

Sargon mounts up and grabs the lead rope of his packhorse after he settles himself in the saddle. He curiously watches Silverfish mount: the elf grabs the reins of his horse and ties them in a knot. He then jumps, landing his left foot in the stirrup, grabbing a rope that is in front of the saddle, tied around the horse by Tymothy. Silver then jumps up, landing on his stomach in the seat; he swings his short legs around and sits himself up all in one motion. The squire is impressed.

"That's pretty slick, Silver, but your horse is not moving. You would be in a mess if your horse took off running before you were in the saddle," Sargon says.

"That has happened before. That's why I tie the reins and have this rope to hold on to," Silver says as he unbuckles the left stirrup, then buckles it way up high. He sets it down then slides his foot in it. The right stirrup has already been adjusted. "I get off the same way … yes, I know it's time consuming. It is just what I have to do to make it work," Silver says to Sargon as the others mount up. "I just have to make sure I'm not close to any trees when I jump off."

Silver smiles, and the others chuckle at the elf as he mimics hitting a tree with his head.

The group leaves the castle and rides for a couple of hours to the area where they were the previous day, except for Chan, who runs the whole way. Exel, riding lead, keeps a sharp eye out for any bugbears they may have missed and is relieved to see there are none.

Sargon pulls off his left gauntlet, putting his hand on his chest with three fingers pointing to his right. This is the sign for east; Exel nods then starts heading eastward toward the coast. They continue on this course for about an hour; there is a sweet, acrid stench in the air. Exel stops and waits for the others.

"What is that smell?" Sargon asks.

"That's why I stopped. It's horse—actually, horse innards. Stomach, to be exact. They cook it with the grass fermenting in it. That is the sweet smell. Perequine love it; it's a treat to them. I need to ride ahead to see where it is coming from. Hard to tell in these dense woods." Exel quietly says, "At least the wind is in our favor."

"Boy, that's rank," Bjorn comments.

"What is that smell?" Silver asks as he rides up from behind.

"Shhh. It is possibly the perq's lair," Sargon says quietly, shushing the elf.

"I thought maybe you soiled yourself after drinking that swill Father Yor gave you." Silver looks at Sargon and gets a dirty look from Father Yor.

"Funny, where did you get that Dog Rose anyway, Father? That flower does not bloom until greenway?" Sargon asks, speaking of the spring.

"I got it from Sven," Father Yor answers.

"Who is Sven?" Sargon asks.

"He is Calador's candlemaker," Father Yor explains.

"How old was that mess?"

"Oh, probably a couple of years," Father Yor answers.

"Great, you gave me a rotten elixir to drink."

"It worked, didn't it? The marks on your neck are gone, and your speech is clear."

"True," Sargon clarifies as he feels his throat.

"What are we waiting on?" Chan walks up.

"Exel is looking ahead," Sargon answers as he looks at the impatient monk.

The pathfinder rides ahead about a hundred yards, then quietly walks his horse back to the group.

"There is an old tower ruins ahead. There are two perequine at the entrance standing guard on both sides of the door," Exel reports. We can ride up to where I was and leave the horses. There are no pit traps around the area.

"Let's go," Sargon commands.

The group proceeds forward to the spot that Exel was at earlier, the edge of the woods about fifty feet from the tower. Everyone dismounts and arms themselves while Chan waits, leaning against a tree and looking bored.

"Stay ... watch the horses," Sargon quietly tells Tantor.

"Take them out," Sargon orders Febor and Exel. Exel shoots an arrow through a perq's head, nailing it to the wall as Febor simultaneously shoots his crossbow at the other perq, hitting it in the left eye and dropping the animal.

Another perequine walks out, seeing the fighters, and lets out with a loud squeal.

That perq is shot with two arrows, one through the left eye, and the other glancing off the creature's thick skull between the perq's eyes. The eye shot drops the animal.

A very large perq walks out with a maiden in front of him as a human shield, holding a dagger to her throat.

"Gollwng eich arfau," the large alpha male says.

"What did he say?" Sargon asks, looking at Exel, Bjorn, and Chan, who are walking closer to the perq. "I couldn't make that out."

"Gollwng eich arfau ... nawr," the perq says again in a very commanding tone.

The men all have a bewildered look on their faces.

"Damn it, Chan. You are our linguist. What the hell did he say?"

"I speak human languages, not animal," Chan says as he creeps a little closer.

"Bjorn?"

"It is too broken to understand," Bjorn says as he watches the animal.

"It's too guttural for me to understand., Exel says, standing with an arrow notched.

"Maybe we should have brought the good friar after all," Febor adds.

"Help me," Emma pleads as she begins to sob. Her dress is tattered and torn. She has dried mud on her face, looks like she has not eaten in days, and smells really bad.

The frustrated perq grabs the maiden's dainty right hand, slicing through her palm with the dagger.

Emma shrieks in pain. Chan kicks the dagger from the perq's hand.

The quick-thinking monk pulls her away from the animal. Bjorn grabs the maiden in his arms and runs away. Chan catches the dagger and thrusts it into the perq's left eye. The soft leather armor is a welcome addition for Chan, but it is useless against head attacks as the perq backhands the monk, knocking him to the ground.

Sargon and Bellgrad lunge toward the alpha male with swords in hand. The perq pulls the dagger from his eye and slashes at Bellgrad.

SSSCCCRRRAAAPPPEEE. The dagger does not penetrate Bellgrad's armor.

The soldier swings his sword, aiming for the head. The hit deflects off the thick skull and hits the animal's armored shoulder, doing little to no damage.

"HAH," Sargon hollers as he jabs his long sword through the breastplate and into the belly of the perq, pushing the creature into the wall of the tower and knocking his sword back out. Sargon twists the blade as it exits the creature.

Whoo, whoo, whoo ... thud. Bjorn is hit in the back by an axe thrown from inside the tower.

Father Yor runs over to Bjorn, opens his book, and mutters some words. What looks like a mini temple forms around them. They seem to be hidden by the pillars of the temple. Their images appear to be blurry as if looking through old glass.

Sargon slashes at the throat of the perequine but does not cut its head off like he expected. The animal is wounded nonetheless. *Must be dull from the breastplate*, Sargon thinks to himself.

REEEEEHHHH, REEEEEHHHH, REEEEEHHHH. The wounded perq shrieks out in pain as it grabs its throat.

Sargon sheaths his sword and grabs an axe he has tied off on his back and commences to finish off the creature. In three or four hacks, he chops off the perq's head.

Febor the Splendid shoots the perq inside the tower with his crossbow, hitting the creature in the shoulder and sending it into a fury. The animal charges the young soldier with a club. Febor quickly cocks his light crossbow and reloads a bolt just as the monster reaches him.

He points and shoots, hitting the animal between the eyes at point-blank range. The bolt goes through the creature's skull, dropping it in its tracks.

"Oh, I'm sorry you didn't get to hit me," Febor says in baby talk as he looks at the dead perq on the ground.

BAM! Not paying attention to his surroundings, Febor is not so splendid anymore as he is blindsided by another perq who flanked him and cracked him in the head with a club. The soldier has a helmet on, which saves his life, but he got his clock cleaned nonetheless as he falls to the ground unconscious.

Whoosh ... Kerchuck. Bjorn lops off the head of this perq with his axe just as it's about to finish off Febor. "Oh, that's gotta hurt!"

He kicks the creature's head into the surrounding woods. Then he sees two arrows in the back of the perq as the body falls to the ground.

"Oh, I'm sorry. Did I steal your thunder again?" Exel smiles as he looks at Bjorn.

"Shhhh, baby boy taking a nap," Bjorn says as he points to Febor on the ground.

"Are you going to just leave him on the ground there?" Father Yor asks as he walks up.

Bjorn shrugs his shoulders.

POW. POW. Father Yor hits the unconscious soldier in the head with his club.

"What the hell are you doing?" Exel asks as he looks down and sees Febor waking up.

"Oh, my head!" Febor says as he holds his head where Father Yor hit him.

"What kind of healing is that?" Exel asks.

"The painful kind." Bjorn laughs. "Looks like baby boy is not the only one sleepy bye," Bjorn continues as he points to Sargon carrying Chan.

He sets him at Father Yor's feet. Yor pulls a small vial from his robe and waves it under Chan's nose. The monk immediately shakes his head.

"Ugh, what is that?" Chan asks as he wakes up.

"Sulfur." Yor smiles as he helps the young monk get to his feet.

"You did a real good thing, Chan, the way you saved Emma," Yor compliments.

"Thank you," the young girl says from behind Father Yor.

"Well, lookie here!" Exel says as Silverfish walks up, leading his horse with the other horses following.

"Hey, I'm a lover, not a fighter," Silverfish says.

"Okay, lover boy, why don't you go see what is inside," Sargon says as he points to the tower.

"I can do that," Silver smiles as he walks to the tower door.

"Remember, anything valuable comes to me," Father Yor reminds as Silver's smile disappears.

"Father, I want you to take Emma back to Du'tesh. Exel, you and Bellgrad go with the good Father. Chan, you have done enough. Go back with them as well. Take Silver's horse. Squirtal can ride back with me. Bjorn, lover boy, Febor, and I are going to check out this tower."

"There are two dwarves inside—one male and one female. The male has been making them armor. The female cooks for them," Emma explains. "Blathaon is the male's name, and Alberfa is his wife's name. They are prisoners like me."

"Okay, Emma, you ride with me," Bellgrad says as he jumps behind his horse's saddle, leaving the young maiden the seat as he pulls her up with one arm.

"Father, what was that back there? Looked like a miniature temple," Sargon asks Father Yor as he mounts his horse.

"It's the Pillars of Sanctuary. It keeps enemies from harming us while I do my work. It's a powerful spell and can only be used every three days or so," Father Yor says.

"Is the girl hurt, Father?" Sargon asks.

"She will be fine. She just needs food, rest, and a good bath."

"Go, we will be along shortly," Sargon says as Exel jumps on his horse and leads the party away.

Chapter XXII
Mopping Up

Sargon goes to the doorway of the tower. He can hear hammering on an anvil from inside. Looking in, he sees Silverfish talking with a female dwarf who is busy cooking in a huge cauldron beneath a chimney. Silverfish looks in the cauldron and then makes a mad dash outside. The elf starts blowing chunks right outside the tower door.

Silverfish then walks over to Sargon. "Sorry, that stuff she is cooking is awful."

"Exel said what it was earlier. Why did you look?"

"I guess I couldn't help myself. I know, I know, curiosity killed the cat."

"And makes elves puke." Sargon laughs.

"Alberfa says her husband is up on the next floor—there are two perqs guarding him. She also said that there are more prisoners in the dungeon below."

"Let's go upstairs first," Sargon tells the elf as Bjorn and Febor stand nearby, ready for anything.

The old square tower is in bad shape; the wood beams look like they could give at anytime. Dirt seems to fall with every strike of the hammer. Stone stairs hug the walls of the old keep, only wide enough for people to ascend one at a time.

Silverfish creeps up the stairs, remarkably silent. Sargon motions Bjorn to follow. Then he motions Febor to follow behind Bjorn as the squire covers the rear.

The three fighters reach the room to see two dwarves hammering out a breastplate on an anvil. A perq is standing next to them with his back to the fighters. Suddenly the creature turns and throws its axe at the trio. The axe whizzes by Febor's head and into the wall behind him. The soldier raises his loaded crossbow and fires, shooting the animal through the left cheek and into the back of the animal's throat. The perq drops to the floor dead, blood pouring out of the monster's mouth.

"You are pretty handy with that," Sargon compliments.

"Thanks, lots of practice." Febor smirks.

The dwarf doing the hammering points with his eyes toward a tall cabinet on the far side of the room. Sargon catches the clue and points to Bjorn and then to the cabinet.

Bjorn, with axe in hand, rushes over and knocks the cabinet against the wall. This in turn trips up the perq hiding behind it. It roars with a loud squeal as it pushes the cabinet back to the barbarian; the beast rushes out only to get shot center mass by Febor's crossbow. Bjorn pushes the cabinet off himself and swings his great axe. He chops off the snout of the perq then spins around and splits the creature's skull, dropping it to the floor.

"Are there any others?" Sargon asks sharply.

"Maybe more upstairs," Blathaon says as he points to the ceiling, still in shock at the butchering before him. "My brother is down in the dungeon in a cell."

"We will get him after we finish cleaning up," Sargon says as Silverfish searches over the dead perq.

"Wow ... J'avins." Silverfish feathers out the three gold pieces in his hand to Sargon.

"Keep it," Sargon says as he points upward.

Silverfish nods while stuffing the gold in his right boot.

Silver creeps up the stairs to the next floor as Bjorn follows the elf and Febor reloads his crossbow then follows as well.

"Wait for us before going after your brother," Sargon tells

Blathaon, who has grabbed up an axe and nods in agreement.

Sargon makes his way up the stairs to see Bjorn pulling his axe from the body of a dead perq. Another perq close to Bjorn strikes with an axe at the barbarian. Bjorn dodges, and the perq's axe sticks in the floor.

WHOOSH. Thud. Bjorn's attack cuts off the creature's right arm as the monster attempts to retrieve his axe from the floor.

WHOOSH. Kerchunk. Bjorn spins around and chops off the perq's head.

The room is filled with several straw beds. Silverfish is rummaging through the straw.

"I have more J'avins and some Sivs." Silver shows the coins as Sargon just nods. "Look at this!" Silver holds up some polished copper coins. "Looks like someone was passing them off as gold—sneaky," Silver says as he stows away the booty.

"Like Exel said earlier, they like the shiny ... they are too stupid to know the difference," Sargon says as he notices a trunk on the far side of the room. "Go check that out."

Silverfish moves to obey the command. "It's locked," he reports.

"Like that's going to stop you," Sargon says as he looks at the elf.

"Whatever are you talking about?" Silverfish looks up innocently.

"Oh, don't give me that; Father Yor clued me in on some of your exploits," Sargon says, not buying the innocent routine Silver is trying to pass off.

"Hey, this lock has a poison trap in it," Silver says as he looks inside the lock.

"Now how would you know that, Mister Innocent?" Sargon smiles.

"Mister Innocent my ass," Silver mumbles.

"What?" Sargon asks.

"Nothing." Silver grabs some small tools from his belt pouch and starts meddling with the lock. "You see there is a small vial inside? If not opened with the key, it could break open and poison someone trying to get into this trunk."

"Well, can you pick it?" Sargon asks, getting impatient.

"Like I pick my nose ... okay ... there." The lock springs open. The elf carefully sets the lock on the floor then starts feeling around the seam of the lid.

"What are you doing now?

"Checking for more traps," Silverfish says as he finishes. "All clear." He opens the trunk slowly. There are some bottles, a book, and a bag of coins. "Nothing but papers in there. Here is a book of some sort." Silverfish hands Sargon the book as he closes the lid.

"This is some kind of ledger, someone else has been involved in all this and using the perqs to do all their grunt work. There have been a lot of people traded through this tower as slaves. Hmmm ... take the rest of the contents and put it on my packhorse. That includes the money bag ... did not think I saw it, aye." Sargon laughs.

"The rich get richer and the poor get poorer," Silver grumbles.

"Let's get those prisoners down below," Sargon tells the fighters. As he leads the group down the stairs, Blathaon and his dwarven companion join in. They all make their way to the dungeon. They can hear the bleating of goats and smell their stink as they descend.

As Sargon hits the bottom step, a perq lunges at him with an axe. Sargon's shield blocks the blow, pulling a pick from his belt to return the attack. The pick punctures through the breastplate. He pulls it out and hits the creature in the face, the point of the pick stabbing through the creature's thick skull. Sargon pulls the pick free from the perq's face, blood gushing from the wound. The creature blows blood out its snout, spraying Sargon's full helm and chest with blood.

The perequine swings its axe, hitting the squire in the chest. The armor absorbs the blow but now has a chunk missing after the creature pulls the weapon out.

"Let me have him," Bjorn says, spinning his axe in his hands.

"Take him," Sargon agrees as he looks at the hole in his armor. "Damn it." Sargon beats himself up wishing he hadn't worn the armor. He knows that this damage is more than he can skillfully mend himself; it would look like a child had repaired it by the time he was done. He would not do that out of respect for Zeth. He hopes that the blacksmith at Du'tesh Castle is as skillful as Zeth.

The perq swings his axe at Sargon as the squire steps aside to make room for Bjorn. The animal is in perfect position for Bjorn to step in.

Whoosh. Kerchunk. Bjorn lops the head off easily with his double-bladed axe.

The other two remaining perqs are holding prisoners hostage in their arms with daggers to their throats.

"Boy, what cowards! It infuriates me." Sargon grits his teeth.

"I got one," Febor tells Sargon.

"I got the other," Sargon says as he walks up to the perq using the old man as a shield. It takes all of Sargon's strength to pull the creature's hand holding the dagger away from the old man's throat. "Run," Sargon barks as he pries an opening for the man to escape.

Febor shoots the one with a dwarf as a hostage, hitting it in the right eye. The beast falls to the floor. Blathaon comes to the aid of his brother. "Riddance da i chi darn o cachu (good riddance, you piece of shit)," Blathaon says to the dead perq lying at the feet of his brother as he spits on the creature's head.

Once the old man is out of danger, Sargon turns the perq's hand with both of his hands, shoving the perq against the bars of the cell in front of it. He hears cracking as bones in the animal's hand break. Sargon forces the perq's hand into its chest and drives the dagger through the armored breastplate and into the creature's heart. "How you like me now, *sbwriel* (trash)?" Sargon says as the perq fades from the living. "Oh how I hate bullies," Sargon says as he leans against the prison cell to catch his breath.

The one perq left alive throws down his axe and backs to the far wall as Sargon grabs the armor piece that was pulled out from his breastplate off the floor.

"Let him go." Sargon motions the creature to go outside.

The perequine walks past the men then runs up the stairs as the old man walks toward Sargon and the others.

Thwack. Febor puts a bolt through the back of the creature's skull, dropping it on the stairwell.

"Hey, what the hell did you do that for? Animal or not, we don't shoot anybody in the back after they have surrendered. Marxbaq will not stand for that, and neither will I," Sargon condemns the action.

"She is your goddess, not mine," Febor announces.

"Bite your tongue, boy. She watches over all of us," Sargon lectures. "And you as a soldier know it to be true and that one day you will have to answer for your actions. Now go on and get the rest of these prisoners out of here. The keys are hanging on the wall." Sargon points to the wall on the far side of the dungeon.

"Okay," Febor grumbles to himself as he makes his way to the cells. There is a total of eight cells. The first cell holds a male dwarf named Jestin, who also has been making armor with

Blathaon's brother. In the second cell, a human female lies facedown on the floor. Febor goes in to look at her.

"Ugh, she's gone." Febor says as he backs out of the cell, looking like he could be sick. He's clearly taken back by the stench of death.

"Hey, you are not going to pull a Silverfish on us are you?" Bjorn teases Febor as he mimics vomiting.

"That was my daughter, Kiera ..." the old man says. The man introduces himself as Malik. "I have a farm about ten miles away. They took us both, killed my wife as I fought them off. Those bastards starved and raped my daughter. They were going to transport us to Xieg as slaves," Malik says.

"Who was?" Sargon asks.

"I don't know who they are, but they come by every month with a prison wagon full of prisoners," Malik recalls.

"Any idea when they might be back?" Sargon asks Malik.

"They were just here two days ago, they brought that young maiden that the big perq walked outside with. Is she dead? She said her name was Emma, says her uncle is a powerful man."

"She lives, we saved her from the creature. How long have you been here?" Sargon asks.

"A month," Malik says. "They have me help the dwarves sometimes."

"Let's finish up here, Febor.

"Sure."

"Blathaon, sydd yn y dynion oedd yn rhoi'r gorau gan (Who are the men that stop by?)"

"I do not know." The dwarf is impressed with how well Sargon speaks their language. "All I know is what Malik just told you—they come by every month. I know they come from the north and go south to Xieg. They were having us make armor and axes. Axes are quicker to make than swords."

"What about the goats in those two cells?" Febor asks.

"Let the dwarves have them," Sargon answers. "You are welcome to join us—we are going back to Lord Calador's castle. He could sure use a good blacksmith—a dwarven blacksmith at that. Doesn't get any better than that."

"Thanks, but we are going to head back to the mountains to see our families. We have been gone for about two years now ... they probably think we are dead," Blathaon says.

"I'll join you. Tell my brother when you get back, Blathaon," Jestin says. "It's the least I could do for saving us ... I can mend that hole in your breastplate." Jestin points to Sargon's armor.

"Great, sounds like a plan. What about you, Malik? Want to join us? It would be safer than your farm. I'm sure Lord Calador would set you up with a farm close to his castle."

"As inviting as that sounds, I would rather go back home."

"So be it. I think you all are making a big mistake—we can protect you," Sargon objects. "But if you're determined, may Yahmar and Marxbaq watch over you all. Let's go." Sargon finishes his prayer and makes a holy symbol in the air then makes his way up the stairs and out to the horses.

"Jestin, you ride with Bjorn," Sargon says as he walks over and mounts his horse.

Silverfish reaches a hand up and pulls himself up behind Sargon.

Jestin goes over to Bjorn's horse as the barbarian mounts his horse

"Gotcha," Febor says as he helps Jestin on the horse behind Bjorn.

"Thanks." Jestin smiles at the soldier.

"I'll take point," Febor volunteers as he mounts his horse.

"Hold up!" Sargon says, holding up his hand as he spins Tantor around to face the tower. "Let's make sure they make it out okay."

Blathaon, Alberfa, and Blathaon's brother Aneirin exit the tower, each leading a goat by a rope. They venture west toward the Shendo Mountains as Malik exits as well. The old man leads two goats south toward his home.

Sargon smiles as he spins Tantor around and points to Febor, who nods and rides onward toward Du'tesh Castle.

Chapter XXIII
Bad People

had forgotten what a piss ant town Strv is," Garxe says to as he walks into the Firelight Tavern. "I always drop by Hershidon's Castle up the hill if I stop for the night.

"Shhh ... keep your voice down. Don't bring attention to yourself. Although I can't see how you couldn't bring any more attention to yourself than you already are by wearing that plate mail." A stranger shushes Garxe as the nobleman sits at the stranger's table. "I like it here."

"I'll have more ale," the man tells the barmaid as she stops by the table.

"I'll have some wine," Garxe tells the young maid. "You would, I was working with a friend of yours a few days back." Garxe adds, turning his attention back to the man at his table.

"Who?"

"Riechter."

"Oh I like Riechter."

"Figures, he's a man of the woods like you. Why haven't you joined his gang of fools?"

"Nah, I work alone ... so what did you need to talk about that you could not put in a dispatch?" The stranger asks.

"Our business has some problems that need fixing, Waldfrin," Garxe says.

"I told you not to call me that," Waldfrin protests.

"It's your name, moron."

"Not anymore. It's Bas now," Waldfrin says.

"Oh, because the Snake said so? Hah. Well it's going to be Mud if you don't fix our problem," Garxe says.

"Hey!" Bas warns as he puts a finger over his mouth in a shushing motion. The barmaid approaches with their drinks. "So what is the problem?" Bas asks quietly once she retreats.

"Your pets are starving the girls we are selling," Garxe quietly says as he sips his wine. "The men we can send to the mines, but we need the women for entertainment. Can't do that much if they get sick and die."

"We have a couple of nice ones. I saw one of them at Budapeste Castle four days ago ... she is a real looker," Bas brags.

"Oh, and tell your friends to quit having their way with these girls. They are not for them. They need to stay fresh. Fresh and fed—can you remember that? I swear sometimes I think you are as stupid as your friends. Mom must've been with the castle jester—you are not from the same blood as me. Dad is probably shaking his fist at us right now."

"From the Hall of the Fathers?" Bas smiles.

"No dumbass, from hell. My father was not what you would call an honorable man," Garxe says as Bas's smile disappears.

"Our father."

"No, your father was a drunk and a thief, stupid," Garxe says under his breath while shaking his head. "What is the word in the woods?"

"Someone killed some of the perqs from my tower a few days back. That wasn't Riechter was it?" Bas asks. "They were a few miles away near some pit traps, a couple of them were at the bottom of those traps."

"No he was hot on the trail of the Guel boy, but left the woods after getting spooked by some rival pathfinders and going back to Vry. He never mentioned any encounters with perqs."

"The Guel boy? Oh, yes, he is at Du'tesh Castle, squire to Calador."

"Squire? Great," Garxe says sarcastically. He knows that Sargon cannot legally be touched because he falls under the protection of the House of Du'tesh. "Have to relay this to Heyrold," Garxe says then gets up and kisses Bas on the forehead and leaves. "See you later, Brother."

"Hey, what is this?" the barmaid asks Bas as he walks away. She holds three extra shiny copper coins.

"Oh, let me have those ..." Bas says as he pulls four other Pens from his pocket and takes back the shiny coins.

"Thanks," the barmaid smiles at getting the extra Pen.

Garxe rides his horse out of town and heads west to Vry. Pressing his horse hard, Garxe manages to get to the city in the middle of the night. The guards at the front gate of the city recognize him and let the nobleman through, waving at him as he passes. Garxe barrels through town to Heyrold's castle. He jumps off, handing the reins to the stable boy just inside the walls. He is met by the same soldier as before, who leads Garxe to Heyrold's study.

Knock knock. "Come," Heyrold barks. "Yes, what is it? Oh ... Garxe, what brings you back around?" Heyrold looks surprised as the young nobleman walks through the door. "Have a seat."

"Milord, it looks as if Sargon has taken up with Calador. The old man has made the boy his squire," Garxe says.

"Here." Heyrold pours Garxe some wine. "No kidding, his squire ... the old man is smarter than I thought. Yes, I heard about where he was from some of my spies, but I did not know that part of the story. Well, we will have to think of something. You still competing at the upcoming games?" Heyrold continues.

"Of course."

"Well, the boy will have to compete, taking Valagar's slot representing Calador.

"Interesting ... I might just drive a lance right through his head."

Both men laugh at the thought.

"Oh man, it's cold," Bas thinks out loud as he lights a fire. He is camped out about fifteen miles from Strv. He thought about sleeping at the inn, but he prefers sleeping under the stars, surrounded by trees even as cold as it is. He finally gets the fire lit and starts throwing small twigs and gradually putting bigger limbs on it. He sits there enjoying the warmth of the fire and the crackle of the wood.

Grrrrrrrrrrrrrrrrrrrrrrrr.

Bas's eyes are as big as saucers as he beholds a terrible sight. An ice bear appears to be approaching the scout. Bas grabs his bow.

"Grrrrrrrrr ..." the growl is interrupted by human laughter coming from the bear.

"Damn it, Evan. You're lucky I didn't shoot you, stupid ass."

"Man, you should've seen your face," Evan says through tears of laughter. "Looks like you were going to shit your pants."

"Where did you get that bear hide? Ugh, it smells like something dead."

"Not far from here. Yeah, the brains haven't rotted out yet. Two dead bears, must have been a hell of a fight. The other bear had an axe through its skull—and I mean all the way through. Whoever did that was real strong, cut the bear's head in two."

"Must have been in a fight with an ogre or a giant," Bas comments.

"Nah, there are no giants down here. They are all in the Shendo Mountains. Well, there was no sign of anything that big around the area. All I found were horse and human tracks and blood by the stream on some rocks. Exel found two sets of armor and some packhorses. Looked like Sargon and someone else lit out in a hurry on one horse—someone must've been badly hurt with all the blood I saw."

"Sargon?"

"The Guel boy."

"I didn't know his name. Exel was with you?" Bas asks.

"Yeah, what of it?" Evan answers.

"Oh … nothing, just miss the old days." Bas looks into the fire, remembering his younger days when he was training to be a pathfinder.

"Yeah, he had Zeth's daughter Meg with him. She told us all about Sargon. Wow is she a looker."

"Really? What was she doing with you two outlaws?"

"There was more than two of us there. You mean you don't know? Zeth is dead."

"How? Who would do such a thing?"

"Riechter."

"Really? I find that hard to believe."

"Exel saw the whole thing. There is some good news out of it. Riechter got his leg broke."

"Good. I liked Zeth … good blacksmith … used to like Riechter."

"Your brother was there.

"Really? That shitbird! I just saw him, and he did not tell me jack."

"Yeah, well, he was probably too busy talking about himself or all the money he has."

"Hey, that's my brother."

"Exactly. We got Riechter good, though, we led him off Sargon's trail. He had some sap tracking for him. Some of the other guys made some birdcalls up in the trees, spooked Riechter good. I had him in my sights, but some soldiers came up. I did not want to fight that many." Evan mimics holding his bow. "There were probably enough of us to take them out, but why stir up a hornet's nest? Besides, we helped the knight by signaling others further in the woods who helped Sargon by taking out awaiting assassins along the road to Missionwise. You would have loved it using carrier pigeons like the old days. Well, I have no love for Heyrold, especially after the death of Zeth."

"So what have you been up to lately? That was several days ago. I heard about Sargon at Calador's castle," Bas says.

"Well, Landric and I just got back from Darconia," Evan says.

"Darconia? Why would you go there?"

"Exel had us escort some soldier to a General Devalar," Evan says.

"So you are working for Exel now?"

"No, but he did pay us—two J'avins apiece."

"Wow! Where did he come up with that much coin?"

"Dunno, didn't ask. It must have been important. We got the royal treatment after they talked to this soldier in private. I never ate so much in my life," Evan says patting his belly. "There is something that sticks in my head."

"What is that?"

"That bear with the split skull had a horseshoe impression on its head and bite marks on its shoulder," Evan says with a bewildered look on his face.

"Maybe it was a centaur?" Bas smiles.

"What have you been smoking? Or did you pick the wrong mushrooms again?" Evan asks.

"No."

"Well, centaurs are in the mountains. And, besides, they do not wear horseshoes. I could show it to you in the morrow ... it's not far from here," Evan says as he huddles up close to Bas's fire.

"Get that stinky thing away from here. You want to attract a ghoul?

"Wouldn't that be the grandest thing ever!" Evan smiles.

"No, it wouldn't. Have you been breathing in too much of that dead air? I do not want to come in contact with or even see a ghoul," Bas protests.

"Oh, don't be such a sally girl. You wearing a dress now? Boy, you sure have lost a lot of your spunk over the years," Evan says.

"Well, I have pressing business I have to attend to, so I can't go with you in the morrow," Bas says as he lies down next to the fire.

"Okay, I'll go with you then."

"No, no ... I work alone," Bas says and drifts off to sleep.

Chapter XXIV
Vlasko

"Come on, grandpa, waiting on you," Sargon yells to Silverfish as the squire and the others grow restless, waiting from atop their horses just inside the courtyard. The group is about to journey toward Jaymar to deliver Emma to her family. Tantor impatiently paws the brick inlaid courtyard. "Stop it," Sargon scolds his horse.

"I'm coming. Keep your shirt on," Silverfish says as he walks outside.

"Where's Barbye?" Sargon asks, looking at the slow-moving elf.

"She's not coming," Silverfish says as he walks toward his horse.

"Oh, then we're gone." Sargon spurs Tantor, and the others follow suit, leaving Silverfish in the dust as the group barrels out of the castle.

Exel runs his horse ahead of Sargon, taking point.

Silverfish quickly jumps up onto his horse, even faster than before then suddenly lets out a heavy sigh as he looks at the reins tied to the hitching post.

"Got it!" Tymothy walks out of the stable and unties Silverfish's horse and hands the elf the reins.

Silverfish pulls the horse's head around while making a clicking sound and spurring with his short legs. The horse immediately jumps into a run, eager to catch up with the other horses and nearly knocking the elf off its back. He quickly catches up with the others as the rest of the group is going at an easy gallop down the road.

The group continues west to northwest for two hours, coming upon the road going from the port city of Suva to Missionwise. They stay on course, trekking cross-country headed to the road between Suva and Jaymar. They could go the road to Suva and then catch the road to Jaymar from there, but it would be twenty miles out of the way. Plus, they have already sent word to Natanio to meet them at the small hamlet of Vlasko. They ride for a few more hours then come upon the road to Jaymar and ride for another two hours to the small hamlet.

The town is just a stopover and not much more than that. All it has is an inn, a stable, and a blacksmith shop. There are a lot of people in the inn, and it looks like the stable is fairly filled. A couple of stable boys greet the group as they arrive. Sargon flips them a Siv as Father Yor and the others dismount. Music can be heard as everyone follows Sargon into the Banshee Inn. It grows louder as they enter and are enveloped by the noise of the crowd. Tobacco smoke looms overhead as many patrons can be seen smoking pipes. There is a bar on the far side of this massive room. The whole bottom floor of the inn is a tavern. Sargon looks around and sees the bartender flagging him over. Sargon makes his way to the bar.

"We are going to need nine rooms, my good man," Sargon instructs as he flips the bartender a J'avin.

"I only have five ... well, maybe I can find some more rooms." the bartender says with a big grin, as he bites down on the gold piece.

Sargon smirks and turns around to see Father Yor greeting Natanio as Emma jumps into her man's arms. They all sit at a massive table as the squire walks up.

"Sargon! I cannot thank you enough, old friend, for what you have done," Nate says as he stands up and shakes Sargon's hand, patting him on the left shoulder with his other hand. "It sure is good to see you. It has been way too long. Sorry about your family. I always admired your father and adored your grandfather. His passing two years ago was terrible."

"He went in his sleep. The priest said he was at peace when he died," Sargon adds.

"I would have gone to the wedding but did not hear about it until several days later," Nate says as he lovingly squeezes his bride-to-be's hand.

"Well, it's a good thing you did not attend. You would be dead with everyone else," Sargon says as he sits at the table next to Nate and Emma. "Maybe that was the intention, and through the blessing of the gods you were spared."

"Perhaps ... but we are here now," Nate says.

"Thank you for rescuing me—I never did get a chance to tell you that. I surely would have ended up like Kiera if you all had not come along," Emma tells Sargon, looking around at everyone at the table.

"Very sad, that girl dying like that. If we had been a few days earlier, we could've saved her too," Sargon says.

"Yeah, and if the rabbit hadn't stop to shit, the gargoyle wouldn't have swooped down and got him," Silverfish tells Sargon as a young girl stops by. "Yeah, baby, I'll have a pint of mead," Silverfish continues as he grabs the girl's butt.

"Silver!" Meg greatly objects to the elf's behavior. "You'd better not do that kinda thing when I'm not around," Meg says to Bellgrad, who shrugs his shoulders while Silver smiles.

"Don't touch me, you little creep," the girl protests as she backhands Silver.

"I'll have wine." Sargon tells the girl through his laughter.

The rest of the group orders their refreshments and food.

Exel stands up from the table, recognizing someone across

the room. He marches over and greets his friend.

"Evan, you, old dog. How are you?" Exel smiles as he shakes the young man's hand. "I take it your trip to Darconia was a success?"

"Oh, it went great," Evan says.

"What have you been up to lately?" Exel waves a young girl over. "What are you drinking, bub?"

"Ale."

"All right, two ales, please," Exel orders.

"Well, I skinned one of those bears we came across. Not the one with the split skull, but the other one. What happened with all that, anyway?"

"Sargon and Bellgrad were attacked by those two bears. Bellgrad got bit on the shoulder and flung onto the rocks by the creek. Sargon's horse saved his bacon by attacking the bear and driving the axe head through its skull. Sargon of course stuck the axe into the bear's skull at first."

"Wow, that's what I thought. Anyway I put on that bear hide with the head still on it and scared Bas yesterday something good," Evan says.

"Who?" Exel asks.

"Waldfrin."

"Why did you call him Bas?" Exel asks, clearly confused.

"It's not my idea, it's the Snake's," Evan answers.

"Kalius the Snake? He is doing work for the Snake ... Oh that can't be good."

"Yeah, well he was acting really weird yesterday—weirder than usual," Evan says as the young girl brings their drinks. "I work alone ..." Evan mimics their friend.

"What?"

"Just what I was thinking ... that's what he told me last night." Evan takes a gulp of ale. "So I followed him this morning. I pretended to take off heading north, but I doubled back and followed him. He went west of Missionwise to some old castle deep in the Astrid Forest. I saw him talking with some perequine there. I then saw him come out with some girl in shackles and put her in front of him on his horse. I left then came here and was going to go to Du'tesh Castle in the morrow, looking for you. What do you think he has gotten himself into?" Evan says with a concerned look on his face.

"I don't know ... he sure must be slipping if you followed him all day without being spotted," Exel says. "Could you find this castle again?"

"Does a troglodyte smell bad?" Evan asks.

Exel smiles. "I want you to tag along with us then We are going to Jaymar in the morrow. Do you have a room?"

"No, not yet."

"You can bunk with me then. Besides, I still owe you 2 Sivs."

"Do you have your dice?"

"Does a gob shit in the woods?"

"Not if he's underground," Evan answers.

"Let me introduce you to the group," Exel says as he gets up and makes his way back to the table where the party is sitting with Evan in tow.

"Everyone—this is Evan. He's an old friend from back in my training days," Exel boasts.

Everyone at the table acknowledges the young man.

"Good to see you again, Evan," Meg says.

"Again?" Bellgrad asks.

"Yes, he was with Exel and me when we got your horses and armor," Meg answers.

"Amazing what your horse did, Sargon ... to the bear, that is," Evan says as Sargon nods.

"That's nothing, he stomped a bugbear into the ground a few

days ago," Bjorn says.

"Nice!" Evan downs more ale while he sits next to the barbarian and Exel.

"Did you eat yet? We have lots of food coming or get whatever you want—it's on me." Sargon tells Evan then turns his attention back to his friends.

The young girl puts plates of food on the table—a variety of different dishes like grouse, duck, lamb, and elk. Then she places a bowl in front of the elf as Silver starts shoveling the soup into his mouth.

POW. Silverfish gets a slap upside the head by Father Yor.

"Wait." Father Yor gives Silver a dirty look then says a blessing over the food.

Everyone begins dining.

"What is that?" Evan asks.

"Horse stomach," Silver says.

"No it's not ... I know what that awful stuff smells like," Evan says.

"If it was, he would be puking right now. Isn't that right, Drippy?" Bjorn jumps in as he looks at the elf. Silver looks back with a phony smile then opens his mouth like a child, showing the chewed-up food to Bjorn.

"It's fish soup," Silver tells the pathfinder while he stuffs his mouth.

"I'll have some of that," Evan tells the young girl as he points to Silver's bowl.

"You keep pointing like that and you are going to pull back a nub," Silver warns Evan.

Exel signs as Evan belts out a laugh.

"You know it's rude to talk or sign behind someone's back," Silver says.

"But it's so funny, especially when it's about you, half pint,"

Bjorn looks at Silver.

"That's right, gang up on the little guy," Silver says as he holds up an empty bowl.

"Waah, Waah, I want my mommy." Bjorn continues with the harassment.

"Bring me some more, sweetheart," Silver tells the young girl as he smiles at her. To everyone's surprise, she smiles back at the elf.

"I don't know how he does it," Exel tells Bjorn.

"She feels sorry for him," Bjorn answers back.

"I don't care as long as she sits on my face," Silverfish comments.

"Silver!" Father Yor hollers sternly, waving his club.

Bjorn snorts back a laugh.

"What do you think Barbye is going to say about your comments?" Meg asks.

"Yeah, stupid. You have a great woman at home," Father Yor tells the elf.

"Well, don't tell her. And, besides, sometimes Daddy has to roam," Silver says as he watches the young girl return with another bowl of soup for Evan. Silverfish holds out his hands. "What the ..."

"I'll bring yours right away," the young girl tells Silverfish.

"It's like talking to the wall," Father Yor says as he rolls his eyes.

A young man brings Sargon the room keys. The squire distributes out the keys.

"We only have seven rooms." the young man tells Sargon

"Some of you will have to double up." Sargon announces to the group

"Hey, baby, I have a room," Silverfish tells the young girl.

"In your dreams, shorty," the girl replies.

"Ooh," Bjorn and Exel say at the same time.

Bjorn stands up and starts flapping his arms like wings then walks with his arms outstretched like an eagle soaring. Exel drops to a knee and mimics taking three bowshots. Bjorn makes out like he's crashing to the ground.

"Ooh ... got shot down!" Bjorn rubs it in, as the rest of the table laughs and applauds.

Silverfish rubs his eye with his middle finger.

"You see what I have to deal with ..." Sargon tells Nate.

"Yeah, but you're a natural born leader. I bet they are there when you need them. Val tells me you know who is responsible for your family's deaths and wonders if we would support you. The answer is yes—if you need men, or whatever you need, I'm there," Nate says to Sargon.

"Thanks, I don't have any real proof, just speculation right now. I'm going to retire. I will see you in the morning." Sargon yawns as he stands up and makes his way to the stairs at the rear of the inn. He sets a J'avin on the bar. "That is for the food and refreshments," Sargon adds as the bartender smiles and nods. He eyes the table where the rest of the squire's group is still eating and drinking. A young lady at the bar sees Sargon place the gold piece down and confronts him.

"Milord, would you be looking for some company on this cold night? I'm sure it gets lonely with all your travels. I can ease your loneliness," the young lady boasts as she reveals a very supple leg through a slit of her peasant dress.

Sargon stands there awestruck, never having been approached like this before. The wench is extremely beautiful and smells wonderful; she has long flowing dishwater-blond hair going down to the middle of her back pinned back on her left side by a jewel-encrusted hairpin, revealing a very nice neck. She stands about 5'5" with a very heavy chest as well as intoxicating baby-blue eyes that make it difficult to look away. Her face is painted perfectly with plush lips aching to be kissed.

"Unless that is your lady at the table ..." the young beauty says as she eyes his group.

Sargon turns and looks at the table as well. Meg is watching him, but she quickly turns away.

"Yes ... she is, but thanks for the offer." Sargon sees his opportunity to make a quick exit while not insulting the girl. He finds it extremely difficult to turn such an angel away; he wants her badly, but Jessica is still in his mind and in his heart. He cannot betray her ... *love me, love no other.* Her last words are etched in his mind. Sargon makes his escape to the stairs as the wench looks back at the table and sees Meg kiss Bellgrad.

"Why, that son of a ..." the girl says aloud as she turns to her left and plants her face into a muscular chest as she was about to leave. "Why, I'm so sorry," she says, embarrassed, as she takes a step back to see a barbarian warrior in front of her. "But not disappointed," she says as she playfully rubs Bjorn's chest with her dainty right hand.

"Hello, beautiful. What are you drinking?

"Viko."

"One Viko, my good man, and keep them coming," Bjorn says as he puts a J'avin on the bar. He lightly sways then stabilizes himself by leaning on the bar. "It amazes me the way some women want what they cannot have."

"Yes, I noticed that girl watching the knight while she has her man there with her."

"Who says I was talking about her?" Bjorn comments as he stares into the wench's beautiful eyes. "Don't worry your pretty little head about him ... it has nothing to do with you," Bjorn says as he stares into the goddess's eyes. "Oh ... definitely not you!" Bjorn adds as his eyes admire the young beauty.

"You travel with that knight."

"Yes, with all of them." Bjorn points with his head to the table with the group as he nurses a tankard of mead.

"What is wrong with him? I have never been turned away like that."

"He is *skemmdar vörur*," Bjorn tells the girl.

"What? Damaged goods … oops." The girl covers her mouth as she realizes the cat's out of the bag

"Come on … I can spot my people a mile away." Bjorn smirks.

"Shhh." She shushes Bjorn as she leads him away from the bar. "People will think I am trash."

"What? Are you kidding me? You are the most beautiful woman I have ever seen in my life. Zura herself would be jealous of your beauty.

Stop...do you want to curse me? (Referring to the legend that Zura curses any woman that might be as beautiful as her by changing the maiden into a monstrous Medusa.)

No...What is your name, *elskan* (sweetheart)?" Bjorn asks

"I am Eavan."

"It is true. You are gorgeous... sorry."

Eavan smiles. "Let's go to your room."

Chapter XXV
Jaymar

argon steps into the hallway just as Eavan is exiting the room next to his—Bjorn's room.

"Wow, this is awkward. I would not have believed anyone to be awake this early," she says, brushing her hair over her shoulder.

"Nothing awkward about it. Does my heart good to see you again," Sargon says as he pulls off his helm. "Besides, I always get up early."

Sargon smiles. "I'm glad Bjorn and you got together."

"No you are not. I can see it in your eyes," Eavan says softly, stepping toward the squire. "Look, I'm sorry about the death of your wife."

Sargon's smile fades. "Bjorn talks too much."

"You want me. I see that—"

"Shhh." Sargon shushes Eavan and leads her to his room.

"I want you too," Eavan says as she reaches up to kiss the seven-foot-tall squire.

Sargon lightly removes her arms from his neck. "Look, you belong to Bjorn now."

"I don't belong to any man. He's nice ... and fun. You know he paid me two J'avins."

"Well, I'm overlooking that fact," Sargon states and sits on the bed.

Eavan sits beside him, smiling at the compliment. "You are so sweet, but you have a lot of pain. I see it in your face." Eavan gracefully runs her soft hand down Sargon's left cheek.

Sargon closes his eyes, enjoying the touch of a woman again.

But the next moment, he snaps back to reality and grabs the wench's tiny hand. He kisses her palm before letting it go.

He stands, saying, "I have to go and get everything ready for the journey to Jaymar."

"Look me up on your return trip," Eavan says as she lets out a frustrated sigh. "If it's any consolation to you, nothing happened between Bjorn and me. He passed out soon after we got to his room. Give this back to him." Eavan hands Sargon the two gold pieces that Bjorn paid her.

Sargon smiles as he hands back the gold. "Keep it ... serves him right. I gotta see if he is fit to travel. Good day, milady." Sargon bows and exits the room then enters Bjorn's room next door.

"Get up! Come on, drunky do," Sargon says as he shakes the passed-out mountain man. "Ugh, how awful," Sargon says as he catches a whiff of the vomit on the floor next to the bed. "One would think you'd have learned your lesson about drinking too much."

Sargon searches the room and spots a bowl and pitcher of water on a dresser. The squire fills the bowl halfway then throws it on the barbarian.

"OH ... WHAT THE ..." Bjorn sits up with a dagger in his hand as he spits water from his mouth.

"Get up, stupid," Sargon orders the barbarian.

"Oh ... my head," Bjorn moans and grips his forehead.

"Oh, cry me a river. Get up, get dressed, and clean up that puke." Sargon has no sympathy for reckless behavior. He walks out into the hallway and across to Exel's room.

Knock knock. "Yes, we're up," Exel calls from behind the door. Sargon hears dice rattle as he goes to the next room, which is Father Yor's.

Knock knock. "Yes, Sargon I am awake," Father Yor informs the squire.

"Is Silverfish with you, Father?" Sargon asks as he continues waking everyone.

"No, he didn't come in here last night. Chan is here, though."

Sargon is surprised when his friend opens the door before Sargon knocks. "We are up. See you downstairs," Bellgrad informs Sargon. He notices Meg gathering clothes in the background. The squire gives Bellgrad a smirk.

Sargon makes his way to the next room, where Febor the Splendid and Friar Truvey shared a room. Both men are awake.

Sargon makes his way downstairs to see only one to two people moving about. The smell of tea and coffee fill the air as well as a hint of liquor. It is still dark outside as Sargon makes his way to the stable, where he finds one stable boy feeding the horses.

"Get our horses ready! What's the charge?" Sargon likes to pay his debts.

"Three J'avins for the eight horses."

"Three J'avins ... that's robbery! That's seven Sivs and five Pens per horse. I only pay three Sivs per horse in Missionwise," Sargon protests.

"Sorry, milord," the stable boy apologizes.

"It's not your fault. You are just doing your job," Sargon reassures the boy. "Here ..." Sargon hands the boy three gold coins. He then flips the boy a Siv. "That's for doing such a fine job. Oh, and get that gelding over there saddled as well." Sargon points to Nate's horse; he recognizes the horse even after this much time has passed.

"Thank you, milord. Right away." The boy smiles excitedly at the large tip; he hurries to get the party's horses saddled.

Sargon makes his way back inside the inn to see Exel sitting at the table they had the night before. Silverfish is also there, sitting on the young girl's lap.

"Better not let Meg see you like that." Sargon warns Silverfish.

Silver jumps off the girl's lap.

The young girl asks, "Who's Meg? Is that your girl?"

"Go get us some food," Silver says and swats her on the butt.

The girl disappears into the kitchen just as Meg and Bellgrad make their way downstairs followed by Febor, Friar Truvey, and Father Yor.

The group eats breakfast as Nate and Emma make their way down.

"Come join us. We have some tea and coffee."

"Boy, I thought I was the early riser," Nate says with an odd expression on his face, as if he were late for a meeting.

"Here, you gotta try this stuff," Sargon tells Nate as he pours his friend some coffee.

"Wow, coffee! That stuff is expensive."

"Right, Mom! Try it knucklehead. I know your father doesn't have any at your place," Sargon says.

"True, he is cut from the same cloth as your father. Must be a generational thing being so tight with money. Hmmm ... this stuff's not bad. Needs some cream and sugar though."

"Do I need to buy you a dress?" Sargon smiles as he stuffs his face.

"Now boys ..." Emma chimes in.

"Aw, we always cut up!" Nate tells his sweetheart, lightly punching Sargon on the arm. "Just like old times, eh?" Nate winks at Sargon.

"Our horses should be ready to go. I had the boy out there saddle them."

"Wow, time really has changed you."

"Well, I'm a squire now, and I have responsibilities," Sargon says, watching his companions at the table. He looks up in time to see Silverfish fling a spoonful of porridge at Bjorn's face.

"You were a squire back home."

"That's not the same. Reaxl was very relaxed with me. Being his lord's son tends to do that." Sargon snaps his fingers at Father Yor, who pops Silver on the back of the head, sending the elf's face into his bowl of porridge. Bjorn points with his spoon and laughs at Silver.

"You should be happy he is that responsible. That's why I'm here," Emma jumps in.

"True." Nate nods, enjoying his coffee.

"Oh, my poor darling, what happened?" The servant girl wipes Silver's face with her apron.

"That mean, ugly man over there shoved my face into my bowl." Silver plays it off, pointing to Bjorn.

The servant girl gives Bjorn a dirty look. The barbarian just sits there and shrugs his shoulders.

"Oh my, girl, he just wants sympathy ... he did that himself for acting like a child," Father Yor explains.

"Never a dull moment with this bunch," Sargon says as Silverfish sticks his tongue out at the barbarian.

"Do you need to stand in a corner?" Sargon scolds Silver.

"No."

"We're leaving at dawn. If you are not out there you will be left. Right, little man?"

"I'm not going. I'll just wait for you all back here," Silverfish says.

"You'll have to pay for your own room," says Sargon.

"I have money."

"Don't your folks live in Jaymar?"

"Yep ... don't care to see them," Silver says as he continues eating his breakfast.

"Remember they kicked him out for stealing?" Meg reminds Sargon.

"I remember. Afraid you won't get a warm welcome from home?" Sargon asks Silverfish.

"Frankly, I really don't care," Silver says as he starts polishing off a stack of pancakes smothered in maple syrup.

"I would prefer to stay as well," Bjorn tells Sargon.

"So you can sleep off that hangover? Tough ..."

"Drink more coffee." Sargon says, pouring himself more coffee first and then offering some to Bjorn. The man nods and receives more coffee then begins shoveling in maple sugar and adding cream.

Sargon serves himself scrambled eggs then offers some to Emma and Nate.

"Rabbit?" Sargon grabs a plate of roasted rabbit and hands it to Nate. He grabs himself one then offers one to his woman, but she shakes her head.

"I will take some of that bacon," Emma says as she points to a plate in front of Bjorn. He grabs it away from Silver. Sargon makes a face of disgust at the plate of pork.

"Here, milady." Bjorn nods at Emma.

"Thank you. This is the man who pulled me from that creature. He got shot in the back protecting me. How is your back Bjorn?"

"Good as new, thanks to the good Father. A bit painful healing, though."

"What do you mean?" Emma asks.

"He is referring to my club," Father Yor answers with a smile. "I call it slap o' heal. You see, there are healing properties within ash wood. As I hit with the club whoever is injured, the dust and oils from the club are released into the wound. As the club gets older, you have to hit harder to get the same effect. There are also healing elixirs with ash shavings in them that I make. They're also the prime ingredient for healing potions."

"Potions? Isn't that what an elixir is?" Emma is curious.

"No. A potion is an elixir that has been modified by magic."

"Magic ... you are no wizard."

"No, it's magic from the gods. Or, in my case, Yahmar. I haven't made any potions just yet, only elixirs, but I'm working on it. Healing potions are two to three times stronger than an elixir, and they work instantaneously, whereas, an elixir can take hours or days to work. That's why I use stones as well—"

"Thank you, Father. We need to get going." Sargon interrupts, impatient for the others to finish breakfast and irritated by the rambling of the priest. Sargon walks outside to see Sulo's rays have risen above the trees and lit up the town. Nate walks out and joins his friend.

"Are you okay?"

"Yes, I'm okay. Reminds me of my teachers back home when we were younger—just rambling on. It makes my ears bleed," Sargon says as he walks to his horse.

"I don't see any blood." Nate smiles.

"Funny," Sargon answers as he checks Tantor's armored barding and saddle. "Excellent job ... ah ..."

"Smitty, sir." The boy grins.

"Smitty?"

"Yes, I also help the blacksmith."

"Well, good work. How would you like to be a knight's retainer one day?"

"Whoa ... really?"

"Yes, I may call upon you one day. When I become a knight, that is." Sargon leads Tantor out of the stable

"Thank you, milord."

"You shouldn't get the boy's hopes up like that," Nate comments as he walks beside his friend.

"I'm totally serious. He is of the right age, and qualities like his are hard to find. Calador will be knighting me soon with the games coming up. You have to be a knight to participate.

"True." Nate nods in agreement. "Here, boy," Nate flips the boy a J'avin.

"It is not this much, sire. I'll have to get you change."

"Keep the change." Nate smiles as he mounts his horse.

"Thank you, milord."

"Wow, that's very generous of you." Sargon is surprised.

The others soon make their way outside.

Smitty leads out Emma's horse. Bjorn helps the young maiden up, where she'll ride side-saddle. He quickly double-checks the tension of the saddle before moving on.

The young boy leads out Meg's horse next, and Bellgrad helps his woman on her horse.

Silverfish stands on the porch of the tavern, smoking a pipe and waving at everyone.

"I didn't know the elf had a pipe," Febor says to Father Yor.

"He doesn't. He must've swiped it from somebody," Father Yor answers.

Everyone else mounts their horses. Sargon nods at Exel, who leads the group down the road. He breaks into a run, leading the party on a hard ride. Chan runs behind the group but manages to keep up—a lot better on the open road then being slowed by cross country trekking and snowdrifts.

They all ride for the better part of eight hours, reaching Jaymar at late evening. Nate breaks formation and heads to the front upon arriving. The city guards recognize the young nobleman and motion the party through the main city gate. Nate takes lead and guides the party through the city streets and to the castle of Beloges. Emma's uncle is there to meet them.

"My sweet girl, it does my heart good to see you," Beloges tells Emma as he helps her off her horse. "Come in, all of you. I'm sure you are tired after your travels," Beloges adds as he scans the party and motions everyone in.

Stable boys all gather the horses as the group dismounts.

"Oh boy!" Father Yor groans, his sore muscles protesting as he dismounts. Once on the ground, he stretches and squats. "What a ride. That has to be the longest I have ridden before."

"You did good, Father." Bjorn pats the young priest on the shoulder as he walks by, clearly unfazed by the ride.

"I see you are feeling better ... after blowing your guts out a few times," Father Yor says under his breath.

Friar Truvey and Febor laugh as they walk by, following Sargon and Nate into the castle.

"Are you okay?" Bellgrad asks Father Yor as he helps Meg off her horse.

"It just doesn't feel right without the little guy."

"You are not his mother, Yor. Come on inside," Meg tells the priest.

"Perhaps you are right. Hopefully, he won't get himself into any trouble," Father Yor adds as he looks blankly at the horizon.

"Even mothers need a break from their children," Bellgrad says.

Yor laughs and joins the two as they walk into the castle.

Chapter XXVI
Rewards

arling, wake up … the baby is crying. Can you go see what's wrong?" Jessica asks.

"Sure, my sweet bride." Sargon gets out of bed and looks over at his beautiful, Jess, heavy with child number two. Nothing is more beautiful to him than the way she looks right now. He scurries down the hall of the family castle; all the while, the baby cries. It seems as if it takes hours to get down the hall. Sargon opens the door to the nursery and walks in. Horrified, he finds his son being eaten by the same bugbear that ate the other little girl. His son's face is a combination of Jessica and himself.

"NOOOO!" Sargon jumps out of bed and starts pacing, too worked up from the dream. He gets dressed and armored up then heads downstairs. He doesn't know where he is when he goes into the hallway, but he soon snaps back to reality. Quietly, he makes his way to the stairs; it is still dark outside. He creeps down the wooden stairs, the boards making all kinds of creaks and groans in addition to the jingling of the plate mail that Calador is loaning him while his field plate is being repaired. He makes it to the bottom step after what seems like an eternity. He spots the cook as he walks down the hall toward the kitchen.

"What time is it? Sargon softly asks.

"What—" the man startles. "You scared the life out of me, milord." The cook looks out a window. "It's four in the morning."

"Good … How did you know that?"

"Lord Beloges has a clock in the tower outside," the cook adds as he points outside the window.

"Humph ... I will be in the stable," Sargon tells the middle-aged man.

"Oh, okay. Do you want some tea?"

"Do you have any coffee?" Sargon asks.

"I have to make it."

"Thanks," Sargon says then heads outside. He stops for a moment, letting his eyes adjust to the darkness. He looks up and sees the clock in a tower across from the main hall of the castle. *That must've set Beloges back a few Pens*. He thinks to himself. He makes out the stable across the courtyard and walks to the entrance, where he sees Tantor and the other horses. There is no activity; the stable boys must still be asleep.

Sargon walks over to Tantor's stall. A lantern hanging on a nearby post gives off a soft glow, most of its light shielded by the lantern's hood. Sargon raises the hood, lighting up the stable. He sees his friend munching on some hay.

"Hey, old man. How are you, buddy?" Sargon asks as he pats his horse on the neck. "I can't think of any better company right now. Let's get you some food, aye?" Sargon walks to the back of the stable and finds the store of grain. Grabbing a bucket, he partially fills it and takes it to his mount. Tantor whinnies softly as Sargon pours the grain into the feed trough. It's a sound that touches the young squire's heart.

"I had a dream about her again. Seems that you are the only real dear friend I have, and you can't understand me."

Tantor lays his head on Sargon's arm as if he does understand the young man; then he commences to devour the grain, taking huge mouthfuls of the feed.

"Easy there, pig." Sargon laughs and looks around for a brush as he pulls his tobacco pouch from his belt. He puts a chaw in his mouth as he spots a brush on a barrel close to the entrance, then walks over and grabs it. Tantor has already finished his breakfast by the time Sargon makes it back to the stall. He opens the gate, walks into the stall, and begins brushing down his friend.

"Hello?" a voice asks from outside of the stable.

"Hey!" Sargon answers. *Spit.*

"Who goes there?"

"Sargon."

"What are you doing?

"This is my horse, and I'm brushing him down. Who are you?" *Spit.*

"I'm Kjell. I work here," the young stable boy says as he walks toward the squire. "I was wondering if there was a thief or some sort of creature in there."

"Oh, believe me, if there were either, he would stomp them into the ground."

"He is magnificent." The young stable boy rubs the front of Tantor's head. The horse lips the boy's hand in turn. "Ow!" Kjell says as he pulls his hand away.

"He likes you."

"I thought he was going to bite me."

"Nah, he only bites bugbears." *Spit.*

"Bugbears … Wow!"

"Since you're here, you can saddle him and get our other horses ready. I have already fed him, so he is good to go. I'm going to go inside and eat," Sargon starts inside then turns around. "Do you have a bosal?"

"What is that?"

"A hackamore … you know, for training a horse." Sargon is getting impatient.

"Nope, never heard of it."

"A bosal—it's a nose band. You know, for riding without a bit in the horse's mouth." *Spit.* "Don't you train horses?"

"Only Devon does that. He won't be in for a few more hours.

"You are welcome to look in the back room. I've never heard of anyone riding without a bit in the horse's mouth. But what do I know? I just saddle and feed them."

"Tantor there has broken two bits already—once with a bear, the other with a bugbear."

"That's one bad-ass horse."

"Thanks. I just don't want him injuring his mouth while trying to help," Sargon says as he goes to the back room. "I found one." Sargon grabs his bridle hanging on a nail.

Sitting on a barrel, he looks it over while holding the bosal where the bit is. *It won't work,* Sargon thinks to himself. *Spit.* He finds some leather and fashions up a headstall, which he attaches to the bosal; then he attaches the reins. "Here you go. Put this on him," Sargon says as he drops it in the young man's hands.

"Oh, so that's a bosal. I was wondering what that was hanging up by the bridles," Kjell says as he walks over to Tantor's stall.

"I figured I'd find you out here," Bellgrad says as he walks outside.

"I'm about to go eat."

"Let's walk."

"Okay."

Sargon turns and spits his chaw into the grass by the stable. "Be careful with Tantor's face shield. Make certain it's not too tight," Sargon adds as he starts walking.

The men walk about twenty yards from the stable before talking.

"I heard you this morning ... and I heard you the other morning as well. You have been having nightmares, haven't you?" Bellgrad looks at Sargon as they walk.

"Yes ..." Sargon reluctantly admits.

"Look, I owe you my life … twice! That would make me your slave in some customs like Rokia."

"That's a scary thought." Sargon smirks.

"See, this is what I'm talking about. You can confide in me," Bellgrad says.

"You have enough to worry about with Meg." Sargon looks down at the road.

"I would not be able to hold Meg right now if it weren't for you, knucklehead. You risked everything to get me to Missionwise. It's only by the blessing of the gods that your horse did not give out. I heard you when I was in the temple as the soldiers were carrying me away. You told Father Yor you would do anything for me … even give up Tantor. That horse is your life."

"I can always get another horse, but not another you."

"That's what I'm saying—we are more like brothers with everything we have been through."

"True."

"So what have your dreams been about?" Bellgrad asks.

The two men walk around the courtyard as Sargon explains to Bellgrad the dreams as well as the death of Jessica."

"Genzo is tormenting you. That is the way of the enemy."

"Enemy?"

"Yes, Asberdies, Genzo, and Cleko—all the evil gods."

"Haven't I been tormented enough with all the loss?"

"I'm not the one to ask, perhaps you should ask Father Yor. You can also have him chase away the evils spirits from your room tonight. You know what else I think you need?"

"I hate to ask."

"I think you need to take that blonde beauty you were talking to in Vlasko and bed her down."

"I can't. Jessica is still in my heart."

"Jessica is dead, my friend. Besides, I did not say marry the girl—just let her put a smile on your face," Bellgrad advises.

"Perhaps you are right." Sargon smirks as he goes to the door of the castle.

Both men walk in and see the group assembling in the dining room. There are a variety of platters on the table. He finds a place next to Father Yor, while Bellgrad sits by his beloved Meg. Sargon realizes a servant is looking at him.

"Coffee."

"Yes, sir," the servant says as he pours the young squire a cup.

Father Yor holds out his cup, which the servant fills with the hot morning elixir.

Beloges walks into the room. "I hear tell that there is a castle ruins in the Astrid forest west of Missionwise," he announces to the group as he looks at Evan. "There's an old sage here in town that may be able to find it and tell you whose it was. Eat up, eat up. You can see him as soon as you are finished with breakfast. This is for you squire," Beloges adds as he puts a hefty bag of coins in front of Sargon.

"I can't ..." Sargon doesn't want any money.

"I do not want to hear it. You don't want to insult me, do you?" Beloges insists. "Food costs money, so does lodging and the stables. Besides, I would pay a hundred times that to get my niece back," Beloges adds, looking at Emma.

Sargon and Bjorn are in shock.

"Well, thank you, milord," Sargon says as he grabs more meat from the platters on the table. "This is good. What is it?"

"Dog ... no, it's mutton." Beloges smiles.

"You got me there." Sargon laughs as he returns the meat back to his plate. He also grabs some more eggs and biscuits."

"Eat up, everyone. You have earned it. And, besides, you have a long journey back," Beloges says as he gets up and walks to the other side of the table to Chan. The monk is staring up from his food with a confused look on his face.

"Here, young man ..." Beloges adds as he pulls a large curved dagger with a jewel-encrusted sheath from his belt and gives it to Chan. "It's sharp enough and broad enough to go through the tough hide of those perq bastards," Beloges adds with a wink. "Great job, my boy. Emma told me what you did—damn brave thing. Pull the blade, son."

Chan unsheathes the dagger, and the blade bursts into flames. Chan scrambles to re-sheath it. In his haste, his left hand grazes the flames, but it does not burn him.

That is Tönn drekans ... dragon's tooth. It will not burn you as long as you have the scabbard of the weapon. You use this on those perq bastards, and they won't be hitting back." Beloges pats Chan on the shoulder as he circles back around to Bjorn. "I hear tell that you like axes?" Beloges asks Bjorn then he motions toward the doorway of the dining room, where a servant holds a large double-bladed axe. He wraps the blade in what appears to be ice bear hide turned inside out then leans the weapon against the wall. "That is yours, son."

"Be still my heart." Bjorn sits there with his mouth open for a moment then nods to Beloges as he stands up, walks over, and grabs the weapon. "Thank you, milord."

The axe is almost weightless—not what Bjorn was expecting. The barbarian almost hits the ceiling as the bear hide falls away, revealing a bluish blade.

"Don't touch that ..." Beloges warns as Bjorn reaches out to touch the axe-head.

"He's not the sharpest tool in the blacksmith shop, is he?" Beloges smiles at Sargon then pours coffee on Bjorn's fingers, releasing them from the axe.

"It's like touching a frozen flagpole," Bjorn says as he rubs his fingers. *I got to get the elf to touch his tongue to it,* Bjorn smiles at the thought.

"It would have frozen your fingers off if I hadn't released them," Beloges says. "That is Frostbyte. It is said to have come from the Frost Giants of the Shendo Mountains. I don't know about all that—if that were the case, it would be giant sized. I think more likely it came from the dwarves. Anyway, it is yours, mountain man. It should help you out. Be sure to sheath it with ice bear hide."

"I don't know what to say." Bjorn is speechless. "Thanks again, milord. Wow … the handle is iron wood."

"Bjorn, I have an ice bear hide I will give you if you let me use that a while next time we are fighting," Evan says, staring at the axe.

"Sure." Bjorn smiles.

Beloges eyes Sargon, who shovels the last of his breakfast in and gets up to walk with the old knight.

"I cannot express my gratitude enough for such rewards, milord," Sargon says as they walk down the hall away from the dining room.

"Nonsense, my boy. You have brought me back my family. My niece is like a daughter to me. Besides, you all can use those weapons. My days are numbered, and I can't use them anymore. These days are meant for you and your generation. I would want justice as well if my family were murdered. Your grandfather and I fought side by side more times than I can remember. You can count on my help when the time comes. I would love to see Heyrold swinging at the end of a rope, that greedy bastard! He wants to be king of Fegnir, but Duke Rapheal is too blind to see it."

"Who?"

"The Duke of Darconia."

"Oh, I did not know his name. Isn't he actually the rightful king?"

"Yes ... but he is too scared of the other nobles to declare it. But I hear tell that might change with this next meeting after the games. Have you been practicing your jousting?"

"Not yet, milord."

"That's silly of me to ask. Of course you haven't. Are you ready to go? Jeryko is expecting you," Beloges says.

"Who?"

"The sage I was talking about. Sergeant Sverre will escort you there." Beloges leans with one arm against the wall to catch his breath.

"Are you okay, milord?" Sargon sees his grandfather in this old man, imagining he was a grand knight in his day.

"Just old age, my son."

"Let me help you to your study." Sargon sees the room farther down the hall.

He puts his arm around Beloges and helps the worn-out armored knight to his study. "You really should take off your armor when you're at home."

"Nonsense, boy. It's always good to be prepared. You never know when misfortune will fall upon you. Anyway, I am going to die with my armor on, not sick in bed."

"I understand that thinking, milord. I feel the same way. Oh ... wow, you have two family shields. That's eight generations," Sargon says, seeing the shields hanging over the study hearth.

"Get that one down." Beloges points to the shield on the right as Sargon helps him to a chair. Sargon pulls the shield off the wall, setting it on the table next to the old knight.

"This one was my son's," Beloges says as he rubs the raised coat of arms on the right upper section of the brass ceremonial shield.

"He was killed at the Games of Valor last year, right?" Sargon asks.

"Yes, his horse flipped over on top of him as it fell during an open field jousting accident." Beloges studies the symbols. "Another reason I do not like Heyrold."

"That's the initial joust between teams, when they pull the dividing fence? I only heard because Reaxl was very sick and we did not go. He didn't have any brothers or sisters?" Sargon asks, reading the coat of arms symbols of Beloges's son.

"No, I had one daughter who died right after her birth, which also took my wife. That's why I am so glad Emma found Nate. I am passing my title to him at the time of my death. That one is mine." Beloges says, pointing to the section next to his son's. "This one was my father's."

Beloges smiles, remembering his youth and the many jousts he witnessed his father perform. He absentmindedly rubs the section under his son's coat of arms. "And this one was my grandfather's."

Sargon can see the old man is proud as a peacock, remembering the great knight his grandfather was and rubbing the last section of the four. "Put it up," Beloges says as he sits back in his chair, enjoying the warmth of the fireplace and loathing being so old.

"Here, milord." A servant brings Beloges a cup of tea.

"Thanks."

"Well, I am going to go to Jeryko's and see what he has to show me," Sargon says. Then he salutes Beloges and exits the room.

"Send in Father Yor," Beloges says to Sargon as he walks down the hallway.

Sargon enters the dining room and flags Father Yor over.

Yor stands up and walks over to the squire.

"Beloges wants to see you. I think he is quite ill."

Father Yor nods then makes his way down the hall.

"Come in, Father." Beloges waves the young priest into his study.

"Are you unwell?" Father Yor asks as he walks in the doorway.

"I'm well … just old." Beloges laughs. "Wow, you are your father's son," Beloges adds as he looks over at Yor.

"That's what I'm afraid of, milord." Yor looks at the floor.

"Your father was a different person when he was your age," Beloges says.

"You knew my father back then?"

"He was a soldier in my army, started out as a private, very ambitious, and went up fairly quickly in rank. Very likeable guy, broke my heart the day he left to join the army of Missionwise— felt it was his calling from Yahmar … oh, you did not know your father was a religious man?" Beloges says as he sees Yor's expression change.

"No, milord, I was always under the impression that he felt it was beneath him with the stories I have heard," Yor says.

"Don't believe everything you hear. He attended temple services relentlessly. Quite honestly, I thought he might join up with the temple guards and one day become a Templar Knight. I kept up with the goings on from Preador." Beloges smiles at Yor. "You know he met your mother at the temple … well, enough of that." Beloges stops, realizing he is rambling. "Grab that flask over there." He points to the top of his bookshelf, where a dust-covered glass flask rests.

Yor has to stretch to reach it, grabbing it one-handed and setting it in front of the old knight. The container looks very old with a heavy layer of dust and a piece of parchment paper attached with a small rope.

"This is yours … it's about five hundred years old."

"Is that what I think it is?"

"It's a healing potion, but even more important than that is the recipe attached," Beloges says.

"Is it still good?"

"The seal has not been broken." Beloges points to the cork with wax poured over it. I would only use it in an emergency."

"It still has good color." Father Yor grins from ear to ear as he wipes the dust off to reveal a bright-red color in the flask. "I don't know what to say, other than ... thanks, milord."

"You are very welcome, Father. I hope it comes in handy as well as the recipe to make more."

"You are a very good man!" Father Yor says, misty-eyed as he hugs the old man and exits the room.

"Remember, Yor, you might look like your father ... but you are not him nor will you make the mistakes he made. He was a victim of his own greed, and he strayed away from Yahmar— you won't."

Father Yor turns and slowly walks away.

Chapter XXVII
Pretend Knights

t is just on the other side of town," Sergeant Sverre says from atop his horse as the rest of the group falls in behind with Chan walking at the rear. "Let's go!"

"Forward, ho!" Sargon hollers and motions everyone onward. Sargon leads the group down the street and to the other side of town. Tantor prances as the party passes through town, drawing the attention of onlookers. It's not every day the townsfolk see a fully armored heavy warhorse parading through town.

Sargon smirks at the idea that Tantor is prancing because he enjoys the attention he gets; more for his sake than Sargon's.

"That's him ... the Guel boy on that big horse. Arrogant prick, making his horse prance like that," one knight tells another, both sitting on their horses watching as the party passes by. They don't notice Chan standing behind them. "He must really be in love with himself. Better still to put him out of our misery. Let's go." They spur their horses on as Sargon and his companions make their way to the far side of town. Chan drifts behind the two knights as they follow the party.

Sargon and the others dismount their horses as they reach their destination, a small building with a storefront on it. It looks to be a candlemaker's shop by the sign hanging out front and the fragrances emanating from within. The two armored men ride up to an adjacent building, which appears to be a bakery from the smell; they tie off their horses after dismounting. Chan walks to about twenty feet in front of the two men. He drops to the ground and does the flopping crappie, contorting back and forth as if having a seizure in an effort to draw their attention away from Sargon or perhaps lure them in for a strike.

"Jeryko, this is Sargon, Lord Calador's squire." Sergeant Sverre points with an open hand to Sargon as the two men enter the store too. They see an old man with long gray hair and a long beard sitting at a table in the middle of the shop.

Sargon and the sergeant walk around the table followed by the rest of the party. In the background there are various flasks of elixirs and oils on shelves behind a counter; lanterns and unlit torches hang on the walls as well as candles of all lengths and colors. On the table is a hexagon map of Fegnir drawn on bleached burlap. It has an X mark on a hex inside the Astrid Forest.

"I've been expecting you. Come in, come in. Have some wine." Jeryko motions to a pitcher on the table.

"Thanks, but tis too early in the morning, my liege," Sargon says.

"I have a stupid question. Who invented the hexagon way of measurement—it looks like honeycombs to me?" Febor says, looking at the map.

"You are not far from the truth—" Jeryko says.

"It was invented by a monk in Rokia," Friar Truvey interrupts. "Oh, sorry."

"Nonsense, Friar, continue." Jeryko looks at the young friar on the old sage's left side.

"A monk named Brother Diminguez is the one that invented the process. This is back when Lucan was king. He wanted a map of the world put together, and so he charged Diminguez with the task to compile it from all the countries of the world. The monk loved honey, so one day when a scout brought Diminguez a wild honeycomb wrapped in cloth from the pathfinder's saddlebag, the monk noticed the impression of hexagons left behind on the cloth from the honeycomb. This gave him the idea. So he gathered honeycombs, cleaned them out, and filled them with ink then placed cloth over the combs. The rest is history," Friar Truvey says as he points to the map.

"Wow, I'm impressed, Friar," Jeryko says. Sargon rolls his eyes and shakes his head in boredom, wishing for some action. He sighs heavily, seeing the others in the party are impressed with the friar's knowledge and Febor pats the young man on the shoulder. Sargon will soon be regretting his wish.

The two knights outside ignore the convulsing Chan and simply walk around him and through the doorway of the candle-maker's shop.

"Jeryko, we've heard about the ideas you have been spreading around about rebelling against the nobility to incite a civil war."

"What utter nonsense ... it was Beloges that sent these men to me."

"Fuck Beloges!" one of the knights says.

Sargon is taken back by such an outburst and feels something is amiss. It is not to say that knights do not cuss; Reaxl used to cuss up a mean streak at Sargon when he would mess up during training. But it was not "gentlemanly" to carry on this way in public. Sargon recalls a tournament where Reaxl was fighting with staves. He took a hit in the family jewels but did not utter any obscenity, much to Sargon's surprise. Instead, he just teared up and fell to the ground.

"What are knights from Darconia doing here in Jaymar?" Sargon asks, noticing the phoenix markings on their shields and helms—the coat of arms symbol of the capital city. He also notices that the two did not announce themselves. Knights are a proud bunch and will always introduce themselves.

"General Devalar sent us, and we are not here for Jeryko. We are here for you for the murder of your family, Sargon," the other knight comments.

"I am protected under the flag of Castle Du'tesh," Sargon says as he reaches for his belt pouch. *Why did they say General Devalar and not the Duke of Darconia?* Sargon wonders.

"Hold it right there," the knight commands as he points a crossbow at Sargon.

"Easy there, milord ... he is just getting his papers," Father Yor says.

"Shut it, holy man," the knight commands as he now points the crossbow at Father Yor. The priest holds his hands up in utter shock.

"What kind of knights are you two, threatening an unarmed priest?" Bellgrad comments. Even he, a mere soldier, knows that knights would never do this sort of thing.

"Say good bye, Jeryko." The knight points his crossbow at the old sage.

"HIIIIIYAA," Chan hollers from the porch of the shop and kicks the knight with the crossbow in the back, knocking the man off balance. The crossbow discharges, hitting one of the flasks on the shelf.

Sargon immediately notices that the supposed knight overcorrects himself, not being used to the heavy armor—a rookie mistake. "They are not knights, Bjorn!"

The barbarian is standing next to the doorway just inside the shop. He pulls his new axe from his back.

"Easy there, big guy," the knight closest to him pulls a pistol crossbow and points it right at the barbarian's face. "Get your ass over there." The knight motions toward Sargon with the crossbow in his right hand, still carrying the shield on his left.

Bjorn moves over toward the squire, still holding Frostbyte.

The knight with the pistol crossbow turns his attention to

Chan. "Hold still, you little weasel." The knight follows Chan with the weapon as the monk shucks and jives around on the porch.

"Nathair," Friar Truvey says, and the pistol crossbow turns into a snake. The startled knight chunks it out the door and onto the porch. Bjorn takes the opportunity. He steps back toward the knight and swings his axe at his backside. The axe sticks in the back plate of the armor, absorbing the full impact of the hit.

The knight pummels Bjorn in the face with the crossbow. Simultaneously, Chan attacks the knight that was trying to shoot him with a swift kick to the face. The kick hits the helm of the knight, but rings his bell nonetheless. The barbarian just shakes his head and pulls out his axe as the weapon has frozen part of the armor. A big chunk of the armor breaks away as Bjorn retrieves his axe, leaving a gaping hole in the armor.

He swings it at the other knight, but the knight blocks the hit with his shield, dislodging the pieces of full plate from the axe and sending them falling to the floor. Drawing his sword, the first knight spins and attacks Bjorn. The barbarian blocks the swing with his axe, burning Bjorn's hand with the head of the axe. Bjorn shakes it off and swings his axe with both hands at the head of his attacker.

Ching kerchunk ching. The axe slices through the neck guard of the full plate, lopping off the man's head and slicing through the neck guard on the other side. "Whoa ..." Bjorn is somewhat stunned, not expecting that outcome. As the man's body falls to the ground, Bjorn sees Chan retrieve his flaming dagger from the hole he had put in the armor earlier.

Bellgrad leaps at the other armored man, knocking him through the doorway and onto his back as the man's helm flies off.

"Hold it, Bellgrad," Sargon says, making his way to the door. "We need him alive."

But it's too late. The man pulls off the glove from his left hand and sprinkles poison in his mouth from his ring. The man shakes and contorts as the poison does its work.

"That was surely a shock," Sergeant Sverre says, surprised at all the melee. "It is a good thing I was here to witness all of this, otherwise I would not have believed it. How did you know?" the sergeant asks Sargon.

Sargon explains what he witnessed as Bjorn and Bellgrad search the two men looking for any clues.

As Bellgrad inspects the poison ring, he notices the tail end of a tattoo on the man's wrist. The soldier pulls his dagger then cuts the leather straps holding the arm piece to the breastplate and slides it off the dead man. He then rolls up the chain mail beneath to reveal a tattoo of a snake on the arm. "These two surely were no knights," Bellgrad comments as he holds the arm up for the others to see.

"I knew they were not knights ... no honor in their speech to one another. I followed them," Chan says from out on the porch.

"Good job, Chan," Sargon compliments the monk. Chan walks in and nods.

"Sometime a bird flies and not know where it goes." Chan gives a lesson.

Sargon and Bellgrad exchange a look, holding back a laugh.

"Kalius the Snake," Exel states with a strange look on his face, eyeing the tattoo from across the room as he holds his bow and an arrow, which apparently he had notched earlier when the fighting began. "That's who those two worked for—that is his mark. We've been having run-ins with those types. Perhaps one of our friends has gotten mixed up with the Snake as well," Exel says, eyeing Evan.

"I don't understand it ... I don't know who he is. I have never crossed paths with this fellow," Sargon says, looking at the dead men as Bjorn drags the headless assassin out the door.

"I will get some men to take care of this," Sergeant Sverre says as he walks out the door and mounts his horse. "I'm going to have Bargos send word to General Devalar to see if he is missing any men. Go on and finish your business here."

"Someone has placed a hit out on you, milord," Febor tells Sargon. "Those people understand only one language—money." Febor points to Bjorn, who is holding five J'avins from the man he decapitated.

"No guesses as to who that is … that damn Heyrold," Sargon says, shaking his head in disbelief.

"Those men weren't lying about one thing—they did come from Darconia. I hear that's were Kalius's headquarters is," Febor says.

Chapter XXVIII
Vlasko Revisited

id you get your map?" Sargon hollers to Exel, slowing Tantor to a walk. They've been riding hard for the past hour.

"You saw me drawing it out … it's in my saddlebag. Besides, it would be too late if I forgot it back there." Exel says, coming alongside Sargon.

"Friar, come up here," Sargon says as he turns in the saddle to look behind his horse and wave at the young druid.

"Yes, milord," Truvey says as he rides up behind Tantor.

"That was really great what you did back there. I didn't get a chance to tell you earlier, but you probably saved Chan's life."

"Please … with a pistol cross?" Bjorn scoffs as he rides behind Truvey.

"Well, yeah, if he hit Chan in the head." Sargon looks back at Bjorn. "Besides I did not see you charge that guy when he had that pistol pointing at **your** head."

"True," Bjorn recalls.

"So what did you learn from that encounter?" Sargon asks Truvey.

"Things are not always what they seem. I guess the same can be said for the spell I put on that pretend knight's pistol crossbow. It did not turn into a snake—it was just an illusion.

"I did not see any snake," Bjorn comments. "I just saw the fake knight throw his crossbow away."

"I guess you are not as dumb as you look!" Truvey jokes with Bjorn.

"Oh … that's a good one." Exel laughs.

"Hey, I got to make up for Silver not being with us," Truvey says. "Like I was about to say, most all spells that I and my brethren use are non-violent. We only resort to violence when we are attacked first."

"Great ... a tree hugger!" Bellgrad rolls his eyes.

"Yes I have hugged a tree before. Someone's spirit could be trapped in it," Truvey says. "It could be the spirit of someone in your family."

"I never thought of it that way," Bellgrad comments, looking over at Meg.

"You've taken real command of that horse, Father ... I like it!" Sargon compliments Father Yor, who rides up beside Truvey. "Now, we need to stay on point. Febor, what did Jeryko tell us about the castle?"

Febor spurs his horse up behind Father Yor. "Well, the owner's name was Budapeste. He was a knight of the old Order of the King's Eye, the king being Lucan. The knight owned the land from his castle to the sea. Just west of where Darconia sits today, all the way to Lake Moeri and the Ky River."

"There are two orders of the Knights of Lucan. The Knights of the King's Eye was the lower of the two, and the order of knight that Budapeste belong to. Knight of the Brow was the other; but I will not bore you with all these details. What else did Jeryko say about Duke Budapeste?"

"He was an avid collector of exotic animals. It was said that he even had a Ki-rin from the mountains of Euguadia," Father Yor joins in.

"Did you hear that, Chan?" Sargon looks behind everyone to the running monk.

"'Tis a great story ... but not possible. These creatures are pets of Hefnor, God of Wind. They have also been called Qilin. They are a combination of a dragon, a stag, and an ox. They have scales and tough hide and the head of a dragon, the body and antlers of a stag, the tail and strong legs of an ox. They are as big as your horse, milord. They fly as fast as wind, can run faster than any horse, and are about three times meaner. Also, impossible to capture. Very smart too … some are even said to speak. Their mane and hide is said to be made of gold. But I have also heard there are some as red as fire … pets of Sholok, the God of War. Is good bedtime story to tell children, though."

"Have you ever seen one?" Febor asks Chan.

"No, but I have heard stories and seen statues." Chan thinks of stories he heard when he was younger. "There is one story about a group of one hundred miners coming home down from the mountains one day. They were attacked by ten giants hurling rocks. One Kirin killed all ten giants, but not before being overcome by his injuries. He died defending the men. There is said to be a sculpture of the savior in the small mountain village where these men were from."

"Elktor is said to have made some of these creatures as well, but they stay in the forests and their hides are as brown as the soil. Others have green hide to match the trees and plants," Truvey explains.

"Jeryko did say that Budapeste just up and disappeared one day and that anyone living there afterward died mysteriously until the castle was abandoned—said to be inhabited by strange creatures," Bellgrad adds to the conversation. "Maybe some of these creatures got loose and killed the duke."

"Maybe. Well, we know it has perqs living there now. What is the number one rule, Truvey?" Sargon asks, looking back at the young druid.

"Stay together," Truvey responds.

"Excellent."

"Why are we talking about this now? We are still three days

away."

"I wanted to see if anyone was paying attention. It's my job to keep you all alive and make sure that everyone has all the facts. And you can tell Silver when we get to Vlasko," Sargon says as he twists back around. "Let's get to it. They have rested long enough." Sargon spurs Tantor as the rest of the group falls in line, heading east toward the small hamlet of Vlasko. They all ride hard for another couple of hours.

"What did Beloges give you back there, Father?" Sargon asks Father Yor as he slows his horse again.

"It is a potion of healing. I think it is the same as two of the flasks we took from the tower the other day."

"Really?"

"It is bright red, just the same as those you have in your saddlebags. We can check them out the next time we stop. Don't want to risk breaking any while we ride," Father Yor says.

"Good thinking." Sargon smiles.

"You think Silver is okay?" Father Yor looks concerned.

"Guess we will find out soon enough. I did not see any jail or law there. Don't suppose he got strung up in a tree there, do you?" Sargon asks.

"Oh dear ..."

"Quit worrying, Mama Yor." Bellgrad laughs from behind Father Yor's horse.

"Yeah, I suspect they have his body displayed for the whole town to see what happens to thieves," Exel jokes, slowing down in front of Sargon.

"Hey, that's not funny," Yor protests as Sargon laughs and shakes his head.

"Don't worry the good Father like that," Sargon tells Exel.

"Sorry, Father, just having a little fun. He is probably having all kinds of fun with that barmaid."

"What barmaid?" Meg asks.

"Oh ... no one," Exel says as he spurs his horse and disappears ahead.

"What is he talking about?" Meg asks, looking around at the group in front of her.

Sargon spurs Tantor into a hard run as the rest of the group follows.

"What are you not—" Meg's voice is drowned out by the thunderous sound of hooves.

"*Can't hear you.*" Bellgrad mouths as he puts his hand to his ear, running his mount next to his girl. He receives a dirty look as they progress down the road.

The rest of the journey passes uneventfully, everyone in the group avoiding Meg.

The horses slow to a walk as they approach Vlasko.

Father Yor stops his horse while scanning the woods around the hamlet.

"What is wrong, Yor?" Sargon asks as he spins Tantor around to look at the priest.

"I have to go check something out," Father Yor says, motioning ahead. There are glowing candles burning on altars in what look like small shrines scattered throughout the woods. "Come with me," Father Yor says as he cuts a glance at Truvey.

"Follow them." Sargon orders Exel.

The scout nods, breaks formation, and falls in behind the two holy men while the rest of the group rides into town.

"What are you doing?" Truvey asks Father Yor.

"Searching. See all these altars? There is one for your god, Elktor." Father Yor points to a shrine.

"Yes, I think it's great that someone can pay their respects to their deity," Truvey says.

"I agree as long as it's not Asberdies or Genzo," Yor continues as he rides through the woods. "There ..." Father Yor points as he jumps off his horse then grabs some small vials from his saddlebag.

"I do not know what you are doing," Truvey says as he dismounts and follows.

"My job!" Father Yor explains, approaching the makeshift shrine.

"Ugh!" Truvey is surprised by a disgusting statuette of a winged devil sitting on a log about ten feet from the altar. "I'm not feeling very well."

"That's because this is desecrated soil." Father Yor pulls the vials from his pockets. The priest cringes with pain in his gut as he approaches the unholy altar. He takes one of the vials and throws it on the altar. The glass shatters, lit by one of the candles. Father Yor then takes the other vial and tosses it to Truvey.

"What is this?"

"Blessed oil. Throw it," Father Yor commands.

Truvey throws it on the opposite end of the altar. It lights up the other half of the altar and destroys it. Yor then grabs his chesa, holds it above his head, and mutters some words, which causes the fire to double in size for a moment. The pain in his gut ceases as the fire dies down. Walking around the area, Father Yor smashes all the statuettes with his scepter as he chants.

Truvey goes back to the statuette he first saw and smashes it with his mace.

"We have got to go. You will have company soon. I just shot one of their goons," Exel tells the two clerics from his horse about fifty yards away.

"My work here is done." Father Yor finishes walking the area with his holy symbol in the air, exorcising the grounds. He and

Truvey return to their horses, mount up, and head to town behind Exel.

"I was told you would be along soon," Smitty, the stable boy, says as he grabs the horses from the trio dismounting in front of the stable.

"Here you go, my good man," Father Yor says as he puts five pens in the boy's shirt pocket.

"Thank you, milord." Smitty smiles.

Exel, Father Yor, and Friar Truvey walk into the inn; they spot the group at a large table on the far side close to the bar. Silverfish is talking with the others as the trio walk to the table. Father Yor makes out a small group with an Asberdian priest at a table near the one where the group is sitting.

"How are you, Father? It's good to see you." Silver hugs the young priest. "Ugh, you smell like smoke."

"Shh … I missed you too, little man." Father Yor shushes the elf as he returns the hug.

"I heard I missed all the action in Jaymar," Silver says. "Of course I had some action of my own here," Silver adds with a sinister laugh.

"I'm sure I don't want to hear about that." Father Yor rolls his eyes at the elf. "What do you have to do to get a drink around here?" Yor adds, looking around the room. Then he gets up and makes his way to the bar.

"What will you have there, Father?" the bartender asks.

"Mead," Yor says impatiently. "What are you having, Friar?" Father Yor looks at the table.

"Wine," Truvey answers.

"Wine as well, my good man," Father Yor tells the bartender. "Here." Yor puts a Siv on the bar.

"Thanks, milord." The bartender puts two clay jugs on the bar along with two cups.

Father Yor grabs the jugs and cups, turns, and bumps into a man as he was about to head back to the table. "Oh, sorry."

"That's okay, my good Father. I'm a fellow priest myself," the man says.

"Oh really?" Yor says, seeing the man is the Asberdian priest he spotted earlier.

"Look, we are both holy men. I have started a small temple outside of town. I would like to invite you over sometime."

"I don't think so," Father Yor says.

"Well, we are all going to be maggots feasting on rotted flesh when we leave this world, so we should live it up while we can." The priest smiles as he spins Yor around to face the drunken priest. "All they have taught you is a big lie. You won't be serving your god when you leave this world ... I happen to be short on coin, my brother. Could you perhaps make me a donation?" The man's breath smells like a dung heap.

Father Yor has lost all patience. "No, I already took a shit today."

Father Yor leaves the man speechless and walks to the table.

"Hey ... hey, you ..." the drunken priest follows Yor.

"Can I help you?" Bellgrad steps in front of the Asberdian priest.

"Oh, I see how it is ... got your muscle to hide behind."

"Excuse me. I think you need to leave." Bellgrad towers over the priest.

"Yeah ... shitbird it's time to leave before I gut you like a fish. I'll slice you from your nut sack to your gullet. We don't work for Father Yor. He is our friend and a member of our group. Sargon here is our leader, and if we work for anyone, it would be Sargon's lord, Lord Calador," Silverfish says, looking over his shoulder to see no sign of Sargon. He spins his dagger in his right hand.

"That's enough, Silver. You don't have to explain yourself to this joker," Bellgrad comments as he pats the elf on the shoulder.

Some younger men from the priest's table come over and escort the man back.

Silver scoffs as the man staggers back to his table. "Where's Sargon?

"He said he was turning in for the night," Truvey relays.

"I bet. I still can't believe what you told that guy, Father." Silver turns around to look at Father Yor.

Silver relays what he heard Yor say to the Asberdian priest. Everyone at the table erupts into laughter.

"Can't believe you heard that with all the noise in this place," Father Yor says to Silverfish as he sits enjoying his mead, feeling a little embarrassed.

Truvey pours himself some wine.

Meanwhile, Eavan and Sargon are locked in a heavy kiss in the hall outside his room. "Umph," Eavan moans as the squire holds her up against the wall with his left hand, fumbling for the room key with his right. He manages to unlock and open the door, walk her inside, and kick the door shut.

Clunk. Crack! Boom! Laughter can be heard from behind the door.

Chapter XXIX
Father Ola

orning, milord."

Sargon opens his eyes to see his lovely wife, Jessica, lying next to him in bed, her head propped up by her left arm. Her beautiful face morphs until he's looking at Eavan. Sargon comes fully awake, remembering last night's romance at the sight of the headboard loose and leaning against the wall. He remembers the two of them falling on the bed in the heat of passion, breaking the frame. His size and the fact that he was still wearing armor might have had something to do with it.

"What time is it, beautiful?" Sargon asks, caressing her cheek.

"Midmorning."

Sargon considers jumping up but decides to stay in bed next to this *goddess*. It has been a long time since he has awakened this late and felt so well rested.

"Did I satisfy your appetite, milord?"

"I don't know. I haven't had breakfast yet." Sargon laughs and rolls over onto Eavan.

Downstairs, Father Yor looks around, concerned. "I'm telling you, something is wrong ... we never wake up before him, let alone finish breakfast."

"Leave him be. He will be down when he is good and ready. Believe me, no one has earned the rest more," Bellgrad explains.

"He's not just sleeping," Silverfish adds with a devilish laugh.

"Speaking of which ... what's this I hear about you and a barmaid? Was it the girl you were flirting with the other day?"

Meg asks.

"Excuse me? What are you, my mother? How is that any of your concern?" Silver says.

Bellgrad rolls his eyes and shakes his head.

"Barbye is my friend," Meg says.

"So? Do you even know what she was doing when we first met?" Silver asks. "Well … I'll tell you later …" Silver recants as he glances over at Father Yor then gets up from the table and walks outside.

"What's wrong with him?" Meg asks, looking around the table.

"Really? You have to ask? You have spent too much time at home. Look, your concern for Barbye is admirable, but he is right. It is not your place to ask. I would've thought your mother had taught you better," Bellgrad says.

Everyone else at the table looks around the room, trying to ignore the couple.

Meg scoffs and storms upstairs to their room.

"Well … there will be no action for you tonight." Bjorn laughs patting Bellgrad on the shoulder before walking outside.

"What, no words of wisdom?" Bellgrad says, eyeing the rest of the party at the table.

"I'm the last guy to be giving advice about women … heck, I have a girlfriend in every town," Febor boasts as he points to himself with his thumb and shakes his head.

"Don't look at me. Yahmarian priests are celibate. Even if I weren't, I'm not too sure I would want a woman in my life. I hear too many problems from the married folk, not to mention all the drama I have seen with this bunch."

"Sometimes it is better to have two birds in a tree than to understand a woman," Chan relays a lesson.

Bellgrad and the others look at the monk as though he has

lost his mind.

"Women are like nature—just when you think you have it figured out, something changes and throws all your knowledge out the door. What? I wasn't always a priest." Truvey smiles at Bellgrad.

"What made you become a priest of the woods, anyway?" Bellgrad asks the young druid.

A memory flashes through Truvey's mind. A hut on fire. A young girl's terrible screams. *TRUVEY! TRUVEY!* Then the memory disappears as quickly as it came. Truvey stares blankly at the wall.

"Friar. Friar?" Bellgrad looks puzzled.

"I love animals ..." Truvey responds.

"I do too, especially smothered in gravy," Exel comments.

Everyone at the table laughs.

"What did I miss?" Silverfish asks sitting at the table.

"Nothing." Exel smirks.

A plate is set before the elf.

"Are you eating again? We just finished breakfast." Father Yor shakes his head.

"What is that?" Truvey asks, looking disgusted.

"What, are you new? It's a roasted sheep's head—mighty tasty," Silver says with a big smile on his face. He pulls out one of the eyes then begins munching on it.

"Ugh ... I think I'm gonna be sick." Truvey covers his mouth with a hand and runs out the front door of the inn.

"Smooth move, Lumpy," Father Yor scolds Silver.

"What?" Silver asks innocently.

"He's a vegetarian," Father Yor says.

"What's that?" Silver asks, relishing his meal.

"He doesn't eat meat, stupid."

"Oh, well it's a bad day to be him, then." Silver shrugs as he cracks the skull with his dagger and eats the meat from within.

"Boy, you eat like a Troglodyte," Father Yor says as he watches the elf eat.

"Good thing I don't smell like one." Silver smiles.

"No ... you smell like a troll." Chan smiles from his seat next to the elf.

"Here's our illustrious leader," Father Yor says, spotting Sargon descending the stairs.

"Coffee," Sargon tells one of the servant girls as he sits at the table. "Mmm ... something smells good."

"I just had a roasted sheep's head." Silver smiles as he pushes away his plate with a bare skull.

"Okay ... I'll have one of those as well," Sargon says to the servant girl.

Silver's smile fades. He was hoping to disgust the squire too.

"Two eggs as well ... and lamb chops."

The servant girl takes the order and disappears to the kitchen.

"Worked up a hunger, did we?" Silver questions the squire.

"Yes, you could say that ... and why are you staring at me?"

"I just had to see it for myself." Silver smirks as he switches his gaze to Eavan walking down the stairs. "Just wanted to be sure you were not Bjorn's pretty boy."

"No chance of that," Eavan says, sitting down next to the squire. "Tea please, Abigail," Eavan says, smiling at the servant girl waiting beside the table.

She giggles as she heads back to the kitchen.

"Thank you," Silver says, looking Eavan in the eye.

"For what?" Eavan asks as she holds Sargon's hand and leans her head on his shoulder.

"For that ... I haven't seen a smile on his face since I met the guy. He usually looks stern like he has a stick shoved up his ..."

"Silver!" Father Yor interrupts.

"Well, just saying …"

"My pleasure, Silver," Eavan says as she receives her tea.

"You know this fool?"

"Well, yes, everyone knows Silver," Eavan answers as she receives a shearing glance from her lover.

"Not like that, silly. He frequents the inn quite often." Eavan gently nudges his shoulder. "Not my type … I only like REAL men," Eavan whispers. She kisses Sargon's ear and slides her fingers along his inner thigh.

"Okay … okay." Sargon smiles and almost blushes. He feels jumpy at her touch.

From the front porch of the inn, Bjorn hears a whistle coming from the stable. It appears to be Bellgrad, who has been talking with Smitty, the stable boy, about saddling the horses for the group. The soldier nods toward the Asberdian priest from the night before. He and his goons are approaching the inn.

"Get out of my way!" the Asberdian priest tells Bjorn, who is standing with Exel in the doorway.

"Tell your master that I am onto him. He destroyed my temple last night."

"I have no master. And who are you talking about?" Bjorn questions.

"The priest, Father Yor," says one of the goons.

"Like we told your priest last night—we do not work for Father Yor. He is our friend," Bjorn says. "Now, if you want to talk to our leader, Sir Sargon is sitting at the table there with Father Yor," Bjorn adds as he steps away from the door.

The Asberdian priest looks in and sees the armored squire setting next to Father Yor. Father Yor looks up.

"Oh … great," Father Yor says.

"What?" Sargon looks at Father Yor.

"The Asberdian priest from last night. I thought we would be long gone by now," Father Yor says nervously.

"There's nothing to fear, Father. I'm here." Sargon smiles as he reassures Yor. "What did you do?"

"I did not get a chance to tell you last night ... here he comes," Father Yor whispers.

"Sir Sargon, I am Father Ola," the priest introduces himself.

"What can I do for you, Father Ola?" Sargon says, looking up from his breakfast. He sees the priest has two men with him, and he notices Bjorn and Exel tagging along.

"I have a small shrine outside of town, or rather I *had*. It was destroyed last night."

"How does this concern me? I am no follower of Asberdies," Sargon comments as he continues eating.

"I know, but you are a knight."

"Thank you, Father, but not yet."

"Well, you will be soon enough. But you follow in their ways."

"What's your point?"

"I believe your follower there, Father Yor, did this deed," Ola says.

Father Yor is about to open his mouth but is silenced by Sargon's raised finger.

"First off, Father Yor is not my follower. He is my counsel and my confidant, not to mention my friend. Do you have any proof to back up your claim?"

"No."

"Any witnesses who saw him do this?"

"No."

"Well, I'm not the law around here, but it sounds like you are bearing false witness against him."

"He is a priest of Yahmar."

"Yes, and he travels with me and therefore is under my

protection. Good day, sir."

Father Yor is impressed.

Father Ola turns to leave. "*Ragno ... correre,*" Ola says as he slowly spins back around to face the table.

Father Yor eyes the priest. Ola suddenly grabs a handful of something from a bag with his left hand and blows it in Father Yor's direction. "*Maledire te.*" But Bjorn interrupts Ola's spell, giving the man a shove. Instead of hitting the intended target, the powder lands on Truvey, who happens to be sitting to the right of Father Yor.

"SEIZE HIM!" Sargon orders, jumping up from the table.

Truvey sneezes. Bjorn attempts to grab Ola, but the man dodges then runs to the wall and steps onto it as if it were the floor. In the next breath, he's running on the ceiling with blinding speed as his companions follow him on the ground, heading for the door.

Bjorn starts to throw his dagger but stops at the last moment, seeing all the people in the inn and realizing the danger of hurting an innocent bystander. "Get the hell out of here, *skríða* (creeps)," he hollers.

Exel shoots at the priest, but an enchantment protects the man, running like a spider along the ceiling.

Jumping down, the priest stops in the inn's doorway, looks down at his right sleeve, and sticks a finger through the grazing hole made by one of Exel's arrows. Ola laughs at the sight and turns to go.

Exel has an arrow notched and taking aim at the priest.

"No, too many innocents," Sargon says as he pushes down the arrow with his open hand.

CRACK. Chan hits the priest upon the crown of his head, knocking the man out. Father Ola's two companions pull him to safety. Chan jumps back, almost falling backward as one of the men gazes at the young monk.

"Are you okay?" Father Yor asks Truvey.

"I'm okay ... I don't know what that stuff was that he blew on me, but I feel fine," Truvey answers.

"I don't know either, but I got a little on me as well. Perhaps it was some itching powder or something like that."

"What's wrong, Chan? You look as if you have seen a ghost," Sargon tells the monk, who is running toward the group, looking pale and shaken.

"That ... that man with priest was dead. I saw in his eyes," Chan relays, trembling slightly.

"Here, have some coffee." Sargon pours a cup then hands it to the scared monk.

Father Yor makes his way to Chan, rubbing his hand across the young man's head, petting him like a cat. *"Non aver paura,"* Father Yor recites. Chan's trembling stops instantly, and he regains his composure.

"Thank you, Father. I will not forget." Chan smiles at the priest. "I have never encountered something like that before."

"Yes, the living dead can have that effect. That man is probably a wight. He most likely doesn't know he is dead."

"A wight?" Sargon asks.

"A wight, an undead a step up from a zombie or a ghoul. They have the soul of the man trapped with an evil spirit hidden in the background," Father Yor tells Sargon.

"How do you know all this stuff? Surely you have never run into any of them before," Sargon says.

"It's in here." Father Yor holds up the spell book he carries with him. "Bishop Solias had a run-in with many undead. This book is a journal as well as a book of spells."

"So, what does the good bishop suggest we do?" Sargon asks sarcastically.

"Nothing. Pursuing him would only anger the spirit," Father Yor says.

"Nothing?"

"Right. The priest will probably end up being killed once the man realizes he is dead. Wights hate all living creatures, and once the rat is out of the bag, the evil spirit will take control, killing all around it."

"More reason to go after it now," Sargon suggests.

"I think freeing the people enslaved by the perqs is more important right now. Heck, it could be years before the wight realizes what he is. The man still has all the memories and feelings from when he was alive, and apparently Father Ola has done a pretty good job of hiding the man's condition from him," Father Yor explains.

"How can we distinguish him from the living if he is not with the priest?"

"He will have an unending thirst."

"Great, so we just find someone drinking a lot and go bash him in the head. That should be easy in a tavern." Sargon smiles.

"Funny. No, another tell is living in a dark environment. A cave, a basement, etc.," Father Yor says.

"That wight was in the daylight, and he was not harmed," Chan joins in.

"I did not say that light hurts them, like vamps. They just don't like it and will shield themselves from it, especially where they dwell," Father Yor explains.

"Vamps?" Sargon asks.

"Vampires ... the light of Sulo destroys those kinds of undead," Father Yor says.

"We are all ready to go. Smitty has the horses saddled up," Bellgrad says.

"Let's go." Sargon walks out of the inn, the others follow.

Chapter XXX
Father Yor's Unwelcome Return

ho goes there?" asks a soldier from the front gatehouse of Missionwise.

"It's Father Yor and friends," Yor says, waiting impatiently atop his horse outside the city walls.

"Sorry, Father. I'm new, and I had to get one of the other men to verify who you were. There have been bandits on the roadways at night. That's why we have been keeping the gate closed. Come right in. We don't usually get travelers this early in the morning," the soldier says as he and two others raise the portcullis.

"Someone wanted a cold camp last night. Needless to say, we all were eager to get underway this morning. I woke up shivering and told Sir Sargon here that I would give him five Sivs if he would light a fire," Father Yor says, pointing to Sargon.

"Humph," Sargon scoffs. "I was just avoiding unwanted company, like we had before ... Do you have to tell everybody our business?" Sargon scolds Father Yor.

"There sure seems to be a lot of crying going on," Exel says over his shoulder as he rides through the gatehouse.

"Yes, it's making my ears bleed hearing all this bellyaching," Bjorn joins in.

"You two can just shut it," Father Yor protests.

The group rides to the far side of town toward the temple.

"You both leave the good Father alone. I'm cold too," Meg says.

"I'll keep you warm." Bellgrad smiles.

"I'd sooner sleep with Silverfish," Meg replies.

"Huh?" Silver wakes, almost asleep on his horse. "Anytime, baby girl."

"Oh you just shut it, mister, if you know what's good for you," Meg tells Silverfish.

"Everybody shut your piehole," Sargon says. "Yor, you go into the temple, and we will meet you at the inn. Get your supplies and whatever else you need, and don't dally about. We need to get to the ruins as quickly as we can."

"We can all go to the temple," Father Yor says.

"No, the generosity of the temple will have to wait for another day. I will instruct Tate at the stable to leave our horses saddled. We will get a quick bite to eat then we can be on our way. I figure it's going to take us several hours to find this castle," Sargon says as the rest of the group heads to the stable, leaving the two men atop their horses in the middle of the road.

"Morning, milady," Tate says as he grabs the reins of Meg's horse. The rest of the group arrives behind the young maiden.

Sargon and Bellgrad hand over their horses to Tate, instructing him to leave the animals saddled but give them a morning feeding. Father Yor leaves his horse at the stable and scurries off to the temple. He stops halfway up the stairs and begins talking to someone.

Sargon shakes his head as he and Bellgrad enter the Inn of the Choking Gnome with the rest of the party following behind. Sargon scans the almost vacant tavern, searching for a large table. He spots one on the far side, doing a double take as he sees Chan sitting at the table enjoying some tea. *How did he slip by us and get in here so fast?* Sargon thinks to himself.

"How did he get there?" Bellgrad asks the young squire.

"Pretty sneaky. Almost as good as Silver." Sargon stops Bellgrad, who's about to head to the table. "Look." Sargon points with his head at two large men approaching the monk. They look as if they've been drinking all night.

"What?" Silverfish asks as he looks across the room. "Oh, he's gonna kick their asses." He turns and dashes out the door.

"Silver!" Sargon smirks.

"Look at this joker, Zeek," the one man says to his friend as he looks at Chan.

"You're a long way from home, ain't ya, gwiddy?"

Chan calmly sips his tea, ignoring the racial slur.

"He must've just woke up. He still has his nightgown on," Zeek tells his friend.

"That's not a nightgown—it's a robe."

"A robe ... are you some kinda royalty?" Zeek asks. "Hey, I'm talking to you, gwiddy." Zeek grabs Chan's right arm.

Chan grips the man's hand and twists it.

The man shrieks in pain then backhands Chan in the mouth with his other hand.

"There's our cue," Sargon tells Bellgrad.

"Wait."

"Oh my goodness," Meg says, watching a large male approaching Chan. The man is wearing a burlap shirt with no sleeves. It is Bjorn, who had made his way to the hearth and pulled off his armor to warm himself. Meg oohs and aahs as Bjorn makes his way over to Chan.

Bjorn grabs the other man's arm just in time, stopping him from hitting Chan with a number nine sleeper, his heavy wooden club. Bjorn commences to throw the man across the room, where he hits the far wall then crashes onto an empty table. He lays unmoving. Chan puts a walloping on Zeek that the man won't soon forget.

Another drunken goon taps Bjorn on the shoulder then punches him in the mouth as the barbarian turns around. Bjorn just smiles, showing bloody teeth. He returns a much harder punch, sending blood and a couple of teeth flying through the air as well as the man, who crashes down on a table, breaking the legs then falling to the floor.

Another brawler breaks a chair across Bjorn's back. Still holding the club, Bjorn hits the guy in the gut, making him double over. Bjorn gives the brawler an uppercut with the club, sending the man flying backward and breaking another table. The man crashes to the floor, knocked out cold.

"Thank you, but I did not need your help," Chan tells Bjorn.

"Sure ..." Bjorn says, throwing the number nine sleeper on the table.

"What's that?"

"That's what one of your buddies was about to pound you with. You would've been asleep till the morrow."

"I owe you one." Chan smiles at Bjorn.

"Don't worry about it," Bjorn says as he sits next to Chan and flags a servant girl over. The rest of the group gathers around the table.

Sargon orders food for the group; he also gives coins to the servant girl, telling her it is for the damages that Bjorn caused. They all dine for a time without Silverfish. Moments later, Exel appears at the front door of the inn after entertaining company with some old colleagues he found. He flags Sargon to the door and motions across the street.

"What is it?" Sargon asks as soon as he arrives at the door.

"There is something going on at the stairs of the temple," Exel says, eating an apple.

"Damn him!" Sargon curses as he catches a glimpse of Father Yor surrounded by people. "Further delays," Sargon grumbles as he storms outside and toward the temple.

Sargon takes the stairs of the temple two at a time until he reaches a mob chanting "devil worshiper" while throwing rotten fruit and vegetables. A young boy next to Sargon hands the squire a rotten tomato to throw. Sargon tosses it aside.

"STOP THIS NONSENSE AT ONCE," Sargon hollers.

One in the crowd says, "He is a worshiper of Asberdies, milord. How else could he have healed this man here who had the plague? No other priest has ever done that."

Sargon recognizes the healed man from the infirmary when Bellgrad was there.

"He is a great man of Yahmar and blessed by his god. He has saved many lives and *not* by the aid of Asberdies. I have seen with my own eyes the miraculous work he does. He follows the ways of Bishop Solace."

"He was a great man of Yahmar ... but he lived years and years ago," another man in the crowd comments.

"Perhaps he lives again through Father Yor," Sargon says, seeing Silverfish in the crowd throwing the rotten ammo. Sargon stares him down, and the elf drops the rotten fruit and shrugs his shoulders. He leaves, looking disappointed.

"I bless all of you. Perhaps you can see the error of your ways," Father Yor recites, holding his chesa above his head. The holy symbol catches a reflection from Sulo, which diverts sunrays upward in multiple directions.

Through the sunrays, as if opening into another world, a winged warrior can be seen flying above. Sargon gives the archon a salute as the people immediately fall to their knees, begging Father Yor's forgiveness.

"See? I told you. It was Yahmar's power that saved me, not Asberdies," Zeth says to the mob as he waves at the angel.

The archon pulls off his full helm, smirks at Zeth, and returns Sargon's salute. Then he flies upward and disappears. The mob spreads out to let the good Father pass.

Sargon and Father Yor enter the temple. Preador, High Priest of Yahmar, greets the two young men along with several acolytes.

"Yahmar is truly watching over you, my son," Preador grins like a proud father.

"You saw that too?" Yor asks.

"We all did!" Preador says as he hugs his young understudy and shakes Sargon's hand. "Let's get you something to eat."

"I have food waiting for me back at the inn, Your Grace," Sargon says. "I just helped Yor out of a jam. I need to get back." Sargon salutes and leaves.

"We are going to Budapeste Castle, Your Grace," Father Yor tells Preador. "I'll grab a quick bite then be on my way. I do need to get more stones and supplies, though."

"Help yourself to whatever you need and look up Gunther to outfit you with better armor." Preador smiles and points to Father Yor's chain mail.

"Oh ... here," Father Yor places a large handful of J'avins into Preador's hands.

"What's this?" Preador asks.

"My tithes."

"Oh, that's way too much."

"Please, Your Grace, I insist."

"You need money for yourself."

"I still have some."

"Well ... okay." Preador laughs as he puts his arm around the young priest's shoulder and escorts him toward the kitchen. "Your mother would be very proud of the man you have become."

"Do you think she sees me?"

"Most certainly. All she has to do is look out the window of the Hall of the Fathers," Preador answers.

"Right, tending to the cherubs in the back of the hall. The same as Jessica, I suppose."

"Who?"

"Jessica, Sargon's bride."

"Oh, right."

The two men arrive at the kitchen and sit at the table while food is brought out to them.

"I can't believe you were throwing rotten tomatoes at the good Father," Sargon scolds Silverfish as the two eat breakfast at the inn.

"What? I was just having some fun." Silverfish laughs as he receives disappointed looks from the others at the table. "Oh … come on. It was just a little harmless fun."

"Well, you could've stood up for Father Yor. It shouldn't have to be Sargon all the time," Meg says.

"Right, like they are going to believe me," Silver says, pointing to himself.

"Well, you could've tried."

"Not my style, babycakes," Silver says and stuffs some pancakes in his mouth.

"You have no honor."

"Meg!" Bellgrad scolds.

"Hey, big guy, it doesn't bother me. I don't give two shits what she thinks about me."

"Silverfish!" Sargon protests and sips his coffee.

Meg storms outside with Bellgrad chasing after her.

"What's her problem?" Silver says, looking innocent.

"Do you even hear yourself, shitbird?" Evan shakes his head as he gets up from the table. Exel and Febor follow.

"What's their deal?" Silverfish asks.

"Shut up and eat your breakfast," Sargon tells the elf.

Silverfish just shrugs, shoveling even more food in his mouth.

Chapter XXXI
Castle Budapeste

She is going to be okay," Sargon reassures a worried Bellgrad. "It's not like she could go with us—it's much too dangerous."

"I know. I just don't like her being back in Missionwise alone." Bellgrad pulls his horse away as it nips playfully at Tantor's faceplate. The two horses walk side by side as the rest of the group lead their horses behind, cooling them down from a hard ride.

"Enough of that. You need to get your mind right. You will get yourself killed if you are not one hundred percent here," Sargon says.

"Right." Bellgrad's worried look disappears. He looks over his armor and checks his weapons. "Like that plate mail, Father!" Bellgrad calls back to Father Yor.

"Aye, I think it looks great," Sargon says, others in the group voicing their agreement.

"Thanks, everyone. It doesn't weigh much more than the chain mail by itself, although I might need some schooling on fighting with two weapons, Bellgrad. Gunther gave me this sword to use as well." Father Yor draws a long sword and twirls it around with his right hand.

"Well, you're about to get it ... hey, you are fairly handy with that sword," Bellgrad says.

"I don't think this is the time to experience fighting with two weapons, Father. Those perqs are very strong—they can penetrate your armor with one swing of their axes. Grab that extra shield I have on my packhorse. I will help you train with two weapons later," Sargon says.

"As will I," Bjorn says from his position behind the priest. "Anyway, you should not be in direct fighting—you are support. We will need your healing when the blood starts flowing."

"So I should not fight at all?" Father Yor says, frustrated.

"Not what I said. I am saying stay behind us. There will be enough love for everyone when the fighting starts," Bjorn clarifies.

"How do you know?" Father Yor asks.

"Just a gut feeling."

"We seem to have stumbled into a blanket of mist," Sargon says. A light fog swallows the group and turns gradually heavier. There is a persistent familiar noise ahead. *That can't be ... frogs*, Sargon thinks to himself.

Exel and Evan have ridden ahead to scout the area. According to Evan, the castle is massive and can be seen from miles away as it towers over the trees. But that's not the case today. The only thing visible is a lonely mountain off in the distance, its base clouded by fog. Exel comes riding back, and he signs to the group. Bjorn answers, and Exel turns around and heads back.

"The castle is up ahead," Bjorn tells the group. "We need to be quiet. There is a lot of perq activity ahead. Exel counts ten outside, which means there are at least that many inside, if not more."

"You got all that from his signing? He only did three actions?" Sargon looks confused. "I don't see how you could see anything in this soup."

"We need to go," Bjorn says, sighing in frustration at Sargon's ignorance of the silent language. He spurs his horse onward.

The group proceeds for another hundred yards; Father Yor and the others remain silent as everyone checks over their gear while riding. The group dismounts about twenty yards from the castle. It appears to be a massive structure with a drawbridge over a moat. The walls go on as far as anyone can see, which makes the place appear larger than the town of Missionwise. It is hard to make out with the fog blowing in from the mountain. The sound of the frogs becomes louder as the party draws nearer to the castle. *They are usually hibernating this time of year. What the heck?* As he dismounts, Sargon realizes it's warmer around the castle than in the rest of the forest. He can hear rushing water in the distance between the croaking of the frogs. The sound is all too familiar, reminding him of Calador's castle. An aqueduct. *Sounds like the castle is still in perfect working order, at least as far as the water is concerned.* A great fountain can be seen just inside the main gatehouse. Judging by the waves of mist rising from the fountain, it's working perfectly.

"It's warm," Truvey whispers while he squats down next to the moat, dips his hand in, and then drinks. He turns around and smiles at Febor.

"I wouldn't drink that," Febor warns Truvey.

"Why? It's perfectly fine fresh water."

A creature jumps from the water, snapping at the druid. Febor pulls the young man away just in time.

"Wow! Thanks, my friend—"

Febor interrupts, "Shhh. Get down. Looks like a perq is coming our way." Both men crouch behind dead weeds along the bank of the moat. Silverfish looks at the men with an angry expression from his position halfway across the drawbridge. The elf scrambles to hide under the bridge, hugging the wooden beam as the perq walks across the drawbridge and stops just past Silver's position.

Thwack. Thwack. Two arrows fly from the woods, hitting the creature in the head. As the perq collapses into the moat, the water instantly comes to life where the animal fell in. The water looks like it's boiling.

Silverfish pauses to make sure another perq does not come to investigate. Suddenly a giant orange-and-black spider crawls out of a web pocket in the corner of the drawbridge just behind his head. The creature must be three feet across and four feet long and flashes six-inch fangs. Silver scrambles out of his position and slips, causing one foot to hit the water. A fish comes to the surface, exposing a mouthful of razor-sharp teeth. Silver is really moving now. He swings onto the drawbridge and to his feet in one smooth motion then sprints back out to the woods. He throws a dagger, taking out a perq that was coming for him. Two arrows fly overhead as he runs to the party, never bothering to look back.

"I've never seen him run so fast." Sargon snickers to Father Yor, who smiles and nods.

"Ew ..." Sucking wind, Silver rubs his hands across his back and all over his body as if he were covered in ants. "Oh, spiders ... I hate them. And ... and there are fish with teeth in that moat. I think they ate the perq you shot," Silverfish relays to Exel as he catches his breath, shaking violently. "We need to burn the drawbridge."

"Are you mad? We are not burning the drawbridge. That is our only way in and out of the castle. There are innocent women being sold as slaves there, remember? That's why we are here," Sargon says as he mimics hitting himself in the head and making a stupid face.

Silverfish sticks out his tongue.

"Is it rotten?" Sargon asks, ignoring Silver's childish behavior.

"Yeah, that spider was pretty rotten. I think he was figuring I was breakfast."

"No, the drawbridge, numbskull," Sargon says, shaking his head while the others snicker from their crouched positions in the woods.

"Oh yeah, the wood is in great shape. The chains and workings are broken, so it can't be raised. But the wood is not rotten at all … must be iron wood. There is a three-foot orange-and-black spider under that bridge."

"Orange and black? Doesn't sound like any spider from Fegnir," Exel says.

"Sounds like a widowmaker spider from the tropics, like the island of Krau. Those fish are definitely not from here, either. Same as that alligator," Evan explains.

"What's an alligator?" Silver asks.

"That is what attacked Friar Truvey. It's like a small dragon with a really big mouth that lives in the water, but it's from tropical swamps like the eastern part of Cozafied. The warm water must be coming from a hot spring on that mountain up there," Evan says, pointing beyond the castle.

"How is it you know so much about these creatures? And don't tell me you have been to the tropics," Silverfish says with a raised eyebrow.

"No, I haven't. But Exel and I have had run-ins with other pathfinders from those areas," Evan says.

"Remember, Lumpy, Jeryko said Budapeste was an avid animal collector, so there is no telling what else we are going to run into. We see that some of his animals have survived, or several generations have—and that was just in the moat," Exel explains to Silverfish.

"Enough of this sneaking about. Let's go slap steel," Sargon says as he draws his sword.

"Easy, big guy. We still don't know where they are keeping the girls," Exel says.

"True." Sargon looks at Silverfish.

"What … oh hell no!" Silverfish looks around at everyone

looking at him. "I'm not going in there by myself. Not after what I just went through. Send in the two scouts."

"I would, but they have heavier armor on. Exel with plate mail and Evan with chain mail, and you know that makes noise," Sargon explains.

"Why did they change armor?"

"I don't know. Maybe they just wanted to impress you, chucklehead. They figured there would be some heavy combat. Look, I'm sure there is lots of treasure—you know that perqs like the shiny stuff—not to mention what else we might find. Jeryko did say that Budapeste just up and disappeared, and you know he had to have a lot of gold from all those creatures he sold, just stashed away somewhere, ripe for the picking," Sargon explains as he lightly elbows Exel.

"Are you drooling?" Father Yor asks Silverfish, who is staring blankly at the castle wall.

"What? No ... no, but that's a pretty good reason, though, besides those poor girls." Silverfish wipes his mouth on his sleeve.

Bellgrad just shakes his head and rolls his eyes as he draws his sword. Bjorn and the others ready themselves.

Truvey hears a girl giggling in the distance. "Did you hear that?" Truvey says to Febor.

"Hear what?" Febor says, crossbow in hand. He is focused on Silverfish, who is heading back across the drawbridge as Exel and Evan each have an arrow notched, eyes on the elf.

"Oh, must be nothing," Truvey says as he watches Silver scurrying across the drawbridge looking like he has something stuck up his butt.

Silver gets through the main gatehouse and stops at the far corner, looking at a building just inside the gate on the right side. Suddenly, Silver jumps back then retreats across the drawbridge.

"THEY ARE COMING!" Silver hollers, running past the two archers and back to the party. "They must've seen me," Silver relays to Sargon.

Thwack. Thwack. Thwack. Three perequine are shot dead from among the unending stream of creatures pouring through the gatehouse. Chan joins the other archers, armed with a short bow. *Thwack. Thwack. Thwack.* Three more are dropped as the horde reaches the party.

Thunck. Thunck. Febor and Bellgrad each put a bolt through an approaching perq's heads with their crossbows. The creatures keep coming.

Finally! Sargon thinks, smiling with his sword in hand. His smile fades as the perqs run right past them and into the woods. *Ah shit, the horses!* Sargon realizes what is happening.

Swoosh. Thud. Swoosh. Thud. The sounds are followed by a horse's scream that fades into a gurgle. Sargon is sickened to know that a horse has been butchered. He rushes with Father Yor and the others to stop the carnage. He knows Tantor will do his best to defend the other horses, but his great warhorse may be overwhelmed by sheer numbers. There must be at least fifty perqs.

The party gets there to discover one of Sargon's packhorses is the first victim, its head chopped off by an axe. Other perqs are dismembering the horse and carrying off the carcass along with the guts. They ignore Sargon and the others as if they are not even around.

It's like shooting fish in a barrel with a crossbow, the perqs attacking defenseless and unarmored horses ... save one. They did not count on a horse attacking them. Tantor has the perqs stacked up around him like cordwood. He has been kicking, stomping, head-butting, and ripping the throats of these creatures and has managed to keep them tied up as the other horses run away.

The archers and crossbowmen of the group start unloading into the other perqs who were attempting to slip by Tantor to attack the other horses. Sargon carves a way to Tantor through the perequine surrounding his horse. Bjorn chops his way to Tantor as well, swinging his axe back and forth as if threshing wheat. Bjorn's axe, Frostbyte, slices through the heavy perq hide like butter. A perq jumps in the saddle on Tantor's back and chops the armored neck of the horse with an axe. Sargon manages to make it to his friend's aid just before the perq penetrates to Tantor's neck.

STAB. "RHEEEEEE," the perq lets out a horrid scream.

Sargon thrusts his blade, penetrating the gut of the perequine, going all the way through the animal. Blood pours onto the saddle and flows to the ground. The flow increases as the squire retrieves his sword. The perq falls lifeless to the ground. Tantor manages to step on the head of the creature, making a loud *POP* as the horse nervously stomps about. Sargon hops in the saddle.

Jumping over the fallen perqs, Sargon steers Tantor over to the dead packhorse. Bjorn understands what Sargon is doing; he walks over and grabs the squire's lance lying beside all the other gear and supplies scattered about the woods. Sargon is going to make damn sure he kills any perqs before they get to the other horses.

Grabbing the weapon, he spurs Tantor racing toward the horses, careful not to hit any trees with the lance. Sargon makes out one perq running ahead toward the other mounts. He lowers the lance and runs the weapon through the creature and into a tree, leaving the broken weapon and perq nailed to it. Sargon throws the broken half of the lance away and pulls his sword. He lops off the head of another creature while galloping toward the other horses. Seeing no other perqs, Sargon sheathes his sword and grabs the reins of Father Yor's horse. Sargon leads the horse back as the other mounts follow.

Back at the castle, Sargon sees the rest of the party waiting for his return—all except Chan, who walks up behind the horses.

"Well, at least *you* came out there with me. See any other perqs?" Sargon smiles at the monk.

"I find one. He is headless now."

"Great! Where is Silver?" Sargon asks, looking at the group.

"He went searching for the girls," Father Yor relays.

"Not a good idea—"

"We covered him as he went into that old inn," Exel interrupts, walking back across the drawbridge toward Sargon.

"Where is Friar Truvey?"

"He went into that old arena over there," Exel points to the left of the castle.

"By himself? You let him go?"

"I warned him not to go. What was I supposed to do, shoot him?"

"We all warned him, Sargon," Father Yor confirms.

"I'm going to let him have it once he gets back," Sargon says, leaving the horses and walking across the drawbridge.

As if on cue, Silverfish emerges from the second building on the right, a large two-story structure. It looks untouched by time, like Calador's castle.

"I found the prisoners. They are all locked away in separate rooms. It's an old inn with everything intact."

"Well, come with us first. We are going after Friar Truvey. Were there any more perqs?"

"One. I snuck up from behind and gutted him like a fish."

"Good."

"Wow, this place is bigger than Missionwise. It's about the same size as Jaymar," Silver says. He looks around, following the others toward the arena.

The party passes by a large temple, which sits directly across from the old inn. The temple is the same size as the temple of Yahmar in Missionwise. Father Yor cannot distinguish whose temple it is from the outside. He does not have a good feeling about the structure.

"There is much evil in this place," Father Yor tells Sargon, looking around. "The fact this place seems untouched by time can mean only one thing—a ghost, mainly Lord Budapeste. I don't have a good feeling about that temple there either," Yor continues, pointing to the temple.

They take the south entrance of the arena. The place is void of life save one. In the middle of the arena stands Friar Truvey, facing away from the group. It is difficult to see clearly through the fog, but Truvey's robe is easy to recognize. A very deep voice speaks in Dwellnivar and Fegnirian simultaneously. As they approach, the group sees a large figure that seems to fade in and out. Its arm is extended, its hand around Truvey's neck.

Rwyf yma i ladri Yahmar (I am here to curse Yahmar).

Rwyf yma i ladrhau Zura (I am here to curse Zura).

A holl dduwiau eraill Zor (And all the other gods of Zor).

Bydd pawb ohonoch yn marw os na fyddwch chi'n dweud (All of you shall die if you do not tell).

Mae hyn yn dangos ei enw, felly rwy'n dymuno'n dda i chi (This demon his name, so I wish you well).

"A poet he ain't," Silver says.

"Shush!" Father Yor interrupts.

Mae gennych hyd nes y bydd Sulo yn codi yn y bore

(You have until Sulo rises in the morrow).

The demon releases his grip, and Truvey falls lifeless to the dirt floor of the arena, shriveled like a dried apricot.

"NOOOOOO!" Febor roars. He shoots a bolt as Evan and Exel fire at the same time.

The missiles merely pass through the transparent figure as if it's not even there.

"SSSHHH." Silver signals for Bjorn to be quiet. "Truvey's taking a dirt nap!"

"You asshole! He was my friend," Febor tells Silverfish. Bjorn and the others shake their heads.

"Well, you wanted your ghost. Here you go," Sargon says.

"This is not a ghost. It is a demon, like he said ... or rather the shadow of one."

"*A sut yr ydym yn tybio i ddod o hyd i'ch enw?* (And just how are we supposed to find your name?)" Sargon asks the creature's silhouette. It turns to face the squire, and he gets a full look at the creature. It has horns like a bull coming from either side of its head, fangs on the top and bottom of its mouth, wings like a giant bat, and hands like a human. Its eyes are black, and its skin has a greenish tint. The pungent smell of sulfur emanates from the specter. It's a horrible sight to behold.

Bjorn jumps at the demon and hollers, "HAH!" But he merely passes through the figure, his axe doing no damage. He falls to the ground, dust pluming into the air.

"*Dwyt ti ddim* (You're not)." The demon laughs as it floats through the mist.

Sargon looks at Father Yor, who just shrugs his shoulders.

www.ingramcontent.com/pod-product-compliance
Lightning Source LLC
Chambersburg PA
CBHW050857130726
47900CB00013B/190